BAYSIDE
Heat

Bayside Summers
Love in Bloom Series

Melissa Foster

ISBN-13: 978-1948004855
ISBN-10: 1948004852

Cover Design: Elizabeth Mackey Designs
Cover Photography: Sara Eirew

PRINTED IN THE UNITED STATES OF AMERICA

A Note to Readers

I love friends-to-lovers stories, and Drake and Serena's has been a long time coming. These two are perfect for each other in so many ways. I have many fun surprises for you in their story, but two I'd like to mention. The first is for avid Love in Bloom fans who have read every story beginning with *Sisters in Love*, the very first Love in Bloom book. You might remember Abby Crew from *Sisters in White*. In this book you'll be reacquainted with her, and you can look forward to her love story in the future! For my chocoholic fans, I'm thrilled to announce that I have teamed up with Kane's Donuts, located on Oliver Street in Boston, where much of this story is set, and Kane's has created the Perpetual Bliss doughnut just for Drake and Serena! When you're in the Boston area, be sure to stop by and try it out!

I have more fun, sexy romances coming up soon. Be sure to sign up for my newsletter so you don't miss them.
www.MelissaFoster.com/Newsletter

If this is your first Love in Bloom novel, dive right in! All Love in Bloom stories are written to be enjoyed as stand-alone novels or as part of the larger series. You can pick up several free first-in-series novels on my website.
www.MelissaFoster.com/LIBFree

Happy reading!

Melissa Foster

Chapter One

SERENA MALLERY FIDGETED nervously as she walked from the parking lot of Bayside Resort, where she worked, toward Summer House Inn to meet her friends for breakfast. She embraced the sounds of their laughter and of Cosmos, her friend Desiree's scruffy little dog, barking from his perch on the dune overlooking Cape Cod Bay. She spotted the objects of the pup's attention. Her bosses, Rick and Drake Savage and Dean Masters—the owners of the resort—were sprinting up the path toward the inn after their morning run. This was how she'd greeted most days for the past several years, surrounded by her best friends, whom she loved like family. This time next week she'd be living in Boston, greeting the days alone but starting her dream job.

Her nerves flared as she stepped into the fenced-in area beside the inn, as excited as she was nervous to deliver her news.

"Hey, Serena." Mira stood by Emery at the far end of the yard. At six months pregnant, Mira looked radiant in a cute maternity dress. Her skin really did glow. Even her dark hair looked fuller. "Des and Vi will be out in a sec. Is that the shirt you bought in P-town last week? It looks really cute."

Mira was Drake and Rick's younger sister. She and Serena

had been best friends forever. Emery had moved to the Cape last summer. She taught yoga at the inn, and she was still dressed in her yoga pants and sports bra from an early class.

Serena looked down at her flowing white top, with cut-out shoulders and lace edging around the neckline and sleeves. It had quickly become one of her favorites. "Thanks. We have excellent taste."

Emery glanced over as she pulled the elastic from her hair, sending her golden-brown hair tumbling past her shoulders. "I think it looks hot." She shifted her gaze back to Dean, whose eyes were locked on her as the guys approached.

"Stalking your fiancé?" Serena asked.

Emery's eyes lit up. "Look at all that yumminess. Do you blame me?"

She knew Emery was talking about her bearded, heavily muscled fiancé, but Serena had grown up with Dean, Drake, and Rick. There was no doubt they were all good-looking, and as water sports fanatics and hard workers, they kept in prime shape. But the only one Serena had ever crushed on was Drake. She watched him stalking across the dune. His powerful body was covered in a slick sheen of sweat. His thick, wavy dark hair blew in the wind. He always looked like he was in need of a trim, and he never seemed to care, which made him even hotter.

"Morning, Serena," Desiree said as she stepped outside, pulling Serena away from her fruitless infatuation. "I've got cherry-cheese croissants, your favorites." She set a plate of croissants on the table.

Serena's mouth watered. "They smell delicious."

Desiree cooked for them nearly every morning, and it was no secret that the quality of her elaborate breakfasts was tied to the quality of her sex life. Mornings when there was only cereal available, everyone grumbled at Rick. Not that Serena felt bad for him. He and Desiree were blissfully happy, they had incredible careers, and they had each other.

At least I'm on my way to the career I've always wanted. Finding my soul mate will just have to wait.

"You should have heard the headboard banging this morning." Violet set a pot of coffee on the table. In biker boots, cutoffs, and a black tank top, with her colorful arm and thigh tattoos on display, she looked every bit the artist she was—the complete opposite of demure Desiree in her floral sundress. "Sounded like a train was taking down the inn."

"Geez, Violet!" Desiree chided. They might be half sisters, but they were as different as oil and water.

"I see Vi's jealous again," Rick said as he sat down beside Desiree and pressed a kiss to her cheek. "How's my gorgeous fiancée?"

Dean hauled Emery into his arms. "Hey, babe. How was yoga this morning?"

Serena loved living on the Cape, but it was also small and transient, which made for few opportunities to meet guys who weren't just looking for a quick hookup. At thirty-one, after watching most of her friends fall head over heels in love, she wanted a chance at that happiness, too. As a teenager, she dreamed of marrying smart, musically inclined, sexy-as-sin Drake. Even though he had blown her off years ago, making it perfectly clear that she'd been friend-zoned for life, she'd thought again about the possibilities when she'd started working for him at the resort. But he'd never made a move, and four years was long enough for her to accept reality. It was time to move on.

Emery giggled, and the next thing Serena knew, Dean was

hauling Emery against him, kissing her deeply.

"Can we please keep the lovey-dovey fuckery down to a minimum while I'm eating?" Violet asked.

Serena's nerves got the better of her as Drake closed the distance between them.

"Hey, Supergirl," he said as he sat down.

She tucked away the endearment. She'd miss all of her friends, but she'd miss seriously frustrating and insanely hot Drake the most. Of course, there was no way she'd tell him that. As they'd worked together over the past few years, he'd become one of her closest friends. When they were out as a group, he watched over her like a hawk, treating her like a younger sister who needed protecting and making it hard for her to meet guys. It was time she moved on, physically and emotionally. The miles between them should make it that much easier.

Drake grabbed the back of her shirt, tugging her down to the chair beside him, and leaned closer. His masculine scent surrounded her as he said, "Ready to talk about store number five?"

In addition to setting up the infrastructure and handling administrative work for the resort, Serena helped Drake with the design, layout, and administration of his chain of music stores. The grand opening of his fifth store was a few short weeks away, and today they were finalizing the store layout.

"Definitely," Serena said. "But I think it's time you start calling it Bayside Music and Arts."

"Good point." He poured her a cup of coffee, then poured one for himself.

As everyone loaded up their plates, she felt queasy at the prospect of delivering her news. Before she could lose her nerve, she blurted out, "I'm moving to Boston for an interior design job."

Her friends fell silent, and all eyes turned to her. Her stomach pitched. The girls looked confused. Rick and Dean were exchanging displeased glances and eyeing Drake, whose jaw was clenched so tight, it had to hurt.

Oh God. She felt like she was betraying everyone and reminded herself she wasn't.

"You guys knew I took the job at the resort only temporarily, to help get it off the ground," Serena reminded them. "That was four *years* ago, and I told you last summer that I was applying for interior design jobs to finally get my career moving in the right direction."

"Yes, but I thought you were looking around here. You're moving to *Boston*?" Mira said with a pained expression. She'd been Serena's best friend since childhood, and they'd always been there for each other. She placed one hand on her burgeoning belly and said, "I'm happy for you, but I'm going to miss you."

"I know. I'll miss you, too," Serena said, feeling the heat of Drake's stare. She tried to distract herself from looking at him by mentally ticking off a list of things she had to do to get ready for her impending move. At the top of which was finding someone to fill her position at the resort. She hoped to still help out with the music stores. "I promise to come back as often as I can and of course when the baby is born, and we'll FaceTime *a lot*."

"You better," Mira said in a softer tone. "Our new baby will need Auntie Serena around, and Hagen will miss you so much." Hagen was her eight-year-old son.

"I'll miss him, too," Serena said.

"Poor Matt," Mira said. Matt was her husband. "Forget gaining baby weight. I'll probably pack on another twenty pounds from ice cream as I eat my sadness away."

"Enough guilt tripping. This is great news," Rick said with a genuine smile, which faded as his gaze shifted to Drake. "It's what you've always wanted." He seemed to direct his comment at Drake instead of her, as if reminding him of her plans.

"I know. Ever since I was a little girl. Isn't it fantastic? I'll miss you guys so much, but I couldn't turn down an interior design job with Kline, Heinan, and Bruce, or rather, KHB. They're one of the most sought-after design firms around."

"You've wanted a career in the big city for as long as I've known you," Desiree said. "So even though I'm going to miss you, I'm happy you found something so amazing."

"Boston?" Violet said. "Our small-town girl's growing up."

"Congrats, Serena," Dean said as he draped an arm around Emery's shoulder. "I appreciate all you've done for us."

It wasn't lost on Serena that Drake hadn't said a word. "Thank you. I still can't believe they called. I had almost given up." She'd interviewed with KHB last winter and had thought they'd written her off. The resort had only a few winter clients, which had freed her up to get back into the industry by working part-time for Shift Home Interiors. Although she loved the work she'd done for Shift because it included space planning and helping to set up offices from scratch, and not just decorating work, the owner had recently had a baby and cut back to working only part-time. She couldn't afford to hire Serena full-time. But even with a degree and several years of design experience prior to her current job, most of the bigger firms had turned her down.

Cosmos ran into the yard and leapt into Desiree's lap. He

began licking her face, making them all laugh. Except Drake, who remained stoic and still beside Serena, save for the muscles bunching in his jaw. She might as well get the worst part of it over with.

"There's one tiny hitch," Serena said, finally meeting Drake's gaze. "They want me to start next week."

Drake dropped his fork with a *clank*, a scowl twisting his handsome face into a mask of frustration. "Next *week*?"

"Hard to lose your fuck buddy, huh?" Violet mumbled.

Emery choked on her drink. Dean patted her back, chuckling along with Rick. Mira went wide-eyed, and Drake turned a scowl on Violet.

Serena rolled her eyes. She was used to Violet's insinuations. There was no doubt that she and Drake were close. He'd always looked out for her, but that didn't mean they were sleeping together—despite the fact that Serena had spent too many nights thinking about what it might be like to have his strong arms wrapped around her and those piercing eyes boring into her...

Drake's dark gaze slid to Serena, and her stomach skidded to a halt. Yeah. She needed to get out of town all right.

"I'm sorry. I did everything I could to try to get more time," she quickly explained. "Two employees left them without giving notice, and they basically said if I couldn't start right away they'd have to hire someone else. But don't worry. I'm going to start interviewing right away to fill my position. I've been collecting résumés for months. I'll start interviewing candidates tomorrow. I know I can get Harper to fill in at least part-time if we don't find someone before Friday." Their friend Harper Garner was a screenplay writer, and she was supremely organized. When Serena had first mentioned looking for a job,

Harper had offered to help. "I'm sorry, Drake. I'll turn it down if you really think it'll cause a problem for the resort."

"Don't be silly," Rick said, shifting a narrow-eyed look to Drake. "You were there for us when we needed you most, Serena. We'll figure things out."

"No sweat," Dean agreed.

"I can help out part-time, too," Emery offered. "I'd just have to rearrange a few classes, but it's doable."

"I'm sure, between all of us, we'll be just fine," Rick reassured Serena. "This sounds like a great opportunity for you."

The air rushed from her lungs. "Oh, thank God. I didn't want to turn it down. I don't know if I'll ever get a chance like this again." She looked at Drake and said, "Don't worry. I'll still help get the music store up and running."

He nodded curtly. "Have you told Chloe yet?"

She and her sister, Chloe, had practically raised each other while their mother was out looking for a man to foot her bills. Chloe was the director of the Lower Cape Assisted Living Facility (LOCAL), and she was as determined to succeed as Serena was. Serena knew Chloe would be happy for her, even though it meant she was moving away. "I haven't had time yet. They just called me this morning with the offer. I'm really sorry about giving so little notice."

Drake grumbled something she couldn't make out.

Violet pointed at him and said, "Maybe if she *were* your fuck buddy she wouldn't be leaving."

"That's not true!" Serena snapped. "And I would never be anyone's fuck buddy, least of all Drake's."

She didn't even want to try to figure out what the screwed-up look Drake was giving her meant.

"Whatevs, little one," Violet said. Then she glared at Drake and said, "Tell her you're happy for her. Your resort will survive without her. More importantly, I'm hearing a reason to party."

"A goodbye party!" Emery said. "Yes, definitely. Mira, can you go to Undercover if you don't drink?" Undercover was a nightclub in the next town over, owned by Harper's brother, Colton.

Mira patted her belly and said, "My baby is portable for the next three months. It goes where I go, so I'll be there."

Drake leaned closer to Serena and said, "I'll drive you to the party so you can drink."

"Okay," she said, hoping that meant he wasn't as upset as he looked.

Violet pushed to her feet. Her coal-black hair draped over her shoulder as she leaned across the table for another cherry-cheese croissant. "Keep up the headboard banging, Rick. These croissants are the *bomb*."

"Oh, I plan to." Rick pulled Desiree close and whispered something in her ear that made her blush.

"I'm out of here, sis," Violet said. "I'm heading to Hyannis to pick up supplies." She strutted across the grass toward her motorcycle.

"And we have a music store to get in order." Drake pushed to his feet and pulled Serena up by her arm.

"Hey. I haven't eaten." Not that she could eat anyway. Her stomach was all knotted up. "And I need my notebooks for the store."

"Aw, shit," Rick said. "She poked the bear."

"And we have to deal with the bear after she leaves." Dean stroked his beard, his serious blue eyes locked on Drake, who was glaring at both of them. "Hey, Serena, you sure you can't give us three months' notice? Or maybe a year?"

Drake glowered at him and grabbed a croissant. "We'll get your notebooks and you can eat on the road. We have work to do, and apparently only a week in which to do it."

THE RIDE TO the music store was painfully tense. Music blared in the cab of the truck while Drake looked like he was chewing on nails and Serena pretended not to notice as she added items to her to-do list. She stole a glance at him in the driver's seat, where he sat with his arm on the door, his jaw tight. He had a dimple in his right cheek that appeared only when he was angry or frustrated, and the darn thing was so sexy, there were times Serena had pissed him off just to see it. That little *tell* hadn't disappeared since she'd mentioned leaving, and right now it was more heartbreaking than sexy.

Getting on better footing with Drake suddenly became her number one priority. They had a lot to do before she left, and if he was angry, it would be that much harder to get everything done. Besides, she truly, deeply cared about him, and the idea of leaving things unsettled between them cut her to her core. She set her phone in her lap as he slowed to a stop, waiting for a break in traffic so he could cross to the parking lot of the new store.

"Sorry about giving you guys such short notice," she said. "I asked for a month, but they said they needed me right away."

He shifted a tight look to her. "Mm-hm."

"Drake, you can't be that mad. You know I've been looking for a new job for *months*."

"Yup." He sped across the road, into the lot, and threw the truck into park in front of the store.

Those dark eyes slid to her for about half a second before they both climbed out of the truck. He strode purposefully toward the door. She hitched her bag over her shoulder, and despite the uneasiness between them, she did what she always did. Her eyes coasted down his broad shoulders and back, and as he unlocked the door to the shop, her gaze moved to his butt. She was forever trying to figure out how the hot hunk of a man before her was the same person as the lanky teen she'd fallen for when she'd been a silly high school freshman and he'd been a cool senior with *all* the pretty girls after him. She couldn't help it. She'd crushed on him for so many years, it was as much a part of her as the way she craved cookies dipped in milk.

Only she told herself she no longer craved Drake in the same way she once had, with a fluttering in her chest or holding her breath at his every word. No, things had changed a long time ago. She'd grown up, but that didn't mean she couldn't appreciate a little eye candy from her first crush.

Drake held the door open and motioned for her to pass through.

"You keep grinding your teeth, they're liable to break," she said as she walked into the nearly empty space.

"I'm not grinding…" He shook his head, and a half scoff, half laugh fell from his lips. It was a familiar sound, one that said he was annoyed but also amused.

He was a broody guy sometimes, but it was always driven by a clear cause, and he didn't mince words, play games, or hold grudges. She liked and respected those things about him, which was probably what made them such good friends. Neither one took shit from the other.

"Oh, good," she said as she set her bag on the counter. "You've gotten over yourself."

"Over *myself*?" He paced the floor.

"Yes! So I got another job? You know I've always wanted to do interior design."

He crossed his arms, leveling a serious stare on her. "I'm happy for you, but it leaves us—*me*—in a lurch. I'm just trying to figure it all out." He waved at the space. "I've got to get my arms around doing this alone."

"You've opened four other music stores."

"*We*, Serena. *We've* opened four other music stores."

"What...?" She thought back to the first store he'd opened, during her junior year of college. She'd helped him revamp it and had come up with a theme that they'd since carried over to the other stores. "That's not true. *You* opened the first one. I just helped make it attractive after you made it look like a garage."

"Exactly. It was a joint effort," he said sharply.

"I guess you're right." She stepped closer, knowing the best way to center his mind had always been to be near him. She knew he was calculating project times, divvying himself up between the resort and the store. Some guys were like bears, all claws and scare tactics. They bullied their way into projects, creating more havoc than good. Drake was a methodical thinker, as fierce and powerful as any man she'd ever seen, but he didn't attack. He was like an eagle ready to land, circling his prey until he knew the exact second to swoop down and make a clean getaway. She admired those qualities in him as a friend and as a businessman.

"But this isn't new to you, Drake," she said calmly. "I'm not leaving you high and dry. I'm here now, and it's only Monday. I have five or six more days before I go to Boston, and you know damn well I'll work every minute to get as much arranged as I can. And then I'll be only a phone call away. I love working with you and setting up the stores. You know that."

"Do you?" His voice was tense, but his eyes filled with something much deeper.

Curiosity? Longing?
Wishful thinking much?

"Are you really asking me that?" she challenged.

FUCK. WHAT AM I doing? Drake had no idea when he'd stopped seeing Serena as just a friend—*again*—or when he'd begun noticing her womanly curves, the way she twirled her hair around her finger when she was sleepy, or the wanting look that came over her sometimes when they were working together late at night. But when the thrum of heat he'd felt when they were teenagers returned years ago, he'd known he had to mentally draw a line between them. He'd once again promised himself he'd never stand in her way or hold her back. She'd had big dreams since she was a kid, and after what she and her sister, Chloe, had gone through when they were growing up, he was bound and determined to make sure she achieved everything she ever wanted.

No matter how much it stung that he couldn't be on that list.

But as he gazed into her entrancing eyes, shades of sea green glimmering against soft cocoa, even with his promise in mind, he was powerless to stop the guilt-inducing questions from coming out.

"Then why leave? You left your first interior design job because you were bored, remember?" Serena had worked for several years as an interior designer right after college, and after boredom had consumed her, she'd spent the next two years helping a retail company establish their offices in Hyannis. She'd been on fire, and lucky for Drake and his partners, when that job ended, they'd been able to swoop her up to help them get Bayside Resort off the ground. The last thing he wanted was for her to go backward in her career.

"Yes, but that was years ago, and it was a tiny firm where *all* I did was decorate. KHB has *huge* clients. They assured me I would be an integral part of the client teams, involved with all design-management decisions, not just picking out fabrics and pictures. If I ever want to make a name for myself, it's *the* place to do it."

He was glad she'd thought it through, but that didn't take away his heartache over her leaving. "You've been doing interior design for months with Shift. We gave you an office in the community center so you wouldn't have to drive to Hyannis. I thought you were happy here." He'd even sent her a number of design clients over the winter, hoping to help her get off to a good start so she could build a reputation for herself.

"I *am* happy, and I appreciate everything you've done for me, giving me the office to work out of and sending clients my way. And I love helping you get the music stores up and running, taking a blank slate and creating something amazing like we did with the resort. All those cottages, the office, the community center...We made them gorgeous and homey enough so customers feel like they've come home when they arrive each summer. I *love* doing that, and I adore our friends. You know I do. But I need *more*, Drake. I need something of my own. The resort just doesn't need me anymore."

But I do.

Every iota of his being wanted to give her *more*, but he couldn't give her the *kind of more*—the career—she wanted. He turned away to try to regain control of his emotions.

"God, Drake, what do I have to *say* to make you understand?"

He faced her again, and she crossed her arms. Her long dark hair lay sexily over her bare shoulders, contradicting the angry press of her lips. The look summed her up perfectly. She could be tough as nails or sweet as sugar, depending on the situation. She'd spent her life fighting for everything she'd ever had just to overcome a mother who worked too many hours in order to keep a roof over her girls' heads and spent her nights prowling for men. There was no way in hell he was going to make it any harder for Serena to chase her dreams.

With a softer tone, he said, "There's nothing more to say, and I'm sorry I was a dick. It was totally selfish of me. Let's get started on the space designs. I'm sure you've got a billion things to take care of before you leave."

"Whoa. That was a complete turnaround. You sure you're not going to secretly chain me up in the office or something so I can't leave?"

"Or *something*," he said with a laugh.

"Why are you laughing?"

"Because I don't chain women down to get them to stay."

Her jaw dropped open. "But you do...*chain women down*?"

He didn't respond.

"Oh my *God*! You do!" she said. A hint of intrigue in her eyes warred with the shock on her beautiful face.

"Tie, not chain," he clarified, struggling against an image of her bound to his bed, her hungry eyes and her fuckable mouth begging him to take her. As he'd done for years with such fantasies, he gritted his teeth, forcing the thoughts away, then added, "And only if they ask me to."

"They *ask* you to?" She mouthed, *Wow.*

Jesus, why did he say anything? "We are *not* having this conversation."

"How did I not know this about you?" she asked incredulously.

He grabbed her bag and handed it to her. "Dig your notebook out of there, Supergirl. It's time to get to work."

Her beautiful eyes were wide with curiosity that he wanted desperately to satisfy. "But—"

"Serena," he said sharply, leaving no room for negotiation. "We are *not* going there."

Chapter Two

SERENA RACED FROM the file room into her office Wednesday evening and grabbed her phone, typing a quick group text to Mira, Desiree, Emery, and Chloe. *Leaving in five minutes. I'm sorry!! I promise I'll be there soon.* She was supposed to meet them in Orleans in five minutes to shop for clothes for her new job, but Drake was still behind closed doors with the last interview of the day. She hoped that was a good sign, considering he'd nixed the first two candidates she'd brought in.

Drake's door opened, and Serena shoved her phone in her purse, trying to read his expression.

"Thank you for coming out," he said to Mina, the petite blond applicant. "We're interviewing for the rest of the week, but we'll get back to you as soon as we make a decision."

Something in his tone told Serena he'd decided against her.

"It was a pleasure meeting you." Mina shook his hand, and then she offered her hand to Serena. "And thank you, Serena. Good luck with your new endeavor."

"Thank you. We'll be in touch." She watched Mina leave, and the second she was out the door, she turned a stern glare on Drake. "What's wrong with her?"

"We can't have a *Mina* around here. We'll get her confused

with Mira."

Serena hoped he was kidding. "Seriously? You can't tell the difference between a petite blonde and your tall, brunette sister?"

He shrugged. "She's too..."

"Experienced?" she said sarcastically as she gathered her notes for the music shop and shoved them into her bag. "Drake, she worked for three summers running the office for a cottage community. How can that *not* be good enough?"

"She didn't lack experience," he said casually. "She lacked *personality*."

"She was sweet and friendly. What more do you want?"

His lips quirked up. "Sweet and friendly will never cut it when something needs to get done. We need sweet, *strong*, and *warily* friendly."

"What does that even mean? And when did you become a psych major?" She grabbed her bag and dug out her keys.

"You've worked here for years. Do you really think *sweet* will cut it when Rick and I disagree and she needs to intervene or make a final decision? Or how about when guys come in and hit on her? Will *friendly* send the wrong message? Will she be able to deal with a handsy renter?"

"She won't have to. You always bulldoze anyone who comes near me."

"She's not you," he said, and stalked into his office.

"Well, maybe you can pretend she's your younger sister or something."

He looked over his shoulder, glowering at her.

Serena stifled a laugh. "I'll miss that scowling face when I'm gone. Maybe you can send me a selfie every once in a while." They texted each other often, hung out after work, and were partners in all their group activities with their friends. But the idea of Drake sending a selfie made her laugh.

"Oh, I'll be in touch. Don't worry. Someone's got to look out for you."

"My *butt* they do."

"How about we keep men away from your ass," he said a little too sharply.

"Ha ha," she said sarcastically. "You're going to *hate* not being able to watch me like a hawk, aren't you?"

He was glowering again.

Teasing him was so much fun. "How did you ever survive when I was away at college?" As she turned to leave she remembered how often he'd come to visit Mira when they were away at school. She spun around, gaping at him. "Oh my God! You weren't visiting your sister—you were checking up on both of us, weren't you?"

A cocky smile spread across his face. "Like I said, someone has to look out for you."

"Geez. You're…" Her phone vibrated with a text, and she snagged it from her purse as Chloe's name appeared on the screen. "Shit. I've got to go. I have to shop for clothes for my new job, find boxes, and start packing. It's going to be another late night."

"You okay, Supergirl?" he called after her.

She turned, struck by the concern in his eyes. Not for the first time in the last twenty-four hours, and probably not for the last, sadness swept through her at the reality that the friends who were as close as family and *the man* who had been always there for her would no longer be just a few minutes away.

This is my dream job, my chance to have a better life, she reminded herself.

Breathing deeply, she said, "I will be," and headed out of the office.

The drive to The Now, a new upscale boutique in Orleans, was long enough for Serena to pull herself together about leaving and to think about the clothes she needed to buy. Business-appropriate clothing for the small beach community was a world away from the posh clients she was sure to work with in Boston.

"Uptown Funk" was playing in the boutique when Serena arrived, immediately lifting her spirits. Colorful skirts and blouses filled racks and dressed mannequins. The walls were lined with upscale fashions of varying styles. At least it wouldn't be hard to find a few nice outfits.

A tall blonde called to her from behind the cash register. "Hey there. Welcome to The Now."

"Thank you!" Serena spotted the girls in the back of the store and weaved around the racks toward them. Chloe, having come directly from work, looked elegant as always in a simple blue shift and heels. Mira looked fresh and gorgeous in a cute maternity sundress, which was similar to Desiree's more revealing outfit. Emery wore her usual yoga pants and tank top. Serena should have felt like she fit right in with her blousy top and miniskirt, but she was still so harried from her busy day, she was sure she looked as frazzled as she felt.

"Finally!" Emery said. "I was beginning to think you and Drake had decided to *christen* the music shop."

"You're getting more like Violet every day. We weren't even there," Serena said flatly. "He took forever interviewing a girl for my position. I'm sorry I'm late. It's been an insane day."

"Did he hire her?" Mira asked.

"No, the big dork. He said she didn't have the right personality. She was *too* sweet and *too* friendly. Can we please not talk about Drake? He's pissing me off. I can't believe how much work there is to do before I leave. Between organizing the office so the next person can walk in and understand how we do things, setting up the new Bayside Music and Arts, and nailing down everything for my move, I swear I'm going to lose my mind."

"Don't lose it before the wedding, please," Desiree said. She and Rick were getting married in September.

"No promises if Drake keeps being a pain," Serena said.

Chloe sifted through a rack of blouses and asked, "How many lists have you made?"

"One for the music store, one for the resort, and one for the work I just finished up for Shift Home Interiors," Serena said proudly.

Chloe arched a finely manicured brow. She was as blond as Serena was dark, but she wore her hair in a cute pixie cut and had a soft, pretty face to pull it off. "Keep going, baby sister. I *know* you've got more—like what to pack, what to buy, what you don't want to forget…"

Serena groaned and began looking through a rack of dresses. "So I'm a list maker. It keeps me sane."

"I make lists, too," Desiree said.

"Not me," Emery chimed in. "I'd lose them, or one of the cats would steal them."

Emery and Dean's cats, Tango and Cash, were always stealing things. Emery told tales of missing underwear, keys, jewelry, anything the little thieves could get their paws on.

"Serena's been making lists since she realized there were certain kinds of boys she needed to avoid." Chloe grabbed a sharp-looking royal-blue blouse and held it up to Serena. "I love this color for you."

More precisely, she'd started her list with Drake Savage and all his finest points, followed by all of his faults.

"That's a fantastic blouse." Emery snagged an off-white skirt from a rack. "Pair it with this skirt."

"Wait," Serena said. "How much are they?"

Chloe gave her a *get serious* glare. "Serena, you have more money than you'll ever need. You can afford nice clothes for your classy new job."

"I don't want to dip too much into my savings. How much is the blouse?" She'd been tucking away four hundred dollars a month since she'd started working full-time after college, with very few exceptions. She figured she couldn't miss what she didn't have, and she was right. She'd never missed the hundreds of dollars she stowed away in her bank account, and now she had a nice nest egg. Before the job in Boston, she'd dreamed of buying the cottage she was renting. She loved living around the corner from the beach, even if she had to trek through the woods to get to it. But dipping into her savings made her nervous. She'd allotted one month of her usual savings for new clothes, and if she was careful, she could build a whole wardrobe around it.

"Twenty-eight dollars," Chloe said. "And you're trying it on."

"And the skirt?" she asked tentatively.

"Same," Emery said. "We know how thrifty you are, but come *on*. They're beautiful, and you need to look the part in Boston. What size? Six?"

"Eight," Serena said. "I've got curves, woman."

"Curves Drake has noticed a *lot* since I moved here," Emery pointed out. "He seemed really pissed at breakfast Monday, and even this morning he was edgy. Now that you're leaving town, I think you should fess up about your tryst with him. That man is *so* possessive of you—don't tell me you've never banged him."

Serena rolled her eyes. "Would you please get off the Drake train?"

"Hey!" Mira covered her ears. "I don't want to hear this!"

Serena pulled Mira's hands down and said, "You'd be the first person I'd tell, even if you didn't want to hear it. I told you about the duet, remember?"

Desiree and Emery exchanged a curious glance as they all moved to another group of clothing racks.

"The dreaded duet," Chloe said. "Please don't bring that up. She was a mess for weeks."

"I was not!" *It was months.* She focused on the professional-looking cap-sleeved dress in front of her.

Chloe sidled up to Serena and said, "I wanted to *kill* him."

"*What* are you talking about?" Emery demanded. "What *duet*? The guys had a band as teenagers, right? Did you sing in it?"

"No. It was just stupid kid stuff." *Like the way I used to listen to them practice, pretending I wasn't counting the number of times Drake glanced my way.* "Drake and the guys had entered their band in the beach talent show, and I asked Drake to do a duet with me." Even now, when Drake played the guitar, Serena was thrown right back to those early years. There was always a moment of reflection, a longing for what she'd missed out on, and then the sting of rejection would hit, bringing her firmly back to the present.

"Those beach talent shows were the *best* for meeting guys from other towns," Chloe pointed out. "You were so swoony over Drake back then, and he was so full of himself. I wanted to choke the life out of him after he ditched you."

"He *ditched* you?" Desiree's eyes widened. "I can't even imagine him hurting you on purpose."

"He was just being a teenager," Serena said, as if it were no big deal, although back then it had been a very big deal. She chose a black dress from the rack and moved to another display. The girls moved with her.

"A week before the talent show, there was this...*moment*," Serena admitted.

"A fuck-me-baby *moment*." Emery waggled her brows.

"Emery, please..." Mira pleaded.

Serena sighed. "No. We were singing outside one night, just the two of us, rehearsing for the duet. We were singing 'You're the One That I Want' from *Grease*, and I was foolishly crushing on him, like holding my breath every time he looked at me. I saved for months to buy those fake leather pants and heels so I could look like Olivia Newton-John in the movie."

"It was painful to watch her lusting after my brother," Mira said with an empathetic expression. "I love him, but teenage boys are just..."

"Horny assholes?" Emery suggested. "I've got three brothers. Trust me, I have heard it all."

"They're just *unaware*," Mira said diplomatically. "Drake was more serious than most boys, but when it came to girls..." She shook her head.

"Luckily, that swoony, stupid crush didn't last long," Serena said. *At least not in a way anyone else could see.* Secretly, it had taken far too long before she could even imagine being with any other boy. She'd faked moving on for Mira's sake, and eventually she *had* moved on. *Mostly anyway.* But it hadn't been quick or easy. "You know that feeling when your insides are churning and you can feel your blood heating up inside your veins? In that moment, under the stars, I remember feeling like I couldn't breathe or hold on to a single thought. Like my whole body was on overdrive."

"I *love* that feeling," Emery said.

"Yeah, well, I've never felt it for anyone except him." Serena's thoughts lingered on those memories. The excitement and nervousness that had made her entire body tremble felt as real and present as the hangers in her hand.

"Is that *true*?" Mira asked.

Serena realized everyone was looking at her like she'd just exposed her deepest secret, and she mentally replayed what she'd said. *Shitshitshit.* "I meant I hadn't *felt it* for anyone except Drake *until then*." She waved her hand as if she hadn't slipped up and revealed the truth. "There have been *plenty* of men since that awful night."

"I can attest to that," Chloe said. "The girl was determined to get over her crush."

Serena gave herself kudos for pretending to move on so well.

"You go, girl," Emery said. "Don't let being ditched hold you back. There are always more fish in the sea. But I still want to hear about *how* he ditched you."

"It was that night, right after that crazy, breathtaking moment when we both leaned in. I was sure he was going to kiss me. I *saw* it in his eyes, could feel it in my bones. And then suddenly he pulled back without kissing me. He looked almost mad, which was confusing as hell to a ninth grader thinking I'd finally landed the guy I was crushing on. Then he broke my heart. He told me he couldn't do the duet and that he shouldn't have agreed to it."

"What the fuck?" Emery snapped. "What a dick move.

Sorry, Mira. I love your brother, but really? An almost kiss and then he backs out a *week* before the event?"

"Right?" Chloe rolled her eyes. "When she finally told me why she was so upset, I confronted him, and he said he'd overcommitted and the band thought it would hurt their chances to win if he entered twice. I gave him *all* my fury."

"You and me both." Mira laid another blouse over Serena's arm. "I gave him a hard time on a daily basis even after the talent show. Serena was devastated, and it was as infuriating as it was embarrassing that my brother was the one who had hurt her."

"I never held it against you." Serena picked through another rack of skirts to try to push those sad memories away. She chose a few styles, loading them into her arms. "It was a long time ago."

"And he's amazing to you now, so clearly you guys have worked through it," Desiree said. "That's what matters most."

Sure, if by worked through it you mean never spoke of it again.

Desiree held up a black wrap dress with a red sash. "I know Vi doesn't wear dresses, but don't you think she could pull this off for the wedding? I know she won't wear anything that's not black."

"She'd probably use that sash to tie a man to her bed, so yeah," Emery said. "I think she'd wear it for that reason alone."

Serena's mind chased that *tie* right back to Drake, and she felt her cheeks heat up. She dipped her head so the girls wouldn't notice.

"Oh my God." Chloe gave Serena a deadpan look. "You're still thinking about Drake tying you up, aren't you?"

Serena cringed.

"What?" Mira's eyes widened.

"He made a comment the other day. Obviously I never should have told Chloe about it." Serena glared at Chloe. "Way to go, sis."

"Wait. Is there more to you two than you're letting on?" Mira asked.

"Secret tryst," Emery said in a singsong voice.

"No!" Serena insisted. "What is wrong with everyone this week? We were *joking*! I said something about him chaining me down in the office so I wouldn't leave, and he said he didn't have to chain women down." She lowered her voice and said, "He *ties* them down, but only when they *ask*."

Laughter burst from Emery's lips, which made them all crack up.

"Oh, no, no, no," Mira said, taking a step backward. "I can't even…"

"Seriously? Drake has a dark side?" Desiree asked. She was the most proper of them all, and yet, according to her delicious breakfasts, she had an amazing sex life.

Chloe whispered, "I wonder if he has a red room."

"Stop!" Mira said with a laugh. "He's my *brother*. If he has a red room, I don't want to know about it." She turned to Serena and asked, "Does he have a red room?"

"No! I don't know!" Serena said. "But it *is* surprising, right? I can't stop thinking about it."

"I *knew* it," Chloe said. "You're still into him, aren't you? You never blush, and you're blushing like you're back in high school."

"That's called *surprise*, not interest." Serena headed for the dressing room with all four of them on her heels. "So, none of *you* knew he was into that?"

"No, but a little sexy bondage isn't *red-room* dark. I can see him doing that." Emery lowered her voice and said, "Dean and I *explore*, and it's amazing."

"Okay, first of all," Mira said, "Dean is like a brother to me, and I try to stay as far from my brothers' sex lives as possible. Can we *please* change the subject? It's bad enough that the breakfast table is like a banner announcing the quality of Des and Rick's bedroom antics."

Emery sidled up to Serena and said, "I think you should *do* him before you go to Boston," in a rushed whisper. "See if he ties you up and report back."

"Ohmygod." Serena pushed through the dressing-room curtain, trying to ignore her suggestion—and wondering what it would be like to *do* Drake.

DRAKE SAT ON the dunes with Dean and Rick, shooting the shit while the girls were out shopping. He took a swig of his beer, turning toward the breeze whipping up from the bay as the salty air washed over his skin. The sense of peace it usually brought was one of his favorite things about living on the water. But tonight it failed to settle the chaos wreaking havoc in his head. He pulled out his cell phone, reading Serena's text from earlier for a second time. She'd been trying on outfits for her new job and texting him selfies taken in the dressing-room mirror, asking if they made her look frumpy or if they were *too sexy* for her new job. Didn't she know she could never look frumpy, and even if she did, she'd still be the most beautiful woman he'd ever seen? And as far as too sexy went, hell *yes*. Everything she wore was too sexy if he wasn't there to keep guys away, but he'd never tell her that. Instead he'd responded with,

You look great.

"Serena again?" Rick asked.

"She's nervous about her new job." Drake was worried about her moving, too, and not just because he'd miss the hell out of her. She'd always dreamed of living in a big city, but he had a feeling she was in for a surprise. She'd gone to college at University of Massachusetts in Dartmouth, which was more of a small town than a big city. Interviewing in Boston was a lot different from living there.

Rick plucked a piece of dune grass and said, "The grass is always greener, right?"

Drake had never seen the allure of big cities. They'd grown up in Hyannis and had lost their father in Cape waters during a freak storm when they were teenagers. While Rick had moved to Washington, DC, to try to escape the painful memories, Drake had traveled enough for his music stores to know that the Cape was where he belonged. This was where his roots were, and if he had it his way, he'd remain there until the day he'd be buried at sea, just like his father.

"That grass-is-greener shit is the biggest farce there is," Dean said. "If you're unhappy, the grass is greener elsewhere. When you're happy, that happiness fertilizes your grass so it's always lush."

"Christ, Dean." Drake shook his head. "When did you start talking like a man in love?"

"The day Emery Andrews showed up on my doorstep asking to use my bathroom."

"And then saw long-dong naked man and moved in," Rick reminded him.

Dean grunted out a curse. "Don't be an asshole."

Emery had moved to the Cape last summer and had stayed

with Violet for her first night. When she'd woken up in the morning, she'd found a naked man in the kitchen, and Dean had immediately moved her into his cottage.

"Sorry. Lifelong failing." Rick took a drink of his beer.

"You've got that right," Dean said. "Did I tell you Em wants to get certified as a SUP yoga instructor?"

"What's SUP yoga?" Drake asked. "Do they talk smack while posing?"

Rick chuckled.

"Stand-up paddleboard," Dean explained. "She thinks it will be the next big thing out here. She'll probably try to get the girls to be her guinea pigs the next time we go out on the water. Do you think Serena will come back to go boating with us? If not, we have to find you another fake girlfriend or you'll be the odd man out."

"Shit," Drake mumbled. "Now who's the asshole? Serena's not my fake girlfriend."

They did everything as a group, and Serena had always been his other half. They'd shared Jet Skis and kayaks, doubled on surfboards, and teamed up in doubles events during bonfires. He didn't even want to think about doing those things with someone else.

"Does that mean you're finally going to tell her how you feel about her?" Rick asked.

Drake shook his head and took another swig of his drink. "Nothing to tell."

"Mm-hm. That's why the back of your truck is full of boxes," Dean pointed out.

"She mentioned needing boxes. Big deal."

Rick set his beer bottle in the sand and leveled a concerned gaze on Drake. "Come on, bro. Are you seriously going to try to play this off like we're idiots? We live here. We work here. We've seen how close you two have gotten."

Drake gripped the bottle tighter.

"You're just going to let her walk away like she means nothing to you?" Rick challenged.

Drake pushed to his feet. "Let her walk away? That's not what this is, and you know it. This is her dream. Who the hell am I to stand in her way? What the fuck do you want me to do? You were both there when she was growing up. You know what her life was like, how hard she worked to fit in with everyone else because her mother was too fucking busy to take care of her and Chloe. You think I want to be an hour and a half away from her?" He paced.

"Then what *do* you want?" Dean asked so casually it pissed Drake off even more.

He stopped pacing. "Not to be given shit by you two. She's not walking out of my life. She's walking into the start of hers. Do you even realize how lucky we were that she helped us get this place off the ground?"

"Yeah, we do." Rick rose to his feet. "Unfortunately, you've wasted four years being too chickenshit to tell her how you feel."

Drake grabbed him by his shirt with both hands. Through clenched teeth, he seethed. "I'm not chickenshit, you asshole. I'm man enough to not fuck with her head."

"You want to hit me? Get your aggression out? Go ahead," Rick challenged. "But it won't help."

Drake shoved him away as his fingers curled into fists. "I don't want to hit you. Don't you get it? She was *always* temporary. We knew she was heading out of here at some point, and if she were mine, it would fuck up her plans."

31

"Dude." Dean put a hand on Drake's shoulder, and Drake shrugged him off. "Whoa, Drake. We're on your side. We didn't know you'd thought it through. But even so, how can you be so sure she can't have both?"

"Because I know Serena. I was there when she broke her arm on the skateboard when she was eight, and I was there that night when she got back on the skateboard, determined to prove to everyone that she couldn't be dissuaded from making the jump she'd spent all day practicing. I was there when she was fourteen, watching over her as she walked home alone after work at the diner—where she was paid under the table so she could save up for college—because she refused to rely on anyone else to drive her or walk with her to and from work. She's stubborn, and she's driven. Do you really think she'd even consider going to Boston if she and I had been together the past four years? The last thing she needs is to choose between her heart and her dreams. I have never—and I will *not ever*—do that to her. If you know what's good for you, you won't mention this again."

They both held their hands up in surrender.

"And what about you?" Rick asked. "What happens to your heart?"

"I'm fucking fine. Don't worry about me."

Rick's phone rang, and as he withdrew it from the pocket of his hoodie, Drake sent him a silent warning, reiterating the message to keep this bullshit to himself.

"Hey, baby," Rick said into the phone as Dean's phone rang. "Great. See you soon."

As Rick ended the call, Dean looked at his phone. "It's Em. Girls must be done shopping." He put the phone to his ear. "Hey, doll."

Drake grabbed his empty bottle.

"Sorry, man," Rick said. "But at some point you've got to stop looking out for *her* and look out for both of you."

"Leave it alone, Rick," Drake warned.

"Just sayin'. You're almost thirty-five. Soon you'll go gray, and then how many chicks are going to want you?"

"Getting women has never been an issue for me," Drake ground out as his cell phone vibrated. "This is a choice, Rick. Don't you get that? Making her life harder to make mine easier is not the kind of guy I am. I'm out of here."

As he headed back toward the resort, he pulled out his phone and read Serena's text. *OMFG. Know where I can get boxes this late?*

See, asshole? Drake thought to himself. *I know exactly what she needs.*

Chapter Three

SERENA DROPPED THE movies she was holding onto the floor and checked her phone for a response from Drake. Nothing. He was clearly pissed at her for taking the job in Boston, despite his efforts to appear okay with it. She groaned and tossed her phone on the couch. Tired, hungry, and sad about moving away from everyone she loved was no way to approach packing. Serena and the girls had shopped until the stores closed, and then Chloe had left to prepare reports for work the next day and the others had wanted to get back to their men instead of grabbing something to eat. She went into the kitchen and poked her head into the refrigerator, cursing herself for forgetting to buy milk. She opened the pantry and stared at the shelves until everything blurred together.

Ugh. Nothing looked good.

She grabbed a bottle of wine—a poor substitute for milk and cookies—and filled a glass. She polished it off without taking a breath, then refilled her glass and carried both into the living room. If she had to pack, she didn't have to do it sober. She sat on the floor by the couch and picked up a movie. *How to Lose a Guy in 10 Days.* She hated that movie, but Emery loved it. She set it in the box and picked up another. *Animal*

House, one of Drake's favorite movies.

Drake.

You big pain.

She'd known he'd drive her crazy finding a replacement, and she didn't blame him. It would be as difficult for her to adjust to a new boss as it would be for him and the others to adjust to a new person in her position. Serena had met her new boss, Suzanne Kline, the daughter of one of the owners and the only corporate namesake running the show, when she went in for her interview. She was friendly enough, but she definitely had an edge to her. Serena had been mentally preparing herself for the difference between the laid-back environment at Bayside and the professional nature of KHB. She was ready, or at least she hoped she was.

She set the movie in the box and picked up *Fifty Shades of Grey*. Drake had watched it with her as payback for her watching *Dirty Harry* with him. He'd made her promise not to tell the guys he'd seen it, and now she wondered about his sexual habits.

What had he been thinking while they watched it?

She drank her wine and picked up her phone. After taking a picture of the cover, she texted it to Drake with the caption *If you make replacing me hard, I'll tell the guys about this.*

She finished her glass of wine and set the movie in the box, remembering how they'd watched the whole movie cuddled beneath a blanket. Not once had she felt like he wanted her sexually or that he'd been uncomfortable watching it with her, which she'd made peace with over the years. But after Emery had spent all evening cornering her, trying to secretly convince her to sleep with Drake, she couldn't stop thinking about the desires she'd thought she'd long ago stopped giving any serious consideration to.

Three hard raps at her door startled her to her feet. Breathing too hard, she went to the door and peeked out the sidelight window. Relieved to see Drake, she let out a pent-up breath, only to stifle it again when he lifted his face and she saw tension written in the creases around his eyes and the telltale dimple in his cheek. She opened the door, and he barreled in, bringing a gust of tension with him. He carried a bag in one hand and a bundle of flat boxes in the other.

"You send that to the guys, and I'll send this to the girls." He set the flat boxes against the wall and handed her his phone.

She glanced at the picture he'd taken at Undercover a few weeks ago. She was sticking her tongue out and shoving her finger into her mouth, like she was gagging. In the background Rick and Desiree, Matt and Mira, and Dean and Emery were slow dancing and gazing lovingly into each other's eyes. "You wouldn't dare!"

Drake's deep laugh wound around her. "Bet they'd love seeing your reaction to their kissy-kissy-lovey-dovey dance." He set the bag on the coffee table.

She looked at the picture again, unable to stop smiling. "I'll tell them I was making the face at *you*, not because of them."

"Yeah, they'd believe *that*." He grabbed his phone and pocketed it. His gaze drifted around the room, landing on the single box she'd begun packing. "Wow. You're really making a dent in packing, huh?" He picked up the bottle of wine and cocked a smile. "Serena's little helper? Is it that bad?"

She groaned. "I hate packing as much as I hate grocery shopping. Thanks for bringing boxes. I set an alarm on my phone for noon tomorrow so I wouldn't forget to pick some up. I totally flaked on picking them up before shopping, and then I was tied up too late with the girls."

Drake smirked, his eyes darkening.

She realized what she'd said and rolled her eyes. "Not that kind of *tied up*. Although, you never did finish telling me about your dirty deeds, *Mr. Grey.*"

"I'll plead the Fifth on that one." He reached into the bag he brought and withdrew a half gallon of milk.

She squealed, pleasantly distracted from her dirty thoughts. "Thank you! How did you know I needed milk?"

"You always need milk. Besides, I figured you'd need it with these." He pulled out a package of snickerdoodles from Because We Can bakery, which was open 24/7.

"I *love* you!" She snagged the cookies and headed into the kitchen. "I take back everything bad I have ever said about you."

"You've said bad stuff about me?" he asked as she took two cups down from the cabinet.

She gave him a deadpan look and poured the milk. "Do you need a list?" She handed him a cup and said, "I called you a pain right before you arrived. Or, to be more accurate, a *big pain.*"

"Ouch." He gave her a cookie and took one for himself. "I guess that's only fair. I called you stubborn."

She touched her glass to his. "A toast to *big stubborn pains* and snickerdoodles." She lifted the glass to her lips.

"You are the only person I know who can drink milk after wine and not get sick."

"I've got mad cookies-and-milk skills. What can I say?" She waggled her brows and bit into the cookie. "Mm. This is just what I needed. The perfect dinner."

"You didn't eat dinner?" He pulled out his phone. "I'm ordering us a pizza. You figure out where we should start packing."

"Drake, you don't have to—"

He stepped closer, his body brushing against hers. She felt her nipples rise to greet him. That was new—*and nerve-racking.* Her body hadn't responded to him like that in years.

She glanced up at his authoritative expression, and she knew arguing with him would get her nowhere. Given the way her body was suddenly all lit up inside, she also worried their bickering might further confuse her lonely hormones. Maybe she needed to push *finding a man* to the top of her to-do list when she got to Boston after all.

"You're so good to me," she finally managed.

The edges of his lips curved into the smile she'd fallen head over heels for all those years ago, and he said, "Someone's got to be."

Her own mother had ignored her enough for her to know that wasn't true. Nothing was a given in this life, especially being cared for.

"That's what friends do, Serena," he said, once again re-minding her where she was firmly slated in his mind.

She stepped back, putting space between them and remind-ing herself how foolish she was being. It was like ninth grade all over again. "Well, that's not really true, but I'm glad you are."

He set that concerned stare on her again. "You're easy to be good to, Supergirl. Don't ever let anyone make you think otherwise."

That made her feel all kinds of good, and also a little awk-ward. They were still standing in her kitchen, and she couldn't drag her eyes away from his.

"We've been so busy," he said, breaking the silence, "I ha-ven't had time to ask if you've found a place to live in Boston or if you need help moving."

"Thanks, but I'm keeping the lease on my cottage until it ends in October so I can come back and help with the music store and see everyone. KHB owns a block of furnished apartments walking distance from the office. They let their first-year employees use them at a reduced rental rate, so there's no heavy moving. I should be all set with just a few suitcases and boxes."

He nodded, looking a little disappointed, and said, "Good. I'm glad you're all set, but if you need help, just let me know. Day or night, whatever you need, you know I'm here."

Why did she feel like she might cry? "What will I do without a friend like you in Boston?"

A genuine smile crawled across his face, stealing most of the disappointment from his eyes. "Throw yourself into your career so you can shoot to the top of your field. I want that for you, you know."

Her chest filled with love for him. Not hot-and-bothered fuck-me-now lust, but deep-seated, fill-her-heart-up love for the man who understood her, liked her despite her faults, and had always supported her decisions. Even when she wasn't sure if she could pull something off, he always pushed her to try. He may have blown off her romantic notions all those years ago, but look where they were now. She wouldn't trade this for the world.

He grabbed the box of cookies, slung an arm over her shoulder, and headed for the living room. "And come back on the weekends, of course, so I have my partner in crime to hang out with."

WHEN THE PIZZA came, they polished it off, along with half the cookies, while they packed Serena's movies and books, reminiscing about old times and talking about her new job. She had never been one of those girls who was always on a diet. It was just one of the many things that set her apart from most of the women Drake knew. He glanced at her, sitting with her back against the couch, knees pulled up despite the miniskirt she wore, which bunched around her thighs as she flipped through an old yearbook. One bare foot rested on the other, her toenails painted a pretty shade of pink. A flash of memory sailed into his mind from when they were young, when she and Mira would paint each other's toenails in his parents' living room. They'd sit on the floor facing each other, painting with tiny sparkly nail polish brushes while they talked about Lord only knew what. Something that made them giggle a lot—he remembered that. After they finished their nails, they'd do their hair and then insist he and Rick watch their silly fashion shows. That was a hundred years ago, and he remembered it as clearly as if it had just happened. Back then Serena's eyes had seemed too big for her face, her lips too full, like she'd accidentally been given an adult's features. But the beauty gods sure knew what they were doing, because by the time she was a teenager, she was flat-out *stunning*. As a guy filled with too much testosterone, that had proven problematic when they'd go to the beach and Serena would wear one of her skimpy bikinis. Drake had spent much of those early summers waist deep in the frigid sea.

"Drake, look at this." Serena's voice pulled him from his memories.

He moved beside her against the couch. "Is that your senior year?"

"Mm-hm. This is the guy I went to prom with, Rod

McDale." She pointed to a guy with longish hair like Drake's. He had on a Black Sabbath T-shirt and jeans, and he was leaning over a keyboard.

Drake's gut clenched.

"I saved every penny I earned for a whole year to afford the dress I wanted." She flipped a few pages to the part of the yearbook that featured pictures from prom.

His eyes were immediately drawn to a photograph of a group of girls standing arm in arm, wearing bright, sparkly dresses, but all he saw was Serena's beautiful face, caught midlaugh as Mira and whoever the girl was on her other side kissed her cheeks. Serena wore her hair pinned up, with side-swept bangs, and her cheeks were flushed. The yellow halter-top dress with a thread of gold beneath her breasts might have looked simple on anyone else, but on Serena it looked elegant. On her wrist she wore a corsage of white roses, and a strange beat of jealousy pulsed through him.

"You're the prettiest girl there," Drake said honestly. "He was a lucky guy."

She tilted her chin up, studying his face for a long moment. "Want to know a secret?"

"Not if you're going to tell me that he's the dude who stole your virginity or something equally disturbing."

"Like I'd share *that* with you? Get real." She shook her head. "Never mind."

"Aw, come on. I was kidding. Tell me your secret."

"No. Forget it." She closed the yearbook.

"Come on, stubborn girl." He took the yearbook from her and opened to her senior picture. "I want to know a secret about this cutie pie in the tasseled hat."

"It's embarrassing, and you'll just make fun of me."

41

He touched her cheek, guiding her face toward him again. "No, I won't. Tell me."

An uncharacteristically shy expression came over her. "I called to ask you to go to prom with me," she said so quietly he tried not to breathe, for fear of missing it. "Not as a *date* date, you know, but as friends. We always had fun together, and I figured…"

His chest constricted. "Why didn't you?"

"Call you? I did." She paused, her gaze skittering nervously around the room. "But you told me about the trip you'd planned to the West Coast with your friends from school."

"Serena…" He wanted to tell her he would have gone with her, but he knew that wasn't true. He'd been in his third year of college, and she was just graduating high school. He'd matured, gained experiences she'd had yet to enjoy and conquer. He'd had too much experience as a man to be with her then, especially when she was just starting her life, gearing up for college. And then, by the time she was old enough that it felt appropriate to be with her, she'd had her heart set on achieving more than a life on the Cape.

"Why me?" he asked. "As I remember, you had plenty of punks sniffing around every time I came home to visit."

"Yeah, and you scared them all off!"

"Hey, I was away at school for months at a time. You had enough time to hook up without me around."

"And I did," she said too nonchalantly, making him wonder just how many guys she'd been with.

"Do *not* tell me about them."

"Oh, *please*. You were probably hooking up with all sorts of women at college. Don't even pretend you were bothered by not being here to watch over your fake sister." Her eyes

42

widened, and she jumped up to her feet. "I just remembered something I have to show you!"

She snagged her phone from the couch and shoved it in her pocket. Then she grabbed his hand and tugged him to his feet. "Come on."

He followed her down the hall toward her bedroom.

"I have a shoe box with stuff from the guys I went out with in high school and college. It's hilarious."

"I don't want to see that." He stopped walking.

"Yes, you do! It's funny. They're not love notes or anything."

She grabbed his wrist and ran into the bedroom.

He swept his arm around her waist, hauling her against him. "I don't want to see it."

They both laughed as she struggled and twisted.

"Okay, okay!" she said between giggles. "Then let me show you the pictures from when Mira and I made you and Rick play wedding with us! You were such a handsome groom, and you have to see how serious Rick was when he officiated the ceremony. It's way funnier than the high school guys."

She wrenched free and went into the closet. He'd been in her bedroom so many times, he could navigate around the king-size bed and matching oak dresser and nightstand with his eyes closed. He had carried her to bed when she was too ill with the flu to walk or too drunk to manage it and dozens of times when she'd fallen asleep in front of the television as they watched movies. He knew that when she was sick she hated using flat sheets, preferring the softness of her comforter against her skin, and that she needed the closet light left on in order to fall asleep, because she had never quite gotten over her fear of the dark. Who would know to do those things for her in Boston?

Fuck, I hate this.

His gaze swept over the new fancy clothes and silk lingerie littering her bed, tags still in place. The empty shopping bags lay forgotten on the floor. He diverted his eyes from the lingerie, but not before imagining her wearing the sexy black lace panties he'd seen by her pillow, her bare breasts brushing against his chest as she lay beneath him.

"Drake? I think I might need you," she called from the closet.

Not in the way I want you to.

Biting back his desires, he went into the closet and found her standing on a stool, teetering precariously on her tiptoes while she reached for a stack of boxes. He wanted to run his hands up her long legs, to feel goose bumps chase his fingers and her flesh grow warm as he brought his lips to her skin, taking his first taste of her.

Jesus. I'm a fucking prick. She's days away from making her dreams come true, and all I can think about is making her mine.

"It's okay," she said, stretching farther to reach the topmost box. "I think I got—"

She swatted at the boxes, sending them flying through the air as she lost her balance and fell into his arms. Dozens of pictures, cards, and other memorabilia sailed down around them. She was breathing hard, her soft curves pressed against him. Her beautiful hazel eyes blinked up at him, an intoxicating mix of amusement and heat. In the space of a second, he saw dozens of images of her, laughing, crying, eating, lying in the sun. What felt like a lifetime of loving her culminated into one split second.

"Drake," she said breathlessly, passion swimming in her eyes.

He knew he should hold back, knew he didn't have the

right to mess up her plans, but he was powerless to resist the desires stacking up inside him. He lowered his face toward hers, and a shrill alarm sounded, jolting him back to reality.

Her eyes widened with shock and something bigger. *Panic?*

"Fuck," he ground out as he set her on her feet, the annoying alarm still sounding from her phone as she pulled it from her pocket.

She was shaking a little. Her cheeks were beet red, and her eyes were trained on her phone, like she didn't want to, or *couldn't*, look at him. Had he misread her? Seen only what he wanted to see?

"I must have accidentally set the alarm for midnight instead of noon. It's so late…"

"I'm sorry, Serena. I shouldn't have—"

"You didn't—" Her eyes flicked uneasily up to his. "I appreciate you helping me pack and bringing all that stuff."

Damn it. He'd made her uncomfortable. "Serena…" He wanted to tell her how he felt, why he'd almost kissed her, but that would only make her more uneasy. Instead, he motioned to the mess at their feet, trying to find safe, stable ground, and said, "Want help cleaning up?"

She shook her head. "It's late. I'm fine."

He wasn't an idiot, and she was anything but *fine*, but he knew she needed him *gone*.

He hiked his thumb over his shoulder, silently cursing himself, and said, "I'll take off. See you tomorrow at the office?"

"Yeah. Um, I have some stuff to take care of for the music store in the morning, remember? But I'll be back in the afternoon. We have interviews scheduled."

Back to fucking business.

Was it really better that way?

Chapter Four

RICK'S AND DRAKE'S voices escalated behind Drake's office door Thursday afternoon. Serena cringed. She had been training Harper for the past few hours, and the guys had been in there nearly as long. For the umpteenth time, Dean's calm, stern voice rang out with, "Cut the shit," before their conversation became muffled once again.

"Is it always like this?" Harper asked in a hushed whisper.

"No," Serena reassured her. "They don't always see eye to eye, but they rarely raise their voices. It's just a really tense time with my leaving so quickly."

Between interviews, coordinating the layout for the music store, and packing, Serena had little time to breathe, and it seemed the more people she interviewed, the tenser things became. Drake had been running hot and cold since she'd gotten there today, either giving her clipped responses or being overly playful, and she knew it was because of last night. She hadn't slept a wink. Had stayed up all night vacillating between wanting to call and bitch at Drake for doing exactly what he'd done to her back in ninth grade and being too embarrassed to see straight. Had he told Dean and Rick about their *almost* kiss? Was that why they were fighting? Or worse, what if he *hadn't* been thinking about kissing her last night, and she'd freaked out for no reason? What if he'd been leaning down only to whisper something? *Oh God.* She could see him doing that so clearly, making fun of her falling into his arms like a bad rom-com movie.

"I'm sorry," Serena said. "They really are great guys to work with. I wish we'd done this earlier in the week, when tempers weren't so high."

"No. It's fine. I work in film, remember?" Harper said confidently. She was a lot like Desiree, a beautiful blonde with a sweet demeanor. But just like Desiree, Harper was strong and could stand up for herself. She was also an earthy, hippie girl who never got flustered, which meant she'd do just fine working with the guys.

Serena felt a streak of unexpected jealousy. She was *really* being replaced. As much as she wanted to go to Boston, it made her feel a little like a torn-out page in a notebook. She'd served her purpose, but no one was irreplaceable.

"In film, everything escalates," Harper said. "People raise their voices at the littlest things. I'm used to it." She looked down at her notes and said, "What else should I know?"

They'd already covered the office organization, client relations, contracts, and emergency contacts, including plumbers, electricians, and others.

Serena leaned closer and lowered her voice, even though she knew the guys couldn't hear beyond their own battles. "Dean is the peacemaker. If they're all three in the office and Rick and Drake get into it, just glance at Dean, and he'll settle them down. But when he's not here, it's best to let them hash it out, unless they're out here, in your space. When that happens, step between them. It's a visual reminder that they're not alone and there's a female in their presence. They'll usually calm down like scolded children or take it behind closed doors."

Harper laughed. "Men are so funny. It's like they think it's fine to be Neanderthals when they're alone, but if a woman is around they want us to think they're cool, when really we just want them not to kill each other."

Serena thought about that. "When I was in college I worked at a clothing store, and my boss would bitch a blue streak at anyone, anytime, anywhere. He was shameless."

"That would suck."

"It did, but these guys aren't like that. If they're arguing, you know it's about something that's really important to them. Don't get concerned or take it personally if they storm out of the office. That usually means they can't control their emotions, so they go outside and end up running a few miles while they yell at each other. They typically come back in better moods. Sweaty, but smiling."

"Maybe I should try that instead of yoga. Did you hear that Emery is going to start a couples yoga class?"

"Why does everything happen when I move away? I would love to see her get the guys out there. Actually, I've seen Dean and Emery do yoga together, but they make it look sexy and romantic."

They talked about exercise for another few minutes before circling back to Harper's new duties. Serena's thoughts lingered on the idea of doing yoga with Drake, his big hands guiding her, keeping her steady as they exchanged energy. But she quickly pushed those thoughts away. They were all wrong, especially today.

After Harper was all set to start working Saturday and had left the office, Serena got busy with the music store designs.

Rick and Dean stormed out of Drake's office, startling her. Dean blew past and walked directly out the front door. Rick paced like a hungry tiger beside her desk. Serena glanced into Drake's office and saw him standing with his back to her, arms crossed, staring out the window. Was he thinking about last night, too? Wondering why she'd turned into a fumbling dork around him?

"He's in a crappy mood," Rick said.

Tell me about it. "You all survived. That's a good sign."

"For now." Rick stopped pacing, his face a mask of irritation. He had the same dark hair as Drake, though he wore his short. They both had dark eyes, like their father, but until Desiree had come into Rick's life, his eyes had always seemed tortured. Rick had been only fourteen when they'd lost their father, and while she knew Drake and Mira had long ago dealt with their grief, Rick had bottled it up until he'd wanted a shot at a future with Desiree. Desiree and Drake had finally helped him through his grief, and he'd been a different man ever since.

"How many more candidates do you have lined up for tomorrow?" he asked.

They'd interviewed several people for her position, and Drake had found something wrong with each and every one of them.

"Two. But don't worry. Harper agreed to work from eleven until three each day until we find someone. That'll get you through the busiest hours. I've contacted temp agencies, but Drake doesn't seem very receptive to that idea."

He nodded. "Harper's fine. Thanks for all your hard work. Listen, I know you're crazed, getting everything done for the music store and the resort and trying to figure out how to move your life to Boston, but I just want you to know how much we appreciate all that you've done here. Don't let Drake's pissy mood mislead you. You know how he hates adjusting to new things. This is hard on him. He's going to miss you a hell of a lot. We all are."

"We both know that's not true," she said quietly. They'd made major design changes at the last minute when they were redecorating the cottages, and he'd never flinched. "Drake has no trouble adjusting to change. He has issues with me leaving him in a lurch. But thank you for the kind words. I know how much you appreciate my helping out. I've loved every minute of it." She stole another peek into Drake's office. He was sitting at his desk now, watching them. His eyes were sad, and the smile that appeared was clearly feigned. She quickly shifted her attention back to Rick. "I'm going to miss all of you, too. Even the growly one in there," she said more lightly than she felt.

"Desiree said the girls are helping you finish packing tonight. Is there anything us guys can do to help?"

"Other than showing up for the goodbye party tomorrow night? That's all I really need. A happy send-off, because I know I'll cry all the way to Boston despite being excited to start my new job."

"That I can do, but no tears, please. You'll only be a short drive away, and I have to deal with my brother losing his mind. I'm not sure I can deal with both." Rick stepped around the desk and embraced her. "I'm going to miss your smiling face."

Serena breathed deeply, trying to ease the emotions bubbling up inside her. "Thanks. Now my makeup will smear."

"You don't need it anyway," he said as he dug his keys from his pocket. "I'm heading down to Yarmouth for a meeting. Text if you need me."

"Okay. I hope your day gets better." She inhaled deeply,

grabbed the design swatches and catalogs she'd collected for the music store, and her laptop, steeling herself before heading into Drake's office.

He was standing by the window again. She wanted to confront him about last night, to get it all out in the open like they usually did when something was bothering them. But her pulse was racing just thinking about actually saying it out loud. And if it hadn't been an *almost kiss*, she could do without another dose of mortification.

"Drake? Do you have a minute?"

"Sure." He turned around with a cold expression that quickly warmed to *tepid*.

She swallowed hard, as hurt as she was angry. "I have all the design elements for the shop, but I want your final okay before I approve the orders." She set the books on the desk, spread out the fabric swatches, and opened her laptop, glad to have something to focus on besides the questions zooming through her mind. Drake moved beside her, standing so close she felt his tension as her own.

"You sure you're okay to do this right now?" she asked. "We can go over it later or tomorrow morning if you need some time to...*process* whatever happened with Rick and Dean."

"I'm fine." His lips tipped up just enough for her to know he *wanted* to be okay with their interactions, but clearly it would take as much effort for him as it was taking for her.

She leaned over the laptop, navigating to the site she wanted to show him. "I know we agreed on the sofa already, but I found this one and contacted the distributor. If you like it, they have one that was custom made for another shop, but that customer ended up going with something else. I like the rounded back, and it's a little longer than the other, but it would really help define the sitting area. People like things that are unique, and I think the shape alone will encourage people to stay longer, pick up a music book or an instrument, and get comfortable. The more time spent in the store the better. We always say the key to returning customers is developing friendships, right?"

He leaned over her shoulder, his chest brushing against her back, sending her mind reeling to last night, when she'd been teasing him about showing him pictures and he'd tugged her against him. She'd laughed from the teases, but also as a cover from the awareness of his hard body and the strength of his arms, which had gripped her in unexpected ways. She'd wanted to turn in his arms, to confront him about why he'd pushed her away all those years ago.

"Yes, *we* do," he said in a low voice that she swore oozed with seduction. "That's a very cool couch."

Ohmygod. I'm doing it again. She pushed those lustful thoughts away, telling herself it *wasn't* seduction she heard but the sound of Drake restraining his anger over her quitting. Or maybe over last night's miscommunication? *Oh boy.* Now she was dizzy.

He leaned forward a little more, pressing his body more firmly against hers. "What would we tie it to?"

Shit. She hadn't imagined it. Her mind swam back to his comment about tying up women, and she breathed a little harder. *It's official. There are some things a person says that can never be forgotten.*

He reached for the fabric swatches with one hand and placed his other hand on her hip, warming her through the thin material of her skirt. He touched her all the time. Why was she suddenly noticing it so much? And why did she have butterflies in her stomach? *No, no, no.* This could not be happening.

"One of these?" His warm breath sailed over her cheek.

"Yes, for the chairs."

"Ah, makes perfect sense. I like this one." He held the swatch of distressed burgundy leather and slowly rubbed his thumb over it.

She imagined his thumb sensually stroking her skin.

"How about you?" he asked just above a whisper. "Do you like leather?" He dropped the swatch and picked up the shinier fabric sample. "Or something softer?"

"I...um..." Her mind went straight to the gutter. "That one's great," she said quickly. "I thought about mocha, but everyone uses shades of brown. This adds a splash of color, and I found these great lighting elements that can be ordered in any color." God, now she had verbal diarrhea. She fumbled with one of the lighting books, opening to a marked page to try to distract herself from her overactive hormones, which were on freaking fire.

"Lights," she said too breathily, and flattened her hand on a page.

Drake put his hand beside hers, covering the tips of her fingers with his own. Sparks raced over her skin. She lifted her gaze to his, and the air between them thickened with desire as it had last night. Confusion and lust muddled her thoughts.

So much for steeling herself against all of the emotions last night had unleashed.

"You okay?" he asked casually.

"Mm-hm." *Just feeling ridiculous for thinking last night meant something.* "It's just been a crazy few days. Sorry." She shifted her gaze to the lighting book, trying to pull her head out of the darkness she'd fallen into, and leaned forward a little more, purposely causing her hair to fall around her face and blocking his view of her. "These are the lights I'm thinking about. The shelving units and the hardware to hang the instruments should be installed this weekend. I figured I'd come down next Friday night and work through the weekend to help get things set up." Even though she couldn't see his face, she felt the heat of his stare, and her words continued tumbling out nervously. "If we order the furniture today, it will be here in time for the grand opening, which we also need to talk about. I've spoken to the newspapers and the local radio stations. We're set for two weeks from Saturday, on the twelfth."

He moved her hair over her shoulder. She held her breath at the intimate touch.

His brows were knitted as he studied her face. "You talk like you're on speed only when you're nervous or drunk."

"Not true," she lied.

He shifted positions, leaning his butt on the edge of his desk beside her. He reached for her hand, holding it gently, and brushed his thumb over her skin in the same slow rhythm he'd stroked the leather, rooting her in place. "Talk to me, Super-girl."

"Don't call me that." She pulled away and crossed her arms, angry that he was so calm and upset with herself for caring. "I don't feel very *super* anything right now." She wanted to shake him, smack him, or run as fast and as far away as she could. The trouble was, she also wanted to climb him like a ladder and take the kiss that had taunted her for far too long. All those emotions tangled together, twisting and turning inside her until she felt like she might explode.

His eyes remained deathly calm, trained on hers. "Because of last night?"

"What do you think? I'm so fucking confused and angry right now I can't see straight," came out before she could stop it, each word laced with venom. "What the hell was that last night? I felt like I was back in ninth grade again!"

"Ninth gra—"

"Do not tell me you don't remember the night you backed out of the duet!" Angry tears burned, but she forced them back. "You leaned in and—*forget it!* I'm not reliving that moment either. But I deserve an answer about last night."

"I'm sorry!" he growled. "I didn't mean to—"

"Oh, now it was a *mistake?*" The pain in her heart brought fresh tears. With trembling hands, she began gathering the swatches and books from the desk.

"No, Serena." He grabbed her arm.

She wrenched her arm away. "Don't," she warned. "I feel like I don't even know you anymore."

He hauled her closer, ignoring her struggles. "You know me better than I know my fucking self. It wasn't a mistake, okay? It just wasn't fair to try to kiss you when you're about to move away."

She twisted out of his grip again. "You're damn right it's not."

She slammed her laptop closed, stacked the books on top of it, clutching it all to her chest, a barrier between them. She was breathing too hard, tears slipping from her eyes. "I was so damn in love with you as a kid. Do you have any idea how hard it was when you turned me away back then? Well, I'm not a lovesick teenager. This time *I'm* in control, and there's no way I'll let this throw me off course. Do you have any idea what kind of trust it took for me to accept this job with you in the first place? How hard I had to fight my feelings for you to make it work?

It's been *four years*, Drake. We have been working side by side for *four years*, and now that I'm finally moving on, you pull this shit?"

"I wasn't *pulling* anything."

He stepped closer, his eyes boring into her with so many emotions she could drown in them. Hurt and confusion gnawed at her. He must have noticed, because regret rose in his eyes, and he ground out a curse.

"Damn it, Serena. Can we just fucking talk without you bolting?"

"Fine!" she shouted. "You've got two minutes." *Before I start crying.*

"You are my best friend, my partner in crime. The last thing I ever want to do is hurt you."

She squared her shoulders as a tear slipped down her cheek. She swiped at it and said, "Here's a fun fact for you. You failed. *Epically.*"

He shifted his eyes away, gritting his teeth, and when he looked at her again, the raw torment in his gaze cut straight to her heart.

"I'm truly sorry, Serena," he said in a softer tone. He lifted his hand as if he was going to reach for her. He must have thought better of it, because he pulled it back and said, "Don't let my stupidity ruin our relationship."

"Friendship," she clarified. "Why did you do it? Do you have any idea what kind of slap in the face it was for you to do that to me for a second time?"

"I wasn't thinking. No, that's a lie." His voice escalated. "All I ever do is think about you. Why do you think I didn't kiss you when we were teenagers?"

"Because you wanted faster, hotter, older girls," she said

without hesitation.

He scoffed. "Seriously? No. *Wrong*. Because I was about to go off to college, and you were just starting to...You were only..." He turned away and ground out, "Fuck."

"Only...?"

"Fourteen or fifteen," he said angrily. "I know it sounds like I wanted older girls, but it wasn't just our age difference. It was *everything*. I was going to college, and you were on the cusp of figuring out who you were as a person. I didn't want to take those experiences away from you for what could have only ended badly. You'd have wanted a guy who was there for you, for Friday nights, parties. *Prom*. And I was a stupid kid going off to college. I would have hurt you without trying. Gotten drunk, made a mistake. Everyone that age fucks up, and I couldn't do that to you."

"You're saying you did it to *protect* me?" She needn't have asked, because she knew it was true. That's who he was and how he did things, but it didn't make it hurt any less.

"And maybe protect myself?" he said with so much honesty, it hurt to hear. "Our lives were about to move in totally different directions."

Realization dawned on her. "Like now?" She tried to swallow past the emotions thickening her throat, but it was like trying to choke down a golf ball.

"Of course like now," he seethed. "Our timing *sucks*. When you started working here, we were finally both adults, on equal ground, only we weren't. I had achieved what I wanted, and you were right there for me, by my side, helping me. But you *rightfully* made it clear that you were only here temporarily. Do you have any idea how hard it was for *me* because of that? Not that I'm complaining, because I don't hold any of this against

MELISSA FOSTER

you in any way, but you need to know it wasn't easy working beside you, having everything I wanted except the part of you that would have made us real."

She could barely breathe, afraid to trust her ability to decipher his words.

"But you were biding your time before moving on to bigger, better things, as you *should* have been," he clarified. "I *want* you to succeed. I want your dreams to come true and for you to know that all your efforts to parent yourself, to work your fingers to the bone for a prom dress, school books, and tuition weren't for nothing."

He paced in front of the window, the truth burning like acid.

"I have feelings for you, Serena. You must have known that," he finally said. "But I'll never be the kind of selfish man who puts you in a position to choose between work and a relationship. You struggled, working your ass off your whole life for this type of opportunity. If we had kissed, there would be no holding back for me, and you'd be left wondering *what if* you had stayed in a job you didn't really want. And then you'd regret it and probably resent me. The worst thing I can imagine is seeing that in your eyes day after day, knowing I had the power to change it and was too selfish to do so."

She felt her heart slicing down the middle.

"So, yeah, I fucked up twice by almost kissing you," he said apologetically. "But I realized my mistake, and I hope it's not too late to salvage our friendship."

She didn't even know how to respond and stood dumbfounded, swiping at her tears. Even with his feelings for her, he was playing the part of her protector, and the worst part about it was that he was right. Every damn thing he said was probably what would have happened if they had kissed—all those years ago, or last night.

"I'm sorry, Serena." He gently touched her arm, his voice thick with regret. "What can I do to make it up to you?"

"Nothing. I'm fine." *Just an idiot.* "I'd better go." She stumbled toward the door in a haze. "I'll write this stuff up and have it on your desk in the morning."

Chapter Five

SERENA STARED ABSENTLY at the chocolate chip waffles on her plate Friday morning, listening to the girls laughing at Emery's ridiculous yoga jokes. This was Serena's last breakfast with her friends before she moved. They'd helped her pack last night, and she'd been so upset over what had happened with Drake, she'd refused to talk about her new job at all. If she talked about work, her mind raced right back to him, and she was afraid she'd tell them everything. Packing had taken only two hours, but the girls had hung out on the patio with her until almost two o'clock in the morning. By the time they'd gone home, she was feeling a little better.

Then came the silence.

And the sight of her life boxed up and ready to move.

She'd thought she might hear from Drake, but he hadn't reached out. Reality had crashed down on her again, bringing with it more tears. She wasn't sure which was worse. Wondering if he'd never felt the heat between them, or knowing he'd chosen not to act on it, regardless of his reasons.

"Are we allowed to talk about work today?" Mira asked carefully, bringing Serena's mind back to the present.

"Sure," she said blandly. She could handle a conversation

about work, couldn't she? Soon the guys would be back from their run and Violet would come barging in with her racy comments, and the world would be right again.

Except her world was too upside down to ever feel right again. She knew she'd have to get used to a *new normal.*

Ugh. New normal.

The term made her feel like a divorced woman.

"Do you think the guys will hire someone today?" Mira said.

"Are you kidding? I thought this was going to be easy. I've brought in six people I thought were perfect, but according to Drake, they were either too young, not strong enough communicators, or maybe they just breathed too heavy. Who knows." Serena sighed, remembering how thankful she'd been that she'd found so many qualified candidates so quickly and how deflated she'd felt after Drake had interviewed each one. "You know the daughter of the lady who runs the mini golf in Orleans?"

"Diane?" Chloe set down her juice glass. "Her grandmother lives at LOCAL. I see her all the time."

Chloe rarely joined them for breakfast, but Serena was glad she was there today.

"Hagen loves Diane. Matt takes him there on the weekends when I'm working." Mira worked for Matt's father at their family's hardware store. "If Diane is there, she always gives him free ice cream."

"Her daughter Daphne moved back to Eastham last fall from Wilmington, North Carolina, where she ran a small resort like Bayside. She'd gone through a divorce after having her little girl and wanted to be closer to her family. It must have been a bad divorce, because she changed her name back to Zablonski. Anyway, she's been working for Ocean Edge Resort in Brewster, and she doesn't like how big and impersonal it is, so Diane gave her my name. She's ideal for the job, but Drake said she would probably get overwhelmed." Serena rolled her eyes. "She worked at *Ocean Edge*, only the biggest, most glamorous resort on the Cape. That place has way more rooms and cottages than we do. She was unflappable. I think he's making it difficult on purpose. But that doesn't make sense, because he's never been like that."

Although he'd broken her heart last night, he'd been completely honest with her, and as much as she hated it, it still didn't warrant what she'd implied.

"You're right," Mira said. "It doesn't make sense. It's not his style to make things hard on others. He's a *fixer*. Remember how he stepped in after our dad died and helped with everything?"

Serena felt a stab of sadness. She and Mira had been thirteen when Mr. Savage had fallen overboard during a freak storm and was lost at sea. Rick was fourteen, and Drake had been almost sixteen. It had been a treacherous time for all of them, as Mr. Savage had been like a father to Serena and Chloe. At an age when other kids were out causing trouble and thinking only of themselves, Drake had been focused on making sure everyone else was okay. Including Serena.

"I remember sleeping over at your house shortly after your father died," Serena said. "We were bawling, and Drake came in to comfort us. He dragged us outside—"

"Because everything is easier under the stars," Mira and Chloe said at the same time Serena did.

"I forgot you were there," Serena said to Chloe. Although Chloe was Rick's age and she was close with Mira's family, she'd always had her own group of friends.

"I didn't sleep over," Chloe said. "I had been out at a party that night and saw you guys in the yard when I was coming home, remember?"

"I remember now."

"Drake's just going to miss you," Desiree said. "At least that's what Rick said. He said even Drake doesn't realize how much he'll miss you."

"I'm going to miss him, too. If I don't kill him before I leave." Serena turned toward the dunes so her friends wouldn't see her sadness.

The rumble of Violet's motorcycle drew their attention. Violet pulled off her helmet and shook out her long black hair. She tucked her helmet beneath her arm and crossed the lawn toward them.

Emery leaned forward, lowering her voice, and said, "Where has she been this morning?"

"She didn't come home last night," Desiree said quietly.

"Really? Who was she with?" Serena asked. Violet's mysterious life outside of the inn had always intrigued Serena.

"No idea," Desiree said. "But she never tells me anything about her personal life."

"What's the matter?" Violet said as she approached. "You're looking at me like I'm a unicorn."

"Nothing," Desiree said. "Want some pancakes?"

Violet picked up a pancake from the plate in the middle of the table and bit into it. "Thanks."

"I think I know why he's having trouble replacing you, Serena," Mira said.

"Are you still pondering Drake?" Violet asked as she pulled out a chair and sat down. "For smart women, you girls sure are dense. He's a guy. He wants to fuck her. Is that so hard to understand?"

"Violet!" Desiree snapped.

Serena's cheeks burned. She couldn't tell them that he'd pretty much admitted to that last night *or* that it was never going to happen. It suddenly felt too personal—and embarrassing.

"Even if it's true, can you please temper it, Vi?" Mira said exasperatingly. "He's still my brother, and I have a different theory. If you take the friendship out of the equation and think about it purely from an employer's standpoint, he's worked with Serena for so many years; he probably just doesn't want to lose her."

"Maybe," Violet said. "But he still wants to take her six ways to Sunday."

"Ohmygod," Serena said, covering her face.

Ignoring Violet's comment, Mira said, "Serena, you're an amazing multitasker and you do the job of two people, so part of him probably *does* worry that someone else might get overwhelmed. Any boss would feel the same way. You guys have become seriously symbiotic on every level. That's hard to find in a friend, much less an employer-employee relationship. Like me and Matt's dad at the hardware store. And you're *never* in a bad mood, which is amazing considering you have to put up with my brothers."

"I'd like to challenge that statement," Chloe chimed in. "My little sister can be one bitchy mama."

"Shut up!" Serena knocked Chloe with her shoulder. "Don't let Chloe's sharp clothes and sweet pixie haircut fool you. She may be elegant, but beneath that polished exterior are the fangs of a viper and the claws of a wolverine."

"*Psst!*" Chloe made clawing motions with her hands, and they all laughed. "I'm not that bad. But feel free to tell that hot surf instructor of yours that I'm *spicy*! That man has got a body that won't quit."

"Brody Brewer?" Serena couldn't hide her shock. "Are you kidding? You always go for suit and tie guys. Brody acts like he's forever twenty-one. I'm not sure he'll ever grow up."

Serena spotted the guys jogging up the path toward the inn. Matt was with them today, and they were all shirtless, their bodies glistening from their efforts. Drake's eyes locked on hers, sending her emotions reeling. She was vaguely aware of the girls talking, but she was captivated by his serious expression, like he was trying to keep his emotions in check. But *which* emotions was the question. Was he struggling to be friendly? Or was he fighting to keep from letting their attraction get the better of him?

They jogged into the yard, and Drake looked away from Serena.

"Hey, gorgeous." Matt bent and kissed Mira's cheek, then her burgeoning belly. "Hello, baby."

Serena's heart would have melted if it weren't beating so hard she thought she might pass out. Drake pulled his phone from his pocket and focused on that, while Rick and Dean kissed their fiancées and sat down beside them.

"Suit and tie guys are great," Chloe said, and it took a second for Serena to realize she was responding to her earlier comment. "But every once in a while you've got to cut loose with a boy toy."

"Cut loose? We like *ties*," Emery said, snuggling up to Dean while eyeing Serena.

Oh Lord, please let me evaporate into thin air.

"Whoa. What conversation did we walk into?" Rick asked.

Drake grabbed a glass of water and guzzled it down, pacing

instead of sitting down. Violet reached for another pancake, her gaze moving between Drake and Serena.

"I disagree about the cutting-loose thing," Mira said, reaching for Matt's hand. "From my experience, one ex-professor is better than any boy toy could ever be."

Violet dramatically sniffed the air, and all eyes turned on her. "Do you guys smell that?"

Everyone sniffed.

"What?" Dean asked. "I don't smell anything except Emery's sweetness."

"Nope. Not that." Violet walked behind Serena and sniffed the air. Then she moved toward Drake and did the same. "Yup. That's the distinct scent of sexual tension."

All eyes turned to Serena and Drake.

Drake looked like he was chewing on glass.

He shifted his gaze to Serena, and she searched for a hint of a joke or a shred of happiness to hold on to. In her eyes, he would always be the perfect mix of shirt-and-tie guy and sexy, fun boy toy. But when he ground out a curse and stormed out of the yard, she knew she'd never experience either one, and she wondered if their friendship could ever recover.

AFTER AN EMOTIONALLY grueling day, Serena gathered her things, taking the cards she'd bought for each of her bosses out of her purse. The office was too quiet. Rick and Dean had left for a meeting, promising to see her at her goodbye party at Undercover later. Drake had gotten a call from someone named Sterling and had left when she was on the phone without so much as a goodbye. She had no idea if he still planned to drive her to the party—or if he'd show up at the party at all for that matter. He'd managed to avoid her for most of the day, except for brief interactions after each interview, when he'd shake his head, shrug, and mumble an excuse for why the applicant wasn't right for the job.

She left Rick's and Dean's cards on their desks, and her stomach knotted as she went into Drake's office, remembering the first day she'd joined them. They hadn't even set up desks yet. Drake lived upstairs from the office, and his apartment had been as bare as the office. She'd quickly remedied both. She'd known how much Drake missed his father, and he'd told her many times that he felt closest to him on the water. For that reason, she'd decorated the office and Drake's apartment in rich woods with nautical undercurrents throughout.

Clutching the envelope, she headed upstairs to his apartment. It had been a struggle to keep her emotions in check when she'd helped decorate his apartment, wondering if she was choosing sheets and pictures for other women to enjoy. But she'd never actually seen Drake bring any women home. She knew he dated, but as far as she knew, he'd never been a player or the type of guy to hook up with random women. She hadn't thought about that too much recently, because Drake had made it clear that she was only a friend, but now, knowing what she did, she wondered about his personal life. Was her impression of him skewed by wishful thinking?

She'd dated a few guys over the past four years, but they'd all left her wanting something more. Only she didn't know what *more* was. It was like an itch she couldn't scratch. Had Drake had his itches scratched? Had women spent the night at his apartment and he'd been careful to shoo them out before she arrived at work?

She ran her fingers over the blue envelope, tracing the white rope and anchor over the hard ridges of the key to his apartment she'd put inside. Why hadn't he ever asked for it back? She opened the old-fashioned mail slot on the door and hesitated. *This might be it. Our final goodbye before I leave town.*

Well, if this was it, it was his choice, wasn't it? His loss.

She slid the envelope into the slot, and then she hurried out to her car and drove away from the office. At a time when she should be celebrating her future, all she could do was cry. She didn't even try to stop, because at this time tomorrow, she'd be far away in a new city, making the fresh start she'd always dreamed of.

Her mother's voice, the voice she rarely heard anymore, whispered through her head. *What you wish for today may not be what you truly want tomorrow.* She and Chloe had been young, wishing on the dried seeds of dandelions, and in a rare moment of parenting, their mother had doled out that truthful piece of advice. She'd gone on to explain that she'd always wished she would become a mother, but she hadn't realized it would be so hard. It was one of those eye-opening moments when Serena's little-girl heart had ached so badly she'd gotten on her bike and pedaled straight over to Mira's house. She'd seen Drake in the yard, and rather than let him see her tears, she'd pedaled all the way to the creek, almost two miles away. Drake had shown up on his own bike a few minutes after her, and when she'd asked how he'd known where to find her, he'd said, *Anyone who knows you would know where you were going.*

She pulled into her driveway, and all that sadness turned to frustration. She had sworn she wasn't going to let this thing with Drake lead her astray, and here she was, completely entrenched in thoughts of him. *No way.* This could not happen.

She couldn't afford to be sidetracked when she started her new job.

My new life.

A sting accompanied the thought, but as she'd learned to do years ago with her mother, she buried the sadness that came with her leaving and told herself that whatever Drake did or didn't do tonight should have no impact on her. She had a car and could drive herself to the damn bar. She just wouldn't drink much.

She went inside and walked directly past the sealed boxes, into her bedroom. She showered, taking her time to meticulously apply Nair everywhere *just in case* she found someone worthy of distracting her from Drake. She dried her hair, then took extra care applying her makeup. If Drake wanted to shun her because it was too hard to face what they shouldn't have, that was his business. She was going to celebrate her fantastic friendships and the start of something new.

She'd packed most of her nice clothes, but tonight she wasn't looking for *nice.* She dressed in the white eyelet crop top she'd bought right after college, when she'd moved back to the Cape. She hated strapless bras, so decided to go without one, which turned out to be a good thing because, as she laced up the top, she noticed it was a little tighter now. She pulled on the matching miniskirt with a lace hem, leaving her midriff bare, and slipped her feet into a pair of cute strappy sandals. Then she checked her phone for messages, reading one from each of the girls telling her how excited they were to see her tonight—and tried to ignore the sting at not finding one from Drake.

Fuck it.

She put on a pair of gold dangling earrings, a matching necklace, and a handful of bangles. Then she grabbed her keys and headed out to her car.

Chapter Six

DRAKE CLIMBED THE porch steps as the front door flew open and Serena barreled out. He stopped midstride. Her eyes were heavily lined, making the greens and browns stand out even more, and her hair had a just-been-fucked look, a little wild and *very* sexy. It cascaded over her shoulders in natural waves. And holy hell, what was she wearing? Her shoulders were bare, and her top—if he could call it that—was only a few inches from top to bottom. It laced up the center, revealing not only a path of exquisite cleavage, but also her enticingly sexy belly, from hips to ribs. Her skirt stopped just above midthigh, with a tiny row of lace at the edge. His fingers curled with the itch to touch her.

"Drake?" she said with more than a hint of surprise. "I didn't think you'd show up."

He blinked several times to clear the lust from his brain, and when that didn't work, he forced himself to step onto the porch. "Did you think I'd leave you hanging?"

She lowered her gaze and said, "You left early. I wasn't sure…" The hurt in her voice was inescapable.

"Look at me, Serena." He waited until he had her full attention, and then he said, "You were on the phone, and I had to run to P-town to get something, but at no time did I consider standing you up for tonight." He pulled the jeweler's bag from his pocket, hiding it in his hand, and said, "I missed out on bringing you to your prom, and I was going to bring you a corsage, but at our ages it seemed…" This sounded much better in his head. "That's not true, Supergirl. Flowers die. That's why I didn't bring you a corsage. I wanted you to have a going-away present that would always be with you, something that would make you smile when things got tough." He opened the little velvet bag and withdrew the wrap bracelet he'd had made just for her.

Her eyes bloomed wide. "Drake…?"

"I'm sorry I've been a little messed up lately." He wound the long, braided gold and brown leather bracelet, which was accented with dozens of tiny diamond stars, around her wrist several times. As he hooked the clasp he said, "My partner in crime is leaving and I'm not really sure which way is up anymore."

"This is…" Her eyes dampened as she gazed at the bracelet and then up at him. "It's beautiful. Thank you."

"A beautiful woman deserves beautiful things." He repositioned the bracelet so a circular gold charm rested in the center of her wrist. Then he withdrew the accessory chain from the bag and hooked it to the charm. "Spread your fingers, palm down."

She did, her eyes darting up to his, and he imagined giving her all sorts of commands. *Take me in your hand…That's it…Stroke me, baby.*

Holding her gaze, he tried to push away those thoughts as he pulled the chain down the center of the back of her hand and wound the end around her middle finger and then connected it just above her knuckle to the tiny heart-shaped clasp.

"Oh, Drake," she said breathlessly. "I don't understand. Why…?"

"I had it made for you so you always remember that everything is better under the stars. Is it comfortable? Too binding?"

Her eyes darkened, and she inhaled a sharp breath. "What? Um…No. Not at all."

"Good. Then shall we go celebrate?" He offered her his arm, and she wrapped her hand around it, holding her other hand out to admire the bracelet.

Serena fidgeted with the bracelet the whole way to the bar. Her skimpy skirt rode distractingly high on her thighs, making it difficult for Drake to rein in his desires as he turned on to the main drag in Truro, a neighboring town to Wellfleet, and caught her stealing a glance at him. She turned away so quickly, he didn't get a clear view of her face. He'd been fighting himself since he told her how he felt yesterday. He knew he was doing the right thing, but confessing his feelings for her and knowing she was leaving tomorrow had lit a wick that he felt burning down too fast. Every stolen glance, every breath she took in that barely there top felt like it came from his own lungs—and man, he wanted it to.

By the time they reached Undercover, she was nibbling on her lower lip, and that sexy innocence nearly made him detonate.

The lot was packed. He parked at the far end, beneath an umbrella of trees, and turned toward Serena. She was still staring straight ahead, her face a mask of apprehension, which tore at his gut. Was it him, or was it her leaving that was causing her distress?

He took her small hand in his and brushed his thumb over her warm skin, memorizing it to hold him over when she was gone. The gold chain sparkled against her sun-kissed skin. "Talk to me, Serena."

She turned to face him with worry in her eyes. He gently pulled her across the seat, close enough that he could almost feel her racing pulse between them.

"Aw, sweetheart, what's wrong? Are you nervous about leaving?"

"Yes," she said softly. "And about *this*." Her gaze fell to the bracelet. "It's gorgeous and sweet, but it's also *confusing*. What does it mean, Drake? On one hand I feel like you're sending mixed messages by avoiding me all day and then giving me this…" She ran her finger over the chain on her hand. "But on the other hand, you don't owe me an explanation about what you're up to at work, and you've given me presents before. This should be no different. But knowing how you feel about me makes it different."

He touched his forehead to hers and slid his hand to the nape of her neck, holding her there as he said, "I'm sorry. I told you I was fucked up right now. I did avoid you today, but only because I can't stop thinking about"—*making you mine, kissing you, sweeping you naked beneath me and loving you until you can't remember why you wanted to leave in the first place*—"things I shouldn't."

"Join the club," she whispered.

His insides flamed at the secret between them. He brushed his lips over her cheek, and she inhaled a ragged breath. It was so sexy, he did it again, earning another seductive inhalation. He drew back so he could see her face, still holding the back of her neck, and she clutched his forearm. Her breasts rose with each heavy breath, and her tongue slicked over her lips, making his mouth water. There was no denying the calculated, seductive move. *Nicely played.* Their eyes locked, and hers narrowed ever so slightly, suddenly brimming with confidence, and if he was reading her right, which he was damn sure he was, also ripe with challenge.

"You're going to make a liar of me if you keep looking at me like that."

"Sometimes a lie isn't a lie," she said breathily.

He couldn't resist pressing his lips to her cheek in a series of light kisses, telling himself her cheek was safe. If he could just have this little taste, he could get through the night and figure out how to lock his desires away again.

Her skin was warm and temptingly soft. She closed her eyes, barely breathing as he kissed her cheek again and again, so trusting and sweet. Her fingers pressed into his skin with every touch of his lips, fueling the battle raging in his head. *Just one more.* He kissed the tender dip just below her ear, and she sighed dreamily. *Fuuuck.*

"Then what is it," he asked, "if not a lie?"

"It's a…" she whispered.

She turned her face, and their lips brushed like a breeze passing over too quickly. The tease ignited sparks beneath his skin. He ran his hand along her thigh, aching to make her *his*, though knowing he shouldn't even be tempting himself with the kisses he'd already taken.

"A…?" he said as he began kissing her neck.

She arched toward him, holding his head, keeping his mouth on her neck. *Oh yeah. That's it, baby. Show me you want me.* He opened his mouth and sealed his teeth over her tender skin, sucking hard enough for her to gasp. He threaded his fingers into her hair, tugging her head to the side so he could take more of her. Her hand fisted in his hair, pulling hard—but not pulling *away*—causing a deliciously erotic sting and making his cock throb even harder. He needed to break their connection or he wasn't going to stop. He'd fought to remain on the right side of the invisible line between them for years, and he was fucking that up. Sending her mixed messages only scratched the surface of why he should break their connection.

"It's a bad idea," she panted out.

Her words, along with the roar of a motorcycle, crashed through his reverie. He released her like he'd been burned. "Bad idea. Right. Sorry." *I'm a fucking prick.*

"No—" She grabbed his hand, leaning closer. "This isn't a bad idea. That's what the *lie* is. We're not making a liar out of you. You just had a bad idea in the first place."

A series of successive taps on the window made them both jump.

"Fuck." He rolled down his window, and Violet peered in. "Hey," he ground out.

Violet's gaze sailed over Serena, and Drake fisted his hands to keep from shifting in his seat and blocking Violet's view of Serena's lust-filled eyes, tousled hair, and pert nipples poking against the thin material of her top.

"You guys coming in?" Violet arched a brow. "Or *coming* out here?"

THERE WERE NO words to describe the feeling of walking into the crowded, dimly lit bar between Violet, who was smirking like she'd caught Serena and Drake having sex, and Drake. Drake radiated sexual energy as he hulked beside her like a bodyguard who'd been told not to touch his charge. He practically growled at the men who dared look at her. They'd been there for a while, and she still hadn't calmed down. She swallowed hard, shifting in her seat. The man hadn't even kissed her on the mouth and he'd practically melted her thong off.

The erratic beat of the music amped up the thrum of heat buzzing inside her as she watched Drake carry their drinks from the bar. His eyes blazed into hers, fiercely sexy and haltingly arresting. She touched the bracelet he'd given her, remembering how he'd held her stare with a wicked look in his eyes as he'd wound it around her wrist. She knew she'd see that look late at night when she was alone in the dark, reliving the feel of his lips on her cheek, his hot breath warming her to her core. But for now she tried to push the memory away, drinking him in as he approached. His cocksure stride drew the eyes of nearly every woman he passed. He looked scrumptious in the black linen shirt she'd given him last Christmas. It had quickly become one of her favorites because he always left the top buttons open, giving her a peek at the dusting of chest hair beneath. Some guys were too hairy, others shaved or waxed their chests, but Drake had the perfect amount of chest hair, and now, as he closed the distance between them like a lion stalking his prey, she imagined what it would feel like against her breasts.

Violet leaned back in her chair. Her black top rose at the hem, exposing an inch of tanned skin above her hip-hugging black leather miniskirt. She took a picture of Drake with her phone. Then she handed the phone to Serena and said, "Don't drool on it."

Serena rolled her eyes and shoved the phone back to Violet. "It's not what you think."

"Enlighten me," Violet said with a smirk. "Because that blond skank is trying her best to seduce him, and he can't take his eyes off *you*."

Serena glanced over, and her insides flamed at the way he was looking at her. And just as quickly, jealousy clawed its way up her spine at the sight of a pretty blonde pawing at his arm. She didn't know what to make of what had happened in the truck, but she knew what she *wanted* to make of it. And she knew that might not be smart for all the same reasons Drake had so diligently outlined for her yesterday.

Her gut twisted as he leaned down and said something to the blonde. This time tomorrow she'd have no idea where he was or who he was with. Panic gripped her. She shifted her eyes to the dance floor to try to calm her nerves. They weren't even a couple. It shouldn't matter what he did or who he was with, despite those few scorching moments in the truck. As it was, she had no idea who he was with most nights. Sure, they texted often, but she didn't pry, and he didn't offer details. She only knew that in the mornings they either met up at Summer House for breakfast with their friends, or he arrived at the resort shortly after her, on his way back from his morning run. She was sure he'd been with women over the years, but she couldn't remember him having anyone by his side even once when they were out as a group.

She glanced across the table at Mira and Matt, their heads bowed as they whispered to each other. Matt must have said something dirty, because Mira's cheeks pinked up and she closed her eyes, which made Serena think of Drake's lips on her cheek. She turned her attention to Emery and Dean dancing too close and slow for the fast beat. A few feet away from them, Desiree and Rick kissed, swaying to the music. They made relationships look easy, like life revolved around them, not the other way around. Why was it so complicated for her and

Drake?

"Shit, woman. You look like a confused little kitten, and I know you're no kitten." Violet pushed to her feet. "We're going to dance this shit out of you."

Dean and Rick came back to the table as Violet yanked Serena up beside her.

"Harper's with the girls," Rick said, and pointed to the three of them dancing.

Serena couldn't suppress her smile. Wearing a short, colorful hippie dress, along with several long, dangling necklaces, Harper looked like a flower child. Her long blond hair swung as she danced like she was on the floor by herself, her arms flailing, her chin tipped up, and her eyes closed. Beside her Desiree danced a little self-consciously in a cute maxi dress, while Emery ground her hips and shimmied in a skintight, bright-blue minidress.

Violet dance-strutted across the floor in her silver-heeled biker boots.

"Mira, want to dance?" Serena shouted over the music as Drake joined them at the table and set the drinks down.

"Yes!" Mira kissed Matt and headed toward the dance floor.

Serena turned to follow her, and Drake caught her by the hand, staring longingly into her eyes. In the next second that longing morphed to something darker, sending her stomach into a wild swirl. She didn't think as she grabbed the drink he'd gotten for her and guzzled it down.

His eyes burned hotter, *hungrier*, as if her nervousness was turning him on as much as his interest was flustering her. She grabbed another drink from the table without a care for whose it was and downed it just as fast, taking comfort in the warmth of the alcohol as it slid down her throat. Drake's eyes flared with a maddening, and equally exciting, appreciation. Never had she been so nervous around a man, so unsure of what she wanted. Or rather, what she *should* do. She knew *exactly* what she wanted—the six-foot-two man with eyes the color of night and lips as unrelenting as a bullying wave, who had stolen her heart when she was just a girl.

She turned and made a mad dash to the dance floor.

She weaved through the crowd, hips and shoulders swaying to the beat, feeling looser by the second as the alcohol numbed the worry out of her. Violet and Emery were slithering up and down each other's bodies in some sort of dirty dance, while Desiree and Mira leaned in close, talking as they moved in purely PG fashion. Driven by the lust pulsing inside her and the tension-easing effects of alcohol, Serena joined Harper in an evocative dance. She gazed up at the colored lights, calmed by the music, feeling it throb and flutter inside her. This was what she needed, to lose herself in something other than Drake, to feel in control again.

"Finally!" Harper yelled over the music.

Serena answered with a bump of her hips.

"Why didn't you tell me that you and Drake were a couple?"

Violet and Emery cracked up.

"What? We're not!" Serena shot a look at Mira.

"Don't look at me," Mira shouted. "I see what Harper sees!"

Harper's brows lifted in confusion. "Then I've really lost my hotness radar, because the way you two look at each other tells a different story."

"It's just a weird night." Serena raised her arms over her head and closed her eyes for a moment to try to lose herself in the beat again, but all she saw was Drake's sinful gaze. She opened her eyes as Chloe burst through the crowd and threw her arms around her.

"Sorry I'm late!" Chloe hugged her, then embraced the others. "Wow. You guys all look amazing!"

Violet smirked. "Don't we always?"

"I know I do," Emery said.

Chloe pointed to Serena and said, "Are you dressing to get one last quickie in before Boston?"

"Something like that." Serena had forgotten what she had on. She did look like she was trying to get lucky. Was that why Drake had finally made a move?

"I thought she'd dressed for Drake!" Harper said as they began dancing.

Violet danced over to Serena and said, "So did he," into her ear.

Serena glared at her.

"She's been dressing for Drake since she realized she had boobs!" Chloe teased. "Why would tonight be any different?"

"Shut up and dance with us!" Serena said, hoping to change the topic.

They danced in a group to so many songs, Serena didn't know when the colored lights had dimmed, and she didn't care. She was a little high and was feeling good. When Harper tapped her on the shoulder and motioned toward Drake sitting at the table watching her like she was putting on a private show just for him, she turned up the heat.

Holding his gaze, Serena thrust out her breasts, rolling her shoulders back, first one, then the other, swaying her hips to the same rhythm. She raised her arms, moving them over her head as she turned seductively. When she'd turned full circle, his face was a mask of wicked intent. His interest made her feel bold and sexy. She sidled up to Emery in an erotic grinding dance. Emery fell right into step, and together they drove Dean and Drake out of their minds.

Suddenly Emery grabbed Serena's hand, jerking her out of her sensual taunt.

Emery's eyes widened as she stared at Serena's new bracelet. "What is *this* amazing thing? Where'd you get it?"

"It's a going-away present from Drake." Serena's pulse spiked again, and she stole a glance at Drake, who was still practically drooling over her.

"He gave you a *slave* bracelet?" Violet asked with more than a hint of shock. "I did not expect that kind of fuckery. *Wow.*"

"What's a slave bracelet?" Desiree asked. "That sounds really offensive, Violet. You shouldn't say that in public."

Violet stopped dancing and gave her sister a deadpan look. "Not *that* kind of slave, Desiree. It indicates a BDSM slave. They relinquish all rights to their master."

"Who would do that?" Desiree gasped, looking at Serena with troubled eyes.

"What? *No!* What are you...? He isn't...*Ohmygod.*" She stormed off the dance floor and headed for the table. The girls followed like she was the pied piper. She stopped, and they collided into her. She turned around as they frantically apologized all at once.

"Please don't say anything, okay?" she pleaded. "I don't need everyone thinking this about me. *Us.* There is no *us!*" *And if he is into slaves, there is definitely no* us.

"We won't," Desiree promised.

"Promise," Harper said.

Chloe laughed. "My lips are sealed, but I totally want to know!"

"I don't," Mira said.

Serena needed a drink. Or *three*. She glared at Violet and Emery.

"*Fine.* Jesus, you guys are so weird." Violet went back to the dance floor.

"Okay, but you have to tell us what he says when we're not around the guys," Emery urged. Then she joined Violet.

Serena thought she was nervous before, but every step closer to the table made her heart race faster. The girls took their seats, chatting with Rick and Dean and stealing glances at her. Her thoughts fragmented as Drake rose to his feet in all his rugged glory—and she pictured him with a whip, wearing leather shorts and a collar.

Shitshitshit.

"Take my seat, Supergirl," he said. "I got you another drink."

She sank down to his chair.

He pushed a glass in front of her and leaned in close, bringing his mouth beside her ear. His chest pressed deliciously against her side as he said, "It was torture watching you dance and not being out there with you."

"What do you want to do? Handcuff me to your wrist?" she snapped in a hushed whisper.

He chuckled against her cheek, and despite her irritation, her entire body heated and tingled in anticipation of his lips on her again.

"Is that what you *want?*" he asked in a low voice.

"No!" She put her hand up, shielding her mouth as she spoke harshly into *his* ear. "I can't believe you got me a *slave* bracelet!"

"What?" he said angrily. "I didn't."

She held up her arm and twisted her hand from side to side, showing him the bracelet. "Violet said it's a slave bracelet."

"She's *wrong*," he said vehemently, putting his mouth beside her ear again. "I'd *never* want you for my slave. I'm not into that shit." The distaste in his voice conveyed his honesty.

"Then why did you get me a slave bracelet?"

"I got you a bracelet I *liked*, something edgy and different, like *you*," he said.

She pressed her lips together, wishing she'd asked Violet if they sold them in places other than kinky sex stores. "Where'd you get it?"

"From a custom-jeweler friend of mine, Sterling. We designed it together two months ago. He's in P-town with his brothers for the weekend. He called the office today. You've talked to him several times. Why?"

Oh boy. Now she felt like an idiot. "I'm sorry." She reached for her drink, and he covered her hand with his, stopping her.

"Before you get blitzed, tell me what's going on." His serious expression rattled her. "Don't you trust me?"

"Yes" came easily, honestly, and with a gust of relief. Luckily, the girls were busy chatting and not hanging on her every word. "Tonight threw me off or something. When Violet said that, it made me think I didn't really know you." She leaned closer and lowered her voice to a whisper. "Are you into that stuff? Slaves and submissives?"

He put an arm around her and pulled her closer. "I'm into *you*, Serena. Do I enjoy a little kink? Sometimes, sure, if my partner is into it, but I'm not into slaves and submissives."

She skipped right over his admission about being into her, because they both knew this thing between them was like a simmering pot ready to explode. "Kink," she repeated. Her mind zoomed through all the kinky things she could think of. What if her definition of kink was different from his? She shielded her mouth again and whispered, "What do you consider *kink*?"

He gave her a *get serious* look and said, "We are not talking about this here."

"Do you make women call you *Daddy*?" she whispered, now more curious than ever about what he was into.

"Don't be sick," he said with a laugh. "I told you we aren't talking about this."

"Oh, yes, we are. I'm leaving tomorrow, and I want to know."

He hauled her closer. She was practically sitting on his lap. He'd never been a close talker, and now it seemed that was the only way he wanted to communicate with her. "I'm not going to educate you in kink the night before you leave town."

The way he said *educate you*, in a lower and more serious tone, made her stomach dip. She loved his reaction so much, she decided to push him even further. She grabbed her purse and dug out her phone. "Fine. Maybe I can find some explanatory pictures of guys with big cocks doing kinky th—"

He snagged her phone, scowling at her. "Enough."

"If you won't educate me..." She glanced around the bar and spotted Harper's brothers. Colton owned the bar and was gay, and Brock owned a gym in Eastham and was straight as an arrow, making him the perfect weapon to stir Drake's jealousy. "I bet Brock will."

She pushed to her feet, and Drake grabbed her hand, stopping her in her tracks. Her nerves flared. She felt like she was standing on the edge of a volcano, taunting an eruption by egging him on, but Lord help her, she wanted to jump in feet-first.

He rose slowly and purposefully beside her, his steady gaze rooting her in place.

"Where are you going?" Chloe asked.

"To dance," Drake said, putting his other hand on her lower back so possessively he could have branded her bare skin.

Chapter Seven

DRAKE CONSIDERED HIMSELF a master of self-control, but Serena was chipping away at it minute by minute. He'd believed he had conquered his desire for her, shelved it out of reach to be fantasized about but never realized. But as they weaved through the crowded dance floor, his sassy, sexy girl clinging to him, colorful lights raining down on an orgy of bumping and grinding bodies all around them, the scent of lust thickening the air, he struggled with his resolve.

Out of eyeshot from their friends, he took Serena in his arms, crushing her softness against his hard frame. His hands splayed across her back, moving down her hips, demanding and possessive, like she was already *his*. Carnal desires flooded him, and he struggled to remember why he'd fought them for so long.

She gazed up at him with a challenge in her gorgeous eyes, rocking and grinding seductively against him. There was no beginning or end to what she did to him. Seeing her, laughing with her, *wanting* her was a continual stream of goodness culminating in an ocean of emotions.

They danced to their own private beat, slow and sensual, then fast and dirty. His hands moved greedily over her hot flesh.

He wedged his thigh between her legs and pressed her hips tight against him, grinding into her so she could feel what she did to him as he spoke directly into her ear. "Touch me."

He put enough space between them to give her hands room to roam, and roam they did, moving hot and hungrily over his chest, ribs, and *oh yeah, baby*, up his face. Her delicate fingers played over his scruff, then down his neck. She closed her eyes, and her lips glistened enticingly as she moved to the beat, exploring his body, getting lost in him.

"Eyes on me, Supergirl."

Her eyes opened, needy and hauntingly sexy. Tangled between their scorching chemistry and unrelenting desire was a whispered warning, telling him to back off. He was going to upend her life if he continued on this runaway train. Their bodies connected from thighs to chest, brushing and grinding, pressing and rocking. He was hard as steel, and she was panting with desire. He lowered his mouth to her neck, breathing in her intoxicating scent. Her fingers curled into the backs of his arms. He didn't kiss her neck, didn't touch her skin with his mouth. His lips hovered over the curve where her neck met her shoulder, breathing warmth there. She went up on her toes to reach his mouth, but he kept a sliver of space between them, enjoying her clawing and arching, her need for more. The song "Strip That Down" by Liam Payne came on, and he pulsed his hips to the erotic beat. His hands slid down to her ass, holding tight.

She grabbed his head, trying to force his mouth to her neck. He clutched her wrist and drew back far enough to see her pleading eyes.

Fuck. This.

He hauled her off the dance floor toward the hallway that

led to the bathrooms.

"Where are we going?" she panted out, hurrying to keep up with him.

He had no fucking idea, because he wasn't about to take her in a *bathroom*.

"Away from prying eyes." He took her hands in his and backed her up against the wall, caging her in with his body, and pinned her wrists above her head. She stared up at him with wide eyes as he lowered his mouth near hers, craving her like a drug.

"I've always known you were the only woman who could lead me to pure, sexual madness," he practically growled.

The wicked smile that appeared on her luscious lips nearly did him in. "Want to *educate* me now?"

"There are so many sinful things I want to do to you right now, but not one of them has to do with *educating* you."

Her smile faded to a seductive pout. "I was hoping you'd tell me what kind of kink you like."

She had no idea what she was doing to him, with her hands trapped, her body exposed for his taking. He did a quick visual sweep of their surroundings. They were in the hallway, shielded by a group of people talking at the entrance. He shifted his hands, holding hers in one of his, as he slid his other up her thigh, cupping her bare ass cheek. Going deeper, he felt the slim line of a thong. Holy fuck he wanted to be inside her.

He brushed his scruff over her cheek and said, "You want to know what I like?"

"Yes," she panted out.

"I like you, Serena. I fantasize about you naked in my bed, lying beneath me while I'm buried deep inside you. I dream about you wearing provocative clothing—stockings, garters, heels, bent over while I take you from behind." He squeezed her ass harder, earning a sharp inhalation. "Straddling my face while I bring you to the brink of orgasm and hold you there until you beg for more, your body shaking so badly you can barely get the words out."

He kissed her neck, and she whimpered.

"I want you on your back while I taste and claim every inch of you." She struggled against his strength as he held her arms up. "Am I too much for you?"

Her eyes flamed. "No. I want to touch you."

His cock throbbed with her plea. "Not yet, Supergirl. You wanted to know what I like, and I want to tell you."

He took her earlobe between his teeth, and then he sucked it into his mouth. She bowed off the wall, grinding against him. He shot a glance at the entrance to the hall, still blocked by the group. *Thank fucking God.* He shifted, blocking her from view, and tugged her hands higher, stretching her body as he slipped his fingers between her legs, feeling the damp material. She spread her legs wider, the challenge in her eyes underscored by the lust there.

He slid his finger beneath the material, gliding over her wetness, and ground out, "Fuck, Serena." His thumb brushed over her flesh. "Bare. Oh, baby. I am going to devour you."

A seductive grin spread across her lips, and he withdrew from between her legs. All the sass went out of her eyes, and the air rushed from her lungs. He brushed his lips over her cheek and said, "When we're both ready, I'm going to take you painfully slow and intensely deep, and then, just when you think you've given all you can, I'm going to take you a little rough and dirty." He drew back and gazed into her eyes. She was so beautiful, so desperate for it, just like him. He knew he was going to burn in hell for this, but he didn't care. Being with Serena would be worth every singed second.

"But first," he said in a low voice, "I'm going to do everything I can to *heighten* and *extend* your arousal, until your skin is on fire and you orgasm from sheer, erotic desire."

He brought his damp fingers to his lips and licked them slowly, watching her intently. Her eyes widened with shock, curiosity, and red-hot *sin*. He lowered her hands and placed her palm over his zipper, holding it there as he slicked his fingers over her lower lip. He dipped his head and ran his tongue along the same path. Her cheeks flushed, and she squeezed his cock through his jeans.

"That's it, Supergirl," he said, trapping her lower lip between his teeth and giving it a gentle tug. There was a burst of noise from beyond the hallway, pulling him from his excruciatingly *hot* trance.

Serena pushed up on her toes, grabbing his arms like she might climb him as she craned to reach his mouth. She was right there, beyond ready, more than willing, but as tempting as it was to devour her, he forced himself to straighten his spine, regaining control before he threw any more caution to the wind. Focusing all his restraint, he took her hand and led her back toward the table.

"What...? Where are we going?" she asked breathlessly.

"It would be wrong to run out of the party when you're the guest of honor."

She stopped cold, eyes wide, and turned back toward the hall. "Then I need to use the bathroom. I can't go out there like *this*."

He gripped her hand tighter, hauling her against him, and slicked his tongue along the shell of her ear as he whispered,

"Why bother cleaning up? I'm only going to get you wet again."

HOW THE HECK was Serena supposed to concentrate after Drake whispered all those dirty things to her? It had been half an hour since they'd returned to the table, and her friends were watching them so closely, they had to know what was going on. She felt like she had blinking lights on her forehead that read TOO TURNED ON TO SEE STRAIGHT. It didn't help that under the table, Drake's hand was plastered to her leg, his fingers moving in a titillating rhythm on her inner thigh. She could barely concentrate enough to answer the questions her friends were peppering her with.

"I want to know all about your apartment when you get there," Emery said. "I can't believe they hooked you up with a furnished place in walking distance to the office. That firm must really be big time."

"They're a leader in their field," Serena said, reaching for her drink.

"Will you be back for the taste testing for the wedding?" Desiree asked.

Beneath the table, Drake took Serena's hand and placed it on his upper thigh. She shot him a warning look and tried to pull her hand back, but he pressed his over it, keeping it in place. She leaned her elbow on the table, hoping to make her hand on his leg less noticeable, but that just brought his hand farther up on her thigh.

He raised his brows, a devilish grin lifting his lips. She glared at him.

"*What* is going on over there?" Mira's eyes moved between

Drake and Serena. "You look like you want to hit him."

"Something like that," Serena said through gritted teeth.

"Taste testing?" Desiree asked again, bringing Serena's mind back to her question.

Drake brushed his fingers between Serena's legs. She lifted her glass and began guzzling her drink.

Violet narrowed her eyes, and with a knowing smile aimed at Desiree, she said, "I've never heard it called that, but *okay*."

Serena spit out her drink, spilling it all over herself and the table. "Shit. Sorry!"

"Oh no!" Desiree handed her a napkin.

Everyone began wiping up the table, except Drake, who reached over to wipe droplets of alcohol from her *breastbone*. His eyes were dark and full of desire, and she was sure everyone was onto them. She swatted his hand away.

"What did you mean, Violet? What's wrong with taste testing?" Desiree huffed out a breath.

"She meant something dirty," Mira explained, turning a questioning look to Serena—and then to Drake.

"Ohmygod." Serena sank back into her chair.

"I always feel like I'm two steps behind," Desiree complained. "You keep changing code words. Can't you just say *sex*?" Desiree asked.

"No!" Serena snapped. "We're not having sex!" All eyes turned to her. "Great. Thanks, Violet."

"I can say it, baby." Rick nuzzled against Desiree's cheek and said, "Let's go home and have sex."

Now Desiree was as red-cheeked as Serena felt.

"God." Serena swiped at her clothes to keep from looking at their knowing stares. "I'm all wet."

Laughter burst from Violet's lips. "This is news to you?

Because you're not going to win any Academy Awards for that performance of innocence—"

"Violet!" Drake warned. "Come on, Supergirl. Time to get you out of those clothes."

"Finally!" Violet lifted her glass in a toast and said, "Proceed with the long-awaited fuckery!"

"Violet!" Desiree chastised.

"We are not *fucking!*" Serena insisted.

Drake shut Violet down with another harsh glare and hauled Serena against him.

"Stop. They already think I'm lying about sleeping with you!" she said in a harsh whisper.

Drake slid a serious gaze over their friends. With his arm protectively around Serena, he said, "Let me make this very clear: Serena and I are *not* sleeping together. We have *never* slept together."

"Well, that's technically not true," Mira said. "You've fallen asleep on the beach together."

"Aw, you guys are so cute," Desiree said as she got up to hug Serena. "You should go home and change out of your wet clothes."

Drake waggled his brows. Serena rolled her eyes as the others got up to hug her goodbye.

"I love you, sis. I'm going to miss you, so make sure you call me a lot," Chloe said. Then she whispered, "And I want details!"

Serena groaned.

"Me too!" Emery said, pulling Serena into a fierce hug. "Have fun *taste testing.*"

"I'm never going to live tonight down, am I?" Serena asked as Mira hugged her.

"Probably not," Mira agreed. "I don't know what's going on between you and my brother tonight, but rest assured, I do *not* want any details."

"That's good, because I don't know what's going on either," she confided. "I love you, and I'm going to miss you so much."

"I have a feeling I'm going to be wiping Mira's tears tomorrow morning when she wakes up and her bestie has moved to Boston." Matt wrapped Serena in his arms. "Good luck. You're going to make us all proud."

"Damn right." Rick smirked as he crushed Serena to him. "Don't worry, Serena. I'll wipe Drake's tears tomorrow."

Drake scowled as Dean moved in for a group hug, squishing Serena between him and Rick.

"All right, you two, that's enough." Drake tugged her out from between them and said for her ears only, "We've got to get out of here before I lose my mind."

"I love you guys!" she said as Drake grabbed her purse. "Save my seat at the breakfast table on weekends!"

Their friends' voices trailed after them as they left the bar. Drake held her closer with every step across the parking lot. She was sure he'd be all over her as soon as they reached the truck. She was so nervous as he helped her into the truck, she felt numb and a little dizzy. He reached across her lap for the seat belt, his chest brushing against hers as he buckled her in, which she appreciated because she wasn't sure she could get her brain to work well enough to do it herself.

Watching her intently, he said, "You'd better stay on your side of the truck, or we might not make it to your place."

He closed her door and went around to the driver's side, while she tried to stop her world from spinning.

The drive to her cottage didn't take long, but it felt like an eternity. Questions circled her brain like a carnival ride, as exhilarating as they were alarming. Why hadn't he kissed her yet? Was this it? Was he having second thoughts and now he was back into doing the right thing? Would he even kiss her good night? Would he come inside at all? Did she want him to?

He parked in the driveway and came around to help her out. She took his hand as she stepped out of the truck, which she'd done too many times to count. On the nights he'd driven her home from outings with their friends, he always walked her up to her door, but tonight she was hyperaware of his tempting, strong body beside her, how tightly he held her hand, and how *big* that hand was.

She fished her keys from her purse, feeling the heat of his stare, and awkwardly unlocked the door. He moved her hair over her shoulder, as calm as a summer breeze, which made her even more nervous as she pushed the door open. She caught sight of the bracelet he'd given her, bringing back all of his naughty whispers.

He took her hand, drawing her against him on the porch. Her wet shirt pressed chillingly against her breasts, but his warmth could have burned it right off. He didn't say a word. He didn't have to. His approval-seeking gaze told her he was offering her an out. Her emotions sped and skidded. She'd imagined this moment so many times, had fantasized about all the things he'd done and said at the bar, but nothing compared to the real thing. Drake's power of seduction was a hundred times stronger than she could have ever imagined.

He splayed his hand across her back, as he'd done when they'd danced, sending tiny shocks rippling through her. He kissed her cheek, and she closed her eyes, trying to calm her racing heart. A kiss on the cheek shouldn't make her entire body plead for more, yet she was going up on her toes, clutching the front of his shirt, breathless and needy.

"How did we get here?" tumbled from her lips as he threaded his fingers into her hair and held on tight, searching her eyes.

He skimmed his lips over her jaw, slowing to press light kisses there, and said, "I don't know." He brushed his scruff along her cheek, abrading the tender skin, and nipped at her earlobe. Each touch of his slow seduction sent erotic sensations skittering through her.

"Do you want to be here?" he asked roughly, tightening his hold on her.

"Yes—"

Heat flared in his eyes, and he lowered his face toward hers, stopping short of kissing her and lingering there like the most sought-after treat, just out of reach, making her breathless and anxious.

"I've waited so long to kiss you," he said in a low growl. He tugged her hair, angling her face beneath his, and slowly traced her lower lip with his tongue. "To taste you."

He kissed the edges of her mouth, pressing his hand firmly on her lower back, his arousal temptingly insistent against her belly. She clung to him as his hot lips touched her neck, kissing and licking, taking his time as he revved her up one sinful second at a time. Just when her legs were ready to give out, his mouth covered the curve of her shoulder in a hard suck, and then he *feasted* on her sensitive skin, grinding against her until she was a boneless, trembling mess.

"Kiss me," she pleaded.

He drew back with a wolfish grin, and in the next breath he was lavishing her shoulder with more taunting openmouthed kisses and grazing his teeth over her skin, causing pleasure and pain to collide inside her. Never in her life had she been so turned on. She arched against him, groping his ass, needing more but not wanting him to stop his masterful seduction. His wicked tongue moved across her breastbone in mind-numbingly slow strokes. She had no idea how her legs carried her, but they stumbled into the cottage, and he backed her up against the door, pinning her there with nothing more than his hungry eyes raking down the length of her with lethal calmness. She was breathing too hard, shaking from fingers to toes, every nerve ending already aflame as he visually devoured her. His gaze crawled north again, lingering on her breasts. Her nipples tingled and burned with the need to be touched by him.

He took hold of one end of the tie that laced up the center of her shirt, and his eyes found hers. "If you want to remain only friends, now's the time to tell me, Supergirl."

Was he nuts? She couldn't freaking speak right then if he'd held a gun to her head, so she began fumbling with the buttons on his shirt to convey her answer.

Without a word, he lifted her into his arms, guiding her legs around his waist, and *finally, hungrily*, crushed his mouth to hers in a penetrating kiss that resonated through her like a symphony. Every insistent stroke of his tongue took her higher; his roughness hit like crescendos as he took their kisses deeper. Just when she thought she would come apart from nothing more than this, he eased his efforts to the sweetest, tenderest kisses she'd ever experienced. He was like the most intense, passionate roller-coaster ride, taking her harder, more demanding, holding her in place with one hand buried in her hair, the other gripping her bottom. He continued his exquisite possession, devouring her fast and then slow, rough and then sweet, until her thoughts fragmented and she gave up trying to think at all.

The next thing she knew, he was on the move, carrying her to the bedroom. She could do little more than cling to him as they ate each other's mouths, and when he lowered her to the bed, he went with her, never breaking their connection.

His strong body pressed down on her, his hands cradling her head as he took their kisses to mind-numbing depths. His kisses were whole-body invasions, causing her heart to beat faster, her breathing to become shallow and then frantic, as she filled with desperation. She clawed at his back, tugging at his shirt with the need to feel his bare skin on hers. She was completely and utterly lost in a frenzy of lust and greed and something much more animalistic.

He reared up on his knees and stripped off his shirt. Her hands were drawn to his chest like metal to magnet, moving over his muscles, through his chest hair. How many times had she imagined doing exactly this? His fingers circled her wrists, and he kissed one palm and then the other, his eyes never leaving hers. His lips were soft and hot, and when he touched them to the underside of her wrist, she held her breath. He sealed his mouth over the sensitive skin, driving her out of her mind by sucking and licking, nipping and kissing all the way from the underside of her wrist to the crook of her elbow and back again. She writhed beneath him, feeling every slick of his tongue like a spear of pleasure between her legs. She never knew mere kisses could have this effect on her, but Drake didn't *merely* do anything. He consumed. Claimed. *Possessed.*

"Drake," she begged. Her thong was drenched, her thighs damp with her arousal. He wasn't kidding. He really would make her come from sheer desire.

He continued kissing and sucking, all the way up her arm to

her shoulder. Then he roughly captured her mouth again, lowering his body over hers. His hard length rocked against her center. She was so wet, so ready, every bit of friction took her closer to the edge. She gasped for breath, and he breathed air into her lungs, unrelenting in his thrusts as he claimed her hands and held them above her head. His scruff abraded her lips and cheeks with the force of his kisses. One hand pushed beneath her bottom, clutching her cheek so hard, it forced her sex open, allowing him to press his shaft where she needed it most, taking her up, up, *up*. She was hanging on by a thread, so focused on chasing the peak, her jaw went slack as she angled her hips.

He tore his mouth away and said, "Don't move your hands."

Before she could process his words, he grabbed her ass with both hands, holding her open as he thrust against her. The rough denim and his hard heat sent her soaring, and when he sank his teeth into her neck, she cried out as a million shiny stars exploded behind her closed lids. Her body bucked, her sex clenched, and he captured her mouth again, kissing her so forcefully, she spun higher, out of control. A litany of indiscernible sounds and pleas flew from her lungs into his. Just when she came down from the peak, gasping for breath, his mouth left hers, and she whimpered like a lost soul.

He blazed his way down her body, nipping and sucking, whispering sweetly as he went, but she was too delirious to process his words. When he reached her shirt, he took the tie between his teeth and tugged it free. Holy mother of sexiness, that was *hot*.

He began kissing her oversensitive skin, and her eyes fluttered closed.

"Eyes open, sweetheart. I want you to see who's driving you wild."

Her eyes flew open with his command, stirring all sorts of passions she'd never known existed. She craved that roughness of his voice, the fierceness in his eyes as he loosened her shirt, and then unthreaded the tie completely. He pushed the two sides of her shirt to the mattress, leaving her bare from the hips up.

"I've waited a fucking lifetime for this. You're gorgeous, Serena."

He dragged the silky tie over her breasts. Her nipples pebbled against the sensual touch, and he lowered his mouth over one taut peak, teasing her with light flicks of his tongue.

"Oh God," she said in a long, heated whisper.

He took her nipple between his teeth and tugged, sending shocks of lightning to her sex. Her hips shot off the mattress.

"Mm. Supergirl likes that."

He did it again, and her eyes slammed closed with the mix of pleasure and pain.

"I love your eyes, sweetheart. I want them on me."

Every word was laced with emotion, but the underlying command was not lost on her, and Lord help her, she *loved* it.

Her eyes opened, and he continued his magnificent ministrations, sucking and biting, loving each breast. She struggled to keep from closing her eyes, and at the same time, watching him was the most erotic thing she'd ever seen. The pleased look he gave her as he tasted her made her even hotter, more desperate for him. Her entire body tingled and throbbed as his mouth moved slowly over every inch of each breast, sucking the underside of one as he groped the other. She'd never known her body was so sensitive, but every slick of his tongue made her wetter. His hips were wedged between her legs, and he angled up, thrusting against her swollen sex in the same rhythm as he squeezed her nipple and sucked her other breast, causing a collision of sensations. She bowed up beneath him, her legs opening wider so he could press harder, and *sweet baby Jesus*, the man knew exactly what he was doing. A searing ache burned inside her, an orgasm fluttering just out of reach. He pinched harder, sucking so roughly a spear of pain shot through her core, exploding in a gust of fiery sensations. She cried out, clutching at the mattress. He didn't relent, holding her at the peak, heightening and extending her arousal just as he'd promised. She quivered and quaked, caught in a web of exquisite sensations. She couldn't breathe, couldn't see, could only surrender to his divine ecstasies, spiraling into oblivion.

She felt suspended by waves of pleasures as his mouth and hands traveled down her body. His fingers pressed firmly into her skin as his lips brushed ever so lightly beside them, on her ribs, her waist, her belly. Every squeeze of his hand was accentuated by a tantalizing press of his lips and slick of his tongue. She was mesmerized by the look in his eyes as he moved from her face to the part of her body he was cherishing, then back again. Every time their eyes met, her pulse spiked, and when his mouth touched her skin, it brought a rush of too many sensations to pick apart.

He pushed up her skirt, and she lifted her hips for him to remove it, but the coy grin he flashed told her he wasn't going to. Instead, he lowered his mouth to her inner thigh, sucking the wetness of her arousal and sending more electric currents coursing through her. He gripped her thighs, just above her knees, spreading them wider as he kissed her knee and up along her inner thigh until he reached her center. He hovered over her sex, breathing her in, and placed a single kiss to the thin material separating them. Then his mouth met her other thigh in hard sucks and tender kisses, all the way down to her knee. Her skin was on fire as he tasted his way back up her flesh, eyes locked on her.

"Drake, you're driving me crazy—"

He dragged his tongue along the crease beside her sex. Her inner muscles pulsed and swelled in anticipation.

"Give me your hands," he rasped, and she did.

He pressed his palms flat against hers, holding them to the mattress beside her, and lowered his mouth beside her sex again, teasing and taunting all around it but never moving her thong or touching her *there*. She hung on the brink of madness as he loved her thighs, belly, and finally, her breasts, taking her expertly over the edge time and time again.

When she finally collapsed beneath him, gasping her way through a thick haze of pleasure, his lips curved into a smile she'd never seen on him before. It was so serene, it felt like she was privy to a secret. She barely had time to process the thought before his mouth came lovingly down over hers, breathing life back into her spent body. She groped at the waist of his jeans, trying to push them down, needing to feel his cock in her hand, on her body, buried deep inside her.

He captured her hands in his and rose up, shadows pushing that secret smile away and sending a wave of anxiety through her.

"But we didn't...*You* didn't—"

He kissed her shoulder, tender touches of his lips, and then he lowered his forehead there, restraint radiating off him.

"Drake, let me pleasure you," she said, trying to ease the worry of whatever was holding him back.

"Shh." He kissed her again, tender and languid, as if her words made it harder for him to resist. "I don't want you to wake up tomorrow regretting a single thing we do."

"I won't," she promised. "I could never regret this. I've waited forever to be with you."

"And you're leaving tomorrow," he reminded her. "Embarking on an exciting new part of your life. I want you to be clearheaded when you start your new job, not distracted by me, or us, and wondering *what if…*"

She flopped onto her back and sighed. "Well, you already screwed *that* up. All these years and I never knew it was possible to have an orgasm without actually being touched *down there*. If you think that's not going to distract me every minute of the day, you've got your head on backward."

He laughed and leaned over her, kissing her again. "If you say orgasm again, I might have to change my mind."

"Orgasm, orgasm, orgasm!" she said as fast as she could.

He pulled her against him, kissing and laughing as he tickled her. They both fell to the mattress smiling.

"You told me all the reasons you couldn't be with me," she said. "And *now* look where we are. You kind of suck at holding back."

"Hey, I've restrained myself for *years*. I think I should be commended for my efforts." He lay beside her, holding her hand, and said, "I couldn't have held back more than I have tonight if my life depended on it."

She grinned like a fool.

"I think you put some kind of weakening agent in my drink." He leaned over and pressed a kiss to the swell of her breast. "Promise me something. If you regret this in the morning, text me and let me know instead of disappearing and never talking to me again."

"How could I not talk to you again? You'd leave a hole in my life, and that would suck. You won't do that, will you? What if *you* regret it? *Ohmygod.* What if you're telling me this because you *already* regret it?"

"Stop," he said with a smile.

"We need a code word," she said hastily. "*Delete.* If either of us regrets this, we'll text *delete* to the other, and then we'll know that we can never think or talk about it again."

"Yeah, *that'll* work," he said sarcastically. He touched his lips to hers and said, "You are all I'll think about from this second on. Your intoxicating mouth…" His lips came coaxingly down over hers, taking her in another toe-curling kiss. "And don't get me started on your body." He sucked her nipple into his mouth, and she arched off the mattress.

"Drake—" She fisted her hands in his hair, holding his mouth there. "Don't stop."

He moved over her, his thick length pressed against her center as he groped and teased her breasts, taking her higher with every tantalizing touch. She clung to his head as he masterfully sent her soaring again. Holy cow. He was crazy if he thought she'd regret this. She didn't even know what *this* was, and she didn't need a definition. It felt too right to question.

He kissed her and loved her, making her feel cherished, sexy, and oh so satisfied. She melted limply into the mattress, and he gazed down at her, his dark eyes holding her captive. A slow grin lifted his lips, and he kissed the edges of her mouth, as if he simply wanted to remember the moment, to see her face. And *holy cow*, what that did to her hungry heart was overwhelming.

Sometime later, as she lay in a foggy state of post-orgasmic bliss, she realized he'd given her pleasure but she'd done nothing for him. "Let me make you feel good."

"You already have," he said, showering her with more kisses. "No regrets, beautiful."

He wrapped her in his strong arms, holding her as they kissed and then running his hand soothingly along her back as they lay together. Most men couldn't wait to get in a woman's pants, and here he was, content with pleasuring her, holding her.

"Okay, sweetheart," he said softly. "I better go before I forget why we stopped."

She clung to him, knowing he was smart to give her a chance to think before they went further and wishing he could be careless just this once. That he'd take the decision out of her hands, as he had when he'd held back. But now she understood his reasoning well enough to realize that this decision was too important for either of them to give in.

He covered her with the blanket and kissed her tenderly. "Get some sleep."

She lay on her side, watching him put on his shirt and wishing they'd been there four years ago. Was she making a mistake moving away? Could this be the beginning and the end of everything she'd ever wanted?

Weren't those the exact questions, the *reasons*, he'd held back for all this time? The reason they hadn't made love tonight?

"You're going to outshine everyone in Boston, Supergirl. I can't wait to hear all about it. I'll come by in the morning to help you load up your car."

"No. Please don't." She swallowed past the lump in her throat caused by the disappointment in his eyes. "I suck at goodbyes. You know I'll cry, and I don't want that. Just let me pretend it's any other day and I'm going on a road trip."

"That feels wrong on so many levels." He sank down to the edge of the bed and took her hand in his.

"It's not. It's the rightest thing you can do."

He sighed and traced the stars on her bracelet.

"I love my bracelet, and I love that every time I wear it I'll think of tonight. Thank you." She wanted to ask him what tonight meant. How would they act when they saw each other again? But part of her knew that too many questions might bring whatever this was between them to a screeching halt.

"I'll lock up when I leave." He touched his lips to hers and whispered, "Nothing could ever delete tonight from my memory banks. Good night, Supergirl."

Chapter Eight

DRAKE AWOKE TO the sound of his cell phone vibrating on the nightstand. He bolted upright, disoriented after being awake for most of the night. He'd been in a state of euphoria when he'd left Serena's cottage, having finally let her feel his emotions instead of hiding them. But when he'd gotten home, he'd been swamped with worry. He'd done the exact thing he'd sworn he wouldn't do. He'd been *this close* to making love to her. Even without that next level of intimacy, he'd crossed every line he'd ever drawn between them—and despite his worries, he didn't regret a second of it.

But that didn't mean he wouldn't worry like a motherfucker.

He snagged his phone, hoping not to see the word *delete*. Relief swept through him as he read Serena's message. *Thanks for the best night of my life. And for making me more confused. xoxox.* She added a smiling emoji.

"Best night, huh? Nice to know I'm not alone in that." Before he could type a response, another message popped up. *And don't you DARE text DELETE or I'll come back and punch you in your orgasm-inducing mouth! Love you.*

A kissing emoji popped up.

Another message bubble appeared. *I meant I love you like I always say to you and Rick and Dean. Not I love you like a boyfriend.*

He sat up on the edge of the bed, smiling as another message came through. *That sounds bad. You know what I mean. See? You definitely confused me! Goodbye! See you this weekend to work on the shop.*

"What have I done to you, Supergirl?" he mumbled as he typed a reply. *So...you like my mouth, huh? Love you too, Supergirl.*

Drake pulled on his running clothes and texted Rick. *Ready to run?*

Rick's response was immediate. *We thought you blew us off. Hurry your ass up.*

A brisk breeze, sunshine, and the sound of the bay kissing the shore were welcome companions as they ran down the beach. Drake looked forward to their morning runs, even in the winter, when the bitter cold brought them to the streets rather than the beach. Running took all the starch out of him before work each day, and catching up with the guys was always a nice way to start the day. They knew when to give each other space and when to push—emotionally and physically. Drake caught up to Rick and Dean about half a mile down the beach.

"You don't look like a guy who finally got his girl," Rick said.

Before Rick and Dean had fallen for their significant others, they'd dish about the women they'd gone out with. There was no way Drake was going to share any intimate information about Serena. "Yeah? Well, you look like a guy who's about to get his ass kicked."

Dean snickered.

"Tabling this discussion," Rick said with a smirk. "Moving on to more important things, like why the hell didn't anyone warn me that there was so much shit to plan for a wedding?"

"Emery said you were having a simple beach wedding," Dean said. "What's so complicated? Get someone to officiate, throw on some nice clothes, and get hitched."

"You'd think so," Rick said. "But Desiree is arranging *tasting sessions* with Brandy up in P-town. Tasting sessions. It's a cake. It could come from the grocery store and no one would care."

"Brandy's doing the catering for our grand opening, too. Don't you remember Serena and I doing a tasting with her last month? And that's *not* a wedding. You really don't understand women," Drake said. "Desiree's probably been dreaming of her wedding day forever, like most women. She wants everything to be perfect."

"I'm glad you understand, because she wants all of us, guys and girls, to go to the tasting. She said our wedding plans should include all our friends." Rick smirked.

"Great," Drake said flatly.

Rick chuckled. "And flowers? Who knew picking them out could be so hard? Desiree set out pictures of different bouquets all over our bedroom. She said she needs to see which one *feels* right."

"I knew I liked her," Dean said. Having previously owned a landscaping business, he was all about flowers and plants. Now, not only did he manage the grounds of the resort, but he also maintained the gardens at the hospital where he'd once worked as a trauma nurse, as well as at LOCAL, where his grandmother lived.

Rick scowled. "You just wait. When are you and Emery

going to tie the knot?"

They split up to run around a couple sitting on the beach, and while Dean and Rick talked about weddings, Drake's mind traveled back to last night, to the moment he'd lifted Serena into his arms and had finally kissed her—and then he revisited every touch, every taste, every one of her sweet sounds. He'd made a damn liar of himself. But now, in the light of day, listening to Dean and Rick talk about their weddings, when he should feel selfish and apologetic, he didn't. And given the chance, he'd do it all over again. That probably made him even more of a selfish prick, especially since he'd been right. On the cusp of what should be the most exciting time of Serena's life, he'd confused the hell out of her.

"Drake!" Rick grabbed his arm and yanked him around a log he'd nearly run into. "Whoa, dude. *Now* you look like the guy who got the girl. What the hell happened? You zoned out for that last two miles."

"Serena," he said absently as the resort came into view. Wow. He really had zoned out. He hadn't even registered turning around. "She happened to me."

"It's about fucking time," Dean said.

"Does that mean you've given yourself permission to be a mere mortal?" Rick asked.

Drake was not in the mood to be given shit. "What...?"

"The other day you said you were man enough not to fuck with her head," Rick reminded him. "It took you four years, but you finally realized you're only human? Jesus, Drake. If I'd have known that all it would take was for her to get a new job, I'd have practically kicked her out the door ages ago. Do you have any idea how painful it was to watch you two together every time we went out?"

Try being in my shoes.

"There is so much sexual tension between you two, I'm surprised you don't leave a trail of fire in your wake," Dean said. "That's obviously why she's never gone home with any of the guys who hit on her."

Good. Drake had been the one to drive her most of those times, but he wasn't fooling himself. She'd never hidden the fact that she'd gone on occasional dates, and each and every time had been excruciating for him.

"Don't get your hopes up too high," Drake said as they slowed to a walk by the inn. "She's on her way to Boston, and my life is here. I meant it when I said I'd never make her choose or stand in her way."

"It's only a half hour flight from P-town," Dean reminded him. "An hour and a half by car without traffic."

"What's your plan? You can't just sleep with her and let it go at that," Rick said protectively.

"Don't you think I know that? I'm the one who"—*loves her. Holy shit. I really do love her*—"has been watching out for her all this time. And we didn't sleep together."

They looked at him like he wasn't making sense.

"Then what's got your nuts in a knot?" Dean asked.

Rick grinned. "That he didn't sleep with her, obviously."

Drake glared at him.

"Come on. I'm starved." Rick started up the path toward the inn. "You can expect eggs Benedict or something equally amazing today, and yes, I expect a thank-you."

Dean scoffed. "Real men don't brag."

The last thing Drake wanted to do was to sit around the breakfast table watching those two make out with their women while his girl was setting up house in Boston. "I'm out of here."

"You going to be around later?" Rick called after him.

Drake turned around. "Yeah. Why?"

"We've got to talk about hiring someone. She's gone, man, and you know Serena. Even if she hates her job, she's not coming back to run the office."

"Emery and Harper agreed to help out, but we need someone permanent," Dean pointed out.

Drake's gut twisted. He hadn't even realized he was holding on to the hope that Serena might come back. Rick was right. She'd see it as a failure. She was all about moving forward. Her voice traipsed through his mind. *I won't end up like my mother, running through quicksand with the hopes of someone else creating a life for me. Every time she got her foot on solid ground, she'd meet a guy and backslide into the muck of wishful thinking. Wishes don't make dreams come true. Only hard work can do that.*

He looked at Rick's and Dean's expectant faces. He'd been pushing away his true emotions for so many years, he had a feeling the ones he'd finally unleashed were only skimming the surface. He hadn't realized how messed up he'd been over Serena's leaving. He was damn lucky they'd put up with his attitude.

"I'll be in the office later," he said. "We'll go through the résumés and bring back the best three candidates. I'm sure one of them will be fine."

He jogged across the sand toward the office, imagining Serena's car parked out front. His heart sank. The exact opposite of the reaction he'd had every time he'd seen it, day after fucking day.

He went into the office and stopped in front of her desk. Harper would be there soon, and then Emery, and then some other person. As he headed upstairs to his apartment, he tried to come to grips with the reality that he'd never again see her beautiful face behind that desk. It felt strangely like one of their connections had severed, even though another one had developed.

Taking the stairs two at a time, he threw open his apartment door, grabbed his phone from the dresser behind the door, and thumbed out a text to Serena on his way to the kitchen. *Just got back from my run. Miss seeing you already.* He grabbed a bottle of water from the fridge and guzzled it down, contemplating the text. He set the bottle on the counter, deleted the text, and typed, *I bet Boston looks brighter with you in it.*

"Damn it." That made him sound like a chick.

He deleted the message and headed for the shower, catching sight of a picture hanging on the wall in the hallway. Mira had taken it right after they'd started working on the resort. He was standing on the office porch having a heated conversation about renovations with Rick and Dean. Serena sat on the steps, her knees touching, making a silly face by sticking out her tongue and crossing her eyes. She was pointing behind her with both thumbs. Her hair was shorter then, and it was spring, too early for the summer sun to bring out her hair's golden highlights, which had always bewitched him.

The resort belonged to her just as much as it belonged to him and the other guys. Maybe more so, since she'd had to figure out how to work with the three of them and overcome so much between each of them to help make *their* dreams come to fruition. They'd fought her tooth and nail when she'd wanted to pretty up the office and cottages to make them more feminine and when she'd instituted procedures that took more time than they would have liked. In the end she'd been right. Their systems were efficient, their project management structure sound. And don't even get him started on the music stores. Had it not been for her, he'd have made a few big mistakes that would have cost him dearly. He had no doubt she was going to excel at her new job, and he would be damned if he'd stand in her way.

He thumbed out the message, *Thanks for putting up with all of us and for putting your heart and soul into the resort and the music stores. They're all better because you had a hand in them. Go kick ass, Supergirl. You've got nowhere to go but up.*

He sent the message, wrestling with the things he really wanted to tell her.

Fuck it. He took a picture of the photograph in the hall and typed the caption, *The dude on the left misses you.*

That was fucking lame. They had never been sappy types.

He deleted the message, took a selfie, and sent it off with the caption *Does this sweat make me look hot?*

SERENA KICKED HER bare feet up on the coffee table in her new loft apartment Saturday evening and sank into the plush, teal-blue art-deco sofa as she video chatted with Chloe and Mira. She had given them a virtual tour and clued them in to some parts of last night's extracurricular activities. Chloe had peppered her with questions, but luckily, Mira had demanded a PG summary. She had gotten away with saying, *Being with Drake surpassed my wildest dreams and we didn't even sleep together.* It wasn't like Serena wanted to share all the details of her and Drake's incredible night, but she knew Chloe would have continued pushing had it not been for Mira.

"What on earth are you eating?" Serena squinted into the

monitor.

"Sushi," Chloe answered.

Mira wiped her mouth and said, "Chicken. Matt and Hagen grilled it with all sorts of veggies. It's delicious. What are you eating, Serena?"

Serena held up a pint of her new favorite ice cream. "BJ's. Kinky Pleasures!"

"I didn't know Ben and Jerry's had that flavor." Chloe lifted her chin as if it would help her see inside Serena's container. "Show it to me. What's in it?"

Serena tilted the container toward the screen. "It's not Ben and Jerry's, and it's full of pieces of chocolate, walnuts, cherries, and toffee. BJ's ice cream serves *only* dirty flavors like Custard-lingus and Obscene Orgasm. That one was white and creamy." She snort-laughed, making the girls crack up. "This apartment building is *insane*. Everything I need is right downstairs, including my dinner." She shoveled a scoop of ice cream into her mouth. "I might never leave the building."

"I don't think your boss would like that," Mira said.

"You're so responsible." Serena's phone vibrated, and Drake's name appeared on the screen. Her stomach fluttered, as it had been doing every time he texted. Although he had yet to text anything about last night or about the card she'd left at his apartment. She read the text and said, "Hold on. I need to reply to this."

"Is that Drake *again*?" Chloe pulled her sweater around her shoulders. She was sitting on her deck, talking to them by candlelight.

"Yes. A bunch of stuff was installed at the music shop today. He's just catching me up, and he's also asking questions about the people we interviewed. It sounds like they're taking another look at the candidates I brought in," Serena said as she replied to his text. She wanted to ask him what last night had meant, and she worried that maybe she'd been too honest with her feelings in the card. *Drake, there was a time when I thought we might end up together. And then I let that thought go. But never fully. Even now, knowing how you feel about me and why you want to keep distance between us, I still can't let it go. You'll always be the first boy I fell in love with. I wonder, though, if you'll also be the last.*

It had felt like the right thing to say at the time. She drew in a deep breath and said, "Can I ask you guys something about dating?"

"Hold on. Let me get away from little ears." Mira got up, carrying her phone.

"I know you mean me, Mom," Hagen said as she passed him.

Mira bent and kissed his head. "Say hi to Auntie Serena."

He looked up from the puzzle he was working on with Matt, and his normally serious blue eyes widened. "Hi! Do you like Boston? Did you go to the library yet? Are you eating ice cream? What flavor? I had ice cream after lunch." Hagen loved libraries, museums, and basically any place where he could learn new facts. Matt and Mira were always taking him on educational outings.

"That's a lot of questions, buddy," Matt said to Hagen, then he turned his face toward the screen. "Hey, girls. How's it going?"

"Hi, Hagen. Hi, Matt." Serena waved. "I haven't gotten to the library yet, Hagen, but I will report back when I do. And I am eating ice cream. It's called—"

"Watch it!" Mira said.

"Yummylicious," Chloe chimed in.

Matt shook his head with a stifled chuckle.

"On that note, I'm taking this call outside." Mira held the phone closer as she went outside and whispered, "Eight-year-olds are like little spies. They collect intel and bring it out at the worst possible time. Just this morning he asked Matt if he remembered to stop by the girls' shop and get new *toys*."

Serena and Chloe howled with laughter. Desiree and Violet had first come to the Cape under the guise of their mother needing help due to her failing health. They'd been tricked into running their mother's art gallery, Devi's Discoveries, which was on the grounds of the inn. They'd later discovered an adult toy shop in the back of the gallery, which their mother had failed to mention owning. They ran that now, too.

Mira sat down on a deck chair. "Poor Matt had to run out and buy Hagen toys so he didn't parrot it right back to everyone else."

"I'm sorry," Serena said, still laughing. "But that's *hilarious*."

Mira narrowed her eyes. "You just wait until you have children."

"Not happening anytime soon for me," Chloe said.

"Me either, but is it safe to ask you my question now?" Serena asked.

Chloe leaned forward, her hazel eyes wide with curiosity. "Ask me anything. I'm like a dating guru."

"You are pickier than anyone I've ever met," Serena reminded her. "That's totally not true. You're like a dating *warning sign*."

Mira laughed. "Okay, okay, you two. Keep it PG, please. Drake is still my brother."

"I know. Don't worry. This isn't about sex. I didn't tell you guys this, but Drake and I almost kissed Wednesday night."

"What?" Chloe snapped. "You withheld that from us?"

"Thank you," Mira said.

"You're welcome. There's more. Thursday, a full *day* before Drake and I even kissed, he told me how he felt about me *and* all the reasons why we couldn't be together. And his reasons made sense. I mean, sort of. The way he said it, I almost felt thankful that we had never hooked up. We talked about that *almost kiss* the summer of the duet, and he said we were in two different places, with him going off to college and me just starting high school. And he was right."

"That's really chivalrous of him," Mira said, "considering most high school guys are out for sex."

"It makes me wish I hadn't threatened him back then," Chloe said softly.

"You threatened him?" Serena and Mira asked in unison.

Chloe shrugged. "You're my sister. He broke your heart. I wanted to punch him, but you know, that would have been like punching a brick wall, and I like my knuckles. So I threatened him instead."

"God, you're awesome. Thank you." They had always had each other's backs, but she'd never known her sister had gone that far on her behalf. "Anyway, he knew I was only filling in temporarily at the resort, and he didn't want to put me in the position of us getting together and then giving up my dreams or being confused about where I was heading and what I was leaving behind."

"He meant *him*, right? Leaving him behind or a relationship with him?" Mira asked. "I hadn't realized full-on big-brother mode was that ingrained in him."

"No, not *big-brother* mode," Serena said. "Responsible-mode or protector-mode. He made it *very* clear that his feelings for me were not big brotherish at all. He said that he couldn't be with me because it would be selfish, and that if we kissed he'd never be able to hold back."

"Well, that didn't stop him last night," Mira pointed out.

"Yes, it did," Serena said honestly. She'd felt his restraint. She'd been ready to go all the way, and he'd put on the brakes. He'd done it again. He'd *protected* her.

The man didn't have a selfish bone in his body.

"Hello?" Chloe waved her hand.

Serena blinked several times to try to clear her thoughts. "Sorry. I was just thinking."

"So what's the problem? That he was right? He couldn't hold back?" Chloe asked. "Because I'd say the man's a god for going years without touching the woman he wanted. Especially since you guys were always together."

"I know he is, and no, that's not the problem. The problem is, I left each of the guys a card Friday afternoon thanking them for everything and telling them that I'd miss them. But since I thought Drake and I had no chance at being together and I was moving away, what I wrote in his was blatantly honest. I basically poured my heart out, and now I worry it was too much. That maybe it scared him off."

"What did you write?" Mira asked.

"How I *really* feel about him. I held nothing back." She wasn't about to tell them what she'd written, but it played in her head like a recording stuck on repeat, just like that old Journey song Drake used to play all the time. The one she'd lived by. "Don't Stop Believin'."

"Well, has he said anything about being scared off?" Chloe asked, bringing her attention back to their conversation. "Has he pulled back? Because he's texted you three times since we started this chat."

"No. He hasn't said or done anything like that, but if I got a card where he'd poured his heart out, I'd at *least* acknowledge it."

"Maybe he's embarrassed," Chloe suggested.

"Ask him," Mira added. "Or I can if you want? He promised Hagen he'd take him sailing tomorrow afternoon. I can ask him then."

"No! Don't, Mira. *Please?* That would be mortifying. We've only had a few hours together. We're not even really dating. I don't know what we are yet. The last thing I want is to make this seem like more—or less—than it is. Promise me you won't even tell Matt. You know the guys talk. Matt might slip up and say something, and then they'll all try to fix us or something."

"Then that's your answer," Chloe said. "If you're confused about it, chances are he is too. And if you poured your heart out, he's probably figuring out how to handle it. Just give it some time."

"I won't say a word, Serena. Don't worry. But Chloe's right. I wouldn't worry about it," Mira said. "I love my brothers, but when it comes to women, they're both a little thickheaded. Look how long it took Drake to finally give in to his feelings for you. He's not going to back off because you like him *too* much."

Serena sighed, feeling better. "You're right. I'm overthinking. I'm so nervous about"—last night—"starting my new job, it's making me overthink everything. Look." She grabbed her notebook from the table and held up her lists, explaining each one as she turned the pages. "I made all these lists just since I finished unpacking. A grocery list, questions I want to ask Monday, clothes I want to remember to bring back next weekend, things I need to follow up on for the music store. I even made a list of suggestions for Justine at Shift to help streamline her processes."

"You are a sick woman." Chloe smirked. "If I were in a new city with no responsibilities for two days, I'd be out exploring, finding out which clubs are the hottest, where to get my morning coffee, where to hang out and get tan…"

And yet here I am, in a new city, wishing I were back at Bayside in the arms of a certain man.

Long after her conversation with the girls, when the streets were quiet and moonlight shimmered in the harbor, Serena lay in bed texting with Drake. She told him about her loft, which was efficient and cozy, though smaller than the cottage she rented at the Cape.

There's a view of the harbor, she texted. *It's not spectacular, but at least I can see water.*

His response came fast. *Are there good locks on the doors? What's the neighborhood like? Safe? Did you find the grocery store? Gas station?*

She smiled at his typical guy questions as she texted. *Yes to locks, and yes, it's safe. I'll go to the grocery store tomorrow. It's only about twenty minutes away. I had ice cream for dinner.*

He texted a scowling emoji. *How will Supergirl survive without an all-night cookie bakery?*

A better question would be how would she survive without seeing him except on weekends? Last night he'd opened a tap, and her emotions no longer eked out only to be swept away. They flowed like a river. But she had no idea where she and Drake stood, so she tried to keep those thoughts to herself and changed the subject. *Did you eat cookies on my behalf for dinner?*

Her eyes slid around the bedroom, thinking about how

lame it was that she wasn't asking what she really wanted to know. But she was nervous, and he was taking a long time to reply to her text, which made her even more worried. She tried to concentrate on how different the loft was from her cottage. She entered the cottage directly into the living room, and she had a real bedroom. She entered the loft between the laundry closet and galley kitchen on the left and the bathroom on the right. The bedroom had two entrances, one from the kitchen and the other from the living room. Neither had a door, and the bedroom walls stopped about a foot from the ceiling, allowing moonlight to stream in. It felt strange, but she thought that was probably normal, since it was new to her.

Her phone vibrated, and she read Drake's text. *No cookies. The only thing I want to eat is 100 miles away.*

"Ohmygod!" She pressed the phone to her chest, eyes slammed shut, an unstoppable grin on her face. The card *hadn't* changed his feelings.

Or had it? For the better, maybe?

She couldn't live like this. She had to know what they were doing, where they stood.

She thumbed out a message before she could chicken out. *You know I suck at not knowing where I stand with ANYTHING, so I have to ask…What are we doing?* She pushed send and held her breath.

Every silent minute that passed felt like an hour. After five minutes, a fissure formed in her heart. She set her phone beside her pillow, contemplating backpedaling with an apology, or saying he didn't need to answer. She closed her eyes, and her phone vibrated.

With her heart in her throat, she opened and read his text. *Texting. You should get some rest. You'll need your energy for grocery shopping.*

A kissing emoji popped up, and then a sleeping emoji with the message, *Good night Supergirl.*

"What the fuck?" she seethed into the darkness. "You can't practically start sexting and then go all big brother on me." She started texting exactly that and suddenly realized what she was doing.

She was *chasing.*

Her mother *chased.*

Serena did *not.* Not even for *him.*

She set her phone on the nightstand and burrowed down deep in the blankets. A minute later, the first warm tears slid down her cheeks. As she drifted in and out of her thoughts, it was Drake's handsome face that accompanied her, his rough voice threading through her mind: *Nothing could ever delete tonight from my memory banks.*

Except maybe a hundred miles...

Chapter Nine

DRAKE'S PHONE RANG at a little before two o'clock in the morning, and Serena's name flashed on the screen. He felt bad for the way he'd left things with her, but he'd had to get his head on straight and make a decision once and for all before answering her question. He put the phone to his ear, and before he could get a word out, her panicked voice rang through.

"Drake! Someone's banging on my door. What should I do?"

He clutched the phone tighter. "Slow down and look through your peephole."

"Okay," she whispered. "I'm so scared."

"Breathe, Serena. What do you see?"

"Hold on."

He listened to her hasty breathing through the phone, the frantic slide of the locks and chain, and then she was punching his chest, crying.

"You scared the shit out of me! You bastard! Why…?"

He dropped his bag inside the door and gathered her trembling body into his arms, closing the door behind him. He held her tight, kissing her tears away as she clung to him, gasping for air.

"I'm sorry, sweetheart. I'm sorry. You asked what we were doing, and I had to say this to your face." He drew back, cradling her face between his hands, her warm tears colliding with his thumbs like accusations. He'd driven like a bat outta hell to get there, and he was glad he had.

"What *are* we doing?" she demanded.

"What we should have done ages ago." He lowered his lips to hers, and she smiled and cried against them, breaking his heart and then healing it again with the eagerness of her kisses.

He lifted her into his arms and opened his eyes long enough to navigate to the small bedroom. "I found your card this evening. It had slid behind the door. Thank you for never letting us go." As he lowered her to the bed, he said, "Everyone needs one person they can count on. Someone who isn't a lover or a parent. Someone who can watch out for them with nothing clouding their vision. I wanted to be that person for you."

"Maybe I'm not like everyone else," she said sweetly, *confidently.* "Because I want you, and you are that person for me."

He kissed her again, slow and deep, feeling all the chained-up pieces of himself unshackling. "I was never a selfish man, but with you, I'm shamefully selfish," he whispered, pressing tender kisses to her chin and cheek.

"Be selfish with me, Drake. I can handle it. I *want* to handle it." Her gaze turned fierce, and she said, "But if you ever scare me like that again, I will *not* forgive you."

He couldn't suppress a chuckle. "Says the girl who was sleeping in *my* favorite beach shirt. When did you steal that?"

"If you're *good*, maybe I'll tell you," she said lustily, and lifted the bottom of his shirt. "Off, please."

He tugged his shirt over his head and tossed it to the floor. She reached for him, and he knew every moment of his life, every decision he'd ever made on their behalf, had been the right one at the time, just like *this*.

"Is that a challenge, Supergirl?" he asked as he lifted her shirt over her head, leaving her bare, save for her pretty panties. He clutched her waist with both hands, lifting her off the mattress, and shifted her toward the head of the bed. He lowered his mouth to her breast, teasing her roughly with his teeth and hands, the way he'd learned she loved.

She arched up, fisting her hands in his hair while pushing against the back of his head, pleading, "Harder, oh, *oh*!"

A loud, surrendering moan left her lungs, making his cock throb. He shifted positions, rocking his steel shaft against her sex as he devoured her breasts.

"Oh God...*Drake*," she pleaded breathlessly.

He captured her mouth, thrusting and grinding against her center. He read her noises perfectly. A high-pitched whimper told him he'd hit the spot, and her nails carving into his skin told him to press harder, move faster. Soon she was soaring, bucking and crying out into their kisses. He fucking loved that.

He rose, grabbing both sides of her panties. "These have got to go."

He tore them off and rubbed the silk against his cheek, loving the flare of heat in her eyes as he drank in every sexy inch of her. She was shaved bare, her center glistening with desire— all for *him*. She'd unleashed every ounce of possessiveness he had been stowing away, and now there was *no* holding back.

"Fuck, babe. You are stunning." He dragged the silky panties over her thighs, around her sex, making her center clench with anticipation. "Do you know how many years I've dreamed of this? Of you lying naked beneath me?" He ran her panties lightly up her side, and she squirmed with the tickle and tried to cover up. "Move that hand, sweetheart. Next time I'll use your panties to bind those pretty little wrists of yours."

"Do it," she begged, and lifted her wrists.

He grabbed one wrist and sucked the underside of it, earning more sinful pleas. "I need your hands on me tonight. But we'll get there," he promised, and stepped from the bed.

He dug his wallet from his back pocket and tossed it on the nightstand and then stripped off his clothes. She licked her lips, her eyes locked on his cock, as he climbed onto the bed and knelt between her legs. Just the thought of her hands on him made his body throb. She reached for him at the same time he roughly spread her legs. Her eyes darted up to his, and he caught her hand before she touched him.

"Now I'm in a quandary, Supergirl. I want your hands and mouth on me, but I'm so fucking hungry for you, I don't think I can wait."

He dragged his tongue across her palm. Then he sucked her fingers into his mouth and swirled his tongue around them. She breathed harder, looking so sexy, so beautiful and trusting, he ached with love for her.

"Just let me touch you for a second," she pleaded.

Oh yeah. Every damn second of his life had led to her, all right. They were made for each other. He guided her hand to his cock, covering it with his own. She gave his shaft a series of tight strokes. His hips bucked, fucking her fist, and she quickened her pace, squeezing tighter as she stroked the head. He gritted his teeth at the immense pleasures.

"What do you like?" she asked breathlessly.

"*Fuuuuck*, baby." He grabbed her hand. "I like you. Everything about you, and right now I'm half a second from burying my cock in your mouth and coming down your throat."

Her eyes narrowed. "Do it."

"Christ, you are a dirty girl. I'm *not* coming in your mouth before you come on mine."

"Just one little suck?" She scooted up to a sitting position and ran her tongue slowly across her lower lip, then along the sweet bow of her upper lip.

His cock wept to get in her sexy mouth.

When she reached for him, he didn't stop her. She guided his cock into her mouth, and holy fucking hell, she sucked and swirled, following her sweet, hot mouth with a stroke of her hand. The sight alone was enough to make him come. She took him to the back of her throat, her eyes locked on his with a look as devastatingly sexy as it was challenging. She quickened her pace, and he was right there with her, pistoning his hips as she fondled his balls, until a rush of pressure skated down his spine, and he knew if he didn't pull back, he'd lose it.

Losing it was *not* an option.

He withdrew from her mouth, earning a gasp and a whimper, which he silenced with a fierce kiss.

"You're a fucking goddess," he ground out as he swept her beneath him.

She leaned up and nipped at his lips. "What took you so long to notice?"

"Baby, I've known you were my kryptonite forever."

He kissed her again, slow and deep, enjoying the feel of her nakedness against him. And then he kissed her longer, because he was in no hurry to relinquish her mouth. His cock rubbed against her center, slick with her arousal. Every rock of his hips earned a moan, a quiver, a gasp. She was so sensual, so alluring, he craved seeing her shiver and quake. He kissed his way down her neck, over her breasts, loving every inch from ribs to belly button. He lowered his mouth to her inner thigh, kissing and sucking, making her squirm and moan. Her intoxicating scent overwhelmed him, unleashing more carnal urges. He lifted her knees, spreading them wider, and devoured the tender skin all around her sex until she was clawing at the sheets.

"*Please*, Drake. I can't take it. I need your mouth on me."

She arched off the mattress, reaching between her legs. She pushed her fingers over her wetness, and he grabbed her hand.

"You're not rushing me, Serena." He sucked her fingers clean, her essence bursting over his tongue like a long-awaited celebration.

"God, your mouth," she said greedily.

"You want my mouth, baby?" He slicked his tongue up along her glistening center, earning another sinful moan. "Like this?"

He circled the apex of her sex, adding pressure to her most sensitive nerves, over and over again. She inhaled a series of small, sexy gasps.

"Or like this?" He sealed his mouth over her swollen sex, plunging his tongue into her tight heat.

"Yes!" she cried out as he took her roughly, *devouringly*, and used his hand to add pressure where she needed it most. "Oh God, *Drake*!"

Her hips bucked, her sex clenched around his tongue, and a stream of sultry, erotic noises sailed from her lips. He read her body perfectly, moving with her, finding, exploring, and *enjoying*, all of her pleasure points. He held her at the peak, knowing just when to ease up and when to give her more. She was like the finest, most exquisite instrument he could ever learn to play, and he would become an expert.

When she finally collapsed to the mattress, he loved his way up her body as aftershocks quaked through her. She shivered at the nips and sucks he stole on his way to her glorious mouth. When his lips covered hers, she didn't pull away at the taste of her arousal lingering on his lips or the ferocity with which he kissed her. She rose beneath him, trying to take even more.

They both came away breathless. There were so many things he'd thought he'd say at this incredible, important moment. He'd profess his love for her, promise not to hurt her, to support everything she wanted in her career. But as he gazed into her trusting, loving eyes, he saw that she already knew all those things.

He reached for his wallet.

"Don't," she said softly.

The plea in her eyes made his heart feel impossibly fuller.

"Have you been unsafe with anyone?" she asked.

"No. Never," he said honestly, and the rest of the truth poured out. "I hoped we would eventually get our timing right. I was always careful."

A sweet smile lifted her lips. "I've waited my whole life to be with you, and I'm on birth control—"

Her words were lost in the eager press of his lips as he gathered her in his arms, gazed deeply into her eyes, and said what perhaps she didn't yet know. "I'm yours, Serena. I've been yours since you set your mesmerizing eyes on me and nervously fumbled your way through asking if I'd sing a duet with you. I wanted you desperately then, and I regretted holding back, but it brought us to this magical place and time, and I will not let you down again."

He lifted her into the cradle of his arms, kissing her as their bodies became one. Nothing could have prepared him for the surge of emotions engulfing him or the intensity of their connection as they found their rhythm. They didn't rush as they explored angles and depths, their bodies moving in exquisite harmony. Lust spiked through him with every seductive gasp, every erotic touch. When her orgasms crashed over her, one after another, like they'd set off an avalanche, the way she clung to him, crying out his name, was the most intense pleasure he'd ever experienced. Their passions mounted, desire stacking up inside him until he felt it throbbing through his veins, simmering beneath his skin, and when she bit down on his shoulder, he surrendered to his own powerful release.

Sometime later, as they lay tangled together, Serena drifted off to sleep and Drake wondered how they'd managed to give each other so much for all those years without ever giving each other *this*.

Chapter Ten

THE MORNING SUN snuck into Serena's loft as slow and sweet as a cove kissed the shore, bringing the most glorious morning of her life into focus. She lay nestled in Drake's warmth, his strong arms holding her tight even as he slept. He smelled heavenly and manly, like all the good things in her life wrapped up in one. She wanted to turn around so she could see his face as he slept peacefully beside her, feel his breath on her cheeks. But at the same time, she didn't want to move and break the spell they'd fallen under. What if things changed between them? What if it became awkward?

What if they changed for the better?

The urge to know was too strong to ignore. She turned within the confines of his arms and found him awake, smiling sleepily.

"Hey, Supergirl." He pressed a kiss to her lips.

Her heart somersaulted at the emotions in his voice. Gone was the underlying restraint, the pretense of being only friends, and she liked this *much* better.

"Did I wake you?"

He shook his head. "I've been awake for a while, wondering how long I had to wait before I could make love to you again without you thinking I was a letch."

"What if I like your lechery? We have years to catch up on, and we *are* going to be apart until next weekend. That leaves a lot of time for my body to forget how good you feel."

He moved over her with a wolfish grin, his hardness pressed against her center, and her entire body reached for him. He laced their hands together, pinning hers beside her head, and began teasing her, burying only the head of his cock and moving in and out torturously slowly. He pushed deeper, stroking over the scintillating spot inside her that made her lose her mind.

He nuzzled against her neck and said, "You think you'll forget, huh?"

"Uh-huh," she said breathlessly. "Maybe you should keep reminding me."

His wicked mouth claimed hers, kissing the fib right out of her as he drove her to the brink of oblivion and then sent her soaring to the clouds.

Later, after they'd loved each other thoroughly in her bed and again in the shower, greeting the day in a way she'd only dreamed of, Drake pulled on a pair of tan shorts and a green T-shirt, both of which hugged him in all the best places.

"What are you gawking at?" Catching her watching him in the mirror as she put on a pair of dangling peach earrings to match her peach-and-white tie-dyed tank top and khaki shorts, he circled her waist from behind.

She turned in his arms, so full of happiness she thought she might burst. "I've been crushing on you for so long, I keep expecting you to vanish or for me to wake up from the best dream ever."

His low laugh was music to her ears. He kissed her again,

and then he swatted her butt. "This is no dream, sweetheart. Come on. Let's go find your grocery store and explore." He dug a palm-sized notebook from his backpack and handed it to her. "I started a list for you…well, for *us*."

"A list?" She flipped to the first page, taking in his familiar all-capped handwriting.

HARBORWALK

INSOMNIA COOKIES (OPEN UNTIL 3AM!)

FANEUIL HALL MARKETPLACE

THE CHEERS BAR (CHEERS BEACON HILL)

INSTITUTE OF CONTEMPORARY ART

DUCK BOATS

FENWAY PARK

BOSTON TEA PARTY SHIPS & MUSEUM

AQUARIUM

BLACKBIRD DOUGHNUTS

"You found an all-night cookie place?" She launched herself into his arms. "When did you have time to do this?"

"When I couldn't stop thinking about you and your new life and I realized how much I wanted to be a part of it. I want to explore Boston with you and see your gorgeous smile and your eyes light up when you see some of those things for the first time."

"Who knew you were so romantic?"

"Definitely not me," he said as he pushed his feet into a pair of loafers. "But you're annihilating everything I thought I knew about myself."

"I prayed to the devil to get you to stop being so restrained around me. Where do you want to start exploring?" she asked excitedly.

He checked the time on his phone. "I promised Hagen I'd take him sailing today, so I have only a few hours. I've got to be on the road by noon, and I want to make sure we get your groceries so you don't have to stress over that."

She'd forgotten Mira had mentioned the sailing trip. Knowing he drove all that way just to be with her when he had to rush back made their time together even more special.

"I'm Supergirl, remember? I can get my own groceries, and according to the handy-dandy list you made me, Insomnia Cookies will make sure I don't starve. I say we explore."

He chuckled. "Okay, Supergirl. Exploring it is."

She put on a pair of cute sandals and they headed outside. It was a gorgeous, cool morning, made even brighter by the feel of Drake's hand claiming hers.

"Let's head toward Faneuil Hall Marketplace and see what we can find," she suggested.

"I'm yours until noon. You lead, I'll follow." He leaned in for a kiss.

How could something as simple as a kiss make her swoon like a schoolgirl? Yet here she was, grinning so hard it hurt, her heart racing like he'd just proposed, as they crossed the street.

"Are you nervous about tomorrow?" he asked casually.

"Yes and no. I'm confident about my skills, but I am a little out of my element here. I hope my creativity hasn't become too Cape Coddish."

"It's not like you've only been decorating beach cottages with Shift. And look at what you've done with the music stores and the resort. I don't think you're too Cape Coddish at all."

She waved at the high-rise buildings, the traffic on the four-lane streets. "I know, but there's definitely a difference between the corporate business world on the Cape and here. That's what I'm nervous about. That and fitting in with city people."

"Look around you, Supergirl." He motioned toward the people walking by. "They're just people."

"*City* people," she pointed out. "They think differently than we do."

"And you have always thought big. You're the perfect blend of corporate woman and beach girl." As they waited for a light to change, he gathered her in his arms and said, "I'll tell you what. Anyone gives you a hard time, you send them my way. And next weekend, when you come home to help with the music store, I'll make you feel better."

"Now, that sounds promising."

The light changed, and a few minutes later they crossed over the water and stopped to enjoy the view. It was so different from Wellfleet, with all the tall buildings along the shore and no sandy beaches.

"It smells different from Wellfleet," she said. "But it still makes me feel closer to home to see the water."

Drake put his arm around her and kissed her cheek. "I'll bring sand next time. We'll fill up a baby pool with it and put it on your balcony. Do you have a balcony? I don't remember seeing one."

"No, but I read about a rooftop deck. We can put it there, throw on bathing suits, and…It still won't be home," she said. "But if you're with me, it'll be close enough."

They talked about the music store as they continued walking.

"Did you connect with Carey?" she asked. Carey Osten was a free-spirited musician and record aficionado who had helped Drake run several of his stores over the years. Carey traveled often, and usually lived in his old Dodge van. Though he owned a cell phone, he wasn't married to it like most of the people they knew. Sometimes it took him weeks to return calls.

"He got back to me yesterday. He's on his way back from California. He'll be at the opening, ready to run the store. I confirmed with Cree, too. She's all set." Lucretia "Cree" Redmond was in her early twenties and dressed like a mini-Violet. She had an affable personality without the snark Violet so proudly touted. Cree played several instruments, and although she worked for their friend Sky in her tattoo parlor in Provincetown, she had agreed to also work part-time at the music store.

"I spoke to Cree, too, and Maddy and Evan. That's a few more things off our to-do list." Madison Barber was in town for the summer visiting her sister, Lizzie, and had also agreed to work part-time at the music store. She was in her early twenties and lived in Harborside, Massachusetts, not far from the Cape. She and Evan Grant, the son of their friends Bella and Caden, had graduated from college together in Harborside. Evan lived and worked full-time on the Cape and had offered to help out with the grand opening.

They talked about the minutiae of opening another store—supplies, insurance, modifying the employee handbook, and a number of other things. Drake was as organized as Serena was, and even when they disagreed, they always found a way to compromise. She loved how in sync they were when it came to business. *As long as that business isn't me leaving the resort*, she mused.

"Check out Kane's Donuts!" A young guy handed them a flyer with mouthwatering pictures of doughnuts and a coupon for twenty percent off.

"Where is *this*?" Serena asked. "We have to go there!"

Drake kissed her again. "That's the look of surprise I adore."

He was stealing so many kisses, acting like they'd always been a couple, and Serena realized, in many ways, they always had.

The guy gave them directions to the doughnut shop around the corner. The aroma of cinnamon, chocolate, warm pastries, and coffee surrounded them.

Serena moaned, clutching Drake's arm. "I want to bathe in this smell."

His eyes darkened, and he pressed his cheek to hers, speaking in a rough voice. "I'll fill your bathtub with doughnuts. You bathe in it, and I'll lick you clean."

He gave her neck a little bite, sending sparks skittering through her.

Oh boy. How was she going to eat now?

"Hey there, lovebirds," the pretty blonde said from behind the counter as she set a tray of powdered doughnuts behind the glass display. She wiped her hands on her apron and set one hand on her hip, flashing a friendly smile. "What can I get you?"

Her warm blue eyes swept over them as they drooled over the delicious-looking options. Drake didn't hesitate, ordering for both of them.

"We'll take two iced coffees, a Chocolate Orgasm, and a Boston cream doughnut."

"I like a man who knows what he wants. For here or to go?"

"To go, please," Drake said, pulling Serena against his side. "We've got a lot of ground to cover before noon."

Serena read the description of the Chocolate Orgasm. The name alone was enough for her to get excited, but the description—a decadent chocolate-cake-style doughnut filled with rich, creamy chocolate pudding, dipped in Hershey's chocolate syrup, and rolled in crushed chocolate cookies—had her licking her lips.

"Ah, tourists, huh?" the blonde said as she carefully put the doughnuts into a bag.

"I just moved here from the Cape." Serena nudged Drake. "Which means Drake's the tourist."

After she made their coffees, they followed her down to the cash register. "Well, I'm Abby. I hope you'll come back often. It's nice to get to know new faces."

Drake paid and said, "I have a feeling you'll have a hard time getting my girlfriend to stay away."

Serena's heart skipped at *girlfriend*. It sounded even better coming off his lips than she'd imagined.

"A fellow sugar fiend," Abby said. "I look forward to seeing you again…?"

"Serena," she said. "And this is Drake."

"Enjoy your orgasm," Abby said, and then she went to help another customer.

As they left, Drake tugged Serena closer and whispered, "Silly baker put a hole in the middle of the Chocolate Orgasm instead of giving it a creamy center. Guess that means I get to dip my chocolate in your cream."

Heat spread through her chest at his naughty innuendo. "How do you know I want the Boston cream doughnut?"

His scruff hit her cheek again, and in a voice that nearly melted her panties off, he rasped, "Because you told me to 'do it' last night. My girl likes a creamy mouthful."

She gasped, and he chuckled.

"See what happens when you unleash the beast? Too much

for you, Supergirl?"

"Never." And now all she could think about was him *doing it.*

Half an hour later, Serena was still riding a sugar-and-Drake-high as they explored Faneuil Hall Marketplace. It was like they'd walked into another world, full of colorful shops, brick-and-stone courtyards, and historic buildings, all of which gave the area a festive feel. They moved with the crowds, shopping and checking out kiosks.

"This reminds me of a bigger, upscale Provincetown," Serena said. "Only different."

"I like how you relate places to home." He looked over the heads of the people around them, leading her through the crowd to a kiosk selling sunglasses. He chose a pair of bright purple shades and put them on Serena. "Now, that's high fashion."

She glanced in the mirror, beside which was a pair of green sunglasses and a straw hat. She snagged them both and put them on him. "Are you ready to hit Palm Springs, darling?"

They tried on several pairs of funky sunglasses, teasing each other and being silly, and finally bought matching gold-framed glasses. Hers had pink lenses and his had blue. At the next kiosk, Serena bought a hair clip and put her hair up in a messy bun to get sun on her shoulders. Drake immediately claimed the bare skin with a series of scintillating kisses.

They moved from one shop to the next, and when they rounded one of the three main shopping buildings, they came upon street performers.

"Let's watch!" Serena dragged Drake toward a couple doing acrobatics in the middle of a crowd. A short distance away, a man hung upside down wearing what looked like a straitjacket.

"Look!" She headed that way.

Drake laughed. "You're like a little girl in a candy store."

"I can't help it. This is so fun." She was mesmerized by the escape artist manipulating his way out of the restraints. The crowd cheered, and she clapped and bounced on her toes. She turned toward Drake to hug him and realized he'd been watching *her*, not the show.

He lifted her off her feet, smiling into their kisses. When he set her back on her feet, he kept hold of her, gazing into her eyes with a look she *felt* rather than *read*. It was like he was seeing more of her than anyone ever had.

"What?" she asked tentatively.

"It feels good not to have to hide when I want to look at you or touch you."

Did he have any idea how much that meant to her? "You sure do know how to make a girl walk on air," she said as she wound her arms around his neck. "Now kiss me before I climb you like a tree."

And he did.

Thoroughly.

Just as she felt herself walking on air, he pulled out his phone and checked the time, making her painfully aware of their morning together coming to an end.

HAVING LOST TRACK of time, they had to hurry. There were so many things Drake wanted to say and do, but suddenly words evaded him. On the walk back to Serena's apartment, he tried to ignore the pang of longing already forming in his gut. He contemplated backing out of the sailing trip with Hagen in order to stay with Serena a few hours longer, but he couldn't do that to his nephew. But leaving Serena also felt like the wrong thing to do. They'd only just come together. He'd lived practically every day of the last four years with her by his side. Five days apart seemed like an eternity, and he hadn't even left yet.

When they crossed the harbor, she thanked him again for driving up from the Cape, and he heard a hint of sadness in her voice, tugging at his heartstrings even more. By the time they reached her block, they were holding each other tighter, walking slower, as if they could delay the inevitable. He wondered when he'd become such a wimp that he couldn't push the heartache away. She'd opened Pandora's box, and the trouble was, he didn't want to close it, or push any of his emotions aside any longer.

Across the street from her apartment building, a group of people were playing music on the grass. Serena's eyes lit up and she opened her mouth, like she was going to say something. In the next breath, the light in her eyes dimmed. He knew she was worried about time. He had to leave right away, but there was no way he'd leave without a smile on his girl's face.

"Come on," he said, and headed across the street.

She hurried to keep up. "You can't be late for Hagen."

"I'll drive fast."

They stepped onto the sidewalk and crossed the lawn to the group of musicians. A guy and a girl lay on a blanket taking selfies, a banjo resting by their feet. Beside them, two guys were playing guitars and a girl held a saxophone, singing along. A few feet away, a woman with long hair was teaching a redheaded man to play the guitar.

Serena snuggled against Drake's side and said, "Remind you

of home?" Their go-to event with their friends had always been bonfires on the beach. Sometimes all of Matt's siblings and in-laws would come, along with Harper's siblings and some of their other friends. Drake and the guys would play the guitar, making up songs as they went.

"Almost." What he wanted to say suddenly became very clear. He waited for one of the guys to set down his guitar. Then he pulled out his wallet and said, "Excuse me. I'll give you a hundred bucks if you'll loan me your guitar so I can sing my girlfriend a song."

The guy's eyes widened. "Sure, man. Take it." He held out the guitar, and Drake gave him the cash.

"Drake!" Serena's beautiful eyes widened with shock.

He leaned in and kissed her. "This is for you, Supergirl."

He played the tune for "Chasing Cars" by Snow Patrol, modifying the lyrics just for her. He was vaguely aware of the guy who had lent him the guitar videoing him singing.

I'll do it all
Just for you
Every day

I don't need
Anyone
Or anything else

Emotions brimmed in her eyes. He continued playing the guitar as he kissed her cheek and then fell back into the song.

When I'm with you
Just by your side
Everything feels right

It's become clear
What to do
How to feel

How can we have just begun
When it feels like you've been here all along?

He sang a few more verses, and as the last words left his lips, tears streamed down Serena's cheeks and trembling hands covered her mouth and nose. He lowered the guitar in one hand, and she threw her arms around his neck.

Cheers and applause rang from a crowd that had formed out around them.

"I *have* been here all along," she said through kisses. "Just like you have."

"And I always will be."

Chapter Eleven

I BET PICKING out an outfit to wear the first day of work is ten times harder than choosing a wedding dress! I have to run. Tell everyone I say hi, and when Drake gets back from his run, give him a big sloppy kiss on the cheek for me! Serena sent the text to Desiree, shoved her phone in the messenger bag Mira insisted she buy at The Now, and headed into the elevator of her office building. She was still on an adrenaline high from her time with Drake. Starting her new job added a dose of nervous energy to the adrenaline.

She was *buzzing*!

Two sharply dressed men in suits entered the elevator, flashing friendly enough glances before returning to their conversation. The taller of the two glanced over again. His bright green eyes held a silent greeting. She imagined Drake standing next to her, growling at the guy, and suppressed a giggle. A pretty, painfully skinny blond woman and a lanky, bearded guy wearing thick, black-framed glasses and skinny dress slacks stepped in, standing against the side wall. Serena smiled, feeling confident in her red pencil skirt and white blouse. They smiled, then tipped their heads, whispering to each other. She felt like the new girl at school.

KHB inhabited the top three floors of the fifteen-story building. Reception and administrative support was on the thirteenth floor, the designers inhabited the fourteenth, and the executives were on the fifteenth. One of the suited men stepped off the elevator with her and headed through the glass doors like he was on a mission. Too busy talking into his phone, the man didn't say hello to the receptionist, Carolyn, whom Serena had met during her interview.

Carolyn sat pin straight, a black headset at the ready as she efficiently and professionally answered several calls. She held up one finger with a practiced smile, but her eyes gave away her happiness to see Serena. Her professionalism coupled with the severe cut and the model-perfect shine of her black hair, expertly applied makeup, and French manicure gave off a slightly hoity-toity vibe. But Serena knew better. Carolyn had been leaving work when Serena had left after her interview, and they'd had coffee together downstairs. She was easy to talk to, and it had become clear that her prim persona was merely a front she put on as a representative of the company.

Carolyn ended her call and stood up quickly, leaning across the desk and waving her hands. "Get in here and hug me!" she said quietly. "I was so happy when they said they hired you. You look amazing."

"Thank you! I'm so nervous. I have no idea where to go."

The phone rang, and Carolyn held up her finger again as she answered it and settled back into her seat. After sending the call to its recipient, she said, "Don't be nervous. You'll do great. You're starting with Chiara Twain, our human resources coordinator." She pronounced the woman's name *Chee-ar-ah*. "She's relatively new, too. You'll love her. After you fill out a mountain of paperwork, she'll show you around the offices, and then she'll bring you down to meet with Suzanne. I'll let Chiara know you're here."

Carolyn answered another call, and Serena stepped back from the desk to wait, feeling a little more at ease. Several people came through the reception area. Some flashed tight smiles, but others were too busy on their phones to notice anything as they crossed the hardwood floors to the white marble reception desk.

"Serena?" An energetic blonde hurried across the floor in her sky-high heels as though they were flats, her hand outstretched. "I'm Chiara Twain, your go-to gal for all things human resources related. Everyone mispronounces my name, so just think of a cheering cheetah. *Chee-ar-ah.* Shall we get started?"

"Yes, thank you." She wished she could rush through the human resource part of her day and race upstairs to get started, even though she liked Chiara.

As they weaved through the elegant offices, their heels silenced by plush carpeting, the din of busy employees filled the air. Chiara spoke in a hushed tone as phones rang out around them and people hurried past. The thrill of it all eased Serena's nerves, and she tried to remember every face on the way to Chiara's office.

"I haven't been to the Cape, but it's on my bucket list," Chiara confided. "I'd imagine, though, that you might experience a little culture shock with the move. I know I did when I moved from Reno last month."

"It's definitely different. At the resort we wore whatever was comfortable, and there is no Boston Design Center, that's for sure." Boston Design Center was the region's premier destination for luxury interior furnishings and featured more than three hundred and fifty thousand square feet of showrooms. Serena had been there when she'd interned during college, and she and Justine, the owner of Shift, had also visited on occasion.

"I could get lost in BDC," Chiara said as they entered her office. "I went there once with Laura, one of the junior interior designers you'll be supervising, just to check it out. I have no idea how designers can choose from all the selections there."

Serena was still a little shocked that she was going to be supervising a team of two. She couldn't imagine not having her hands on every piece of the design process, but Suzanne had reassured her that she'd never feel like she wasn't in control.

"Let's get the paperwork out of the way first." Chiara set her up at a desk with a ton of paperwork, an employee handbook, and a designer's code of conduct booklet, which seemed to be the ABCs of ethics for designers.

That should come in handy on the nights she couldn't sleep.

Almost three hours later, after a not-so-brief orientation meeting and a tour of the fifteenth floor, they finally stepped off the elevator on the fourteenth floor. While the thirteenth floor, where clients entered, was decked out in calming and elegant earth tones, and the executive suites were even more luxurious, though a bit too drab for Serena's taste, the fourteenth floor was alive with color and activity.

"Welcome to your new home," Chiara said as she led her through the office. She pointed out the coffee room, conference area, and the resource room, which had catalogs, brochures, fabric swatches, and more. Light hardwood floors and glass walls on the exterior offices gave the space an open, airy feel. "As you can see, this floor is set up for collaborating."

"Yes. The work flow is perfect." Serena took in the U-shaped workstations, each boasting a splash of color on chest-height privacy screens. Designers were bent over their desks, talking on the phone, working on plans, or leafing through catalogs. Across the room, a woman and a man stood before a whiteboard, hashing out design elements. There was a vibrant hum of activity, just as she'd imagined.

"Your office is the second from the right." Chiara led her to a group of people gathered around a table discussing design elements. "Hi, guys," Chiara said. "This is Serena Mallery, our new senior interior designer."

Serena recognized three of them from the elevator that morning.

"I thought I picked up the scent of *newbie* in the elevator," one of the suited guys said. He was tall and handsome, with closely shorn brown hair and wily green eyes she bet probably opened a lot of bedroom doors. His lips quirked up in a coy grin. "Welcome to the mayhem. I'm Gavin."

"Nice to meet you," Serena said.

The thin blonde she'd seen earlier said, "And I'm Laura, a junior designer. Spencer and I are on your team." She motioned toward the bearded guy.

Spencer waved. "You can call me Spence. I'm looking forward to working with you."

"Thank you. I can't wait to get started." Serena followed Chiara into her gorgeous new sunny office.

"Why don't you set your things down, and I'll let Suzanne know you're here."

She stifled the urge to do a happy dance and glanced out the window at the streets below. She was so excited. She had to quell the urge to take pictures to send to Drake and the girls. She set her bag on the credenza behind the sleek light-wood, extra-wide desk, and as calmly as she could, she said, "Thank you so much, Chiara. Maybe we can have lunch one day."

"Are you under the impression you'll have *downtime*?" Chiara lifted her brows. "Seriously, lunches are crazy around here, and our senior designers often save lunches for client meetings. But maybe we can grab a drink after work sometime."

"Sounds great."

A few minutes later Chiara brought her into Suzanne's office, which was three times the size of hers.

"Welcome to KHB," Suzanne said as Chiara left the room. She waved to a leather chair across from her desk. "Sit down and get comfortable. Let's get you up to speed."

Serena guessed Suzanne to be in her late thirties. She had olive skin and sharp brown eyes. Her dark hair was pulled back in a sleek bun, and she gave off an aura of sophistication. Her finely fitted gray suit and expensive heels further underscored her business-savvy nature. But it was her confidence and assertiveness that Serena had first noticed during their interview. Suzanne didn't mince words, and Serena respected that almost as much as she admired her design abilities.

"Do you have any questions before we dig in?" Suzanne asked.

"No. I'm ready and excited to take charge of my first project."

"Great." Suzanne picked up two folders from her desk and handed them to Serena. "You'll be working with two major clients. Seth Braden, the president of BRI Enterprises, a major retail conglomerate, and Muriel Younger, a principal attorney at Younger, Lynch, and Ryan. We've worked with both of them before. All of the information you'll need is in the files. Seth has just taken on a partner, and he's doing a full-scale rebrand and redesign, and Muriel has expanded her offices and is taking over another floor in her building. You have a meeting scheduled to see Muriel's offices Wednesday. I assumed you'd want some time to get your head wrapped around that job before meeting with Seth. He's awaiting your call, but no pressure to get started yet. He's out of town until next week. Since your last visit to the Boston Design Center was some time ago, I've asked Gavin Wheeler, another senior designer, to go with you Friday to help you get acclimated to the way things are done there."

"Sounds perfect. Thank you."

"You'll also be working with two smaller clients." She handed Serena two more folders. "The Wilkinsons are renovating their home library, and the MacIntyres have a small contracting firm. They want to redecorate their offices on an insanely meager budget." She arched a brow. "We took them on as a favor to a big client. Good luck with that one. Did Chiara explain how to report business mileage and expenses?"

"Yes, and she encouraged me to take clients to lunch or dinner. Is that appropriate?"

"Appropriate and expected. The relationships are as important as the work itself. I also assume she introduced you to your team, Laura and Spencer?"

"Yes. She did. They seem eager and nice."

"They're loyal and creative. You've got a strong team behind you. Use them to their fullest extent. I believe you're all set." Suzanne rose to her feet and held out her hand. As Serena shook it, she said, "Welcome aboard. I'm really glad you're here."

"So am I." Serena walked back to her office—*her* office—feeling a strange sense of euphoria. She was thirty-one years old, and she had finally truly connected with her lifelong love, and now she had the opportunity she'd always wanted. What more could she ask for?

Her stomach growled as she entered her office, where she

found a box from Insomnia Cookies on the desk with a big pink bow tied around it. She opened the card, and her heart filled up with each word. *Congratulations, Supergirl. I bet you didn't eat breakfast. Hopefully these will make it to you by lunchtime. Knock 'em dead. Love, Drake.*

"Someone's got a sweet tooth," Gavin said as he walked into her office.

"I have about twenty-five sweet teeth. The rest are just there to balance things out." She untied the ribbon and set it aside with the card so she could take them home. "Want one?"

"Absolutely. Why else would I be standing here drooling?" He arched a brow and took a cookie. "Are these from your boyfriend or your sister?"

"How'd you know I have both?" She looked over the selection of delicious treats, itching to text Drake but not wanting to be rude to Gavin.

"You're spending more time looking at the cookies than looking at me, which tells me you're not single, and you sort of give off a vibe like you know someone's got your back." He leaned closer and lowered his voice conspiratorially. "Could be the boyfriend, but in my experience, that kind of confidence usually comes from a girls' club."

She laughed. "What are you, the woman whisperer?"

"Something like that." He glanced down at the files on her desk and winced. "She's throwing you feet-first into the fire. Good luck with Muriel."

"Why? Is she awful?"

"Nope. She's a typical KHB client." He pointed toward the left side of her office. "My office is right next door if you need anything. I'm looking forward to our field trip Friday. Plan for lunch. I'll clue you in on how things work around here."

The second he left, she whipped out her phone and sent Drake a quick text. *Can't text too much, but thank you!! The cookies are a poor substitute for your kisses, but they'll do. Miss you like crazy!* She added a winking emoji and a kissing emoji. Then she sat down and prepared to research the mysterious Muriel Younger and powerhouse Seth Braden.

"HEY, LONELY BOY," Rick said as he came through the door of the music store late Monday evening.

Drake hung up the electric guitar he was holding and climbed down from the ladder. "What's up?"

"Just making sure my brother's not crying his eyes out or anything."

Rick and Desiree had gone sailing with them Sunday afternoon, and Drake had told them all about him and Serena. He was pretty sure they would have popped open a bottle of champagne if there'd been one lying around.

Drake scoffed. "Thought I'd get a head start on things."

"Is that code for keeping your mind off Serena?"

"Pretty much. She's coming down for the weekend, and the last thing I want to do is spend the whole time getting the store in order." But they had so much fun when they set up the stores, he felt her absence like a missing limb.

"Makes sense. The grand opening should be fun. Are you still shooting for the twelfth?"

"Yeah. We'll make it in time. Serena's on top of the media and advertising."

"As always." Rick grabbed another guitar and handed it to Drake. "Climb up. I'll hand them to you."

"Thanks." He moved the ladder to the next group of hangers and climbed up. "Where's your soon-to-be wife?"

"We're not joined at the hip."

Drake gave him a *yeah, right* look. He wished he could be joined at the hip with Serena like they used to be.

"She's having dinner with Vi. Sisterly bonding and all that. I figured it was a good time to catch up with you."

"You just saw me at the office." He hung up another guitar and waited as Rick unpacked the next one, wondering what his brother really wanted. "Harper did a good job today."

"She's great. She got in touch with Daphne and scheduled an interview for Friday. It's on your calendar." He handed Drake a guitar with a troubled look in his eyes.

Drake hung up the guitar and climbed down the ladder, meeting his brother's gaze head-on. "What's really going on, Rick? You look like something's on your mind."

"When we were sailing yesterday, I noticed a look in your eyes, like a fleeting moment of panic. You were there for me when I needed you most. You pushed me to get over my demons, and it helped me to move forward with Desiree. I have never regretted giving up my business or moving back to the Cape. I want to be here for you, too, Drake. So whatever that was, whatever I saw, I want you to know that you can talk to me. I'm not that angry guy who can't face Dad's death anymore."

They'd both been on the deck of the boat the night of the storm when their father had fallen overboard and been lost at sea, while their mother and Mira were down in the cabin, out of harm's way. Drake could still hear the howling winds, still feel the cold rain pounding his cheeks, the deluge of waves crashing over the deck in the pitch-black night, and the dense *whoosh* of the boom cutting through the air as it slammed into their father, sending him to his death. The ocean was a destructive, uncaring beast, and it had swallowed him to its dark depths so quickly, none of them could have saved him.

Drake turned away, busying himself with unpackaging another instrument. He hadn't thought anyone had noticed the fear that had risen inside him.

"Dude...?" Rick put a hand on his shoulder. "What's going on?"

He faced the brother who had struggled for so long with guilt over their father's death, who had fought him every step of the way to keep from healing. Until Desiree. Drake had dealt with the grief from his father's death years ago. The only thing he had ever hidden from was his feelings for Serena. And he hadn't hidden from them as much as he'd tried to *outrun* them for her sake. Now that he knew how she felt about him, he was done with that bullshit. But the path from here to a future with Serena was unclear. He was sick of things being unclear or off-limits, and when they were sailing, he was struck by another troubling gray area.

"When we were sailing, all I could think about was what if the unthinkable happened when we were out there. Dad didn't get to say goodbye to any of us. I was so damn focused on our pain and trying to hold everyone together, we never talked about what Dad's last thoughts were. What went on in his mind as the boat keeled and he went overboard? What was he thinking during his last few seconds of life? I don't want my last thoughts to be 'I've wasted years,' or 'Why am I here while she's there?' I can't go back and fix the years we've missed, and it's probably too soon to figure out the second. That's what you saw."

They stood there in silence for a few moments as their painful past wrapped around them. The haunted look in Rick's eyes made him look five years older, and Drake was sure he was guilty of the same.

"I thought about Dad's last moments until I was sick with it," Rick confessed.

"I know. You and I talked about that when you and Des got together, but for me it's a selfish thought. As much as I want to know what Dad thought, I kind of don't." He paused, his confession gnawing at his gut. "But I want to make damn sure I don't regret a thing from here on out."

They worked in silence for a long while, putting up displays, each lost in their own thoughts. Eventually Desiree called, which was Rick's cue to leave.

He embraced Drake longer than usual. When they parted, he said, "Are you thinking of moving to Boston?"

Drake shrugged. "I wasn't," he said honestly. He made enough money with his music stores that he didn't need to work at the resort. But the resort had never been about money. It had been Drake's way of bringing his family back together. Maybe Rick's advice hadn't been too far off when he'd said, *At some point you've got to stop looking out for her and look out for both of you.* Maybe it was time for Drake to stop putting *everyone* else's happiness before his own. "But maybe it's worth thinking about."

Chapter Twelve

"THERE'S SOMETHING VERY wrong about you being dressed to kill when I'm this far away," Drake said in a husky voice that made Serena want to crawl through the phone Wednesday afternoon instead of heading into her meeting with Muriel Younger.

She was standing outside the building. She dipped her head as a couple walked by, so they wouldn't notice the flush heating her cheeks, and spoke quietly into the phone. "If you're lucky, maybe I'll show you what I have on *under* this killer outfit on FaceTime tonight."

He made a growling noise, and she felt it against her skin like his rough, calloused fingers. "Let's make that a promise, sweetheart, not a maybe, because just that thought is going to keep me on edge all day."

"I like you all edgy and hot for me," she said seductively.

"I'm hot for you every damn minute of the day. Two more nights, baby, and then you're mine. I hope you haven't made plans to see anyone else this weekend, because we might never leave the bedroom."

Her head spun with lustful thoughts. "I like that idea, but the girls might take issue with you hogging all my time."

The last few days had been a blur. In addition to researching Muriel's existing offices, studying the layout and designs, and going over the previous presentations her firm had put together over the last few years, Serena began researching the other clients she'd been assigned. She also followed up on the entertainment for Drake's grand opening, verified delivery dates for the furniture and other items that were still on order, fielded questions from both Justine at Shift and Harper, and tried to keep up with the girls back home via texts, but it wasn't like she could keep her phone by her side every second. By the time she fell into bed at night with Drake on the other end of the phone, she was exhausted. Playful dirty talk had always been part of their friendship, but the truth behind their feelings had taken it to a whole new level. He revved her up every single night. They'd never taken it further than a few steamy comments, but the thought of being naughty on a video chat with him made her insides thrum.

"A ravenous man can't be given time limits." His deep voice drew her attention.

"Okay, dirty boy. Wish me luck, because if I stay on the phone with you, I'm going to need a panty change."

"That does *not* make me want to end this call."

"Yeah, me either," she admitted, her temperature rising. "But duty calls. I'll tell you what. If I have time, I'll stop at Kane's and have a Chocolate Orgasm just for you."

"Mm. Chocolate. I'm adding that to my grocery list for the weekend, right alongside *whipped cream*."

"*Oh my goodness*," she said breathily. "Bye, dirty boy."

"Later, you sexy thing, and remember, you've got this. She's lucky to work with *you*."

Serena took a moment to *breathe* before heading inside for

her meeting. She should have known better than to talk to Drake before her first big meeting, but she missed him. Even though he turned her on endlessly, he also calmed her jitters and made her feel confident and capable in ways no one else ever had. Which was exactly how she felt as Muriel Younger greeted her twenty minutes later. Muriel's capped-sleeve Elie Tahari black shift had three spearlike cutouts around the high neckline and clung just enough to her rail-thin frame to be business appropriate. Her coal-black hair was cut in a pixie style, like Chloe's, but while the cut looked soft and elegant on her sister, coupled with Muriel's black-framed glasses and perfectly penciled eyebrows, hers looked severe.

"Serena," Muriel said sharp and fast, as if chastising her. "It's a pleasure to meet you."

Muriel's firm handshake validated Serena's initial impression. "Thank you. I'm excited to get started on your project."

Muriel didn't crack a smile as she headed for the door and said, "I'll be out for the next half hour," without turning to face the receptionist, whom Serena assumed she was talking to.

She followed her out the office door, hurrying to keep up as Muriel sped through another door and up a stairwell to the next floor.

"You're familiar with Younger, Lynch, and Ryan, I assume?"

"Yes, ma'am," Serena said, glad she'd done her research. "It's the largest women-run law firm in the country, the fifth-largest law firm in the region. It was founded by your mother, who is now retired, and you've just acquired two more offices in New York and Philadelphia—"

"You've done your homework," Muriel said as they entered the partially unfinished space her company would soon be utilizing and made their way toward the offices along the exterior walls.

A nearly blank slate. Serena's dream come true.

"We'd like to move our merger and acquisitions team in within sixty days," Muriel said sharply.

"Sixty days will be tight, with the build-out."

Muriel's gaze turned colder. "Sixty days can be done."

"Yes, of course, as long as there are no major last-minute changes." Serena made a mental note to discuss the time frame with Suzanne.

"Your firm has worked with our architect before, Drew Ryder at Ryder Associates. He's expecting your call."

"I'll call this afternoon. I've researched your existing offices and have a handle on your brand and the mood you typically like to set. Are there any chang—"

"If you've studied our brand, then you know there is only *one* mood," Muriel said as she crossed the concrete floor, her Christian Louboutin heels tapping out a fast beat. "We portray utmost professionalism in *every* office, on *every* floor, in *every* location."

"Yes, of course." *Broken record much?* She wanted to offer something new to this woman. If she wanted a rerun of all her other offices, why go with one of the most expensive companies in the area? "I'll make a note that you'd like to carry over the same color scheme as downstairs. What about walls? Glass walls, at least in the conference rooms, would allow for more natural light in the rest of the office."

"And less privacy," Muriel said sharply.

"Noted. Let's talk about the flow of the office. Will there be a reception area on this floor?"

"Yes. Let's go back downstairs and I'll have my assistant walk you through. She can answer any other questions you may have," Muriel said as she walked back toward the stairwell.

So much for Serena's dream come true. She was as hamstrung as a mummy.

Two hours later she returned to her office, scheduled an appointment to meet with Drew Ryder the following day, and headed straight to Suzanne's office. She found her studying floor plans at her desk.

Suzanne waved her in. "How'd it go with Muriel?"

"I'm not sure, actually. She's worked with the company for eight years, and you've designed six suites for the firm. I assumed she might want to freshen things up, but she has no interest in any design suggestions. Do you think I missed something?"

Suzanne waved to the chair. "Sit down. Let's talk." She came around the desk and sat in the chair beside Serena. "Muriel is one of our top clients, and yes, she has a very specific way of doing things. But she expects the same treatment as our less-*controlling* clients."

"Which means a senior designer instead of a junior who would be perfectly competent for the job?" Serena asked.

"Exactly. Companies come to us for our expertise. Some of them truly want the design experience we bring to the table, while others simply want the ability to say we are on *their* team."

"I understand." *Even if I don't like it.* "I'll work up the space plans and meet with Spencer and Laura to get them up to speed. I've scheduled a presentation meeting with Muriel next Tuesday. Would it irk her if I showed her exactly what she's asked for as well as something slightly different on the off chance she might budge?"

"You can try, but it'll be a futile effort," Suzanne said with a shake of her head. "I was once idealistic like you, and I admire your persistence. But don't take Muriel's attitude as a personal affront to your abilities. I only send her the designers I know I can trust to get things right."

"Okay. Thank you. There's one more thing. She asked for a sixty-day turnaround. I know it's possible, but one hitch in the plans and that time line will be shot."

Suzanne rose to her feet. "When it comes to Muriel, there can be no *hitch*, and in my experience with Muriel Younger, there is no wiggle room."

"Okay." Serena nodded. "I do love a challenge."

Serena headed into her office, wishing she'd stopped for that doughnut on the way back to the office. If ever she needed a little pick-me-up, it was today.

Since when is a doughnut better than cookies?

Since Kane's Donuts reminds me of Drake.

There was no time to fret over cravings or ridiculous clients. They were the ones who paid her salary, after all. But there was always time for her *best* craving and her most spectacular *sort of* client. Drake. If only every job were like the resort or the music store.

She pulled out her cell phone and sent him a selfie of a pouty face. *Back at the office without a Chocolate Orgasm. Maybe we can make up for that tonight, xox.*

She returned her voicemail messages, scheduled appointments with the MacIntyres and the Wilkinsons, and then began working on the budget calculations for the law office.

Long after everyone else left for the evening, Suzanne poked her head into Serena's office. "Burning the midnight oil? Have we overwhelmed you already?"

"No, not at all. I'm just putting together the budget for

Muriel's job. Tomorrow I'll do the sourcing of materials and make sure nothing has been discontinued since the last time we ordered."

Suzanne frowned. "That's what you have a team for."

"Oh, I don't mind doing it. I actually *love* that part of the process. Since I'll be out of the office most of Friday with Gavin and then I'm heading home for the weekend, I wanted to make sure I had everything in order."

"Yes, but that's what junior designers are for. They handle the legwork of checking availability and the like. Serena, you've set up entire companies from start to finish. Don't demean yourself by doing lower-level work. You've risen above that. Wear your new crown with pride. People would kill for a senior-design position with KHB."

Great. Now she sounded too small-minded for the job. "Of course, yes. I'm sorry. You're right."

"Don't be sorry. Authority takes some getting used to. You'll get the hang of it, and I promise you'll learn to love the higher aspects of project management. Most of all, the luxurious lunches and dinners you'll enjoy." Suzanne checked her watch. "Speaking of dinner, I've got to run. It's almost eight o'clock. See you tomorrow."

Eight o'clock? Serena gathered her things and headed out a few minutes after Suzanne. But instead of heading home, she decided to get that doughnut after all.

"IS THAT MY sweatshirt?" Drake asked Serena on FaceTime later that night. She looked adorable with her hair all tousled and no makeup on.

"No. It *was* yours," she said sassily. "You loaned it to me on Easter. Remember?"

He smiled with the memory. They'd set up an evening Easter egg hunt in the dunes for Hagen and his friends, and after all the kids left, they'd had a bonfire on the beach.

"Loaned?"

She rolled her eyes. "Whatever. Want it back?" She pulled it over her head, revealing a black lace bra.

"Hell yeah. Now we're talking." He got excited—until he heard the sounds of cars honking and realized she was outside. "Where the hell are you?"

She pulled the sweatshirt back on and said, "On the rooftop deck. See?" She turned her phone, showing him the harbor in the distance. "And check this out." She showed him the lights of the city and then an array of lounge chairs, tables, and gorgeous planters overflowing with colorful flowers. "We need something like this at the resort. Maybe on the roof of the community building? That would be awesome. And check out the decking." She pointed the phone down at the cedar slats beneath her pretty bare feet.

"That's a great idea," he said as she came back into focus and sat down on one of the chairs. "Let's talk about it when you're here this weekend. I'd love a place like that to hang out with you. But, babe, let's not strip in public, okay? I'd hate to have to drive to Boston to kick some guy's ass for wandering up to the roof when you're shirtless."

"Have I told you lately that you're hot when you're jealous?" She blew him a kiss. "But you know I'd never whip my shirt off if a guy were around."

He scoffed. "I've seen you do it on the beach."

"Hey! Hush up about that. We said we'd never talk about it

again." She sipped a glass of wine. "In my defense, I was two sheets to the wind."

"And how's that wine coming along?"

She lifted the glass. "It's my *first* glass, and probably my last. I just wanted to pretend I was home with all of you guys, sitting by the water and bitching about my day, knowing tomorrow would be better."

"You bitched about your days at the resort?" He was only joking. He knew damn well they all did, including him, but he wanted to lift her spirits. "I have an idea." He headed downstairs and out the front door, then jogged toward the dunes.

"Are you going to the beach?" Her eyes lit up. He already missed seeing that in person. "You're so sweet."

"I'm not that sweet. I'm trying to keep from driving to Boston, hauling your pretty little ass over my shoulder, and dragging you back home. Be careful when you tell me what you wish for, because I damn well might make it come true."

She smiled, and it warmed him all over. He walked to the edge of the dune and sat in the sand, turning the phone so she could see the water.

"See, Supergirl? We're under the same stars, separated only by a few airwaves." Turning the phone back toward himself, he said, "Talk to me. What's going on?"

"I don't want to drag you down. It's just a momentary blip on my radar, that's all." She looked away.

"Look at me, Serena. When you aren't telling the truth, you don't look me in the eyes."

"I don't do that." She brought her eyes back to him.

"I know you, Serena. Say what you need to say. I'm all ears, and I want to be here for you."

"It's just that when I took this job, I thought I'd actually be *designing* not just managing budgets and coordinating the efforts of others. I mean, I love the budgets and coordinating and working with architects, even though they usually get annoyed with me for making changes. But what I enjoy most is the actual hands-on sourcing of materials and goods. It's the whole creative wheel, start to finish, that makes it exciting."

The thrill in her voice was inescapable when she talked about the aspects of the job she loved. "I don't understand. You're *not* doing those things?"

"It's probably an anomaly, but I met with one of their biggest clients today, and she didn't want any design input at all. I could have been anyone standing in her office. She shut me down at every turn, then handed me off to her assistant. The whole thing feels impersonal. I know she cares, or she wouldn't be so adamant about how things are done, but her unwillingness to take even a hint of a suggestion makes it feel like she doesn't. She just wants what's easiest and quickest. I'm meeting with her architect tomorrow, which will be another total waste of time. It's not like I can make any changes to his plans. I'm sure she gave him the same directive to make a carbon copy of her other offices. And you know how architects get irritated with designers, so he'll have an ax to grind before I even open my mouth."

"Then he'll be eating crow," Drake said vehemently, "because a gorgeous, smart woman will come into his office and not make the changes he anticipates. Maybe you'll have gained a friend in the industry, which doesn't equate to wasted time."

"That's true. There *is* a silver lining. Anyway, I have a plan to fix this annoying thing of being the *yes* woman."

"Does it include Chocolate Orgasms?"

"Yes. I had one on the way home, in fact. But I needed *more* reinforcements." She aimed the phone down at a half-empty pizza box, and then tipped it up toward her again. "My plan is to gain at least a hundred pounds, stop washing my face so I get acne, and I might stop showering every day. Maybe that will make it so I'm not the face of KHB they shove in front of annoying clients. It should be easy to gain the weight without Emery's yoga classes or evening activities with you guys. But you might want to start thinking about looking for a different girlfriend if you want one that looks good in a string bikini and doesn't smell bad."

He laughed. "God, I miss you. I love your sense of humor. But, uh, what's up with the attitude? You think I'm not manly enough to handle a hundred more pounds of hot woman? I've got news for you. I'd still want you just as much as I want you right now no matter what you looked like. If you smelled, I'd haul your hot sexy ass into the shower, but you know I'd be all over you in there, too."

"Really?" She lay back in the chair. Moonlight shimmered in her eyes, making him miss her even more.

"I wish I was there right now, holding you."

"You're not upset that I'm not exactly in a sex-chat mood?" she asked carefully.

"Not at all, sweetheart. Sometimes you just need to cuddle up in your—*my*—sweatshirt with your man. And don't worry too much about today. This is all new for you, and I'm sure you'll have clients you love and clients you don't, like with any job. But if anyone can make a difference, it's you. So just give it your all and see where you land in a few months. Have you talked to Chloe and the girls about this yet?"

"Only Chloe, when I was stuffing my face with the dough-nut. I have meetings set up next week with more clients, and

Friday I'm going with Gavin to the Boston Design Center. That should be fun."

"Gavin, or the design center?"

Her brows furrowed. "Is my guy jealous again?"

"Should I be?"

"No. Although he is cute, clean-cut, and knows how to dress, like all the guys at my office."

"You're not winning any bonus points, Supergirl. Maybe I *do* need to drive to Boston."

She giggled. "He's funny, too, but he has one glaring flaw."

He sighed, knowing she was just pulling his leg. Or at least hoping so.

"It doesn't matter how far apart we are," she said. "No man could ever be *you*."

Chapter Thirteen

"GIVING UP THE legwork makes me feel like I'll walk out of here half dressed," Serena said semi-jokingly to Laura and Spencer Friday morning. She'd gotten to know them over the last few days, and her earlier impression was right: They were eager and easy to work with.

"That could be interesting," Spencer said with a snicker. He leaned back in his chair, one arm hanging down beside him as he drummed a beat on the edge of his chair with his other hand.

Laura rolled her eyes. "He's trying to get fired for sexual harassment."

"Is that true?" Serena couldn't hide her shock. "You *want* to be fired?"

"No. I'm just a line crosser, and Laura's not, so she likes to point it out."

"You probably do have to be careful in big companies like this. We joked around all the time at my last job, but we knew each other really well." *And now I'm sleeping with my previous boss, so there's that.*

"You know I didn't mean it that way, right?" Spencer leaned forward, picked up a pen, and began doodling. "Seriously, though. You don't trust our abilities?" His eyes flicked up to

169

hers. "The previous two senior designers tossed work on our desks and never looked back."

"Oh, no. It's not like that at all," Serena assured him. "I've looked through your portfolios, and you do great work. I'm just used to doing jobs from start to finish. If it seems like I'm micromanaging as we get moving on our projects, I'm really not. You can tell me to back off if it gets annoying. The client counts on us to get this right the first time. How can we do that if we're not all involved?"

Laura had a wary look in her eyes. "You mean, you actually *care.*"

"Of course I care. Didn't the last person who had this job?" Serena asked.

Spencer scoffed. "They loved their lunch hours and client dinners. But like the long line of people who held the position before you, it was a stepping-stone to other opportunities or they got burnt out."

"You're in the hot seat," Laura explained. "As a senior designer, you get all the luxuries of corporate life, and you get to take credit for your team's work. But did the previous designers care about the work?" She shrugged. "They seemed too busy to care about much beyond their next opportunity."

"Well, that's their loss. Or maybe their clients' loss." Serena had known plenty of people like that. She straightened her spine, looking directly at the two of them, so they would know she had nothing to hide, and said, "I can assure you, I will give credit where credit is due, and if anything, you'll see me in the trenches with you, *not* looking down at you."

"Certain people won't like that," Spencer said under his breath.

"That's too bad. Consider me the rebel of KHB, because

unless you want to see me lose my sanity, I can't be that hands-off. The very definition of *team* is a group working together toward a common goal. Do either of you have a problem with that?" Their eager smiles soothed the jitters in her stomach over possibly getting on the bad side of other senior-level employees. "Okay, then. Let's show the others just how awesome our team can be."

They discussed the budgets and interior elements for Muriel's offices, and Serena got the lowdown on how they usually handled projects. She tweaked their processes so they could work as a cohesive team rather than three separate entities coming together at a finish line.

Two hours later, Gavin peeked into the meeting room. "Ready to go on our BDC date?"

Laura's eyes sparked with curiosity.

"After a quick lesson in sexual harassment, I think it's more appropriate to call it an *outing*." Serena winked at Spencer. "Can you give me ten minutes to wrap things up with my teammates?"

Gavin's brows shot up in surprise. He checked his watch and said, "Uh, sure. I was hoping we'd get lunch afterward."

She glanced at the work before her and said, "I'm not sure I can afford the time for lunch. Can we grab something to go on the way back?"

Gavin stammered in agreement.

Serena purposely took her time wrapping things up with Laura and Spencer, making sure they were all on the same page. "I'd like you to go see Younger, Lynch, and Ryan's space Tuesday. Can you guys make time?"

They exchanged another astonished glance.

"We don't go see clients alone," Laura said carefully. "Only seniors do that."

"We can shadow you, though," Spencer said.

As much as that bothered her, she understood why the company worked that way. However, it didn't scream *teamwork* to her. If this were her company, she'd want the clients to be comfortable with any of the designers who were on their team. *Although I wouldn't pit Muriel against either of these two.* They were too nice to have to deal with her.

Heck, I'm too nice.

"Okay, then. Clear your schedules for Tuesday afternoon, and I'll make the time to take you over." Serena consulted her client notebook. "Actually, clear your morning and early afternoon. I have an appointment with the Wilkinsons for a library redesign. Shadow me on that visit, too. It'll shorten our lead time for the job if we do it all at once rather than two meetings."

"Suzanne's pretty firm about the initial meetings being only the seniors," Laura warned.

"This is my team, correct?" Serena paused as they agreed. "My team, my directions. I'll handle Suzanne. Younger, Lynch, and Ryan has us on a short leash with an even shorter turnaround time. If we're going to fit other clients into our busy schedules, we have to be efficient."

"Woman, you are *fierce*. I'm going to *love* working with you," Spencer said. "If they don't fire you before we get a chance."

"Mallerys fire things up," Serena said proudly. "We don't get *fired*."

As she gathered her things and went to meet Gavin, she hoped to hell that was true.

THE BOSTON DESIGN Center was everything Serena remembered and more—designer eye candy at its best. Every showroom was more luxurious than the last. Her favorite designers had all their best pieces on display, with incredible selections of drool-worthy fabrics and textures. The fine designs gave off different vibes, breathing life into every showroom. She'd dreamed for so long of being exactly where she was today. She wished Drake, Mira, and Chloe were there to share this moment with her. She could rave to them about the designs and pieces, but she'd never do that with Gavin. She was supposed to be a cool, experienced senior designer, and she worried she'd sound like a novice. Not that Gavin seemed judgmental. He was good company, helpful, informative, *and* entertaining.

"Call ahead next time and I'll set time aside for you," a pretty brunette said to Gavin.

"Thanks. I'll be sure to remember to do that." Gavin slid her business card into his suit pocket as they left the showroom.

"You really are a woman whisperer."

He flirted with *every* saleswoman, but he was *suave* in his designer suit and purple tie, laying on the charm just thick enough to leave the women wanting more. And yet he'd been a perfect gentleman with Serena since she'd told him she had a boyfriend, which showed that he had at least some modicum of morals.

He smirked. "The Wheeler charm is a burden."

"I bet," she said sarcastically.

"Seriously. Just ask my brother, Beckett. He swears fending off women is a full-time job."

"And you?"

A puckish look sparked in his eyes. "A gentleman never tells."

"Ah, so you're a gentlemanly woman whisperer. Got it. Are you from Boston?" she asked as they headed for the elevators.

"No. I'm from Oak Falls, Virginia, where everyone knows your name *and* your secrets."

"That sounds ominous. I guess you had a lot of secrets to escape?" she said as they rode the elevator up to the second floor.

"I wanted more than Oak Falls had to offer," he finally said as they stepped off the elevator. "Not much has changed about how business is done here over the years. But the Market Stalls are pretty amazing."

She followed him toward the west wing. "Nice subject change."

"I have many talents."

Goose bumps rose on her arms as the Market Stalls came into view, featuring high-end antiques dealers with goods from around the world.

"Wow. This is even more incredible than I remember." Being here was exhilarating.

"I know. This is my favorite part. I love the high-end contemporary designs, but there's nothing like finding the right period piece to anchor a room."

"Agreed," she said as they made their way through room after room of an eclectic mix of furniture, lighting, and art from the seventeenth through the twentieth centuries. "There are so many antique shops on the Cape. Some are ridiculous, you know, where they call a 1989 table a fine *antique*." She made air quotes as she said *antique*. "But some are incredible. I love knowing that every antique has a story. I want to know what each piece would say if they could tell us what they'd seen over the years."

"A good shop owner can tell you that." He cocked a brow. "Or make up something."

She laughed. "Yeah. That's true, sort of. But you know what I mean."

They meandered through the displays, commenting on pieces and showing each other which looks they gravitated toward and why. Gavin introduced her to several vendors. He was as charming with the men as he was with the women, and Serena realized he simply knew how to work a room. She'd always thought she was a master at that, but she was more of a hugger and more likely to ask about people's families and personal lives once she knew them well. Those were things she needed to get over in this industry. At least in the heart of Boston, where she wouldn't see clients at the beach, flea markets, or local concerts.

"Where did you source materials at the Cape?" Gavin asked as they made their way back downstairs.

"Locally, of course. At least as often as I could. Someone needs to support the local economy. We may be small, but we have incredible shops. Have you been there?"

"Twice, when I first moved to Boston. But life gets busy, you know? And all the things you hoped to do get put on the back-burner."

"Gosh. I hope not too much. I love my life back home. I'm heading back this weekend."

"Good luck with weekend traffic. It'll take you several hours instead of one and a half."

"Oh, shoot. I hadn't thought about that." She knew how awful traffic was on the weekends. He was right. It would take her forever to get there.

"I can see you stressing. Do you want to call your cookie

beau?"

"His name is Drake," she said with a smile. "I'll call him later. I'm sure he's busy with the resort."

As they left the building, Gavin said, "Do you still want to get food to take back to the office, or did you say that to impress the juniors?"

"I don't need to impress them. I have a ton of work to do, and I happen to like my teammates. So be careful how you refer to them, or I might have to bring out my nasty side."

He held his hands up in surrender. "Hey, I like my juniors, too, but that doesn't mean I'm going to give up my lunches."

"Sorry. I'm still trying to find my comfort zone with the infrastructure of the company. I'm not used to being around the type of people who take credit for the work of others. You should have seen their faces when I said I wanted them to come to an initial meeting with a new client. It was like they wanted to go but thought they'd get their noses swatted with a newspaper. It was pretty awful."

He was quiet for so long, she realized he might be just like the others. "I'm sorry. I didn't mean to insult you. God, foot in mouth much?"

He chuckled. "Relax. I was just thinking about how I felt when I first came on board and how much I've let go since then. I know what you mean. It's unfortunate that they've learned their place, but fortunate for them as far as job longevity goes. I know a great café by the office where we can get food to go. Let's take a cab and talk on the way over."

They flagged down a cab, and as they rode to the café, Gavin filled her in on the ins and outs of the office.

"Here's what you need to know about KHB. Like any business, there are two distinct areas that matter. Quality of work and image. KHB prides itself on working with the upper echelon of the business world, which is why we get clients like Younger, who want our name behind them. And that's cool. You know, KHB has made a name for itself and achieved something not many companies could. But it comes at a price. A few days after turning in your billable hours, Suzanne will come talk to you. She'll advise you to take your clients to BDC and rack up as many billable hours as possible. That makes the clients feel special and also fills the well."

"I get it. Clients want to be treated like they're worth every penny they pay, and the company wants to suck them for every penny they can. But I'm still hung up on the taking-credit thing. Do *you* take credit for your junior designers' work?"

He shook his head. "No. But most of the seniors do. It's the way the game is played."

"Not in my book. That's why I'm taking them with me to that meeting. Why visit twice when we can do it in one shot and cut down on the...? *Oh man...* That's about billable hours, too, isn't it?"

He shrugged, but his facial expression confirmed her thoughts.

A few minutes later the cab pulled over to the curb, and she said, "Why is everyone pushing client lunches? They're not billable."

She went for her purse, and Gavin pulled out his wallet.

"I've got it. Company expense." He paid the driver and asked him to wait. Once they were on the sidewalk, he said, "Client lunches...Employees need to eat. What's more advantageous for the company? That we eat while having one-on-one time with our clients, making them feel special, which equates to marketing for KHB, or that we shoot the shit with each other in the break room?"

"*Everything* is about money?"

He pulled open the door to the café and said, "Welcome to the world of big-city business, Cape girl. You want to know why I treasure my lunch hour?"

"Sure, but if it has to do with money, please lie to me." She stepped into line beside him.

"We work our asses off from morning until night most days. Lunch is the only time we can put it all away and turn off the designer side of our brains. Let me ask you something. Why did you become a designer?"

"Why did you?" she threw back, giving her time to decide just how honest she wanted to be about her family life.

"I've always loved putting things together, whether it's fash-ion—"

"I have noticed your penchant for nice threads," she teased.

"Part of my charm." He waggled his brows. "Clothing, spaces, fabrics. I love it all. Your turn."

"I wanted to make my *mark*."

"*Mark?* Like a Serena Mallery *brand?*"

"Kind of. I didn't have much growing up, and I always craved the basic things in life—a family *unit*, a decorated bedroom, cute school supplies like the other kids had. My mom was never around, and my sister, Chloe, and I took care of each other. We created our *family* with friends and their parents, and we found ways to fit in. When I realized I couldn't buy nice things, I began changing *everything* I could get my hands on, making it special. Making it my own. As a kid it was bedazzling a notebook, painting my room, or writing on my shorts to start a trend instead of following one. I worked as a teenager, scraped together every penny, budgeted it out, came up with plans months ahead of time to make sure I had a dress for the prom and all that silly stuff that seemed so vital back then. And since I couldn't buy things to decorate, I lived vicariously through my friends and their families when they redecorated rooms in their houses. One day it all came together and *clicked*. I realized I had *vision*, and I liked the nuts and bolts of bringing things to life."

They ordered sandwiches to go, and she told him about working with Drake to open the music stores and the upcoming grand-opening celebration.

On their way out of the café, he said, "You do realize that this is a whole different world, right? You'll get clients that you have full control over, but you'll have a lot of Muriel Youngers, too. But don't worry. You're just starting out here. Those things you love might change."

"No, they won't. I know where my heart lies. In all the years since I started college, I've never once been bored or become disenchanted with what I do."

They climbed into the cab and he said, "Then why did you leave your last company?"

"Bayside Resort? Because I helped them set up the entire resort from scratch, from the billing to marketing strategies. We designed every office, every cottage, every *room*. There was nothing left for me to do except help run the day-to-day operations. I wasn't *bored*. I worked with good friends I've known forever, and I met new people all the time. But it was time for me to achieve my own success."

"And you think this is it? Working for KHB?"

"I'm not sure," she said honestly. "It's too early to tell, but parts of it, maybe. What about you?"

"This is a step in a ladder for me. I'm thirty-one years old."

"Me too," she said.

"Really? And you haven't outgrown your cookie habit?"

She wrinkled her nose at him. "I'll never outgrow that."

"Good. Some things should always be part of who you are. For me, it's family. I know what I want to end up with. A wife who understands marriage won't always be easy, because the last thing I need is a diva who has no idea what being a family really means, more reasonable hours, and—like everyone else— something of my own."

"Laura said the last two senior designers left for bigger, better opportunities. Is this a stopover for *everyone*? Is that why it feels like something's missing?" She didn't even realize she'd nailed down her feelings to something being missing until just then. She'd never felt like something was missing at the resort. Her need to move on was driven by her job, the one she'd been hired to do, being completed. She'd readied the resort for someone else to walk in and run the areas she'd set up and managed. But had she felt complete for so long there because of Drake? Because of her friends?

"Until you own your own business, I think everything is a stepping-stone."

"I guess that's true." Wasn't everything in life a stepping-stone to *something*? Like school was to a career and dating was to marriage?

"My guess is the reason it feels like something's missing is because you're looking for small-town friendships, loyalty, and comforts in the big city. Like I said, that might change. I've seen good people like you become hardened, disloyal, and impersonal in a matter of months."

"How did *you* escape it? You seem pretty down-to-earth."

"I keep my eyes on the prize. I may not know what that prize is right now, but I have faith in myself. I know one day my future will become clear. My small-town roots have kept me grounded. I might want more *professionally*, but the day I walk out the doors of KHB for the last time, it's not going to be as a lesser man."

DRAKE PACED AT the end of the resort driveway waiting for Serena to arrive home Friday night. She'd texted when she'd reached the roundabout in Orleans, which was only a few minutes away, and he'd been edgy ever since. The drive had taken her an extra hour and a half. He expected her to be tired and irritated, and he told himself to chill out and try not to devour her the second he saw her.

Headlights appeared at the end of the road, and he jogged into the street, every nerve aflame, his fingers curling in anticipation of holding her again.

Her window was down as she rolled to a stop beside him. "Hey, big boy—"

Her words were smothered with a ravenous kiss. So much for holding back. He couldn't resist leaning through the open window and taking the kiss deeper. She clutched at his hair, holding tight the way she must have learned turned him on. Sinful sounds slipped from her lungs, and the car began rolling.

"Brakes," he ground out between urgent kisses.

She slammed on the brakes, pulling him by his hair into another kiss. The sting shot darts of pleasure straight to his groin. His Supergirl was back, and he needed her in his arms. The car rolled forward again, and she grasped the wheel with one hand, still tugging his hair with the other, and slammed on the brake.

"Park," he ground out. "Fast."

He gave her a chaste kiss and sprinted down the driveway beside her car. The second she parked in front of the office, he pulled the door open and she jumped into his arms. Her mouth crashed against his, knocking their teeth together. They both groaned, but neither broke their connection as he carried her into the office and strode up the stairs to his apartment.

Halfway up she pulled back and pressed her hands to his cheeks, her eyes dazzling with heat as she said, "I swore I wouldn't do this."

He grinned. "You and me both. Everyone's at the Beachcomber tonight, if you want to—"

"No! I need to be with you. It's been a *long* week."

"Thank Christ," he ground out.

He reclaimed her mouth as he opened the door to his apartment and pushed it closed with his hip. She wriggled from his arms, and they tore at each other's clothes, stumbling toward the bedroom. They tumbled to the bed in a tangle of nakedness, eating at each other's mouths as he aligned their bodies and entered her in one hard thrust. They both stilled, their eyes connecting through a blur of lust and so much more.

"Don't move," she said breathlessly. "I just want to stay right here, feeling all of you."

He buried his face in her neck, breathing her in. "How is it possible that I've missed you so much?"

"I don't know. I look for you at every turn. When I'm in my office, I wish you'd come in after your morning run, shirtless and sweaty, with that look in your eyes that always made my heart go crazy."

He kissed her cheek, then brushed his lips over hers and said, "You mean the damn-I-want-you look that was immediately followed by an I-need-a-cold-shower grimace?"

"Yeah, that's the one."

He lifted one of her hands to his lips and pressed a kiss to each of her fingers. Then he settled her hand beneath his on the mattress and did the same with her other hand. "This is the first time you've been in my bed, and I want to remember everything about it. Your hair spilling over the pillows, the feel of you beneath me, the look in your eyes."

"It's not the first time," she whispered. "When we finished decorating your apartment, I lay right across the bed, staring up at the ceiling while you were talking with Rick, remember?"

"I do, actually. I remember wondering if he'd think I was a dick if I asked him to leave so I could try to seduce you."

"Liar." She grinned.

"You're right. I wondered if he'd think I was a dick if I told him to leave and flat-out took advantage of you."

Passion simmered in her eyes. "God, how I wish you had."

She leaned up as he lowered his lips to hers, meeting him in a slow, sensual kiss as they found their rhythm. The feel of her softness beneath him, her tight heat swallowing him thrust after thrust, nearly made him lose his mind. Their kisses turned rougher. They moved faster, their efforts urgent and possessive. She clawed at his back and wound her legs around his. Her feet slid down his hamstrings, locking just above the crook of his knees as he drove in deeper. He wanted to do everything, to touch her everywhere, at once. This, her, their coming together, was truly and utterly perfect.

He pushed his hands beneath her hips, lifting and angling, so he could hit the spot that would make her lose control. He quickened his efforts, and her head fell back. Her eyes were closed, her lips parted as she clung to him, stealing gasps of air as they made love to their own passionate beat. A sheen of sweat covered their flesh as he pounded faster, took her harder. He felt tension mounting in her thighs, creeping up her torso, until her whole body was taut, her heels digging into the back of his legs. Her eyes opened, and she held his gaze, sending his heart into a spiral of emotions. His girl knew just what he wanted—what he *needed*—to see and feel *all* of her.

"I adore you," he said passionately as his mouth covered hers in a greedy kiss.

He struggled, holding off his own release as her inner muscles pulsed tight and hot around his shaft. Pressure mounted at the base of his spine, throbbing and burning with every thrust. Her nails cut into his flesh, sending spikes of desire darting through him.

She tore her mouth away, pleading, "*Come with me.*"

He abandoned all restraint, following her over the edge, into a world so full of Serena, it was all he could do to remember how to breathe.

They lay together afterward, Serena's fingers trailing lightly over his skin as she nuzzled closer and whispered, "I have to pee."

He chuckled. "You're so romantic." He kissed her forehead, then patted her butt and said, "Go."

He laced his fingers behind his head, watching her full hips sway as she padded across the floor. She'd never seemed the least bit self-conscious about her body. Most women tried to cover up their bodies, but Serena was comfortable in her own skin. He loved that about her. A whisper of a voice in his head wondered if she'd been like that with all the guys she'd been with. He glanced at the card she'd given him on his nightstand, and he knew the answer didn't matter. Her heart had always belonged to him, just like his had to her.

She came out of the bathroom with a playful expression on her face and grabbed one of his T-shirts from the stack of clean laundry on the chair in the corner. "Mine."

He laughed as he stepped from the bed. "I sure am."

He helped her put on his shirt, which covered far too much of her. Then he gathered her in his arms and kissed the tip of her nose. "I'm glad you're here, Supergirl. Not just for the incredible sex, but I think now I know why I've never brought a woman here."

"You never…? Not once?"

"Not once."

She pressed her lips to his chest. "Because you knew it would break my heart to see them leave in the morning?"

"I never got that far in my thinking. You and I picked out this bed, and you know I always hoped that one day we'd finally get our timing right. It would have felt wrong to bring you into my bed after someone else had been there."

The appreciation in her eyes made the pit of his stomach go all squirrely.

"You just earned major bonus points."

"Good, because I definitely want to collect on them later. I'll be right back." He went to use the bathroom and was pleased to discover the scent of her perfume lingering in the air. Damn, he loved that.

After washing up, he returned to an empty bedroom and spotted Serena standing out on the balcony. She was leaning on the railing, arms folded in front of her as she gazed out at the bay. The breeze lifted her hair from her shoulder, pressing the soft cotton of his shirt to her curves. Her left knee was bent, her toes perched just behind her right foot. She looked sexy and innocent, and she was finally *his*. Drake couldn't resist snagging his phone from his shorts pocket and snapping a picture. *My girl.*

He grabbed a pair of boxer briefs from the pile on the chair and stepped into them. Then he went to her, wrapping his arms around her from behind.

"What's going on in your beautiful mind?" He kissed her neck, and she closed her eyes, relaxing against his chest.

"You. Me. The Cape. Our friends. My new job."

"And here I thought I'd worn you out too much to think."

She turned in his arms. Her hands slid down to his butt, and she smiled up at him. "You did, but now that it's over, all that happiness helps me see things more clearly."

"And what do you see?"

"How lucky I am to have grown up where I did, with a mother who wasn't always around."

Every time he thought about her childhood, his blood came to a slow boil. She didn't see much of her mother, just a quick visit a few times a year. He knew damn well it was because her mother was still chasing men instead of taking care of herself, which pissed off Serena. "Why do you consider that lucky?"

"Because if I hadn't grown up where I did, or if I'd had it easy, I might not have ever gotten where I am today, with friends who have stuck by me and showed me that life could be anything I wanted it to be. And I might not have ever found you."

"It's hard to argue with that sort of thinking, but I still would have liked for your life to have been easier."

"Easy is for wimps." She wrapped her arms around his middle and hugged him. "I'm Supergirl, remember?"

She was the bravest, strongest woman he knew. "That's not

something I'll ever forget."

"Can we bring blankets out here and sleep on the lounger beneath the stars? I miss being outside like this."

"How about we bring the mattress out?"

She bounced on her toes. "Really? You don't mind?"

"Not at all."

"I think you just earned some amazing sexual favors!" She dragged him inside. "Can we order a pizza, too? I'm *starved*."

She was always starved, and for some weird reason, the fact that she never tried to hide it made him happy.

They set up their bed on the balcony, and when the pizza came, they ate it under the stars. He told her they'd hired Daphne. She was starting work in two weeks and would be coming to breakfast Sunday at Summer House to meet the rest of their friends.

"Really? That's fantastic. I liked her a lot, and I know she'll do a great job. So, you're really okay with me living in Boston?"

"I'm okay with you being anywhere you want to be. I know you have some issues with your job, but overall, are you happy there?"

"Yes. I think so. There's a lot to get used to, but today was great. The design center is incredible, and Gavin turned out to be even more down-to-earth than I thought. I like him. He seems honest, and I think he's a good person. I never would have guessed he was from a small town, but after spending much of today with him, I can see it in the things he says."

She set her plate on the deck and said, "I like everyone I work with, and even though my biggest client grates on my nerves, I don't *dislike* her. I just want more freedom to design. I'm taking Laura and Spence to see the nerve grater's space next week, and I'm bucking the system a little by taking them with me to meet a new client next week."

"Why is that bucking the system? I thought they were your teammates."

"They are, but it's not like here, where we're all an integral part of things. Or *were*, I guess. The company is all about prestige and money, so they really like senior designers to meet with clients alone initially, then bring in the team. But you know me. Why waste time with two visits when it can be done in one? I think showing up with a team shows them that they're important enough to have all of our attention, not just mine."

"Just don't get yourself fired, Ms. Blaze My Own Path." He pulled her against him and kissed her.

"As I told Laura and Spence, Mallerys don't get fired. We get fired up."

He nipped at her neck and said, "*Fired up.* Now, that's something I'd like to explore a little more."

"Mm. Think anyone can see us up here?"

"No, but just in case..." He swept her beneath him and pulled the blankets over them. "As long as you keep those sexy sounds you make to a minimum, we should be in the clear."

He kissed his way down her body, slowing to love her breasts, earning one seductive sound after another. He moved up, reclaiming her mouth in a hungry kiss.

"You might want to dial it down a little," he warned.

Her eyes flared with heat. "Maybe you should keep my mouth full so I'm not tempted to make noise."

"*Fuck*, baby. I like the way you think."

He shifted beneath the blankets, lying on his side as she fisted his cock and guided it into her mouth. A groan escaped before he could stifle it as he lowered his mouth to her sex. She rocked against his mouth while stroking him faster, squeezing harder. She cradled his balls, sending a spear of heat down his spine. He arched back, his hips thrusting as another appreciative noise escaped.

She drew back, and he instantly mourned the loss of her hot, wet mouth.

"Christ, Serena, your mouth is fucking insane."

"I'll suck you senseless," she promised like a vixen. The predatory look in her eyes made his cock throb. "But you might want to get busy down there and keep that talented mouth of *yours* quiet."

Chapter Fourteen

SERENA SNUGGLED DEEPER into the warmth of Drake's body as sunlight shone through her closed eyelids. She didn't want to open her eyes. She wasn't ready to let the rest of the world into their private haven. She wondered what time it was. She wanted to have breakfast with everyone and catch up on the last week. She had a busy day ahead. She was having lunch with the girls while Drake worked at the resort, and then she and Drake were going to meet the furniture delivery guys at the music store. Mira had texted earlier in the week to ask if Serena and Drake wanted to see a concert across from Mayo Beach tonight, and Serena was excited to do that, too. She'd had a busy social calendar here, whereas in Boston, so far she'd rarely had time to do anything but work.

Drake's thick arm tightened around her belly. "Morning, beautiful. Did you get any sleep, or did your mind whirl all night?"

He'd fallen asleep holding her, and he hadn't moved an inch, except to hold her tighter every time she shifted positions. She'd lain awake thinking about her job and her life and what it might have been like if she and Drake had been together when she was working at the resort. She'd eventually drifted off to sleep and into dreams woven of moments with Drake.

"There was a little whirling, but I eventually fell asleep." She opened her eyes, then immediately closed them against the bright sun. "Why don't we sleep under the stars all the time?"

"Because we live an hour and a half apart," he said groggily. "And we'd freeze our asses off in the winter."

"But it would be nice in the summer months. I get vacation days. Maybe I can take time off next summer and we can do it then."

He cupped her breast and kissed the back of her neck. "I'm all for it."

"Mommy! There's someone on Uncle Drake's deck! See the feet?" Hagen's high-pitched voice drifted up to the deck.

Serena bolted upright on the mattress, scanning the ground. Mira was grinning up at her, one hand on Hagen's shoulder.

Hagen waved wildly. "It's Auntie Serena! What are you doing up there?"

Drake groaned, his arm snaking around her belly again.

"Hi, Hagen!" she called out as Drake sat up beside her.

"Hi, Uncle Drake! Are you having a slumber party with Serena?" Hagen looked up at Mira and said, "Mommy, can I sleep on our patio tonight? I want to have a slumber party, too!"

Mira said something to him that Serena couldn't hear. Then she looked up at them and said, "You guys missed breakfast."

"Sorry," Drake called out. He leaned closer to Serena and whispered, "I'm not sorry in the least. Let's go inside so I can feast on you."

He kissed her shoulder, making her stomach somersault.

"Shh. Your nephew is *right there*."

He pressed a tender kiss to her neck and said, "He can't hear me."

"But he can *see* you!"

"Okay, buddy boy, time to go," Mira said, turning Hagen away from Drake and Serena. "See you at lunch, Serena!"

"Bye!" Hagen looked back and waved. "Maybe I can sleep on Uncle Drake's deck tonight!"

"Not a chance," Drake said as he brought Serena back down to the mattress and brushed his lips over hers. "Weekends are *ours.*"

"We are *not* fooling around out here in broad daylight." She tried to squirm out from under him to escape the oral assault he was lodging with his wicked mouth, but he pinned her wrists to the mattress.

His eyes turned dark as night as he said, "Couch? Kitchen counter? Shower?"

"Yes, yes, and double *yes!*"

Several toe-curling orgasms later, after they conquered the couch, counter, *floor*, and the shower, Serena realized she had no clean clothes. There was no need to pack a bag to come home when she had clothes at her cottage. She put on one of Drake's shirts, tied it around the waist, and wore her shorts from last night.

"Aren't you missing something?" Her panties dangled from his finger.

"I'm not wearing dirty underwear. I'll run to my cottage and grab a pair." Her phone vibrated. She pulled it from her pocket and read Desiree's text. "Desiree said Violet left us a basket with breakfast on the stairs. I'm starved."

"I've got a meal for you."

She rolled her eyes. "I need sustenance. This girl's got to keep her stamina up to keep up with our sexual activities."

On the steps to the apartment she found a basket filled with fresh fruit, two muffins, and a sealed pink envelope addressed to Drake. She carried it to the coffee table and handed him the envelope. "You and Des, huh? How does Rick feel about that?"

He plucked the envelope from her fingers and tore it open. After reading it, he handed the letter to her. "I think the Girl Squad is after me and Vi's a Peeping Tom."

She read the note as she ate her muffin.

Drake,

Deliver Serena, ~~sated and happy~~ well fucked to Summer House at 11:30 for a ~~wedding dress fitting~~ hen party followed by ~~lunch in P-town~~ a trip to the sex shop.

We'll return her to the music shop at 2:30, and then she's yours for more fuckery until 7:30, when we meet at the Bookstore Restaurant to get sloshed before enjoying the concert across from Mayo Beach.

Do not deter from these instructions ~~or you'll be sorry.~~ except for much needed fuckery.

Love, Bayside Girl Squad

PS: You two horndogs might want to go inside tonight. The noises coming from your deck could bring a lonely woman to orgasm. Just sayin'.

Serena nearly spit out her muffin. "Oh my God! Do you think Violet really heard us?"

"Do you *doubt* it?" He snagged an apple and bit into it, chuckling as he chewed.

"Drake! This isn't funny. What if other people, *paying resort customers*, heard us?"

He hauled her against him and pressed his lips to hers. "Then I'd say they got their money's worth."

"Forget your deck. From now on, we're sleeping at my place." At least there they'd have privacy.

"Until your lease runs out."

She rolled her eyes as she pushed to her feet. "I have to go home and get clean underwear before I meet the girls."

"Let's go." He stood up and grabbed his keys. "And let's bring some of your clothes over, so if we do stay here, you're not stuck going pantiless around other guys."

"You're coming? Don't you have to work?"

"I'm taking a few hours off with my girlfriend," he said, surprising her. Drake hardly ever took time off. "Unless you'd rather go alone?"

She went up on her toes and kissed his lips. "Heck no. I'm alone every night in Boston. That's more than enough."

"Good. Now let's talk about your shopping list."

"Shopping list?"

"For the sex-shop detour."

Oh my...

SERENA AND THE girls weaved around tourists streaming in and out of an array of galleries, eclectic shops, and restaurants on their way to the boutique for Desiree to try on her wedding dress.

"So, you'll just see each other on the weekends?" Emery asked. She and Chloe badgered Serena for the scoop on her and Drake as they hurried along Commercial Street in Province-town.

Serena and Drake had started out as such close friends, it felt like they'd been a couple for much longer than they had. It was a little jarring for her to realize this was the first weekend her friends would see them acting like a couple. That made her acutely aware of everything she said and of the immensity of her feelings toward him.

"Yes. Did I tell you about my teammates?" Serena kept trying to change the subject to work, the inn, yoga, *anything* other than her and Drake, but they kept circling back to them.

"Stop with work already," Chloe said. "We want details about your love life, which I might remind you, you haven't had in a *very* long time."

"No sexy details, please," Mira said as she tried to keep pace with one hand beneath her belly, as if she could make it lighter. "My son nearly got an eyeful this morning."

"He did not!" Serena insisted. "We were just lying there, and we were totally covered up."

"On a *mattress* on his *deck*," Emery pointed out.

"How do *you* know?" Serena glared at Mira.

Mira held her hands up. "Don't look at me. Thank God we weren't out catching fireflies in the middle of the night."

"Mira didn't spill the beans," Emery said. "I have eyes. I was on my way to the inn to teach my early class this morning and I saw something on his deck. A closer look showed me two pairs of *feet* tangled up in sheets."

Desiree gasped. "Seriously? Right there above the office? I thought I was risqué being naughty in the crow's nest at the inn."

"You're still learning how to spell risqué, sis," Violet said as they maneuvered around a family sitting on the front steps of a bakery, eating delicious-looking pastries.

"Serena, you and Drake were *naked* on his *deck*?" Chloe went wide-eyed. "And this is the first *I'm* hearing of it?"

"We weren't naked!" she lied. "At least not this morning when Mira saw us." God, this was embarrassing. How could she joke about sex so easily when it was other people's love lives under the microscope?

"Trust me. You would have *heard* last night had you been within a five-hundred-foot radius." Violet flashed a satisfied smirk.

"We won't make that mistake again," Serena said under her breath as they walked by a crowd that had gathered around three young musicians.

"I should hope not," Desiree said. "What if someone saw you?"

"Someone *did*," Violet said, earning another harsh glare from Serena.

"Oh my gosh," Desiree said. "That's *so* embarrassing."

"It's not so different from everyone knowing about your sex life," Emery pointed out.

Embarrassment flushed Desiree's cheeks. She motioned ahead of them to an alley sandwiched between Puzzle Me This, an elaborate game store that was painted in vibrant shades of purple and pink, and Coconuts, a cedar-sided sunglass store. "Swank, the boutique where I bought the dress, is right down that alley."

Serena was glad for the change in subject.

"We should stop and see Sky afterward," Violet suggested. "I could use a new tat."

Sky Lacroux-Bass owned Inky Skies, a tattoo parlor on the other side of the game store.

"You need another tattoo like I need more yoga clothes," Emery said.

"I would like to stop into the flower shop and talk to Lizzie," Desiree said. "And if there's time, Brandy, too." Lizzie Barber owned P-town Petals and was handling the flowers for Desiree and Rick's wedding. "I know we have to be back in time for Serena to meet Drake, so if we run out of time, it's okay."

"Anything else, Queen Bee?" Violet asked as they turned down the alley.

"Oh gosh. Do I sound like that?" Desiree looked frantically from one friend to the next. "I didn't mean it like that. I just wanted to thank Lizzie for answering all my questions this past week and to confirm the tasting session date with Brandy. The tasting is set for the weekend after Drake's grand opening. You guys are all still planning on coming, right?"

They all answered at once as they approached the boutique, assuring her she didn't sound stuck-up and that they wouldn't miss the tasting. The boutique was located in a narrow, two-story house that had seen better days. Remnants of teal scuffed the wooden siding. The windows were shrouded behind big leafy plants, and a pink diamond-shaped sign hung over the door with SWANK! painted in vibrant yellow.

An adorable blond guy sat on the steps, reading. His hair was several shades of blond, cut military-short on the sides, longer on top, and brushed back from his face in a puffy, trendy style. His white dress shirt was unbuttoned four buttons deep. The sleeves were rolled up to just below his elbows. He wore a stylish pair of navy shorts with white polka dots.

He looked up as they approached and said, "There's my beautiful princess bride!"

He set the book down and pushed to his feet, whipping off his dark sunglasses and revealing soft, friendly blue eyes. Several colorful beaded bracelets adorned his wrist, and a single leather anklet set off his muscular, tanned legs. He slid his feet into a pair of flip-flops and pulled Desiree into an overzealous embrace, air-kissing both cheeks.

"Hi, Donovan," Desiree said.

"I see you brought your entourage this time, and not your prince." He lowered his voice and said, "They're gorgeous, but Ricky's better eye candy for me."

They all chuckled.

"Bet *Ricky* loves that," Violet said snarkily as they made their way inside.

"I'm all eyes, not hands-on, sweetheart," Donovan said. "You must be Violet, the motorcycle-riding, badass sister I've heard so much about." He raked his eyes down Violet's black T-shirt and cutoffs to her biker boots. "Mm-*mm*. Woman, you have got it all going on. I have been searching for the perfect dress for you ever since Desiree told me about you."

"This should be interesting," Emery whispered to Serena.

As Donovan went behind the antique dresser he used as a counter, Serena took in the mayhem that was Swank. Several chandeliers and lanterns dangled from exposed joists in the ceiling. Teal and yellow walls looked as though the color had been drained from them, like aged fruit, and dresses were displayed hanging from simple hooks. Antique dressers were placed haphazardly, draped with scarves, mismatched lamps, and other accessories. Funky racks held dresses, skirts, and blouses of all styles and colors, with seemingly no organization.

Serena grabbed Chloe's hand and said, "Please give me a few hours, some paint, and a really great handyman. I could make this place look incredible, instead of like someone's closet exploded."

"Shh," Chloe chided her.

"I've got your gorgeous wedding dress ready and waiting in the dressing room, princess," Donovan said to Desiree as he came around the counter holding a garment bag. He handed the garment bag to Violet and waved to a row of curtains in the back of the store. "Why don't you two chickies go try your dresses on, and I'll get to know your friends."

Violet sneered at the garment bag. "I'm not wearing any frilly shit."

Donovan huffed out a breath. "Honey, I had strict orders from your sister, who clearly adores you, not to find anything too girly. No frills, fuss, or muss. Trust me, sugar. You're going to *love* this dress."

"I'm *not* wearing heels," Violet insisted.

"He knows." Desiree grabbed Violet's arm and dragged her toward the dressing area. "This is what sisters do when one of them gets married. We try on dresses together. Now, get in there and try it on. If you hate it, you don't have to buy it."

They disappeared behind the curtains. Donovan quickly made his way around the room, chatting with each of the girls. By the time he reached Serena, she could see by the look in the others' eyes that they were all crazy about him.

"You're the Boston transplant," Donovan said as he came to her side.

"I guess that's about right. I'm Serena."

"Yes. The interior designer who's dating Ricky's supposedly hot brother, right?" He waved his hand. "The girls gave me the scoop."

"In *seven minutes*? They got right down to the dirt, didn't they?" She glanced at Mira, who mouthed, *I love him!*

"A smart shopkeeper knows how to work a room." He waggled his brows.

"I love your shop. I hope you don't take this the wrong way, but may I ask why you haven't organized it in a way that would make it easier for customers to find what they're looking for?"

"You mean why does it look like my kooky Grandma Zelda decorated?" He reached up and touched a stuffed cat sitting beneath a gold lamp in the shape of a woman.

"I didn't mean—"

"Oh, yes, you did," he said in a singsong voice. "And you're right. My grandmother Zelda owned this place until she passed two years ago. That's when I took over. I haven't had the time to make it more appealing."

"I'm sorry about your grandmother."

Sadness washed over him, and just as quickly, a smile lifted his lips. "Thank you. I miss her, kookiness and all. She was a wild one until the day she left us."

"Have you thought about hiring a company to help you redesign?"

He wagged his finger at her. "Are you going to give me a sales pitch for your overpriced Boston firm?"

"No, not at all. I was actually thinking about a friend of mine who owns a small interior design firm here on the Cape. Maybe you know of her? Justine Harkness? She owns Shift Home Interior in Hyannis."

"I don't, but I'd be happy to talk with her. Why don't you give me her information and write down your name so I can tell her you referred me?"

She followed him to the counter, where he gave her a pen and a notepad.

"This might be just the kick in the pants I need to get started."

Serena wrote down her name and Justine's contact information as Desiree and Violet came out of the dressing rooms.

"Holy cow!" Emery squealed.

Serena and Donovan hurried over. Desiree twirled in a peach, lace-up corset maxi dress with ruffles from hips to ankles, and Violet crossed her arms over the knee-length, curve-hugging, sleeveless black dress with a slit up the right side.

"What do you think?" Desiree asked. "I still can't believe I found a wedding dress so easily. I wasn't even shopping for one when we found it."

"You look beautiful," Violet said. "It's…" Her eyes filled with warm emotions Serena had never seen. She quickly schooled her expression and said, "It's perfect."

"It's feminine and breezy. I love it," Mira said. "You'll knock my brother's socks off."

Emery touched the ruffles and said, "It's so *you*. It's really stunning."

"You make me want to have a beach wedding," Chloe said. "But for that I'd need a man."

"I can help with that," Donovan offered, making them all laugh.

"Desiree, you are the most gorgeous bride I've ever seen, other than Mira, of course. And, Violet…" Serena was at a loss for words. She must have looked it, because Violet rolled her eyes.

Serena carefully uncrossed Violet's arms and walked around her, visually following the gold metal zipper, which started just below her ribs on her right side and wound around her body, across her lower back, and over her left hip, ending at the top of the slit on her upper thigh.

"Let me show you the pièce de résistance." Donovan took hold of the zipper at her ribs and unzipped all the way around her lower back and over her left hip, revealing a sexy path of tanned skin that snaked around her body.

"Holy cow, Vi. You look like a model," Desiree said. "You should wear dresses more often."

"Right," Violet said sarcastically.

Emery walked around Violet, assessing her, and said, "Seriously, you look like you could catch fire."

"I'd *do* you," Chloe said, "and I'm not into girls."

Violet rolled her eyes again. "You don't have to butter me up. I can wear it for an hour or two, but I'm not wearing heels."

"I almost forgot!" Donovan hurried over to an antique armoire and pulled out a boot box. He opened the top and handed a pair of black, wedge-heeled and fringed ankle boots to Violet. "Harley-Davidson Tybee boots, the hottest boots around for our biker girls. The hidden wedge heel and stylish fringe makes them perfect for dressing up or *leathering* up."

"These are kickin'," Violet said.

Desiree beamed at her. "Really? You're going to wear the dress *and* the boots?" She threw her arms around Violet, nearly toppling them both over. "Thank you! I wouldn't have cared if you wore your leather miniskirt and bikini top, but this means the world to me."

"Whatevs, sis," Violet said with a sigh. "Can I change now? I'm freaking starving."

"Yes. Go!" Desiree nudged her toward the curtain. Then she threw her arms around Donovan and kissed his cheek. "You're amazing! Thank you so much for everything. The dress fits perfectly, and Violet looks like a dream. Now I just have to find heels."

"I might have you covered, too, princess." He went to the armoire and returned with another box. "If you like them, they're my wedding gift to you."

Desiree opened the box, and happiness bloomed in her eyes. "I love them!"

She held up a pair of gorgeous sandals, also with a wedge heel, a shade lighter than her dress, with tiny pearls on the thin strap across the front of her foot and on the thin ankle strap.

"With a beach wedding, you want flats or a wedge, and since Ricky's so tall, I thought you'd want the additional height to be closer to his lips." He winked.

"Can you help me with my wedding dress?" Emery asked. "I wasn't going to do anything fancy, but…"

"How about a triple wedding?" He looked inquisitively at Emery and Serena—as did the others.

"Dean and I are *not* crashing Des's wedding," Emery said. "Count me out."

Serena's stomach twisted nervously. "I…um…no. Drake and I *just* started dating. We're not even *close* to being engaged."

"We'll see about that," Desiree said. "Rick and I didn't date long before we got engaged. And look at Em and Dean. When you know, you *know*."

"Don't fall prey to their pressure," Violet said as she stepped out from behind the curtain wearing her own clothes. "Stay strong, little one."

She'd been strong for so many years when it came to Drake, she sort of hated that expression, but her life was in Boston and his was here at the Cape. "I'm going through enough life changes at the moment. We've only just begun trying to figure out how to be a long-distance couple."

That didn't stop her from thinking about Donovan's suggestion and toying with the idea through lunch at the Red Eye Coffee and Café later that afternoon. Thinking of Drake made her think of making love with him, which reminded her of her *shopping* list. As the girls chatted about everything under the sun, Serena thought about her earlier conversation with Drake about her impending *shopping* trip.

You probably want me to get handcuffs or silk ties. His gaze had nearly ignited, and she'd taken it a little further. *Or maybe edible underwear? Violet told me about a wedge pillow that's supposed to be great for hitting the spot. Not that you have any trouble with that...* She'd always thought herself to be open to anything and fairly well versed in the sexual realm, even if she didn't have hands-on experience with much kink. But with Drake, she had a feeling she came across as a novice. He'd chuckled and said, *Baby, you're all I need, but I'm all for exploring a darker side with you.*

The passion in his eyes, the heat in his voice, and the fact that Drake was the man she'd loved forever made her *want* to explore with him, to test her limits.

"Let's eat quick and go see Lizzie and Brandy," Desiree suggested.

"Remind me to stop into your little pleasure trove of dark and sexy secrets when we get back to Wellfleet," Serena said as casually as she could.

Violet's catlike green eyes landed on her. "Guess you got my note."

"You left her a note, too?" Desiree speared a tomato from her salad with her fork.

"I think Vi modified yours," Serena answered. She'd never been the least bit nervous about wandering around their sex shop. But now, just thinking about buying things to actually use with Drake, made her all kinds of jittery, and she second-guessed her suggestion.

"You modified my note?" Desiree gave Violet a disapproving look.

Violet slung her tattooed arm casually over the back of her chair and said, "Clearly mine made an impact."

Violet's note might have opened the gates to Curiosityville, but it was Drake's interest nudging her through.

DRAKE PUSHED THE couch to the area Serena had laid out in her designs for the reading nook in the music store. She was running late with the girls, but she'd sounded happy when she'd called, and he knew how much she missed them. She'd been right about the couch. The rounded back even made him want to sit down and relax, and the style fit right in with the bohemian theme they used in the stores. Although they maintained the same theme for each of the stores, Serena had come up with unique ideas for setup and furniture that fit in with each of the locations they were serving. For example, his store in Florida used brighter colors and a beachier bohemian theme, while the store in West Virginia was more rustic. As he moved the two armchairs into place, rounding out the reading nook, he thought about how well he and Serena worked together. She hadn't dropped the ball once, even with her move, her new job, and her longer hours, and he hoped she'd be excited to see the store set up and ready for the grand opening.

He rolled out the rug she'd ordered—a funky mix of faded blues, reds, golds, and about a dozen other colors in bold shapes—and centered it between the furniture and the display of music books. Then he stepped back and took it all in.

This location was more than twice the size of his first store, despite the fact that more musical instruments were being purchased online than ever. Drake was constantly adapting his businesses to the ever-changing consumer buying habits, offering online fulfillment as well as school instrument rental programs, on-site repairs, and lessons for beginners. He and Serena had lined up the instructors and marketed to the schools in the surrounding areas months ago. Through his deals with distributors, he was able to offer a wide selection of products in all price ranges. After opening the second store, Serena had suggested he offer only a small collection of vintage instruments that customers could request to have sent to their location. That allowed him to keep fewer of the more expensive, rarely purchased items in stock and ready for purchase within forty-eight hours. She was great at cutting expenses without cutting corners, and it had paid off. He'd gained a solid reputation for high-quality goods at affordable prices.

We've gained the reputation.

The doors opened, and Serena breezed in with a shopping bag dangling from each hand, all sexy bronze skin and a luminous smile just for him. "Sorry I'm late! We got ice cream after lunch and then stopped in to chat with Lizzie and Brandy about the wedding. Brandy had to delay the tasting for a week because of a scheduling conflict, but don't worry—I confirmed the catering for the grand opening. She's all set. Then we went to the sex sh—" She stopped cold midway through the store, and her bags dropped to the floor as she looked around at the instruments on the walls, laid out just as she'd suggested. Violins at the front of the store, horns in the middle, and guitars in the back to draw the most customers through. Drums were in the left rear corner beside the counter. The perfect spot for eager young children to get the bug and try them out.

"It's...*done?*" She schooled her expression so fast, if he didn't know her so well, he might have missed the hurt that had first appeared. "You've been busy. It looks amazing."

"You were right about everything." He closed the distance between them. "The shape of the couch, the layout. I think it's our best store yet." He put a hand on her hip and brushed his thumb over her warm skin beneath her shirt. "*Our* best store."

He realized that was how he thought about everything when it came to Serena, as *theirs.* She'd been there from the very start, when he'd found his love for music, when he'd lost his father and that love of music had turned to a fierce few months of songwriting. She'd been there after college, when he'd been touting his dreams to buy a store, and she'd encouraged him, never once doubting his abilities or afraid of the risk he was taking. Every time someone raised a concern, she'd sing "Don't Stop Believin'," until he heard it like a mantra in his mind. And later, when he'd thought about opening the resort with the hopes of bringing Rick back to the Cape, back into the fold of the family, she'd offered to stand by his side before he'd even brought up the idea to Rick or Dean. She had become his best friend, his business partner, and now his lover. The last thing he wanted to do was hurt her in any way.

"I think so, too," she said. "I can't get over it. You did *everything.*"

"Except the feature displays. We'll figure that out Saturday morning, like always." He lifted her chin and gazed into her eyes. She was trying so hard to be supportive, he wondered if he'd done the wrong thing after all. "I'm sorry, babe. I had all those nights alone. Working here made me feel closer to you. And then I got it into my head that if I finished before the weekend, we'd have more time for us."

MELISSA FOSTER

She wrapped her arms around him and said, "I love those reasons. I was just surprised. That's all."

"And hurt." He kissed her tenderly. "You don't have to hide your feelings from me. I didn't mean to hurt you, but now I see how it might feel like I'm pushing you out or saying I don't need your help. That's not it, though. I hope you know that. This is *me* being *selfish*. I want time for us more than I want anything else."

"More than you want to christen your new office?" She began unbuttoning his shirt. "I've always wanted to know what it's like to bang the boss."

He bent to kiss her and accidentally kicked her shopping bag. "You did take a special shopping trip for us, didn't you?"

He picked up the bag from Devi's Discoveries. She tried to snag it, and he lifted it out of her reach. "What did my dirty girl buy at the sex shop?" He peered into the bag.

"It's not what you think!"

He reached into the bag and withdrew a box of penis cookies. He cocked a brow, grinning at her embarrassed expression.

"I told you! That's a new product Brandy makes and sells in their shop. Do you have any idea how weird it was to look at sex toys with my best friends, who'd know I'd be using them with one of their brothers?" She banged her forehead against his chest. "I'm sorry. But I couldn't do it. I kid a lot with the girls about doing sexy stuff, but I don't want them knowing what you and I do privately. It felt wrong and kind of creepy." She looked up at him with troubled eyes and said, "And then I realized that we're all talking about us like we've been a couple forever, but tonight will be the first time they really see us as a couple, together, kissing, touching. How weird will that be? What happens when I want to climb into your lap? Or sneak off to be dirty?"

His heart swallowed her right up as he crushed her against him. "Do you know how much I adore this side of you? The shier, careful girl? I love your brazen side and the animalistic ways we go at each other in bed, but this is just as sexy."

"Really?" she asked sweetly.

He cradled her face in his hands and said, "Really." He lowered his lips to hers and they stumbled toward the office. "I'm bringing the cookies and eating them off of your body." *Oh shit.* He broke away and said, "I need to lock the door." He handed her the box of cookies and sprinted to the front door.

When he turned back around, she was gone and the office door was open. He finished unbuttoning his shirt as he headed for the office.

He found her standing in a black thong and matching lace bra, her hip leaning against his desk. She crooked her finger, beckoning him closer. He pulled off his shirt and reached for her. She pushed his hand away, shaking her head. She unhooked the button on his jeans, looking up at him through her long lashes as she curled her fingers around the waist of his jeans and boxer briefs and yanked them down to his knees. He grabbed the edge of the desk as he toed off his shoes. He stepped out of his clothes and reached for her again, but she stepped back, shaking her head again. Her long hair shifted sexily around her face as she knelt before him, still holding his gaze, and wrapped her hand around his hard length. The image of her seared into his mind, sending a bolt of lust straight to his core.

"How many years did I think about this very moment, Mr. Bossman?"

She dragged her tongue from base to tip, and he gritted his

teeth. She did it over and over again until his cock was slick. She fisted his shaft, stroking tightly and driving him out of his mind.

"I used to fantasize about things heating up between us while we were setting up the stores," she confessed as she sank lower and dragged her tongue over his sac.

"Fuck, baby. I did, too. Every damn day."

She blinked innocently up at him as she swirled her tongue around the broad crown of his cock. He pushed his hands into her hair, holding tight as she lowered her mouth over his shaft, working him slow at first, then faster, taking him *deeper*. His muscles corded tighter with every hot, wet slide of her mouth. He met each perfect suck with a thrust of his hips. Watching her love him with everything she had sent waves of erotic sensations crashing over him.

When she quickened her pace, he growled, "I want to come inside you," and tugged her up by her hair.

She shimmied out of her thong, and he tore off her bra. Their mouths crashed together, and he pushed his hand between her legs, groaning as he slipped his fingers into her sweet, hot body. He tugged her head and devoured her neck, taking her right up to the brink of release.

"Take me from behind," she pleaded. "Fulfill your fantasy—and mine."

She planted her hands on the desk, stuck her ass up in the air, and spread her legs. She turned her head, looking at him over her shoulder as he moved behind her, aligning their bodies.

"Christ, baby. I'm going to fulfill your *every* fantasy."

He slid one hand up her belly and cupped her breast as he drove into her. He captured her mouth in an insatiable kiss, loving her right up to the clouds. She cried out his name in sheer bliss. A sound he'd never forget. But his love for her was too strong, too intense to let it go at this. When she came back down to earth, he carried her to the sofa and laid her down. He loved her tenderly, passionately, pouring all of his love, all of his strength and devotion, into their connection. And when he finally abandoned all restraint, she was right there with him, riding their waves of ecstasy, until they both collapsed, panting and sated, to the cushions.

They lay squished together on the tiny couch, their legs intertwined, holding each other as their breathing calmed. He kissed her forehead, her cheeks, and finally her lips as he ran his fingers through her hair and whispered, "I could stay right here forever and die a happy man."

Chapter Fifteen

SUNDAY MORNING SERENA tried not to think too much about having to leave in a few hours. Last night they'd had a fun night with their friends at dinner and the concert. She'd been so nervous about how it would feel acting like a couple in front of them, she'd decided to take the fear out of it and claim their relationship in the biggest way possible, leaving no room for awkwardness. When they sat down to dinner on the patio of the Bookstore Restaurant, she'd climbed onto Drake's lap and kissed him long and hard, to the point of being obscene. At first it had taken all of her courage, but once they were lip-locked, her emotions had taken over, making it as easy as breathing. Then she'd turned to their friends and announced, *This is how things are going to be from now on. Any questions?*

Drake sat beside her and pulled her close. "How's my man-claiming girlfriend?"

She liked the sound of that. "I'm great. I can't wait to congratulate Daphne at breakfast." She tried to focus on the positive rather than how breakfast would bring her that much closer to leaving.

He lifted her onto his lap and gathered her hair over her shoulder. "I know you're bummed about going back to Boston.

I can see it. Please stop trying to hide your feelings from me, okay?"

He'd skipped his morning run with the guys both days she was there, and she felt bad about that. At least when they'd been just friends she hadn't messed up his schedule. But selfishly, she was glad he'd stayed with her. They hadn't made love this morning. They'd just lain in bed talking and holding each other, the way they had lain on the beach after the concert and a long walk on the beach last night. They'd talked about everything and nothing at all for hours, and it had been perfectly romantic. When they'd finally decided to turn in for the night, Drake had offered to stay at her cottage instead of at his place, but she wanted to be there among his things, in the bed they'd shared the night before. They'd brought a bunch of her clothes over, which were now tucked safely away in his dresser and hanging in his closet.

She eyed the card on the nightstand, remembering how nervous she'd been when she'd written it. Look how far they'd come.

"I think I liked you better when you were all gruff and not caring about what I felt," she said, and touched her forehead to his. "No, I didn't," she admitted. "But let me lie to myself, okay? Let me tell myself I'm fine, because even though it's hard to leave, I'm excited to meet more clients this week and spend time with my team. I just hate the thought of a week going by before I see you again."

"Me too. But we'll talk on the phone and video chat, and before we know it, you'll be back for the grand opening and we'll celebrate."

"And dance like we did last night?" She rubbed her nose over his, then kissed him.

Their friends had joked with them when they were slow dancing, saying things about how Drake didn't look like he was going to kill anyone as long as Serena was in his arms. She'd loved every second of it—being in his arms and knowing their friends had seen the same look in his eyes she had when they'd danced *before* becoming a couple.

"I loved dancing with you as my boyfriend. It changes everything."

Mira had said the same thing last night, that Drake seemed truly happy and relaxed for the first time in his entire life.

"For me, too, Supergirl. We'd better get going. Daphne's probably already there. She's bringing her daughter, Hadley, and she'll have her in the office this morning while she finishes training with Harper."

He smacked her butt as she climbed off his lap and said, "You know what my favorite part of last night was?"

"Groping me under the dinner table?" She slipped her feet into her flip-flops.

He gathered her against him and said, "The moment you claimed me in the restaurant. That was freaking hot. Almost as hot as christening the office."

"Maybe next weekend we can christen your office downstairs."

He made a guttural sound of appreciation and kissed her. She was going to miss falling asleep in his arms, but she might miss their mornings together even more. She loved waking up to him—his scent, his strong arms wrapped around her, and his raspy morning voice. Showering and getting ready for the day, stolen kisses and smacks on her butt—she felt like she was stockpiling all the little things like a chipmunk saving up for winter.

Drake grabbed their matching sunglasses as they went out the door. She loved that he wasn't embarrassed to wear them. As they crossed the grass, she tucked away the feel of her hand in his, the way he pulled her closer as they walked, and the scents and sounds of the place she'd called home for the past several years.

"There's Daphne," he said, heading toward Summer House Inn's parking lot.

Serena walked quicker. "I can't wait to see her little girl."

Daphne was leaning into the back seat, lifting her daughter out of the car seat. "Hey, you two," she said as she settled Hadley, her adorable ten-month-old baby girl against her rounded hip. A few tufts of brownish hair stuck up from behind a tiny headband with a pink bow. Like Daphne, Hadley had chubby cheeks, but unlike her outgoing mother, Hadley had serious eyes, and her tiny lips were pursed in an almost-scowl, like a discerning adult. She was clearly unimpressed with her newfound situation.

"I'm so glad you made it," Serena said. "Hadley is adorable. Hi, sweetie." She tickled Hadley's foot. The baby's expression didn't change, but she clutched Daphne's T-shirt.

"Sorry we're late." Daphne stood up a little straighter, showing them her T-shirt, on which SORRY I'M LATE was emblazoned across her chest. She lifted Hadley a little higher. I'M THE REASON WE'RE LATE was printed across the front of Hadley's pink shirt.

"That is hilarious," Drake said. "Nothing like being prepared for anything. How can we help?"

"I need to get her car seat and bag. Would you mind holding her for a sec?" Daphne handed her to Drake, and Hadley's tiny brows knitted. She looked at her mother like she was out of her mind. Then she cocked her head, studying Drake's face.

"Believe it or not, she likes you," Daphne said. "She usually cries when anyone other than family holds her."

Drake was a natural with kids. Serena had watched him with Hagen over the years, and with other kids who had come through the resort. But nothing could have prepared her for the unfamiliar desires pinging around inside at the sight of Drake's thick arms cradling the sweet baby girl, making her look even smaller and more in need of his protection. He cooed at her.

Serena tore her gaze away, afraid her ovaries might explode.

"Okay, all set." Daphne threw her bag over her shoulder and held out the baby carrier. "Want to trade?"

Drake tickled Hadley under her chubby little chin, earning a slobbery grin. She had two teeth on the bottom and four on top. "Actually, would you mind if I carried her?"

Daphne looked at Serena like Drake was speaking another language. "Are you kidding? I'm a single mother. I welcome the help. He's a keeper, Serena. My ex didn't want to have anything to do with children, which is the reason why he's my ex."

"Not everyone's cut out for parenthood," Drake said, reaching for Serena's hand as they headed toward the inn.

She knew he was thinking about her mother, but it was all she could do to nod. Her mind was racing with new worries. She had so much she wanted to accomplish before she could even think about having children, but Drake was thirty-four and settled in his career. He'd never hidden the fact that he wanted a family, but if they stayed together, would he be willing to wait until she was settled in hers?

Mira and Chloe rushed over to greet Daphne and fawn over Hadley. Harper had asked them to apologize to Daphne for her. She had to miss breakfast because she had an early conference call about her most recent screenplay.

Serena introduced her to the others. "Daphne, this is Mira, Rick and Drake's sister, and this is my sister, Chloe."

"Hi," Daphne said. "Thanks for letting me crash breakfast."

"I'm crashing, too," Chloe said as she slung an arm over Serena's shoulder. "I'm not usually here this early, but I wanted to see this girly one more time before she goes back to Boston."

"That's sweet. When I left for North Carolina my twin brother and our sister probably threw a party." Daphne laughed and said, "Not really, but my sister was glad to have our apartment all to herself. When is your baby due?" she asked Mira.

"Not soon enough." Mira patted her belly.

"Hi, Daphne," Rick said. "I'm glad you made it."

"Thanks," Daphne said as she set the baby seat down beside the table. "It'll be nice to have friends around again. I've been so busy, I haven't gotten out much since I moved back, and so many of the people I grew up with have moved away."

"With this crew, you'll never be alone," Dean said. "And you might never get your baby back."

"I can deal with a few hours of freedom," Daphne said as she fished around in her baby bag.

Rick sidled up to Serena and said, "It's good to see he didn't scare you away with all that slow dancing last night."

"Quite the opposite," Serena said, remembering how incredible it had felt to be in Drake's arms, dancing beneath the stars. "It's called *foreplay*."

Rick chuckled, then turned to Drake and said, "Practicing?"

"Jealous?" Drake tickled Hadley again, earning another smile. Then Hadley turned an almost-scowl to Rick.

"She's cute. You keep missing our morning runs, and you

might end up with a tiny human sooner rather than later," Rick teased. "I hear it all starts with matching sunglasses."

Drake held the baby up in the air, and she giggled. "What do you think, Hadley? Does it all start with matching sunglasses?"

"In my experience," Daphne said, "it all starts with a back rub."

All the girls laughed. The guys smirked.

"You're going to fit right in," Serena assured her.

Desiree, Emery, and Violet came out of the house carrying trays of muffins, eggs, bacon, and sausage.

"They're here!" Emery said. "Look at that baby!"

She and Desiree hurried over to the table and set down their trays. Then they rushed over to see the baby, while Violet gave Hadley a wide berth.

Serena introduced Daphne to Emery, Desiree, and Violet and told her a little about each of them.

"There'll be a test later," Violet said as she snagged a piece of bacon.

"I've got it," Daphne said proudly, pointing to each person as she said their name. "Emery, yoga instructor and Dean's fiancée. The yoga pants helped with that one. Desiree, Rick's other half, co-owner of this gorgeous inn, and sister to Violet, who is the coolest chick I've ever met. I want to be you when I grow up. I have a thing for motorcycles, and I really want a tattoo with my baby girl's birth date, but I'm afraid to get one."

Violet finished her bacon and said, "There's a cure for that. It's called a few shots of tequila."

As Violet and Daphne discussed tattoos, Drake sat down, bouncing Hadley on his leg, which earned him more sweet baby giggles. He pulled Serena down beside him and said, "She's pretty cute, huh?"

"There really isn't anything sexier than you holding a baby. Seeing you with her almost makes me want to drag you back to the bedroom."

Hadley's brows knitted tighter than ever, and her face turned red. A second later, the smell of baby poop wafted around them, causing everyone to laugh.

"Oh gosh. Sorry." Daphne took her from his arms and grabbed her baby bag. "Babies are the ultimate love-moment blockers."

"You can say *cockblockers* or *fuckery finishers*," Violet said. "I'm pretty sure your little one isn't going to be repeating anything you say anytime soon."

Desiree gave her grief for using foul language in front of their new friends. Rick and Dean were busy harassing Drake about spending so much time with Hadley, and Serena sat back and enjoyed the show. She missed this fun banter, the closeness with the girls and teasing the guys. It was a wonderful morning, and Daphne fit right in. Although Hadley seemed a bit nonplussed with all of her newfound *aunties* and *uncles*, which was what Emery dubbed them, except Drake, whom she seemed to adore.

After Daphne left, they cleaned up and made plans to go tubing after the tasting session with Brandy, which was now scheduled for two weeks after the grand opening.

They spent the afternoon hanging out on the beach, and Serena made a point of lying beside Drake with her hand on his chest to *mark her property*.

Drake lay with his eyes shaded by his sunglasses, his lips curved up in a sinful smile as he said, "How about if I strip down and you put that hand on the property you really want to mark?"

"Hey!" Mira snapped. "How about no naked debauchery when I'm around?"

"It's okay. This is the property I want to mark anyway." Serena laid her hand over Drake's heart.

He placed his hand over hers and pulled her down to whisper in her ear. "Nice cover, babe. Next weekend we'll lie out naked behind your cottage and you can mark *any* part of my body you want."

That gave her something to look forward to.

By late afternoon, Serena was doing everything she could to procrastinate leaving, but she knew traffic would be hell, and she needed time to get ready for her work week. She'd purposefully left her work at home this weekend, knowing she wouldn't give up a second of her time with Drake and that Drake would feel guilty if he knew she wasn't getting her work done. But hey, that was what lonely Sunday nights were for.

After saying goodbye to Chloe and all their friends, Serena and Drake stood beside her car, kissing and murmuring promises to call. Why was she getting teary-eyed? She wasn't the kind of girl who cried at goodbyes.

Drake lifted her chin. She loved that intimate touch, the way it set her apart from all other women. She loved everything he did, like the way he was gazing at her right then, as if he understood and wanted to erase all her sadness.

"I know it's silly, but it's harder to leave this time." She half laughed, half sighed into his chest.

"What can I do to make it easier? Do you want me to come there on the weekends instead? Would that help?"

"No," she said quickly. "I want to see everyone. It's hard leaving you, but it's hard leaving everyone else, too. I'm sure it's just that I haven't found close friends in Boston yet." Even as she said it, she knew that wasn't all that was bothering her. She'd been *replaced*, and Drake hadn't needed her to set up the music store. Life was going on without her. She'd known it would, but thinking about it and experiencing it were two totally different things. And after spending the morning with Hadley, she couldn't stop worrying that she and Drake were on different time tables. She knew she was getting way ahead of herself, but he'd looked out for her best interests for so long, she couldn't ignore the possibility of something so important to him.

"What else?" he asked. "I see a storm brewing in your eyes, and I don't want to let you leave until we talk it out."

"It's ridiculous. Not important." She put her arms around his neck and said, "Kiss me. I'll be fine."

"But I won't be fine knowing you're not *really* fine," he said sternly, and that dimple appeared in his cheek. "If this is going to work, we have to be totally honest with each other. Talk to me, Serena."

"It's just...I really like Daphne, and I'm happy you guys hired her. She'll do a great job, but it feels weird being replaced so quickly."

"Remember how irritated you were when I didn't hire her right away?"

"I *know*," she said sharply. "I told you it was ridiculous."

"No. It's not ridiculous."

"It's reality, and I'm not upset over it. I'm just soaking it in and processing the finality of it." She gazed into his caring eyes and knew she had to be completely honest with him. "There's more. I have to ask you something that's going to seem like I'm rushing our relationship, but I don't mean to. I just don't want to hold you back. You're in your midthirties. Are you ready for a family?"

He cringed. "Can we not call thirty-four *midthirties*?"

"I just meant that maybe you were ready. I know you want a family, and I do, too, one day. But I'm not anywhere near ready, and just like you didn't want to hold me back from achieving my dreams, I don't want to hold you back from the things you want, either."

"I want a family one day, Serena, but I'm in absolutely *no* hurry. I want time to build our relationship as a couple." He brushed his thumb over her cheek and said, "You could never stand in my way, because my path includes you from here on out."

Relief washed over her. "I didn't realize how worried I was about that. But wow. It's like a weight just fell off my shoulders."

He chuckled and lifted her onto the hood of her car. "We're made for each other. I thought you were the one who had to convince me of that." He wedged his big body between her legs and said, "Besides, Supergirl, we haven't had *nearly* enough naked time together yet."

Chapter Sixteen

DRAKE PULLED OPEN the doors to Serena's office building Wednesday afternoon, excited to see the look in her eyes when he surprised her. He couldn't shake the worry about the pressure their relationship was putting on her. Only the evenings brought relief, when they'd catch up and she'd rave about her job and her team. That's why he'd been thrilled this morning when he'd received a call from a vintage guitar dealer who was going out of business. His store was about half an hour from Serena's office, and Drake had jumped at the chance to review his stock.

As he crossed the marble lobby and stepped into the elevator, giving a cursory glance to the guy in a suit standing by the button pad, he thought about their calls the last few nights. Serena's life was falling into place. Last night she'd gone out for drinks with the receptionist from her office and Gavin. He wasn't thrilled about the dude, but he trusted Serena, and if he were honest with himself, he'd rather she had a male coworker looking out for her than no man at all while she was out in a new city at night.

"What floor?" the guy asked.

"Oh, sorry. Fourteen, please."

The guy pushed the button and said, "That's my floor. Who are you going to see?"

"Serena Mallery. She's a designer with KHB."

"And a fine one at that. You're in good hands." He held out his hand and said, "Gavin Wheeler, also a senior designer with KHB."

And the guy who had drinks with my girlfriend last night. He shook Gavin's hand, trying to put the sharp, preppy dresser and Serena together. She was so laid-back, it was hard to picture. "Nice to meet you. I'm Drake Savage."

"Ah, yes. The elusive Drake. The cookie man, resort owner, and the guy who's got her drawing little hearts on her notebooks."

Drake chuckled. "Sounds like my girl. I heard you had drinks last night."

"Someone's got to watch out for the women in this office. Although, from what I've seen, Serena can be a real ballbuster. I doubt many guys could pull the wool over her eyes."

"She's strong, that's for sure."

"Did she tell you she went head-to-head with the big boss this morning for taking her juniors on an initial client visit?"

"No, but that doesn't surprise me. She stands up for what she believes in. Hopefully it didn't get her in any real trouble."

Gavin shrugged. "All I know is that the door was closed for a long time, and when Serena finally came out, I asked how it went and she said if they expect her to run a team, then they need to give her the space to do it right."

Drake cringed inwardly. He'd been around enough to know that some executives didn't like to have their decisions challenged. "That's my girl," he said as the elevator opened on their floor. "She doesn't know I'm here, by the way. I was in the area and wanted to surprise her."

"Come on. I'll take you back to see her."

He followed Gavin through the elaborate offices, which were vastly different from their offices at the Cape, and exactly what Serena had always talked about getting into. Guys in suits and women in professional dresses and slacks moved busily about. He was glad he'd thought to clean himself up a bit and wear slacks and a dress shirt.

Gavin pointed across the room to a glass-walled office. "That's her office, but she's probably still in the conference room with her team."

He led Drake down a hall to a glass-walled conference room. Drake took a moment to watch Serena through the glass. She was dressed in a curve-hugging white dress with a black panel down the center and high heels. Her hair was pinned up in a sexy twist as she leaned over a set of drawings, talking with a skinny blonde and a tall, slim, bearded guy. His pulse ratcheted up, not just because she looked hot as hell in that dress, but also because Serena had made it. Whether she was testing her boss's patience or not, she was making a name for herself in one of the biggest design firms in the industry. His heart filled with happiness, and he vowed once again to do everything he could to support her success. He prepared himself to give her a kiss on the cheek and *not* grope her fine ass.

"Look who I found in the elevator," Gavin said as they walked into the conference room.

Serena turned, and her whole face lit up. "Drake!" She threw her arms around his neck and kissed him square on the lips. "You're here! Why? And your *hair!*" She ran her hands over his new short cut.

"I think she's glad to see you," Gavin said.

Serena took a step back and said, "Sorry. I'm more than glad. *Shocked*, in the very best way."

"I've got to make a few calls," Gavin said. "It's nice to meet you, Drake."

Drake shook his hand again. "Let me know if you're ever on the Cape. We'll grab a beer."

"Sounds good," Gavin said on his way out the door.

"I can't believe you're here," Serena said again. "Why are you here?"

"I'm checking out some vintage guitars about a half hour from here and thought I'd stop in and surprise you."

She touched his hair again. "And you cut your hair?"

"I figured I should clean up for your fancy new digs."

"I love it," she said. "You look very hot and very professional. Now please grow it out again." She turned her back to the others and gave him a quick, seductive wink that brought a wave of awareness to his entire body.

"Anything for you, Supergirl."

"Supergirl?" the bearded guy said. "That's the perfect name for our chief."

"I'm not a chief," Serena insisted. "We're a team. One for all and all for one. Spencer, Laura, this is Drake. Drake, these are the talented designers I told you about. The best team a girl could ask for."

Spencer stood up to shake his hand. "It's nice to meet you. How do you keep up with her? She's a whirlwind." He was tall and lean and looked like he belonged at a chic coffee shop with a laptop. He was what Rick called a hipster, with his black-framed glasses and wearing a navy shirt with a white-diamond pattern, a brown sport coat, and dark skinny slacks.

"That she is," Drake said proudly. He would find it hard to

keep up with the fashion of the city, but Serena had seamlessly made the transition.

"No, seriously. She comes up with ideas that blow everyone out of the water," Spencer explained.

"Serena's a great boss," Laura said. She stood to shake his hand. She was pin thin and also fashionably dressed in a pair of taupe slacks and a ruffled white blouse.

"*Teammate,*" Serena corrected her.

"*Boss* who doesn't mind bucking the system," Laura said. "Serena took us on an initial client visit, which we never do. It's amazing how much more we gleaned from hearing the client's initial thoughts on the project." She pointed to the designs and catalogs spread out on the table. "We're only a couple hours into this project, and look. We've almost got it nailed down. She's taken the collaboration process to a whole new level."

Serena looked blissfully happy, fully alive, the way she had when she was in the design and coordination phase during their first year of business. The way she looked each time they opened a music store. No wonder she was sad when she didn't get to help bring all of her ideas to fruition with him for the grand opening. He'd unknowingly stolen that joy from her.

"That's awesome," he finally said. "Serena's a remarkable woman. Can I take you all to lunch?"

Serena winced. "I'm sorry. I wish we could, but we have to leave in twenty minutes to get over to the law office we're designing. I wish I'd known you were coming. I could have rearranged our schedule."

"Don't be sorry," he said, masking his disappointment. "I'm glad I got to see you and meet your team."

"We had the *best* meeting this morning for a home-library renovation. And Laura's right. We're cruising right along with it."

"I'll get out of your hair." He put a hand on her hip and bent to kiss her cheek.

"I'd rather you got tangled up *in* my hair," she whispered in his ear.

He lifted her hand to his lips and pressed a kiss to the back of it, holding her gaze and wishing he could pull her into his arms and kiss her properly.

"I'm just going to walk him to the elevator," she said to the others.

"It was great meeting you both," he said. "Good luck with your projects."

"I still can't believe you're here," Serena said on the way to the elevators. "My two worlds have collided, and I couldn't be happier."

The elevator arrived, and he said, "Wanna bet?" as he pulled her inside.

He hit the CLOSE DOOR button, and the second the doors closed, he captured her mouth, crushing her to him, and she was just as ravenous for him. Their hands moved over each other's bodies as they made out like they'd never get enough.

"God, I miss you," he said, kissing his way down her neck.

She ran her fingers over the short sides of his hair. "I need your hair to hold on to."

He chuckled and kissed her lips again. "I'll grow it back. The way you were talking about sharp-dressing, clean-cut guys, I figured you might be into the look."

"I'm into you, Drake Savage. I am utterly and completely *yours*."

The elevator doors opened, and they jerked apart. Two guys in suits gave them an amused look. Serena's lips were pink and puffy from their urgent kisses. Thank Christ she didn't wear lipstick.

Serena cleared her throat as the two men stepped into the elevator. "Hi, Joe, Kev. This is my boyfriend, Drake. He just stopped by to say hello." She was beaming as she looked at Drake and said, "It was good to see you." She stepped off the elevator, stifling a giggle.

"Shine on, Supergirl. Talk to you later."

As soon as he was back on the street, he called Kane's Donuts. "Hi, Abby? I met you the other day. Do you deliver?"

"We sure do."

"Great. I'd like to order a dozen Chocolate Orgasms…"

LATE FRIDAY AFTERNOON Serena sat across from Seth Braden, the president of BRI Enterprises, and his new partner, Jared Stone, feeling like she'd hit the jackpot, despite having her ass handed to her *again* earlier that morning when she'd told Suzanne she wanted to bring Laura and Spencer with her to another initial client meeting. There was no time to worry over Suzanne's refusal. For now she heeded her request. At least long enough to figure out the best way to sell her on the idea.

She focused on her new clients, who wanted to be involved every step of the way, from the space design right down to the colors of the trash cans, and they were giving her complete freedom of design. Seth had been featured as one of *Forbes*'s most eligible bachelors a couple years ago, and it wasn't just for his wavy brown hair, killer blue eyes, or the whole hot-nerd thing he had going on with black-rimmed glasses, a plaid shirt, and a patterned sweater that looked like it had been knitted by his ninety-year-old aunt. He was a brilliant investor, and based on the last hour, he was about as laid-back as someone who did nothing but lounge on beaches all day. While his tattoo-sleeved, jeans-clad, Adam-Levine-lookalike partner, Jared, hadn't stopped moving since he sat down. If his jaw wasn't jumping, his knee was. A chef by trade, Jared owned several restaurants as well as clothing stores. They were an unlikely partnership, which made them that much more interesting. They'd come together and formed Nova Initiatives, a line of retail operations and restaurants.

"We want something new, *fresh*." Seth scratched his scruffy jaw. "As you know, my brand is a bit more elegant than Jared's edgy, eclectic vibe. Do you think you can combine the two without seeming over the top with either?"

"Or being too trendy?" Jared added. "I hate trendy."

"I'm confident that my team and I can come up with unique options to combine your brands in a way that speaks from your heart."

Seth sipped his coffee, watching her intently. "I work with a lot of designers, and you're the first to mention an *organ*."

She stifled a laugh, remembering Drake's earlier text—*I'm thinking about adding organs to the store*, to which she'd replied, *Really? I've been thinking about a skin flute.*

She cleared her throat to get her head back in the game and said, "You're both clearly passionate about what you do, and passion comes from the heart. It would be a mistake for me to ignore that vital organ when coming up with the concepts for your business."

The two men exchanged an appreciative look.

"Let's talk schedule," Seth suggested.

They scheduled a brief meeting via Skype for Monday, so

she could introduce them to Laura and Spencer, followed by a presentation meeting the following week to discuss concepts. They also set aside a tentative time to visit the Boston Design Center a few days later, assuming they approved the presentation.

She called Drake the minute she left the building and gushed about them as she walked along the sidewalk. "Freedom tastes so good! I can't wait to fill in Laura and Spence and get started. Things are looking up. We're making headway with Muriel Younger's office and our other projects, too."

"That's great, babe. You sound excited."

"I am, but part of that excitement is that it's *Friday*, and after stopping by the office to get my stuff, I get to come home and see you! I cannot wait to get my lips on you."

"Your bed or mine?"

"Mine this time, so we don't have to worry about being seen if we decide to go *au natural* under the stars."

"Sounds good to me. I'll bring over a change of clothes. I have a little something for you when you get here."

She lowered her voice as a woman walked by and asked, "Does it involve nakedness?"

A deep, growly sound came through the phone, heating her up like an inferno. God, she loved his dirty side, and his noises, and his...*everything*.

"Now I'm going to be hard all evening thinking about you naked."

"I like knowing I can get you all hot and bothered. Did I tell you I'm wearing the white lace panties and matching bra that you love? The one with the bows on my hips."

He made another sexy sound.

"Or that I bought thigh-high stockings to wear home tonight just for you? There might be garters involved."

"Jesus, Serena. How fast can you get home?"

"Traffic's going to suck." She lowered her voice as a group of men walked past and said, "I'm going to be starved by the time I get there because I'm too excited to eat."

"I'll be your feast, baby."

"That's what I was hoping you'd say." She flagged down a cab and said, "Safe subject time. I'm getting in a cab." She climbed into a cab and gave them the address of her office. Then she said, "I reconfirmed the bands for the grand opening tomorrow, and we have no last-minute cancelations. I can't believe it, and I can't wait to see it all come together. It seems outrageous that you own *five* music stores. You're like a music store *mogul*. Remember how nervous everyone was when you opened the first one?"

"You weren't," he reminded her.

"Because I knew you'd succeed. You're too driven, too *bull-headed*, not to."

Another call rang through, and she checked the screen. "*Ugh.* That's my boss. Hold on."

She switched to the other call and said, "Hi, Suzanne. The meeting with Seth Braden and Jared Stone went tremendously well. I can't wait to get started. And we're making headway on both the Younger project and the Wilkinsons' library renovation."

"That's good to hear, Serena. I'm calling because I've just been told that you were never notified about the client appreciation day tomorrow. Apparently, the email invitations went out the week *before* you started."

"Oh, that's okay. I don't mind. I have plans anyway. I'm going back home for the grand opening of Drake's music store."

Silence stretched for a beat too long. Serena looked at her phone to make sure she hadn't lost the call.

"Suzanne? Are you there?"

"Yes, I'm here. I'm sorry, Serena, but it's imperative that you're at the event. Your clients will be there, and as a new associate, you're still making a name for yourself with them."

"Yes, I understand, but we've been working toward this grand opening for several weeks, planning it for more than a year. Would it be okay if I asked Laura or Spencer to go on my behalf?" Yet another valid reason to have the junior designers as close to the clients as she was.

Suffocating silence ensued, and panic clawed its way up her chest.

"Serena, if you still worked for Mr. Savage that would be one thing, but you work for KHB now, and you hold a very prominent and important position in the firm. Your employment contract covers these types of monthly events, which are critical to the firm's—and your—reputation."

There was an icy chill to her voice that made Serena's skin crawl. How did people reach a point where they completely lacked compassion? "Yes. I'm sorry. Of course. I'll be there."

She closed her eyes against the sting of tears as they ended the call and she switched back to Drake.

"Babe? Everything okay?"

"Nothing is okay." As she relayed her situation to him, her sadness turned to anger. "I feel powerless, but we both know I'm not. I'm going to talk to her when I go into the office and see if I can change her mind."

"Serena, *don't* jeopardize your job for this. She's right. Your loyalty has to be to KHB right now, and you are building a reputation there."

"Like hell she's right! This is your biggest, most important opening yet, in a town that *means* something to you. This is the opening that matters most, the one where you have pressure to do everything right because so many of the people who will come have known you forever." She knew how proud Drake was to finally feel comfortable enough with his business, his success and practices, to open a store near his hometown. She'd taken extra steps to make sure it was everything he hoped for.

"I know, but it's okay," he said. "I understand."

"Well, don't, because you should be upset, like I am. I would never make an employee miss something they've worked on for so long. We spent months looking for a location, negotiating with vendors, setting up distribution, talking with schools…Tomorrow is the big payoff! It's the moment when we stand back and see it all come to fruition, when *your* community comes together in celebration of what *you've* accomplished. There will never be a repeat of that day. That's *our* moment, Drake. Yours as the owner and mine as your friend who has watched you plan and put blood, sweat, and tears into every element, every decision." She couldn't slow her thoughts as she paid the driver and got out in front of her office building. She stormed inside and pushed the elevator button repeatedly. "I'm going to lose you in the elevator. I'll call and let you know how it goes."

"Supergirl, wait—" he said hastily. "Please don't screw this up because of me. Take a breath. What if she fires you?"

"Then she does, but at least I'm not a doormat." She ended the call and rode the elevator up to the fourteenth floor, preparing to give Suzanne a piece of her mind.

She stalked toward Suzanne's office, replaying Drake's words in her mind, picking them apart until their meaning became clear. *What if she fires you?* She'd been *replaced*. She had no job waiting in the wings. Justine didn't have the workload to hire her. If she was fired, she'd be left scrambling to find another job.

Fuck.

She slowed her pace as Suzanne's office came into view.

Thoughts of her mother barreled into her. Her mother had spent her life chasing men to take care of her instead of taking care of herself, backsliding at breakneck speed. As much as Serena loved working at the resort, and working for Justine at Shift, she didn't want to go backward and be an employee for either company again. She'd built her life around moving *forward*, striving to achieve her next goal. Sure, she'd put it on hold to help Drake and the guys, but she was also growing while working with them, honing her skills, learning about business. It had been a definite move forward.

Was she going to put her job on the line over being unable to see Drake? Was that why she was so upset?

No. This confrontation wasn't about going home to see her boyfriend, or even about missing his biggest moment yet. She was standing up for herself, demanding mutual respect for human beings, their time, and their happiness.

She straightened her spine, lifted her chin, and knocked on Suzanne's door. Suzanne waved her in. It was after six on a Friday afternoon, and Suzanne had contracts, site plans, and proposals—hours of work—spread out in front of her. Did the woman do anything other than work?

Suzanne lifted her gaze. Her hair was pinned up in the severe bun Serena had gotten used to. She had a pencil tucked above her ear and wore a strand of pearls around her neck, adding even more class to her black-and-white dress. "Yes,

Serena?" she said with an air of dignity, clearly unconcerned about whatever Serena had come to say.

Why wouldn't she be? The last two senior designers had walked out without notice. It was nothing she hadn't dealt with before. Serena was a number on an employee log. A cog in the wheel. She could walk out tonight and Suzanne would have her position filled in a matter of days.

But Serena wasn't the type of person to walk out without notice, and she sure as hell wasn't going to give Suzanne a reason to fire her—or the impression that she'd stand for being treated like her plans didn't matter.

"I'm going to attend the event for KHB tomorrow," she said confidently. "But I want you to know that I don't agree with the way you handled this situation. We have worked hard to achieve the opening of this music store, regardless of where I currently work. Years of learning from one store to the next have built to this, and opening a store in the area in which Drake lives is a huge achievement, as you can imagine, since you have several locations. If this were my company, and I were the boss, I would never expect an employee to give up something so meaningful for an event that takes place on a monthly basis." She held her breath, trying to read Suzanne's expression.

Suzanne pressed her lips together in a firm line. Then they tipped up at the edges, but her eyes turned cold. "Your thoughts are duly noted, but you *aren't* the boss." She turned her attention back to the documents on her desk. "Was there something else?" she asked without looking up at Serena.

"No." It took everything she had to hold it together and walk out the door instead of laying into her. The trouble was, Suzanne was right.

Serena wasn't the boss.

Chapter Seventeen

DRAKE CAME OUT of the stockroom of Bayside Music and Arts Saturday morning reveling in the familiar adrenaline rush that had accompanied each of the last four grand openings. Carey and Cree were busy setting up displays featuring the instruments they expected would draw the most attention. They were holding down the fort tomorrow, too. Drake knew he'd be a mess worrying about how sales went the first week, and because he tended to stress over those types of things, he planned to stop by late afternoon for a quick check-in, rather than spending the entire day watching the clock and counting customers.

"Hey, boss." Carey carried an electric guitar in one hand and a display stand in the other. Tall and lean with longish brown hair, an ever-present tan, and warm green eyes that made women want to know more about him, he was a good friend always willing to pitch in with the music stores. "Evan and Maddy are outside. They're ready to go set up the road signs. Unless you need them for the exterior first?"

"I think we can handle it. We have plenty of time before people start arriving, and they usually trickle in anyway. Given the weather forecast, I'd imagine we'll have a light turnout."

"Copy that." Cree looked up from the display she was putting together. Her bright eyes and sunny disposition contrasted with her head-to-toe black, from her raven hair to her clothing and heavy military-style boots. Her Bayside Music and Arts tank top showed off her colorful tattoos. "A day at the beach or a day of shopping? No matter how good the products are, sun, sand, and hot guys in trunks and girls in bikinis always win out. But that's what evenings are for, knocking around music stores and hanging out with your buds."

"Let's hope so." Drake headed outside and found Evan and Maddy loading signs into the back of Evan's Jeep. They looked so young and ready to take on the world, leaning against each other's sides like best friends. Their easy friendship reminded Drake of him and Serena through the years.

Evan pushed from the Jeep as Drake approached. He raked a hand through his brown hair. "Hey."

"How's it going?" Drake asked, though from the blush on Madison's cheeks, he wondered if he'd actually interrupted more than a couple of friends.

Madison tucked her long, honey-colored hair behind her ear and said, "Since it's so early, Carey thought we should put more flyers out before setting up road signs. Is that okay?"

"Yeah. Sounds good." With his first store, he and Serena had done that job themselves. With his second, they'd had volunteers. Now they had volunteers, paid staff, and caterers. More importantly, they had each other in a much bigger way. If Serena couldn't be there, at least he could feel a little closer to her by having her traditional grand-opening breakfast. He handed Evan a twenty-dollar bill and said, "Can you grab a few snickerdoodles for me?"

"Sure." Evan pocketed the cash. "Sudden sweet tooth?"

"Something like that."

A few minutes after they pulled out, Drake was busy wrapping streamers around the posts out front when Desiree's and Mira's cars pulled into the lot. Their trunks popped open, and then Rick, Desiree, and Emery climbed out of Desiree's car and Chloe and Mira stepped out of Mira's. They grabbed bags from the trunks and headed for the store like the cavalry, each wearing a Bayside Music and Arts shirt.

"Where do you want us, bro?" Rick asked.

"Where'd you get those shirts?"

Rick flashed a cocky grin. "We have our ways."

"The opening doesn't start for another hour and a half," Drake reminded them as they all said hello at once.

"We know," Mira said. "Serena told us what happened. I'm sorry she couldn't be here. She was so bummed. But don't worry. She gave us strict instructions on what to put where, and she said you'd put the black streamers out front. Too depressing." She bumped Drake with her hip, and he stumbled back. "Let us do this part, big brother. You're supposed to set up the sound stage."

The sound stage was a new addition to their grand openings, one Serena had insisted upon. She'd even spoken to the local police and arranged for a traffic cop so the event wouldn't cause road issues. They'd argued about that. Drake didn't think they'd have enough customers to warrant a traffic cop, but Serena had been in a stubborn mood, and she hadn't given in.

"You're *all* here to help?" Drake turned as Violet's motorcycle roared into the lot. "Who's watching the inn?"

"We forwarded the phones to the service and put up signs for the opening," Desiree said. "Customers can track us down here if they need us."

Violet climbed off her bike and whipped off her helmet. "'Sup, dude? I'm ready for a major party, so where do you need me?"

"Uh…" Overwhelmed with their support, he stammered.

"Serena said Drake shouldn't do the decorating," Emery said as their friend Leanna's old Volkswagen van pulled into the parking lot. "The balloons are here! Vi, why don't you help Drake since you know more about sound stuff than we do."

"You got Leanna to help?" Although Drake was good friends with Leanna and her husband, Kurt, he hadn't seen them in weeks. "I could have picked up the balloons."

Chloe set her hand on her hip with a *get real* expression and said, "In your *truck*? *Please.* Leanna actually wasn't able to help. She's picking up her sister, Bailey, at the airport. She just lent us her van."

Harper and Daphne climbed out of the van as Dean's truck pulled in and parked beside it.

"Balloon girls, ready to help!" Harper announced.

"I'm babyless for a few hours. This is going to be so fun!" Daphne waved to Dean and Rick. "Hey, guys."

Drake turned to Rick and asked, "Did you know they were all coming?"

Rick smirked and shrugged in response.

"Who's watching the resort?" Drake asked. He didn't know if he should be thankful or feel like an idiot for pulling everyone away for the grand opening. He thought they'd all stop by at some point, but he'd never expected them to put their lives on hold.

"We took a page from Des and Vi's innkeeper's book, turned the phones over to the service and hung up signs for the opening." Rick patted Drake's shoulder and said, "Relax, bro.

The grand opening of your Cape store doesn't happen every day. It's reason to celebrate."

Violet grabbed Drake and Rick by the arms and dragged them away from the girls. "If I were you, I'd lie low and keep my mouth shut. Serena gave an hour-long how-to session over FaceTime this morning with all sorts of pictures of the layout and shit." She looked at Dean and said, "C'mon, muscles, you're with us."

Drake pulled out his phone. "I need to call her. We usually set up with just us and a few employees. We don't need this many people."

Violet shoved his hand down. "Of course you don't, but Serena called Desiree and Mira, and they rallied the troops. Take it like a man. Your woman wants to help from afar. If you make her feel bad for watching out for you, I'll break your arm."

"Damn, girl," Dean said. "You're vicious."

"What? I've got newfound respect for the woman. It takes balls to move away from everyone you know and start over." Violet waved toward the girls hustling around the front of the store, setting up signs by the road, tying balloons to every railing they could find. "Look at them and tell me it didn't take guts. I spent my whole life moving from one place to the next as fast as I could, and I'm not sure I could leave these neurotic, noisy, naive hen partiers for anything." She headed for the trailer with the stage equipment. "Enough sappy shit. Let's get this show on the road. We're setting up the sound stage beside the building."

Hours later, a local band was playing on the stage, the parking lot was packed, and there was standing room only inside and outside the music store. Drake, Rick, and Dean had kicked off the celebration by playing the first song on the stage. It had sent Drake's mind back to their early days as a band, when they'd had dreams of going off and cutting record deals and living the high life. Those dreams had been short-lived. Losing their father had changed everything.

The police had set up barricades around the area behind the stage and blocked the rear entrance from the back road to keep the flow of traffic moving in only one direction. Brandy had set up the food in a tent on the grass, which was also overflowing with people. She'd shown up with two catering vans, and a second shift had brought more food and supplies about twenty minutes ago. Drake had never seen so many people turn out for a music store opening. Serena must have anticipated the inordinate number of sales they'd experience, because she'd given Mira instructions on how to handle incoming stock, and a truckload of deliveries had shown up right before the opening. Drake thought it had been a mistake, but Mira assured him that it was on Serena's list.

Brandy sidled up to him with a plate of food. She was a vibrant, big-boned redhead with a mass of corkscrew curls that were currently trying to escape from their tether at the base of her neck. "Hey, handsome. Serena said I was supposed to make sure you ate and didn't spend all day taking care of everyone else and stressing out."

"I can't eat. Look at this turnout, Brandy. Have you ever seen anything like it?"

"Not for a retail opening. You know, Serena should be an event planner. I might have to pick her brain." She nudged the plate into his hands and said, "Eat the sandwich. You need to stockpile energy for the next time you see her."

He smiled, imagining Serena telling her to say that. "She knows how to get me to eat."

"Actually, she didn't say that," Brandy said with a mischievous grin. "But you're *male* and, you know, that makes you pretty easy to figure out."

He sighed and bit into the sandwich. "*Mm.* This is fantastic."

"Roast beef with horseradish, tomato, watercress, arugula—all the things you love."

"Thank you. I appreciate all that you're doing today. Do we have enough food?"

She peered in the direction of the catering tent. "We do. It's two now and you're closing down at six thirty, right?"

"That's the plan, but I honestly can't see us kicking people out. I don't mind paying more to keep from running out of food."

"We won't run out," she said as Rick joined them. "Serena expected this big of a crowd. I've got to get back to the tent. Rick, make sure he finishes that sandwich, will you?"

"Kick-ass turnout, bro," Rick said as she walked away. "How are you holding up?"

"I have no idea," Drake said honestly. "I think I'm in a state of shock. I wish Serena were here to see it all. She must not have told me everything she did for advertising, because we've never had a turnout like this."

"She loves you, Drake. You know that, right? She said as much in the card she left me when she moved."

"She left *you* a card, too?"

"She left one for me and one for Dean," Rick said. "I figured she left you one, too. She thanked us for being good bosses and said she appreciated everything we did for her. But in mine, she also said not to let you get so wrapped up in life that you forget your first love—*music*."

Drake shook his head. "Like I could ever forget that?"

"That's the point, man. I was thinking about why she'd tell me that, and then it dawned on me. Remember when we first opened the resort, how busy we all were with the renovations and all the paperwork and bullshit that went into getting it off the ground?"

"Man, that was a crazy time." There had been months of digging through paperwork, hiring contractors, meeting with attorneys and insurance professionals to make sure they understood the ins and outs of the business and liabilities. Serena had been with them in the trenches. In fact, she'd been the one to suggest meeting with insurance reps to find out what they *didn't* know.

"Then you remember how she used to traipse up to your apartment and grab your guitar in the middle of all the crap we were dealing with."

The memory brought a wide grin and a wave of longing. "I remember. We'd be bitching about how exhausted we were or about whatever mess we were dealing with, and she'd hand me the damn guitar, sit on her ass, cross her arms like the stubborn, beautiful woman she is, and say she wasn't going to move until I played."

"Exactly," Rick said. "She *knows* you. She wanted me to watch out for the most important part of you. And even though she's not here, she's still doing it." He pointed to the back road, where a line of police cars was escorting a black Suburban.

"Holy shit. What's going on?" Drake pushed his way through the mass of people toward the commotion, but the crowd moved with them, shouting and cheering. Drake grabbed Rick's arm. "What's happening, Rick? This is *my* opening. I've got to know what's going on."

"Control freak," Rick hollered back. "Just go with it. Live in the moment."

He led Drake around the back of the stage to where their buddy Caden Grant, Evan's father, who was a police officer, was standing guard alongside several other members of Wellfleet's finest. The Suburban parked, and a tattooed guy stepped from the vehicle. The crowd went wild, pushing forward and shoving Drake into Rick.

"Holy fuck," Drake said with awe. "Is that who I think it is?"

"Boone Stryker," Rick confirmed, holding his phone up as he videotaped Drake's reaction. Boone was the lead guitarist in Strykeforce, Drake's favorite band. "You can thank your girlfriend for this one. She pulled some major favors with just about everyone connected to him."

Drake's chest constricted. He pulled out his phone, then realized Serena was at that damn company event. "She's going to miss it!"

"That's why I'm videoing it!" Rick hollered over the noise of the crowd. "Wow. She really did knock the wind out of you with this one."

Drake looked into the video camera, his emotions bowling him over. "Baby! What have you done? You should be here!" His gaze coasted over the sea of people, and his heart swelled. "I love you, Supergirl, and I will thank you properly when I see you!"

"That's what I'm talking about," Rick said with a laugh.

Drake couldn't shake the awe inside him. "Baby, how did you do this?" he hollered into the video as the crowd pushed him toward the barricades. He'd read in a magazine that Boone and his wife, Trish, an actress, were both on hiatus and spending time with their son. That was just a few weeks ago. How had she managed this? "I wish you were here! Babe, there are no words! Thank you!"

Rick and Drake barreled through the crowd, catching sight of Boone helping his wife out of the vehicle. She carried their little boy, J.R., in her arms. Drake had read that he was six or seven months old now and was named after Boone's father, Jeremy Rykerts, which Drake remembered because he hoped to one day honor his own father in the same way.

An entourage surrounded Boone and Trish as they made their way up to the stage with the rest of his bandmates. Stagehands were busy setting up equipment and mics. *Whoops* and cheers filled the air as Boone stood centerstage, his arm around Trish. Their baby wore a black-and-white onesie and a bandanna around his head.

"Drake!" Caden waved them toward the barricades. He said something to the officer next to him, and then he made his way over to Drake and Rick and told them to come through.

They climbed over the barricade while Caden and several other officers kept the rest of the crowd back.

"What's the plan?" Drake asked, feeling like a fanboy, gawking at his hero on the stage. Boone had come from nothing, *literally*, and had taken the music world by storm. Drake's idol was standing before him, his brother was by his side, and they were surrounded by loads of people he knew—and hordes he didn't—and all Drake could think about was the absence of the only woman he wanted by his side.

Rick shrugged, but his smirk told Drake he knew *exactly* what Serena had been planning all along.

"How did all these people know he was coming and I didn't?" he asked Rick.

"Boone tweeted earlier today."

Tweeted. Jesus. Serena had long ago hired a social media assistant to handle their social pages for the store and the resort. He'd forgotten they even had them.

"Thank you. Thank you so much." Boone's deep voice cut through the din of the crowd, and more cheers rang out. "Thank you! My beautiful wife and I are so happy to be here to celebrate the opening of Drake Savage's Bayside Music and Arts!" The crowd went crazy. "That's right, so make sure you head inside before you leave and show your appreciation. Buy something from the man who brought this show to you! And just to make it even more enticing, I'll be autographing purchases for thirty minutes after my set."

More applause and shouts rang out.

"Before we get started," Boone said as he gazed out over the crowd, "I'd like to bring Serena Mallery and my man Drake to the stage. Let's hear it for Serena and Drake!"

The crowd chanted, "Serena and Drake! Serena and Drake!"

The air rushed from Drake's lungs.

"Go on, man." Rick nudged him in the direction of the stage, videoing once again.

Drake's head spun as he crossed the stage.

Boone was a formidable guy, and as he embraced Drake, he said, "Congrats, man. I'm happy for you."

"Thank you. Thank you for coming."

Boone put a hand on Trish's back and said, "This is my wife, Trish, and our little man, J.R."

Trish opened her arms, giving Drake a warm hug. She was tall and slim, with long dark hair, and dressed in jeans and a pretty blouse, there was not a bit of pretentiousness about her. Their little boy reached for Drake and clung to his shirt. He had a fake tattoo of a heart with *Mom* written across it on his tiny arm.

"I guess you get to hold J.R.," Trish said as she handed him the little boy. "Serena said you were amazing with children."

A collective *aww* rose from the crowd.

"Where is Serena?" Trish asked. "I was looking forward to meeting her. We've been talking about this event for months."

Months? Serena had set this up for him before they'd even come together as a couple? Drake's heart broke even more for her to have missed it.

"She got held up in Boston, but she wishes she could be here." The baby reached up and touched Drake's cheek with his soft little hand. Drake glanced in the direction where he'd left Rick and was glad to see him standing by the stage, still videoing.

Boone handed Drake the mic and said, "Sell your business, man. Now's your time."

As Drake looked out over the crowd, holding the baby in his arms, he spotted friends, neighbors, and too many strangers to count. He had no idea what he was supposed to say in a moment like this, but when he lifted the mic, his words came easily. "Thank you all for coming out for the grand opening and to hear Boone play. Unfortunately, you've missed out on meeting one hell of a special woman. My girlfriend, Serena, got tied up in Boston, but she's the one who pulled this incredible event together and made it possible for you to see this legendary musician."

Cheers and shouts ensued.

"I hope you enjoy the show," Drake said, and handed the mic back to Boone. "Thank you for coming out today. I can't tell you how much this means to me." He stepped away.

Boone grabbed Drake's arm. "Where do you think you're going?"

Trish took the baby from Drake and said, "Have fun!"

She hurried off the stage as another guy handed Drake a Fender Stratocaster guitar and a pick and set up a mic. Drake shot a look at Rick, who was grinning like a fool, just like he was. He mouthed, *Holy shit. This is really happening!*

"I think you know this one," Boone said as he grabbed his guitar. He put the mic on the stand, and the pianist began playing "Don't Stop Believin'."

Adrenaline pumped through Drake's veins as his fingers hit the strings, and for the next few minutes he played like he'd never played before—and every single note, every single breath he took was for Serena.

SERENA SCHMOOZED, SMILED, and said all the right things at KHB's Client Appreciation Day, but the entire time she'd thought about nothing other than wanting to see Drake's face when he opened the front doors of the store to customers for the very first time and the moment Boone showed up and Drake finally met his idol. He'd told her he wouldn't text during her work event, and he hadn't. She hoped that for once in his life he was enjoying the day and not worrying about her. She had dozens of messages from the girls with pictures of the opening. It looked just as fantastic as she'd hoped it would. They were lifesavers, helping out at the spur of the moment. Rick had sent a link to a video he had uploaded to YouTube of Drake hearing the news about Boone, meeting him, and playing onstage. She'd shed tears of happiness while watching, and she'd noticed that the video already had more than eleven thousand views. Trish had told her that one tweet from her and Boone would make the news of the event go viral. She must have tweeted about the video, too. Serena was sad not to have met Trish and Boone in person, but Trish had left her a message saying they were sorry they'd missed each other and they'd like to plan a trip in the fall and catch up, when there weren't as many tourists around.

"I know you're upset about missing Drake's surprise and his grand opening," Gavin said as they headed into the parking garage after the KHB event. "But you did well in there. Your clients, and your team, *love* you."

"Thank you. You did, too," she said as they entered the garage. "I can't believe they do this *every* month. Don't you get sick of it? It seems like more of an excuse to eat expensive food, drink, and brag about KHB's newest design awards than anything else."

Clients had showed up in droves, and Suzanne gave each and every one of them a good bit of attention, which Serena was actually impressed by. "I can see the value in doing it every once in a while, but every month seems like overkill."

"Hey, if I were Suzanne, I'd do something once a *year*, and I'd invite current clients as well as past clients."

"Yes! Exactly. Fewer events could yield higher returns, bringing back past clients and making everyone want to attend because it's special. I spent my internship working for a design firm in Dartmouth and learning from my sixty-plus-year-old boss. That man had been around. He's since retired and sold his company, but he believed grassroots marketing efforts and personalized service went a lot further than putting on airs. And I have to tell you, that shaped my thinking."

"That's a good thing. Companies who rely on spending to earn end up having more trouble when economies tank." Gavin pointed to his car. "That's mine."

"Enjoy the rest of your weekend, and I'll see you Monday."

"You too. And, Serena, I know it seems like you're constantly fighting the system, but I want you to know that I appreciate the fact that you stand up for what you believe in. You're a refreshing change to have around and a good reminder of how much *I've* changed." The sincerity in his eyes shone in stark contrast to the usual lightheartedness she saw.

"Really? What happened to your small-town roots keeping you grounded?"

He shook his head with a wry smile. "A stubborn chick showed up and unknowingly made me realize that I accept bullshit even when I don't agree with it. Maybe it's time for me to change that."

She took a few steps toward the row her car was in and said, "Why do I have the feeling I'm going to be blamed for something bad in the near future?"

He laughed as he unlocked his car and waved.

She sat in her car and watched the video of Drake again. Elated for him, she sent off a quick text before leaving the garage. *More than 11,000 views. I'm dating a rock star! I'm not above kicking the shit out of fangirls, so don't get any ideas, Mr. Hottie. Xox.*

Two and a half hours later, she climbed out of her car at the resort and inhaled the salty sea air. She followed the undercurrent of smoky wood toward the Bayside community center, where Hagen was sitting on Drake's lap roasting marshmallows beside Mira and Matt. Emery held a stick over the fire, and behind her Dean stood with one hand on her shoulder, talking on his cell phone. Serena's entire being exhaled, releasing all her stress and disappointment.

Hagen hopped off Drake's lap, and as Drake took the marshmallow off the stick, Hagen spotted Serena. He dropped the stick, getting sticky marshmallow all over Drake, and sprinted toward her, yelling, "Auntie Serena is here!"

"Don't touch her—" Mira called out.

She scooped Hagen into her arms. Her eyes met Drake's as he rose to his feet, pushing away all the shadows in her heart. A bottomless sense of peace came over her, and she knew this was where she was meant to be. This was *home*. But her life had become complicated, and she had no idea what *home* really meant anymore.

"Hey, kiddo!" She kissed Hagen's cheek.

"We're making s'mores," he said as he wriggled free. "Uncle Drake is using two pieces of chocolate instead of graham crackers because we ran out. See?" He held up his sticky chocolate fingers.

Mira rushed over. "I'm sorry! I tried to stop him."

Serena looked down at the forest-green V-neck dress she'd worn to the event. There were little chocolate handprints on her hip and shoulder and a chocolate smear across the three sheer lines of material at her waist. After spending the day doing her best to look and act professional and comfortable, being prim and proper and saying all the right things, careful to sit with her knees together and watch her language, she couldn't help but laugh.

She ran her finger along the chocolate on her dress and touched it to Hagen's nose, earning silly giggles. "I wonder if you can convince Uncle Drake to make me one, too? I think chocolate will go a long way tonight."

"Uncle Drake, will you make her a s'more?" Hagen ran to Drake as he approached and tugged on Drake's shirt.

Drake reached down and patted Hagen's head. "I'll make her anything she wants, buddy."

"Hey, gorgeous." Drake reached for her hand, pulling her against him and kissing her smiling lips. "I didn't expect you tonight."

"I couldn't stay away," she said honestly. After watching the video again, all she'd wanted was to be in his arms.

"You blew me away today, Supergirl. I want to hear all about your day."

He kissed her again, and all she could think about was how he blew her away *every* day with his endless patience and encouragement.

Drake looked down at her chest pressed against his sternum. "I'm getting marshmallow in your chocolate."

She lowered her voice and said, "Careful. If you get any on my skin, you might have to lick it off."

Heat flared in his eyes. "Hagen," he said without taking his eyes off Serena. "Let's get busy melting those marshmallows. Uncle Drake has an *insatiable* appetite. We might need to use the whole bag."

Chapter Eighteen

DRAKE AWOKE TO Serena's soft lips kissing their way down his stomach. He didn't even try to suppress his smile as he threaded his fingers into her hair, loving the feel of it—and her hot mouth—against his skin. He'd wanted to take her home the minute he'd seen her beautiful face appear in the darkness last night, but they'd stayed at the bonfire catching up with the others for almost an hour before they'd finally turned in.

She pressed her lips to the head of his cock. He groaned as she continued kissing and licking his hard length. She was the most sensual, honest, enticing woman he'd ever met, and every evening without her was torture. Not because he needed sex, but because his life was not complete without her by his side.

"God, baby. You feel so good."

She buried his cock in her mouth, following her lips with tight strokes of her hand, obliterating his thoughts. His hips rocked as she took him right up to the edge of madness.

"Baby, I'm gonna lose it," he warned, gritting his teeth against the mounting pressure.

She withdrew his shaft from her mouth, watching him as she dragged her tongue from base to tip. Spikes of heat skidded through him.

"Not yet, you're not," she said haughtily.

She straddled him in all her naked glory and sank slowly down over his shaft, burying him in her tight heat. He pulled her down for a kiss, and she turned, guiding her breast into his mouth instead. Fuck, he loved her confidence. She liked it a little rough sometimes, and he was right there with her, teasing and sucking as they loved each other wild. When that wasn't enough, he held on tight and swept her beneath him, driving in deeper.

"Hold my wrists," she begged, sparking all sorts of deliciousness inside him.

As his fingers circled her wrists, pleasure and passion brimmed in her eyes, so different from the joy that had radiated off her when he'd seen her in her office. That happiness had driven him to toy with the idea of buying the guitar store that was going out of business in Boston. Leaving the Cape had never been in his plans, but as he'd come to realize, neither had a life without Serena.

"I love you, Supergirl," he said vehemently. "I have loved you for as long as I can remember."

"A big YouTube star like you?" A rascally look rose in her eyes. "I bet you say that to all the fangirls."

"Only the really special one who loved me before I was famous."

The emotions in her eyes told him how she felt before she said another word. But when she said, "I loved you when you were a skinny teenager carrying around a beat-up guitar and too cool to like me back," sweetly and honestly, he got all choked up.

"I was never too cool for you. You've always been out of my league." He pressed his lips to hers, then said, "And just so we're clear, sass-mouth, other than family, you're the *only* woman I've ever said those three words to."

He lowered his lips to hers as they found the groove that bound them together. Their passion mounted, their kisses turning possessive and rough. He released her wrists with the need to be closer and cradled her in his arms.

"No," she pleaded. "Keep holding tight."

He snagged her lace bra from the floor where they'd thrown it last night and wound it around her wrists, binding them tightly. He pressed his hands to her arms, pinning them above her head.

"You're fucking gorgeous, Supergirl."

Wickedness danced in her eyes as he reclaimed her mouth, more demanding this time. Her softness conformed to his hard frame as her legs circled his body, meeting each thrust with a rock of her hips and a lustful moan. He quickened his pace, and she struggled against his hold. One flash of her eyes told him she was enjoying it as much as he was. Her muscles tensed and her breathing shallowed as her climax took hold. Her body pulsed and thrummed around him, drawing him right to the brink of madness. He needed her arms around him, wanted to feel her nails digging into his skin. He unbound her wrists, and she clawed at his back, bowing up beneath him with every thrust.

"Yes, yes, *yes*," she cried out.

He crushed his mouth to hers, loving her through every pulse and quiver of her climax.

"Open your eyes, Supergirl."

Her eyes flew open, filled with darkness so alluring, so lustful, his mouth watered.

Her words shot out like a command. "Take me *harder*, rock

star."

"I'm going to take you every which way I can." With his eyes locked on hers and his fingers curled tightly around her hips, he said, "Turn over."

She rolled onto her belly, his every fantasy come true. The woman he loved, every gorgeous curve his for the taking. He ran his hands up her outer thighs, kissing each cheek as his thumbs grazed her slick center.

"So trusting," he whispered as he pressed kisses to the base of her spine all the way down to curve of her bottom. Then he spread her cheeks and dragged his tongue along her wetness. "So sweet."

He nudged her thighs open wider, giving him better access, and taunted her with his mouth, then tasted his way up her soft bottom. She squirmed and whimpered, spreading her legs wider. He dipped his fingers into her swollen sex, then withdrew and used his tongue. She pushed her ass back, greedily seeking more, and when he brought his slick fingers to her forbidden entrance, she stilled.

"Don't worry, baby. I'm not going to cross any lines you don't want me to."

She pushed up onto her hands and knees, gazing at him over her shoulders. "I want you to cross them all."

His words played in his head—*you're the only woman I've ever said those three words to*—and he knew she'd also be the last.

A *LONG* WHILE later, they stumbled, sated and more in love than ever, over to Emery and Dean's for breakfast.

"I still can't believe Emery wanted to host breakfast," Serena said in a hushed whisper as they neared Dean and Emery's cottage. Emery wasn't teaching yoga that morning and had announced at the bonfire last night that they were hosting breakfast today. "She can't boil water without setting off the smoke alarm."

It was *almost* the truth. Emery *had* set off the fire alarm at her and Dean's cottage twice over the winter. The first time she'd forgotten to put water in the pot and burned it while taking a bath. But the second time, from what Dean had claimed, it was just as much his fault as Emery's. He'd found her in the kitchen wearing only her panties while she was cooking eggs, and they'd ended up in the bedroom for a *very* long time.

"Don't worry, babe. I'd never let you go hungry. I've got about nine inches of man meat for you."

Drake pulled Serena closer, kissing her bare shoulder. He loved this particular sleeveless sundress. It was black-and-white and pattered like a bandanna. The top fit like a tube top from the eighties, clinging to her, while the rest was loose and short. She looked like she belonged on the beach, which was his favorite place to observe her. She was a beach girl at heart, and as he pondered that thought, he realized she hadn't been out on the water in a while.

"*That* doesn't fill me up," she said. "It only makes me hungrier for *real* food."

He leaned down and kissed her.

"Hey, lovebugs," Desiree called from behind them.

They turned and greeted Desiree, Rick, and Violet. Desiree and Rick looked beyond happy, holding hands and smiling. Desiree's hair was pinned up in a ponytail.

"Don't you mean hump bunnies?" Violet smirked. Her

raven hair was wild and loose around her shoulders. She wore her typical summer duds, one of her many black bikini tops and a black miniskirt, along with her biker boots, of course.

"Violet!" Desiree chastised. "Why do you always have to make something nice sound dirty?"

"Who says dirty isn't nice?" Violet shot back.

"I'm with Vi on this one. Sorry, Des," Serena said as they stepped onto Dean and Emery's patio.

"Hey, are we still planning to go tubing after the wedding tasting a week from Saturday?" Drake asked, thinking about getting Serena back out on the water.

"Yes," Rick said.

"We'll need it after all the *wedding gushing* I'll have to listen to," Violet added.

Dean came outside carrying a tray of bowls. "How's it going?" His hair was sticking up all over, he was shirtless, and he had a big red hickey on his shoulder.

Emery followed him out, looking flushed and carrying several boxes of cereal. "This is the *last* time we host," she said a little breathlessly. She dropped the cereal boxes on the table, set her hands on her hips, and said, "Hosting breakfast is *way* too much pressure."

Drake squeezed Serena's hand. "Maybe my girlfriend should give you a lesson in planning." He still couldn't believe she'd not only set up the store and their usual grand opening while living hundreds of miles away, but she'd managed to book one of the biggest rock stars around and had kept it a secret.

"Yeah, here's a hint. Don't give up sex to feed other people." Serena looked around nervously. "Oh geez. For a second I forgot Matt and Mira were taking Hagen to the go-karts today. She has given me strict orders never to talk about our sex life around her."

They all laughed and began pouring cereal into their bowls.

"Why don't you two go finish your fuckery and get cleaned up," Violet said to Emery and Dean, who were standing at the other end of the table, kissing and whispering. As they disappeared into the house, Violet turned her attention to Serena. "What you did for Drake was beyond kick-ass. I'm sorry you missed it."

"You've been there for everything big in his life," Rick said. "It stinks that you couldn't be there."

"Tell me about it." Serena poured milk into her cereal and pushed it around in her bowl. "But what really matters is that *he* got to experience it. Thanks again for all your help, for keeping the secret, and for all the pictures and the video. It wouldn't have gone over so well without your help."

"Listen, what's a small-town girl to do when things get tough and you're working hard to get your fill. Don't stop believin', right?" Rick chuckled.

"Absolutely," Violet said. "You've got to hold on to that feeling."

"Otherwise it just goes on and on," Desiree chimed in with a pleased-with-herself sparkle in her eyes.

Drake laughed. "All right. I get it."

Serena belted out the chorus to "Don't Stop Believin'," and they all joined in. Drake scrubbed a hand down his face, trying to hide his amusement. He was so in love with her, and every playful thing she did made him fall even harder.

Desiree rushed over and pushed a napkin in front of Drake, fluttering her lashes, and spoke in the breathy voice of a teenager. "Can I get your autograph, Mr. Rock Star?"

"You guys are fools," Drake said goodheartedly.

Desiree hugged him. "Fools who love you, *best* soon-to-be-brother-in-law in the world." She went around the table hugging each of them. When she got to Violet, Violet rolled her eyes. "One day you're going to be the hugger and I'll be the huggee."

"Don't hold your breath. It's going to take a long time for me to get over you bringing Mom out for your wedding." Violet shoved a spoonful of cereal into her mouth.

"You heard back from her?" Serena asked. "She's coming?"

Desiree gave her a deadpan look. "Just because she sent a postcard that said she'd be there doesn't mean she won't forget by the date of the wedding. I'm not getting my hopes up." Their mother, Lizza Vancroft, was as flighty as a seagull.

"I really hope she comes," Serena said. "Mostly because it means she's still making an effort. You deserve that, Des. But also because it'll be fun to see Violet get all edgy and uncomfortable when she can't take part in any fuckery."

Violet scoffed. "Lizza is the *queen* of fuckery. Where do you think I learned it?"

"Well, people can change," Serena said. "Remember, don't *ever* stop believing…"

Everyone burst into song, and Drake couldn't help but join in, too.

After Drake was called a teen heartthrob far too many times, he and Serena went to the Wellfleet Flea Market to see Leanna so Serena could thank her for lending them her van. Leanna made Luscious Leanna's Sweet Treats jams and sold them at the flea market and in restaurants and stores. The flea market was held in the parking lot of the drive-in theater, hosting vendors from all over, selling antiques, clothing, jewelry, video games, and just about everything else under the sun.

They walked hand in hand through rows of white vendor tents. It was a scorcher of an afternoon. The type of blistering heat that radiated off the pavement and reeked with humidity. If Serena didn't have to leave soon, he'd take her out on the boat for the day, make love to her in the afternoon sun, and dip in the water to cool off. *One day soon...*

Serena stopped to look at a pair of earrings. "Chloe's birthday is coming up. She loves opals."

Drake just loved watching her do anything, which was seriously ridiculous, but as true as anything had ever been. He looked over the necklaces and found a pretty opal. "How about this with those earrings? From both of us?"

"You have good taste, rock star. But then again, you're with me, so..." She glanced up at him and said, "We already knew how good your taste was."

He tickled her ribs. She squealed and tried to get away, but he hauled her in and kissed her fiercely. "I love you, you pesty thing."

"You *chose* me. What does that say about you?"

"That I have incredible taste."

She grinned. "Isn't that how this all started?"

They bought the earrings and the necklace and moved on to a display of used paperbacks. Serena held up a thriller by Leanna's husband, Kurt Remington. "Look what I found." She opened it to the dedication and read it aloud. "For my sweet Leanna and my precious Sloan. You are my treasures." Sloan was their little boy.

She set the book down and gazed up at Drake. "His *treasures*. That's so romantic. But I prefer being *your* Supergirl. That has always felt romantic to me."

He pressed his lips to hers and then he took her hand and

they continued down the row. "Want to know a secret?"

"Always. Secrets are sexy."

He looked at her out of the corner of his narrowing eyes.

"What? They are. Think about it. Secrets are things you tell only to very special people. That alone makes them sexy."

"I guess you're right, because this one is about my sexy girl. I used to wonder what it would be like to bring you to the drive-in. I'd picture the normal stuff, you know, making out in the back seat and all that. But because I was wicked jealous of every guy I heard about you going out with—"

"*What?* Even when we were younger?"

"Damn right."

She pressed her body against his side and kissed his cheek. "I love knowing that about you. Tell me more."

"It was torture, and even worse now that you're grown up. Anyway, I thought about how proud I'd feel to strut around here with you on my arm, making all the other guys jealous. Like I am now."

"You see me differently than anyone else does. I doubt any guys are looking at me that way." She pointed to an older man with a protruding belly, sitting in a lawn chair beside a table of antiques. "Except maybe him." She waved to the man, and he nodded.

"Right." Drake turned her by the shoulders and said, "Ten o'clock, dark-haired guy stealing glances, and just beyond him, that bald guy was checking you out the last two times we stopped walking."

"The dark-haired guy isn't bad," she said playfully.

He pulled her against him, glaring at her even though he knew she was kidding.

"Kiss me, you proud peacock. Claim your woman."

And he did.

Ravenously.

They finally found Leanna's booth, where she was surrounded by a crowd of customers who were tasting and buying jams. Leanna talked animatedly to each person, spouting off ingredients and flavors. She was perhaps the messiest person Drake knew, and also one of the sweetest. She was always in a constant state of disarray, with jam on her clothes and tousled hair, while her husband was the neatest, most organized man on the planet.

"Hey, you two!" Leanna finished helping the customers, then came around and hugged them both. "Oh gosh. Sorry." She tried to wipe jam off Drake's sleeve, where she'd accidentally smeared it.

"No worries. Hagen got me worse last night," Drake assured her. "How are you?"

"I'm great." Her gaze moved between him and Serena. "How are *you* guys? Together, huh?"

"I'm a lucky guy," Drake said proudly.

"Darn right you are, and don't you forget it. Serena's a catch."

"Thanks, Leanna, and thank you for all your help with the opening," Serena said.

She waved her hand dismissively. "Oh gosh, anytime. We came by after the flea market, and there were so many people. It was wild! And, Drake, I always knew you could sing, but holy cow. You're a YouTube sensation. You sounded awesome."

"Thank you. Luckily Boone's voice drowned mine out."

"Hardly," Serena said.

"It was pretty crazy. I still can't believe Serena pulled it off without me even having a clue." He draped an arm around Serena and kissed her cheek.

"Actually," Serena said, "Leanna's the reason I was able to get Boone to come. She hooked me up with Kurt's sister, Siena, who is married to Cash Ryder. Cash is Trish's brother. That's how I made the connection. And they were all so nice and willing to help me connect with Boone."

"From what I've heard, they had a blast," Leanna said. "Trish said they're hoping to come back to the Cape in the fall and meet up with you?"

"I hope so," Serena said. "I *really* want to meet them in person."

"Let me know if you guys put something together. If we're back in the city, we'll come for the weekend." Leanna and Kurt lived on the Cape during the summer and in New York City the rest of the year. "I'd love to see them, too."

They talked for a while longer, and Leanna sent them home with a few jars of Sweet Heat, Strawberry Spice, and Frangelico peach jam, their favorites.

On the way back to the truck, Serena asked, "Do you want to stop by the music store?"

"Only if you'd like to see it. Carey texted earlier. They're pretty busy today."

Serena was quiet for a moment, and when they reached the truck, she said, "As much as I would like to see it, I'd rather go someplace and hang out. Just the two of us. I feel like my life has become a mad dash, running from one place to the next. Not that I mind, and I know I did this to myself by moving to Boston, but I really want some downtime with you, without any pressure from other people or work or anything."

That sounded perfect to him. "I've got just the place."

"I JUST HAVE to grab something really quick," Drake said when he parked in front of the office of Bayside Resort. "I'll be right back."

He gave Serena a chaste kiss, and she watched him jog up the steps and disappear into the office. The scents of the sea and the sounds of families brought life to the otherwise-still air. She closed her eyes and tipped her face toward the sun. It was warm without the breeze rushing in the window as they drove. She thought about how much her life had changed. She had almost always spent at least some time at the beach each day, whether she and her friends were taking walks, sitting around a bonfire, or lying in the sun listening to the water kiss the shore. She missed eating lunch on the dunes and kicking off her sandals after work to go down to the beach with Mira and Hagen or with the girls. Sand between her toes had been a daily occurrence, and she'd taken it for granted. Had she done the right thing by moving away? While she'd always had dreams of working in a big design firm, she hadn't been one of those people who disliked the Cape and wanted to escape it. She just wanted to do her own thing, to move forward and make her mark.

She heard the office door close and opened her eyes. Drake was descending the steps with a blanket draped over his shoulder, carrying his guitar case. His shorter hair gave him an edgier look. His scruff did that normally, but the close cut made his jaw seem sharper, his eyes more cutting. He opened his door and set the blanket and guitar behind the seat.

"Now that you're a rock star, you can't leave home without your guitar?"

He scoffed. "Would you expect anything less?" He reached over, unhooked her seat belt, and hauled her across the bench next to him.

"What took you so long?"

He kissed her. "You look beautiful in my truck."

"As opposed to outside of your truck?" she said sassily.

"There, too." He slid his hand beneath her hair, gazing at her like she was a precious jewel he couldn't believe he'd gotten his hands on. "All the little things I've thought about for so long are finally coming true. This is going to sound cheesy, but every time I see you looking a certain way, or in positions where I never thought we'd be, you look even sexier to me. You've been in my truck a million times. But coming out of the office and seeing you smile when you notice me and being able to openly enjoy that feeling? That's pretty fucking incredible. And *this*? You and me?" His lips came tenderly down over hers. "Pure perfection, Supergirl."

Serena felt like she was riding on air as Drake drove down to Hyannis and parked on a side street. Serena knew exactly where he was headed, and she was touched so deeply, it was all she could do to watch him as he grabbed the blanket and guitar and reached for her hand. He led her down the overgrown trail toward the creek she'd frequented as a kid, and all the worries and questions in her mind subsided. Her beautiful man knew exactly what she needed.

Drake lifted branches for her to duck under and held her hand as she climbed over rocks and around fallen trees. A pungent, marshy smell greeted them when they stepped into the grassy clearing near the edge of the creek. The rickety old dock was still there, slanted as ever, missing decking in the same places it had been when she was young. He took his guitar out of the case, and she realized he'd brought the first guitar he'd ever owned, from when they were kids.

He reached for her hand again and said, "Come on. Backstreet Boys are calling us."

"Ohmygod," came out with a squeal. "Are you kidding?"

A coy grin slid across his face. "You know I'm not. You and Mira made us listen to that damn CD all the time."

"Oh Lord." She went with him onto the dock, holding his hand as she stepped over the missing slats. She kicked off her sandals and sat on the edge, her feet dangling over the inky water.

Drake remained on his feet and began strumming the tune to "I Want It That Way" as he kicked off his flip-flops and sang, "Yeah-eah." He winked and sang, "You're my fire, Supergirl. My only desire."

He changed the lyrics and sang about how they *weren't* two worlds apart and how he could reach her heart when she told him what she wanted.

Moved by his humor, his voice, and his generous, loving soul, she jumped to her feet and danced as he sang. When the song ended he went right into "Larger than Life," once again changing the lyrics to speak of them, and then directly into "When I Come Around" by Green Day and then "What I Got" by Sublime. She sang with him, both of them dancing as he played. He parlayed that song into "Little Red Corvette" and then about a dozen more songs from their youth, fast, slow, funny, romantic. She danced and sang until her cheeks hurt. And later, breathless and happy, they sat on the dock for a long while, talking about their childhoods and their current lives and everything in between.

"This is why we need a rooftop deck on the community center at the resort," she said as she lay with her head in his lap.

He leaned down and kissed her. "Let's not talk about work right now. This is our time, and there's something I've been wanting to do for way too long."

"I'm not stripping naked on this dock."

He cocked a brow with a seductive glimmer in his eyes. God, she'd do anything with him.

"*Maybe*," she relented.

"No wonder I love you." He pressed his lips to hers and said, "Honestly, I wasn't even thinking about that until you said it. Sit up beside me."

He helped her up and handed her the guitar.

"When we were supposed to sing that duet, you asked me to teach you the guitar," he said as he helped her position the guitar properly. "It was such a weird time, and I knew if we got that close, I'd have an even harder time keeping my hands off you."

She ran her fingers along the neck of the guitar, remembering how brokenhearted she'd been when he'd said he didn't have time. "I was so awkward back then, and even though I had no idea what to do with the body I'd developed, I was hopeful it might have caught your attention."

"It *did*, and that was the problem. You weren't awkward at all. You rocked those curves under those secondhand shirts and shorts you dolled up. You could have had any guy you wanted."

"There was only one I wanted." She cradled his guitar. "You're really going to teach me to play?"

"Yup. Then maybe you can play me those songs you wrote when you were a teenager."

Her eyes widened. "How do you know I wrote songs?"

"Do you really think you and Mira were quiet when you'd spend the night? Two thirteen-year-old girls hunkered down around your notebooks giggling about lyrics. And at night, when you thought no one could hear you, you sang so loud, I bet the neighbors heard them."

"No way! And there were only three songs."

"*Way*, Supergirl, and I know there were only three, but you sang them endlessly. I think my favorite line was 'boyfriends with big muscles and lots of brains.'"

She snort-laughed and covered her face. "I forgot about that!"

"I assume that was me, and if it wasn't, then *lie* to me, okay?"

"They were all about you," she gushed. "Because they were about the love of my life, so even if I didn't know it then, you were always on my mind."

He moved closer, angling himself so he could put his arms around her from behind, and repositioned her hands. "Be loose. Get comfortable with the instrument."

"If you say 'make love to it,' I'm going to bite your neck."

"Oh, baby. Make love to it," he said in a raspy voice.

She turned and bit his neck, then sucked, leaving a tiny mark that she knew would fade, but the groan it earned was one she'd not soon forget. She tenderly kissed the red spot, then leaned against him and said, "How did you know I needed this?"

"Because I love you, and when you care about someone, you usually know what they need."

"If only all life's answers were that easy."

"Maybe we can find whatever answers you're looking for in

the music. Now, make love to the guitar."

She nudged him with her elbow. "Watch it, buster."

He taught her the basics, and later, when they were back at his place and she was getting ready to leave, he set his guitar in the back seat of her car.

"I can't take that to Boston. It's always been with you."

"I want you to learn on the same one I did. Besides, you're part of me now, so in a sense, it's still with me." He brushed his lips over hers and said, "Thank you for arranging for Boone to fly in and for fighting traffic and coming home last night. I'll come see you next weekend so you don't have to drive back again."

"I would love that. We can knock a few things off of our explore-Boston list. Thank you for today. It was just what I needed. Now the week won't seem so long. I'm going to practice the guitar, but you know I have no music for my ridiculous thirteen-year-old-girl songs."

"Ah, but *I* do."

"What?" She was stunned. "You're kidding, right?"

"Nope. They're written by my ridiculous teenage-boy heart."

"Why didn't you tell me?"

He held her tighter. "Because I can't reveal all my secrets to you at once."

"Yes, you can! If you wrote them back then, then we really *are* meant for each other."

"You doubted that?" He looked perplexed.

"No, not at all. But you know what this means. When you come up next weekend, we'll have to play your music to my songs."

"There's nothing I'd rather do." He nuzzled against her

neck and said, "Except maybe make my name come off your lips in the throes of passion."

She clung to his shirt, wishing they had another night together. "That does *not* make me want to leave. I want to spend all my nights in your arms."

"I'm far more selfish than you are. I want you in my arms at night, I want to see your beautiful face every morning, and I want to monopolize every minute of yours in between."

Chapter Nineteen

"DO YOU THINK it's possible to have a happiness hangover?" Serena asked Chloe over the phone more than a week later. She leaned back in her office chair Tuesday afternoon, looking out at the cloudless sky and thinking about how busy last week was and how glad she was that Drake had driven up for the weekend. He'd brought buckets of sand and a baby pool, just as he'd mentioned the first weekend she'd moved to Boston. They'd sat on the rooftop deck Saturday evening with their feet in the sand, and later, they'd lain on the sand stargazing. It was heavenly.

"I think you mean an *orgasm* hangover," Chloe corrected her. "You said you didn't even leave the apartment Sunday until he left to come home."

"But we went out on Saturday," she reminded her. "We had breakfast in the café downstairs—"

"After hours of sex, I'm sure," Chloe interrupted. "It's totally unfair that my baby sister gets more action than I do."

"Let me just enjoy this moment of achievement." Serena listened to Chloe's heavy sigh. "Anyway, we spent most of Saturday out. Remember the list I told you Drake made? We went to the Institute of Contemporary Art and hung out at the bar the show *Cheers* was based on. That was cool. And after lying out under the stars on the rooftop deck of my building, we had Insomnia Cookies. It was a perfect weekend. So maybe it's a duo hangover of happiness and orgasms."

"Okay, before I choke on my jealousy, how's work these days? Any more confrontations with your boss?"

"Kinda sorta, but last week was amazing. The clients I told you about, Seth and Jared, loved my team, of course, and our concepts, and *everything* I showed them at the design center. I think they're my favorite clients, although the Wilkinsons are close. They're the home-library remodel project. The husband is hilarious, and the wife rolls her eyes at him, then asks me to do whatever he wants anyway. They're really cute together. It's like she just wants him to be happy."

She told Chloe about going out with Laura, Spencer, Chiara, Carolyn, and Gavin for drinks and karaoke last night. She'd had a good time, but with the exception of Gavin, it wasn't anything like going out with her friends from home. The others were nice, but a little too buttoned-up for her taste.

"That's a bummer," Chloe said. "But hopefully you'll meet other people."

"I do like the girl who runs Kane's Donuts, Abby Crew. She's divorced, and she bought the doughnut shop on her own. I'm a little envious, to be honest. She doesn't have to report to *anyone.*"

"Oh God, Serena. How many doughnuts are you eating that you know this woman's entire life story?"

"Probably too many, but it's more fun to eat doughnuts and talk to her than eat dinner by myself. Besides, I like her. She's easy to talk to. Oh my gosh. I almost forgot to tell you! Remember my first client? The attorney, Muriel Younger? She decided she wants glass in her conference rooms after all."

"The woman who wanted *no* creative input? She reminded me of the *Devil Wears Prada* boss."

"That's the one. Her assistant called last week to tell me. I was afraid her architect, Drew Ryder, was going to chew me out for even suggesting it, but he was really cool. I actually think we might use him for Seth and Jared's project."

"Aaaand…? The *kinda sorta* run-in with your boss?" Chloe pushed.

"It was nothing, really," she lied, because she didn't want to hear Chloe tell her how she needed to take a step back and play the corporate game, like Mira had. She was still having a hard time wrapping her head around doing things in order to eke out billable hours when it seemed a waste of her time.

Serena's office phone rang, and she said, "Chloe, I've got to take that."

"Okay, go. And, sis, don't get too big for your britches," Chloe said. "You need that job."

"I *know*. Gotta go. Love you." She ended the call and picked up her office phone. "Serena Mallery."

"Serena? This is Crystal Bernard returning your call."

"Yes, thank you." She flipped through her notebook and found the notes on the client Suzanne had referred to her yesterday. "I've been trying to reach you about remodeling your pool house. I've got some time available later this week if you're free."

"Actually, we're in the Hamptons until late Friday night. We were hoping you could come by Saturday."

Shit. She didn't want to miss the tasting for Desiree's wedding and going tubing with her friends Saturday afternoon. "I have a prior appointment on Saturday, but I can do any day next week."

"That won't work," Crystal said sharply. "We'll be in town for only the one day, Saturday. We're leaving Sunday morning for my niece's wedding, and then we'll be gone for two weeks. We know exactly what we want, and I'm sure it will take only a few minutes."

Nothing ever took only a few minutes, especially if Serena was going to gather enough information to actually start working on the job. "Perhaps it would be better to do this when you return in two weeks and aren't pressed for time?"

"No. We must do it now," Crystal said, and listed a litany of reasons why she had to meet Saturday or move on to another designer.

Serena was *this close* to telling the snooty woman to do just that when Suzanne peered into her office. She waved Suzanne in and reluctantly told Crystal she'd be there Saturday morning. "How is eight o'clock?" Maybe if they met early enough she could still make the tasting.

"That won't work. I have an appointment at the salon. We can do eleven o'clock, and please don't be late. My husband has a difficult time with people who aren't punctual."

Despite her frustration, Serena feigned a smile and agreed, quickly ending the call.

"Sorry, Suzanne. That was Crystal Bernard. I'm meeting with her Saturday at eleven."

"Good. The pool house project." She crossed her legs and flicked an imaginary piece of lint from her skirt.

"Yes." Serena wrote the appointment in her calendar beside Desiree's tasting session, trying to ignore the tweak to her heart. "Was there something you needed?" *Like maybe giving me more difficult, time-sucking clients?*

"I just received a call from Seth Braden. It appears he and Jared Stone are quite pleased with you."

"The feeling is mutual. They're a joy to work with, and their project is coming along nicely."

"I'm glad to hear it. Muriel Younger also contacted me. It seems she's taken your advice for a change in her new offices. Kudos to you."

Serena sat up a little straighter, soaking in the compliment. "Thank you."

Suzanne rose to her feet and said, "I know we have our differences of opinion, but when it comes to professionalism and quality, I'm glad to hear we're on the same page." She headed for the door and said, "Good job," as she walked out.

Serena's mouth was still hanging open when Gavin wandered into her office.

"What are you gaping at?" He sat down in the chair across from her.

"A compliment from Suzanne."

"Nice. Pocket it away. They're few and far between. You're heading back to the Cape again this weekend for that wedding-cake thing, right?"

"Nope. Thanks to the Bernards, I'm stuck here checking out their pool house."

"Aw, that bites."

"No kidding," she said with a sigh. "We were all supposed to go tubing, too. I haven't gone tubing in forever. Why do I feel like my life is passing me by while I make everyone else's life prettier?"

He gritted his teeth. "Because it is?"

"Thanks," she said sarcastically. "You want to know what's worse?" She lowered her voice and said, "When that new client said she would take her business elsewhere, I was ready to let her. Until Suzanne walked in."

"I have something that might make you feel better. Be right back." He left her office, and when he returned, he placed a big chocolate chip cookie on her desk.

She snagged the cookie. "Where'd you steal this from? Are there more?"

Gavin closed the door.

"Oh no. You're not going to get all creepy on me, are you?" She couldn't resist teasing him. They'd had lunch together a few times and had become close, sharing the trials and tribulations of their days and getting to know each other better. He was not the least bit creepy, but his confused expression was hilarious. He reminded her of Rick and Dean, funny, a little protective, and he never crossed lines with her. She had a feeling he missed his own family and friends back home, because he loved hearing about her trips home and about her friends.

"What do you think it is? A *nookie cookie*?"

She laughed. "If it is, you should know that I have a mean knee."

He sat down again and shook his head. "I bet you do. Eat the damn thing. I want to tell you something." He leaned forward, elbows on knees, and said, "A headhunter contacted me last week about a job with Taylor, Fine, and Rickter."

"Shut up!" She couldn't hide her surprise. "They're our biggest competitor."

"I know. I met with them yesterday, and today they offered me the job."

"Great. So my best friend in Boston is leaving." She shook the remaining cookie at him. "Can you please go steal about five more of these for me?"

"Relax. I'm not taking it." He sighed loudly and sat back.

"What? Why not?" She came around the desk and sat in the chair beside him. "They're bigger. They have more awards. It would be a step up."

"Listen to Cape girl go all bigger is better on me."

Her mouth dropped open again. "I don't understand."

"If you got an offer from them, would *you* take it?"

"No, but that's because I haven't decided if I'm cut out for this type of company. I love the work, but it's very...*prestige* driven, and I'm not like that." She waved at his designer suit and said, "You fit right in, and you never go head-to-head with your superiors. You know how to play the game."

"*That* is why I'm not going. I'm *not* prestige driven. Or maybe I've become that way, but it's not who I want to be, and that's on you, girly. You reminded me of the person I used to be, and now I'm determined to get back to being myself."

"Oh, no, no, *no*." She got up and paced. "You *cannot* put this on me."

"I'm *thanking* you."

"Thanking me? For what? Making you think you're *too* good?" She flopped back down into the chair and covered her face with her hands. "I need more cookies. I can't take this. First I have to miss out on the wedding-cake tasting of one of my closest friends and a day of tubing because of some snotty client. And now this is just the guilt icing on the fucked-up cake."

He grabbed her hand and moved it away from her face. "Stop. This is a good thing. I called my old man this morning and had a long talk with him. I haven't made the time to do that in months because of this bullshit job. This is a good thing for me. Like I said before, I don't know my path yet, but I know I'm finally heading in the right direction. I think we should go out and celebrate."

"Oh, good. Maybe I can find a small dog to kick along the way."

"Serena, stop it," he said with a coaxing smile. "I'm being serious. This is all good."

"It won't be when you realize you just turned down your only opportunity to earn more money than you're earning now. Then you'll hate me for opening my big mouth at all."

He looked at her like she was being ridiculous. "I have enough money. I'm taking my cue from the rational girl I met a few weeks ago. You might know her. Stubborn, mouthy, refuses to let anyone walk all over her?"

"Didn't you get the memo? That girl got trampled over and is missing Desiree and Rick's wedding-cake tasting."

"Then let's get the hell out of here and go find her before word gets out." He pushed to his feet and hauled her up to hers. "It's time to celebrate new directions."

She grabbed her things from her desk and parroted, "*New directions.* Desiree and Rick are starting a new direction; they're getting married."

"Great. Let's celebrate their upcoming wedding."

"Drake has a new music store, and Emery and Dean are getting married." There were lots of reasons to celebrate, but she worried about Gavin making the wrong decision.

He grabbed her arm and headed for the elevators. "We have to get out of here before Suzanne comes back and corners us into discussing something boring."

"Mira, my bestie, is having another baby. That's another new direction."

"Yup." He pushed the elevator button. "See? We're due a drink or two."

The elevator arrived, and they stepped inside. As he pushed the button for the lobby, she said, "What if I accidentally ruined your life by saying those things to you?"

"What if you saved it?"

She thought about that as they rode down to the lobby. "Okay, so there's a fifty-fifty chance I shouldn't feel guilty. But either way, you're going to leave this company eventually. Then who will I commiserate with?"

"Suzanne, if you're not careful."

Chapter Twenty

BY TWO O'CLOCK Saturday afternoon, Drake was getting worried. He finally gave in and called Serena. She answered after the third ring.

"Hi." She sounded like she had a mouth full of cotton.

"Hey, Supergirl. You okay? Where are you?"

"*Mm-hm.* Hold on." There was a long silence. "Sorry. I was eating a doughnut."

Why did that make him happy? *Because it makes her happy, of course.*

"I have to put you on speaker to talk to Abby. You won't believe what she did. Hold on." She put him on speakerphone and said, "Are you there?"

"Yeah. I'm here."

"Okay, Abby, tell Drake what you just told me."

"Hi, Drake. Serena and I have been talking for a few weeks now, and she's always raving about you, how much she misses you and how happy she is when she sees you. Well, you get the picture. Anyway, I was making a new doughnut, and it reminded me of you and Serena."

"A *doughnut?*" Drake wasn't sure if that was a good or a bad thing.

"Just listen, Drake," Serena said.

"It's yeast-style, which means it's puffy and light," Abby explained. "I filled it with creamy Belgian chocolate pudding, which is sweet and rich like the beginning of a relationship. I topped it with Taza chocolate frosting, which is a little coarse but truly delicious, and made right in Somerville, Mass, which also reminded me of you two, because you've known each other forever. It dawned on me that *coarse and delicious* is like the ups and downs of relationships. You know, after the blissful beginning, when real life peeks its ugly head in. And then I topped it with dark and white chocolate pearls, which are shiny and beautiful. They're rich and scrumptious outside, but when you bite into them, they have a tiny cookie center and pack a little crunch. Like yours and Serena's relationship, it's heavenly, but the distance—*real life*—adds a bit of crunch to it. I call the doughnut Perpetual Bliss, named for you and Serena, because at the end of the day, it's the love between you that puts that smile on her face. I hope that's okay."

Drake couldn't believe what he was hearing. His girl had talked about their relationship in such a way that she'd inspired a doughnut? Was there anything she couldn't do? "Okay? It's amazing, Abby. Thank you. I can't wait to try them."

"They're delicious!" Serena said loudly, and he imagined her radiant smile and that luminous spark in her eyes. "Hold on one sec, Drake."

He heard her thanking Abby.

She took him off speakerphone and said, "I'm leaving her shop now. I just love her! Isn't that just the coolest thing you've ever heard? A doughnut named after *us*."

"Yes. Beyond cool." *Just like you.*

"Sorry I didn't call earlier," she said. "The meeting took

forever. My client's husband was more than an hour late. Can you believe that? After she told *me* not to be late? Anyway, when we finally finished, I was starved, so I went to eat at that place we got sandwiches by the doughnut shop. And then, well, Kane's Donuts. You know…"

He chuckled. "Yeah, I do."

"I'm on my way home now. I'm just going to change and then drive down. How was the tasting? Did the girls have fun? Are you out on the water?"

"The tasting was good, but everyone missed you, and yeah, we're on the water. I miss you, babe. Call me when you take off."

"Okay. Love you."

"Love you more." He ended the call and turned to their friends. "We've got to move fast. She's walking home."

He started the engine on the boat and sped toward the overpass on Seaport Boulevard.

"There she is!" Rick pointed toward the road.

Serena was walking toward the overpass, looking hot in a sexy red dress, high heels, and the sunglasses they'd bought together. She had on the bracelet he'd given her. Her hair was pinned up, and she wore a happy expression. Drake imagined she could still taste that doughnut. *Their* doughnut.

He turned on the boat's PA system and spoke into the mic. "Attention, Supergirl! Serena *Supergirl* Mallery!"

Serena's head whipped in their direction, and she ran toward the overpass, grinning and waving. Her hair tumbled out of its tethers and over her shoulders.

"Ladies and gentlemen, please clear the way," he announced. "My girl's coming through."

The people on the overpass cheered and clapped as Serena

ran to the railing. She grabbed it with both hands and hung over, yelling, "You're here!"

Desiree, Emery, Rick, Dean, Matt, Mira, and Hagen waved from the deck.

Serena squealed as a crowd formed around her. "You're *all* here!"

"Hey there, beautiful," Drake said into the mic. "We missed you. Head on down to the boardwalk. We'll pick you up there."

She took off running in her heels like they were sneakers. Their friends, and people on the overpass, *whoop*ed, cheering her on and waving. Drake's heart was so full of her, his chest ached.

Hagen jumped up and down. "I can't see her!"

Matt lifted him up so he could see better.

Drake put the mic in front of Hagen, and the little cutie said, "Go, Auntie Serena. Go!"

A few minutes later Drake climbed over the railing by the boardwalk, and she leapt into his arms, pressing her smiling lips to his. Mira captured the whole thing on video.

"You're crazy! I love you!" Serena said between kisses, her happy, salty tears slipping between their lips.

"Crazy in love with you, baby. Did you think I could go tubing without my girl? My sun goddess? Not a chance."

"Hurry up!" Mira urged. "Before we get in trouble for stopping here."

"Come on." Drake knelt and removed Serena's heels and handed them and her bag over the railing to Emery. With Dean and Rick's help, they lifted Serena over the railing and onto the boat, where all the girls hugged her at once.

Hagen wiggled from Matt's arms and hugged Serena's legs. His bright-blue life preserver made it difficult for him to get close. "We brought you cake!"

"Cake! I love cake!" Serena said, hugging him back.

Desiree pointed to a box with several pieces of cake in it. "We brought the tasting to you!"

"You're the best friends ever!" Serena said, hugging everyone again. "The *best*! I can't believe you're all here!"

When she finally landed in Drake's arms again, she wrapped her arms around his neck and opened her mouth to speak, then crushed herself to him, hugging him so tightly, he didn't know how she could breathe.

"Thank you," she said against his chest. "I might have to strip down to my bra and undies, though. I have no bathing suit."

"I brought one. Shorts, sandals, even your hair stuff to pin it up, just in case."

She gazed up at him, her hazel eyes brimming with love. "Just when I don't think I can stand another minute away from you, you make everything feel possible. If I'm your Supergirl, you're definitely my Superman."

"I like Superman!" Hagen piped in. "Can I call you Superman, Uncle Drake?"

Everyone laughed.

Gazing into Serena's eyes, Drake said, "You can call me anything you want, buddy." He leaned closer to Serena and whispered, "As long as you call me *yours*."

"I love you, Drake Savage," she said as she pressed her lips to his. "You are my perpetual bliss."

"Guess what, Serena? We're sleeping in a hotel tonight!" Hagen said excitedly, pulling them from their reverie. "But you're sleeping on the boat with Uncle Drake and everyone else. I wanted to sleep on the boat, but Mommy said it's too uncomfortable for her with her baby belly. But that's okay. I love hotels, too. We're going to order room service."

Serena and Mira shared a laugh. Mira patted her belly and said, "I need my creature comforts."

"We're sleeping on the *boat*? All of us?" Serena bounced on her toes. "Mira, you guys can stay in my place if you want. I don't have room service, but there are stores on the ground floor of my building, including BJ's ice cream." She waggled her brows at Hagen. "And Insomnia Cookies delivers all night!"

Hagen's eyes brightened. "I *love* cookies! Please, Mom? Please can we stay at Auntie Serena's and get cookies?"

As Mira bent to talk to Hagen, Serena leaned closer to Drake and said, "This is the best day ever!"

"You seem to say that a lot." And he couldn't love hearing it more.

She wrapped her arms around Drake's neck and said, "Must be because you make me so happy."

"Look at them. Where is Vi when we need her?" Mira grabbed Serena's hand and lowered her voice. "Before you two get all handsy in front of my boy, let's get you changed into a bathing suit."

"Oh yeah, *that'll* help," Dean said sarcastically, making all the guys laugh.

"Where is Vi, by the way?" Serena asked.

"At the inn," Desiree answered. "She said she'd never survive overnight on a boat full of lovebirds."

"What did she really say?" Serena asked Mira.

Mira glanced at Hagen and said, "Pretty much that, but a little more descriptive and inclusive of the F-bomb."

"Aw, Mom cussed!" Hagen said.

Serena and the girls went belowdecks so she could change

into her bathing suit, and Drake drove the boat out into the harbor.

"Look at me, Superman!" Hagen hollered into the wind. He was sitting on his knees on a cushion, eyes closed, the wind blowing his hair away from his face and plastering his shirt against his little chest.

He reminded Drake of Rick as a kid, always wanting everyone to see what he was doing. "This is pretty cool, huh, buddy?"

"I love it!" Hagen grinned into the wind.

"No more *fake* girlfriend for you," Dean said as he sidled up to him with Rick and Matt.

"Damn right." *No more fake anything.*

He'd been thinking a lot these last few weeks about what he wanted, and at the top of that list was a life with Serena. Everything else could fall into place *around* that.

"You know, I had concerns about this whole long-distance relationship thing," Matt admitted. "But you two make it look easy."

"It's anything *but* easy," Drake admitted. "Every night apart feels like a fucking week, but don't tell *her* that." He glared at each of them in warning.

"Dude, we'd never do anything to make things harder for you guys," Rick said. "How can you fix that? She's pretty set in this job."

He glanced at the cabin to make sure the girls weren't heading up and said, "I've been looking at places in Boston. Think you could manage the resort without me on-site during the week? And maybe some weekends?"

"We can make anything work," Dean reassured him.

"I...uh...whatever it takes, man," Rick said.

Drake didn't miss the hesitation in Rick's voice, and he had a feeling he knew why. "I know I just sold you on moving back home, but what can I say, Rick? *She's* my home. I didn't realize that then, but I know it now."

"Right. Of course," Rick said. "I'm not worried about me. Can *you* be happy here? You've never wanted to leave the Cape. You hated being away for college."

The girls' voices floated up from the cabin, chatting excitedly about the Perpetual Bliss doughnut as Serena climbed the stairs in her crocheted bikini top and cutoffs. Their eyes locked, and her luscious lips spread into a mile-wide grin that reached into his chest and caressed his heart.

"All I know is," he said to Rick, "I can't be happy without her."

THE BALMY AFTERNOON was perfectly breezy out on the water. They went tubing, whipping over the water at breakneck speeds, as carefree as summer afternoons were meant to be. They swam in the frigid sea, and Serena clung to Drake as he teased her about being shark bait and how one tug of her bikini string would make him a happy man. She baked in the sun with the girls, giggling about their men and talking about weddings and futures. The guys tossed teasing barbs, their hearty laughter filling the air. Hagen was back and forth, hanging with the girls as much as the guys. When Mira got too warm, they went into the cabin, where she put her feet up, and the girls took turns rubbing her shoulders and feeling the baby kick. Desiree talked about having babies with Rick, and Emery said she could wait on little ones. The day could only be more perfect if Chloe, Harper, and Violet were there. But the girls said Chloe had been called into work, and Harper's screenplay had finally been optioned. She was preparing to leave for Los Angeles later that week, and she didn't know when she'd be back. They were all very excited for her, and she promised to keep them updated on movie news. The timing was perfect, since Daphne would be on board at the resort.

Everyone's life was moving in *new directions*.

Serena's life had taken a new direction, too, as exciting as it was difficult.

As the sun began to set, she sat on the deck with Emery, soaking it all in. Rick and Dean were fishing at the far end of the boat. Mira's and Desiree's voices floated up from the cabin, where they were busy cooking dinner. Matt was in the cabin, too, plucking away at his laptop, working on his next book. Serena looked across the deck at the man who had made today possible. Drake had Hagen slung over his shoulder like a sack of potatoes, earning infectious little-boy giggles. He glanced over, and the jubilation in his eyes made her heart sing. Drake needed these people, their family, as much as she did. She might feel like she was in a constant state of overdrive, racing from one location or one client to the next. Trying to keep up with the demands of some annoying clients and others who brought sheer pleasure, while building a relationship with Drake and trying to maintain treasured friendships. But being on overdrive wasn't so bad when she had the best friends, and the best man a girl could hope for.

After dinner, they docked the boat and went for a walk along the harbor. Serena told them about the pub where she had gone out for drinks with Gavin last night and where they'd sang karaoke with their other friends from work.

"Do we need to check out this Gavin dude?" Rick asked

Drake.

"Nah. I've met him. Seems like a good guy." He kissed Serena and said, "Besides, my girl doesn't cheat."

"She doesn't have to. When you're not around, you send her Chocolate Orgasms," Emery said with a glimmer of mischief in her eyes. She grabbed Dean's hand and said, "I feel a need for one of those coming on."

"What's a chocolate orgasm?" Hagen blinked wide eyes up at Matt.

Mira looked at Emery and mouthed, *Thanks!*

"I think Emery meant to say chocolate *organism*," Matt answered. "She really wants a chocolate doughnut."

"Yes, *organism*," Emery confirmed.

"I want a chocolate doughnut, too, but I want the one named after Drake and Serena." Hagen took Matt's hand, his brows furrowed in concentration. "Dad, I think we need to take Auntie Emery to the aquarium with us next time so you can teach her about organisms. Doesn't she know they have to be alive?"

Matt beamed proudly. "You're right, buddy. I think a group field trip to Woods Hole is in order."

"It's okay," Dean said. "I'll give Em an intense science lesson and teach her everything she needs to know about *organisms*."

"You can borrow Daddy's book!" Hagen offered, earning laughter all around.

Since it was too late for doughnuts, they promised Hagen some for breakfast. Before returning to the boat, they escorted Matt, Mira, and Hagen to Serena's apartment. Everyone admired her view and her chic furnishings, and Hagen couldn't stop talking about how cool it was that her bedroom walls didn't reach the ceiling. But Serena's mind was on anything but furniture and walls. This was the first time her friends had been inside her new apartment. It was crowded, but that made it feel a little more *right*. She hadn't realized how much she'd missed seeing her friends flop on her couch and poke around in her kitchen. She had a feeling she'd think about those everyday things a little more often now.

"We should probably let them get settled in," Rick said as he set a hand on Matt's shoulder. "See you at breakfast tomorrow."

As everyone said their goodbyes, Mira leaned closer to Serena and whispered, "I'd bet chocolate *organisms* are about as close as any of us are going to get to the real thing tonight." She grabbed Serena's hand and pulled her in for a hug. "Drake's a whole different man. It's good to see you two so happy."

"It's nice to be this happy," Serena said. "Have fun with your boys."

"I have a feeling we'll have a wiggly little boy between us all night. But trust me, sometimes that's just as nice as loving my man. *Family*," she said dreamily. "You know it's always been everything to me."

Serena glanced at Drake standing by the door hugging Hagen goodbye. "I know. For all of us, I think."

She hated thinking about saying goodbye tomorrow. The other night she'd confided in Gavin the things she couldn't confide in these friends or in Drake. She knew they'd try to fix her issues or push her to come back home, and she needed time to figure out what she really wanted without that pressure. She'd told Gavin her concerns about working with people she didn't like, missing the casualness of business on the Cape, and hating the hours after she said good night to Drake each evening, when she was alone in her apartment, feeling the distance between them like a villain in the dark. Gavin had all the same business concerns, but it seemed his other concerns, though different, were even bigger than hers. He'd lived in Boston for years and had yet to find close-knit friends who made him want to put down roots. Serena didn't want to be that person five years from now, feeling empty inside and wondering if she'd made the right choice.

As Drake set Hagen on his feet and reached for her, she went willingly into his strong, loving arms. Gavin was seeking his path, and she was clearly, and unexpectedly, still seeking hers. But she knew one thing for sure: She could handle figuring out her complicated life as long as Drake and her friends were in it.

Chapter Twenty-One

"AREN'T GOODBYES SUPPOSED to get easier?" Serena asked as she hugged everyone for the millionth time Sunday afternoon.

"Only if you don't like the people you're leaving," Matt said as he squeezed her against him. "This was fun. I'm glad Drake didn't mind bringing us along."

"I'd never rip my girl off from seeing everyone." Drake pulled Serena into his arms and kissed her.

He looked about as sleepy as Serena felt. They hadn't slept much last night. They'd lain beneath the stars talking and kissing, waiting for everyone else to fall asleep so they could finally, *blissfully*, make sweet, passionate love. Keeping quiet wasn't easy, especially when Drake knew every single pleasure point on her body and always seemed to discover more. Luckily, he was a master at silencing her with delicious kisses that made her body melt and her head spin.

"I love you guys," Serena said as she and Drake made their way to the dock with her work clothes and heels packed away in her messenger bag.

"Where are you going, Uncle Drake?" Hagen asked.

"I'm just going to walk Serena up to her apartment. I'll be

back soon."

"Take your time," Dean said. "We're in no hurry."

"Yes, definitely. Take however long you need," Emery encouraged them.

"Bye!" Hagen waved wildly, until Mira managed to divert his attention.

Serena tried to stave off her sadness as they left their friends behind and made their way to her apartment building.

Drake kissed her shoulder. "How's my sun-kissed girl?"

"My world feels perfect when I'm with you," she said honestly. "And even more so when we're with our friends. I needed the visit so much. I missed being out on the water and acting like fools with everyone."

"Water is to you what music is to me. It'd been so long since you were out on the boat, I figured you needed to fill that well again before heading into another work week."

Music filtered into her ears from across the street, and she remembered their first afternoon in Boston, when Drake had borrowed a guitar and sang to her. She'd thought that was the happiest day of her life, but every weekend they were together was even better.

They headed up to her apartment. As they stepped inside the apartment that had been filled with so much life last night, sorrow shrouded her. Why did it always hit so hard when they were close to their final goodbyes?

Drake gathered her in his arms, and she buried her face in his chest.

"Don't be sad, Supergirl." He stroked his hand down her back and kissed the top of her head.

"I don't even know why I get sad." She tilted her face up and said, "We just had an amazing time. I should be on cloud nine, and I *am*, but I hate the distance between us during the week."

"Five days and I'll be back. You can count on that. You don't have to fight the traffic. Hell, I'll come up during the week if you want me to."

Her phone rang, but she didn't want to move out of his arms. When it rang again, he reached into her pocket and pulled it out.

"It's Justine, babe."

"Justine?" She'd left her a message a few days ago and wondered why she hadn't heard back. "I'll just be a sec. Don't leave, okay?"

He scoffed. "I'm not going anywhere until I see you smile."

She pressed the phone to her ear, feeling better already. "Hi, Jus. How are you?"

"I don't know. Freaking out a little."

"Why? What's going on? Is Ginny okay?" Ginny was her baby girl.

"Yes, she's adorable. It's business stuff. I need a favor."

Serena followed Drake into the living room and sat beside him on the couch. Drake slid an arm around her shoulders, pulling her close. "Sure. Whatever you need."

"I know you're tied up with your new job, but you know that client you referred from P-town? Donovan? He owns Swank?"

"Yes. I really liked him."

"I wonder if you can take on his project. I'm days away from firming up the sale of Shift, and Donovan had nothing but horrible things to say about the new buyers. He refuses to work with them, and—"

"Whoa! Hold on." Serena shot to her feet, her heart racing.

"New *buyers*? You're selling Shift? What happened?"

"Nothing *happened*. Greg and I have been talking about it since Ginny was born. I want more time with her, Serena. I don't want to be a part-time mom."

"But how did I not *know* this?" She looked at Drake and said, "Did you know Justine was selling Shift?"

Drake shook his head.

"Who are you talking to?" Justine asked.

"Drake," Serena said. "Sorry. Tell me what's going on."

"We got an offer from this guy who owns a few small interior design shops in Plymouth and New Bedford. We've been negotiating for two weeks, and we're close to finalizing. I should have papers to review Tuesday morning. I had planned on handing Donovan over to the new buyers, but I obviously can't do that. If you're too busy, it's okay. I can figure something else out."

"I'm never too busy for you. But..." She had so many questions, she didn't know where to start. "How much are you asking for Shift?"

"Not much. Fifty thousand. It's the equivalent of the profit I earn in one year of part-time work. At least it's something, and it'll allow me to have time with Ginny."

"I wish you had told me. I could have thought about scraping the money together or something." Her thoughts whirled with possibilities.

"I'm sorry. By the time we decided to do it, you had started your new job, and I didn't want to mess that up for you. I can take Donovan's job to someone else if you want. It's just that I trust you, and you referred him to me."

"Don't give it to anyone else. I hardly have time to breathe right now, and I could only work on it on the weekends and in the evenings. Although lately I've had to work for KHB some weekends. But I'll make it work."

They talked for a few more minutes, but Serena couldn't process much beyond the questions swimming in her mind. She sank down to the couch beside Drake after she ended the call, still in shock. "She's selling Shift. I can't believe it. She wants to spend more time with Ginny."

Drake put a hand on her leg and said, "And…?"

She closed her eyes for a beat, feeling all tangled up inside. "I don't know. I'm sort of wishing I had known. What if I wanted to buy it?"

"Would you? You've always said you wanted to work in a large company. Isn't Shift small-time compared to where you are now?"

She groaned and stared up at the ceiling. "I don't know *what* I want, or how I could even entertain the possibility. She's asking fifty thousand, and she's close to finalizing a deal. I'd have to get a loan for some of the money."

"I'll *give* you the money if that's what you want to do with your career."

"No." She pushed to her feet and said, "I'm *not* my mother. What we have is too good to mix business with pleasure."

"Serena, don't be stubborn." He went to her. "If this is what you really want, you can have it all. I'll lend you the money—not give it to you—if you'd like. But just make sure you're not thinking about buying it because of me."

She paced, then flopped back down on the couch. "I don't know what I want. I love so many things about my job. But I also really resent some aspects of it. And I hate being away from you and our friends." She jumped up again, too jittery to sit still, and paced the floor. "But I'm not going backward, and I'm not making a career decision based on *us*."

"Hey, I'm not asking you to," Drake said sharply.

Her heart sank. "I didn't mean that. I didn't even mean to *say* it."

"But you thought it." He wrapped his arms around her, his expression softening.

She couldn't deny it, because she had thought it. *Viscerally.*

"Serena, you could never be your mother. All I meant was I know you're not going to make any rash decisions based on us, which is why you need to know what I've been thinking about. I've looked into apartments in the area. I even talked to the owner of the vintage guitar store that's going out of business about buying him out. But after doing some due diligence, I realized it's not a smart investment, so I'm not going to do it. But you need to know that I am more than willing to move here to be with you if this is where you want to stay. There's absolutely no pressure for you to come back to the Cape. You won't be without me for long if you stay in Boston. It's just a matter of choosing a place to live."

Her eyes filled with tears. "You would do that for me?"

"Of course. For us. I love you. I know how hard it is to go back and forth, and this is just the tip of the iceberg. The more well-known you become in the industry, the more in demand your time will become. I want to make things easier for you, not harder. And selfishly, I want every second of the time you're willing to share in between building your career and making a name for yourself."

"This would be so much easier if I were more like my mother," she said as she blinked tears away. "Then I could just be happy working as a waitress somewhere until you came to rescue me."

He cocked a grin. "You have a hard time with *one* boss. Imagine having to cater to every Tom, Dick, and Harriet that came into a restaurant. I have a feeling you'd last about a day before someone griped about you getting an order wrong and you told them to either get in the kitchen and cook their own fucking food or gave them a diatribe about the trials and tribulations of life as a waitress and demanded an apology on behalf of all waitresses everywhere."

She tipped her head back, marveling at how well he knew her. She was so confused. Was Shift even worth thinking about? Was she being impetuous, blinded by how much she missed Drake and her friends?

"I can't even think right now," she confessed, and pressed her entire body against his, wishing she could stay in the safety of his arms forever. "It's all too much. People contemplate these types of life decisions for months, and I'd have to decide right away. I don't even know if I can get a loan, and she's signing papers *Tuesday*."

"You can probably ask her to delay for a week."

"I can't do that to her. She has a bird in the hand, and she's done so much for me. All she wants is time with her daughter. I would never chance ruining the offer she has on a whim. Maybe I shouldn't even think about it. It's crazy, right?"

"You're asking a guy who opened a music store when I didn't have a pot to piss in."

"That just gives me hope, like it's something I *should* think about."

"Maybe you should," he said supportively.

"I don't know. I have a job people would kill for. A job I would have killed for two months ago. But what if I was wrong? What if I don't want bigger and better or the people that come along with bigger, better? What if I'm really meant to blaze my own trail, defined by my own beliefs and creativity?"

"Then that's not *wrong*, Serena. That's a choice. It means you started down one path and it led you to another."

Was this a sign? Could this be the right path for her? "This is so hard."

"I know. But breathe, baby." His lips curved up in a tender smile. "Remember how you said I didn't make myself into a liar by getting together with you after I said I couldn't?"

"Yes. I said your first inclination was just a bad idea."

He shrugged one shoulder. "Don't you see the similarities? Just because you change your mind doesn't mean it was wrong to begin with, or in this case, even a bad idea. This is how you learn and grow, whichever way you decide to go. Just know this. I want you to be happy. No matter where or how that has to happen. Okay?"

She nodded, feeling like she couldn't breathe. "You have to go. Everyone's waiting."

"Hold on." He grabbed her messenger bag and dug out her notebook. "Let's make pros and cons lists and figure this out. I'll text Rick and tell him to leave with the others. I can rent a car and drive home later."

"Drake…" She shook her head and set the notebook on the coffee table. She couldn't make lists when she wasn't even able to see clearly. But Drake was a fixer, and she knew he was doing it out of love. "I adore you. You know that, right?"

"I hear something bad coming."

She climbed onto his lap and took his handsome face between her hands. "Not *bad*. I know you want to fix this for me, or help me fix it, but I think I just need time to think things through. It might be a great opportunity, but I have clients who are counting on me, and buying a business is a *huge* deal. I'm not even sure I *want* to risk my savings—the money I was hoping to use to buy the cottage I'm renting—on a business. I don't even know if I can get a loan that fast. It's about the same amount as a car loan, but I think it's a different process when you're buying a business. There's just too much to try to figure out right now."

"I told you I'd give you—or lend you—the money."

"I know, but please don't offer me that ever again." She softened her words with a touch of her hand. "I could lose my shirt and have to start over, and there is no way in hell I'm going to borrow or take money from you, so please stop."

"But you won't—"

She pressed her lips to his, silencing his support. "I love you for believing in me, but I have to be smart. I have to make a decision that's right for *me*, weigh the risks, second- and third-guess myself. And I need to do that on my own."

His jaw clenched, bringing out that telltale dimple. She kissed the indentation and then brushed her fingers over it. She was fooling herself if she thought Drake—and even her friends—didn't play a role in what she wanted. Or that Drake's happiness and his need to be near his family wasn't of primary importance to her. He'd never be happy in Boston, that far away from everyone he loved. Those were all things she needed to think long and hard about, and as much as she loved him, she couldn't think clearly about those things while looking into his supportive eyes. "Please don't be frustrated with me."

"I'm not. I just wish I knew what the right answer was. I don't want you giving up everything you've worked so hard for just to be closer to me, and I also don't want you staying somewhere that makes you unhappy."

"As much as it hurts to say it, as much as I don't like feeling like I'm on a hamster wheel running back and forth to the Cape, whatever decision I make won't be *just* about you or certain aspects of my job. It's about *me* as a woman, a career person, and a friend. If I learned one thing from my mother, it's that if I'm going to be the type of girlfriend I want to be, I have to first be happy with all the pieces of myself and my life before you can even consider moving to be with me. Big firm? Little firm? Cape? Boston? Those are things I have to pick apart. The only thing I know for sure is that I want *you*, and thankfully, you've made it abundantly clear that you want me, too. I just need to figure out what *else* I want."

"WHY DO YOU look like you're going to kill someone instead of looking well f—" Rick glanced at Hagen and said, "*Loved?*"

Drake gritted his teeth as Mira joined them. He thought he'd be able to get back to the Cape without having to talk about Serena's situation. "Because I don't know up from down right now."

"What's wrong?" Mira asked. "Is the distance getting to you guys?"

Drake wished it were that easy. "No. Did you know Justine was selling Shift?"

"What? No. I haven't heard anything." Mira turned around, and before Drake thought to stop her, she called to the girls, "Did you guys know Justine was selling Shift?"

"No. She is?" Desiree asked.

Emery ran over. "Can Serena buy it?"

"I don't know," Drake answered.

"Why not?" Rick asked. "Then she could be closer to home."

"Rick, you know Serena's always wanted the type of job she has now." Mira put a hand on Drake's shoulder. "You want her to try to buy it, though, don't you?"

"Yes!" Emery said. "I want her to, even if you don't."

Desiree joined them and said, "She'd be great running her own shop."

"That's basically what she did with us, but on a bigger scale," Dean added. "She set up everything, designed all the cottages, the office, your apartment, the rec center…"

"So that's why you're mad?" Mira asked.

"No!" Christ, it was like arguing with a committee. "I'm not mad at Serena. Jesus, Mira, you know me better than that. I stayed away from her for all those years because I didn't want to stand in her way or make her feel like she had to choose between me and her dreams. Do you really think I want to pull her back now?"

"Hey, calm down." Matt stepped between Drake and Mira. "She's only trying to figure out why you're chewing on nails."

"Sorry," Drake ground out. "I don't know why I'm having a hard time."

"Uncle Drake?" Hagen asked sweetly.

Drake turned, meeting his nephew's inquisitive gaze and feeling guilty as hell that Hagen had witnessed him getting upset. "I'm sorry, Hagen. I shouldn't have snapped at your mom."

"I know why you're unhappy," he said with all the confidence of a little boy with an innocent view of the world. "Serena is gone. I miss her, too."

Drake's throat thickened. He lifted Hagen into his arms,

stepping aside for Rick to drive the boat. "You're right, Hagen. I do miss her."

"So bring her home," Hagen suggested.

"I want her with me every day, buddy, but sometimes adults aren't sure if they're going to be happiest in one place or another."

"Daddy moved here to be with us," he said matter-of-factly. "So maybe you can move to Boston to be with Serena. But you need to still come visit us, or I'll miss you both."

"I will, too," Mira said.

"That's good advice, buddy," Matt said as he took Hagen from Drake's arms. "What do you say you and I see if we can spot any fish while Uncle Drake tries to figure things out?"

After they walked away, Emery said, "I bet we can come up with whatever she needs to buy the business. I have some savings."

"Me too. How much does she need?" Desiree asked.

"*No*, you guys," Drake said sternly. "Don't you think I've already told her the money is hers if she needs it? I could buy three companies for her if that's what she wanted. I appreciate you wanting to help, but this is Serena. She's not going to take money from any of us."

"Not in a million years," Rick agreed.

"She doesn't know what she wants right now," he explained. "I just don't want her to make the wrong decision and regret it, whether that's staying where she is, buying this company, or something different altogether. I laid all my cards on the table. The next move is hers."

Chapter Twenty-Two

SERENA TRUDGED INTO the office Monday morning thanking the heavens above that she didn't have any face-to-face client meetings today. She'd been up late last night talking to the girls, who had each pressed her for details about her thoughts on Shift. Chloe had given her the best advice. *Don't think about Mom while you make this big of a decision.* Once she'd taken their mother out of the equation, her thoughts had become clearer. She'd called Drake, and he'd tiptoed around their earlier conversation. She knew it was killing him that she was suddenly unsure of what she wanted to do with her future. Drake was a fixer. A planner. A guy who had stepped back just so she could move forward. It was that, and all the unknowns, that had kept her tossing and turning all night and left her looking like a zombie this morning. Hopefully the makeup she'd used to cover the dark circles under her eyes would do the trick and no one would notice.

She checked in with Laura and Spencer, passed by Gavin at the coffee machine and kept on going, ducking into her office to hide out for the day. She was so exhausted and confused, she didn't trust herself not to snap at Suzanne if the opportunity arose.

A hand with a coffee cup appeared in her doorway. "Is it safe to come in?" Gavin asked in a cartoonish voice.

"The coffee, *yes*. You? Probably not."

Gavin sauntered in with a cocky grin and a cup of coffee in each hand. He guided the door closed with his foot and said, "I'll take my chances."

"You're either brave or foolish." She waved to the chair across from her.

He set a coffee cup in front of her, then sipped from the other as he sat down. He crossed an ankle over his knee, sat back, and said, "Definitely both, but *wow*. You look like hell. Breakup, nookie night, or PMSing?"

"None of the above." She came around the desk and sat in the chair beside him.

"Don't get handsy with me," he warned.

She smiled. "I need advice."

"Should I get cookies?"

"Probably, but there's no time, so just go with it. Let's say you got an opportunity for a new job."

He wrinkled his brow. "Didn't we just play this game?"

"Different job, and it's in a place you love." She sighed. "It's too hard to be hypothetical. I'm exhausted, so I'm just going to say it, but it stays in this room."

He pantomimed slipping something over their heads. "Cone of silence. *Go.*"

"The woman I used to work for, Justine, is selling her company, Shift, the small design firm in Hyannis I told you about. I just found out yesterday. She has an offer on the table and is supposed to sign the papers Tuesday."

He leaned closer, listening intently. "My interest is piqued. That's the place you said you loved working, but they didn't have the business to hire you full-time, right?"

"Yes. But if I bought the business I could market it and, honestly, she said she earns fifty thousand working part-time. I could live off that if I needed to."

"But is she going out of business because the business is failing? Can the local economy handle it? Was there too much competition?"

"No. She had a baby and wants more time with her. I know Justine. I know how much she loves Shift. She built it from the ground up. But when she had her baby, she changed. She became a mom, and I get that."

"Will she let you look at the books?"

"Yes, but I don't even know if I want to buy it."

He blinked hard, like he was trying to make sense of what she said. "Doing what you love in the area you love. What's the issue?"

"A couple things. I have a solid job here."

"With a boss."

She was too tired for games. "What does that mean?"

"You have issues with authority. Did you not know that? Sorry. I thought you did."

She couldn't suppress her smile. "Okay, that's fair. I do, but only when I think my ideas are better."

"Like I said. *Issues with authority.* What else?"

"I don't know. That's the problem. What if I haven't given this place enough time? What if things fall into place and my weekends become my own? What if Suzanne eventually respects me enough to let me handle Laura and Spencer the way I want to?"

He pulled out his phone, navigated around, then handed it to her. "This is my schedule for last month. You tell me—will things change?"

She glanced at the calendar. He had appointments on almost every Saturday, three evenings each week, and on one Sunday. She handed him back the phone. "Then there's the biggest problem."

"I know. The whole too-good-to-be-true thing."

She rolled her eyes.

"No Kane's Donuts around the corner?"

"Crap. I hadn't thought about that. She named a doughnut after me and Drake. *Perpetual Bliss.* Pretty cool, huh? I bet Abby would mail them overnight delivery if I asked."

"First of all, that's wicked cool, and second, maybe you can convince her to move to the Cape."

She sipped her coffee and said, "Look at you, strategizing my life."

"Someone has to."

"That's just it. Nobody has *ever* had to figure things out for me. I've done it myself forever. That's why this is throwing me off so badly." She got up and went to the window, gazing out over the city. "This was what I thought I wanted. A big city, posh clients, and a job with a big-name firm. I wanted everything my mother didn't want to achieve."

She'd told Gavin about her mother the other night, and it hadn't fazed him in the least. He'd said, *Every strong woman I've ever met had a parent who failed them, a parent who did well by them, or siblings to compete with. There's no magic. We all become who we are because of someone else.*

She turned around, taking in his sharp blue suit and shiny shoes. She had fancy clothes, but she still felt like an imposter in them. Her heart would never be in this company.

"I know what I want, and it's not this," she said confidently.

"I want to go to work every day without the fear of being hamstrung by a boss or having to take on projects I don't want to. I don't care about the money. I care about doing what I love and being around family—Drake, Chloe, Mira, Rick, Emery. The whole gang."

"Great. So what's the issue?"

She plunked down into the chair again. "I have savings, but not quite enough, and I'm not sure I want to sink every penny into something so risky."

"I thought you said the business was solid."

"It is, but what if I screw up?"

He laughed, then coughed to cover it. "Wait. The woman who has no issue going up against Suzanne Kline has confidence issues? Bullshit. What's this really about?"

"Okay, fine. I know I won't screw up, but something could go wrong. The building could catch fire. The economy could change."

"Both true. So you get good insurance, and if the economy tanks you get a new job. Or you can sit around here, work six days a week, and hustle to and from the Cape, and if the economy tanks, you start over anyway."

She assessed his words and his expression. She trusted Gavin to be honest. He had no ulterior motives to get her to stay or leave. "So you think this is actually a good idea?"

"You don't belong here, Serena. You keep telling me that in different ways. 'If this were my company, I'd do *this*,' and 'If I were the boss, I'd do *that*…'"

"I know," she finally admitted. "I think I'm just scared to get my hopes up. What if I can't pull it off? What if Justine doesn't want to change course and goes with the other buyer? What if I can't get a loan?"

"Do you *want* a loan?" He sipped his coffee, casually watching her.

"Nobody *wants* a loan. You get them because you have to. She's asking fifty grand, and I have thirty-two, but I'd be left with nothing. I don't have a car payment or carry any credit card debt. I figure I can probably borrow twenty-five and still have a few thousand left of my savings. It means giving up the hope of buying the cottage I've rented for the past several years, but that's a trade-off I think I'm willing to make."

"There are other ways to make businesses work. Would you consider a partner?"

"Like Drake buying the business and me being a kept woman? *Never.*" She crossed her arms against the idea.

"I said a *partner*, not a sugar daddy." He leaned forward and brushed something from her shoulder.

"What...?" She looked at her shoulder.

"Nothing. Just trying to get that big ol' chip off your shoulder."

She sighed. "Okay, I'm stubborn. No secret there."

"Serena, I'm being serious. I think you've got a chance at something awesome. I'd love a shot at partnering with you. I don't have contacts at the Cape, but I've got plenty of contacts here in Boston that *aren't* affiliated with KHB. And in case you haven't noticed, clients like me. I can work the system. I'm an honest guy, and you and I get along well. I know when to toss you cookies and when to back off. I know you're sharp as hell and your ideas are usually spot-on, but when they're not, I know you can handle a little criticism, *if* worded correctly."

"I didn't kick you in the balls when you told me I was going in the wrong direction with that one idea I had for Seth and Jared, did I?"

He shook his head. "That's how I know you're not an ass-hole. We can make this work. We can build something incredible of our own, taking on clients who respect us and, equally important, clients we respect."

"You're serious?" Her pulse quickened with the idea. "You'd move to the Cape? You know sand and designer suits don't mix well."

His eyes narrowed, and he shook his head. "You know I'm itching to get out of here. Let's blaze a path together. *Shift into success with Mallery and Wheeler.* The perfect tagline."

Goose bumps rose on her arms. "*Mallery and Wheeler.* I like it. You're sure? Because you know I have strong opinions."

"I wouldn't respect you if you didn't. Of course, we'd want to review Justine's books, just to make certain everything's on the up-and-up, have a partnership agreement drawn up, and that sort of thing. But I say we make this happen. Why spend our lives working for other people?"

"You know what? I'm in!" She pushed to her feet, feeling lighter than she had in weeks. She thrust out her hand and said, "To Mallery and Wheeler."

There was a knock on the door, and they both turned as Suzanne peered into the office.

"Serena, can I see you in my office, please?"

If Serena looked half as guilty as Gavin, she was in deep shit. But the twisting in her stomach told her she was making the right decision.

DRAKE POPPED OPEN a beer Monday evening and threw a steak on the grill behind the office. He'd spent the day working at the music store with Carey and Maddy. They worked well together, and the store was already starting to get a following of twentysomething musicians who liked to hang out there. He had no doubt that was due to Serena's brilliant surprise and the fact that Boone had signed all sorts of paraphernalia before leaving. They'd sold out of it the same day, but people still came by to see the place where Boone Stryker had played.

His phone rang, and Serena's name appeared on the screen. "Hey, babe."

"Hi," she said breathlessly. "Sorry it's so late. I had a late meeting. I have so much to tell you. Are you sitting down? You might want to sit down for this."

"Nope. Standing by the grill, what's up?"

"I'm doing it. I'm buying Justine's business! Gavin's brother, who's some kind of accounting wiz, looked over Shift's books this afternoon, and we met with an attorney to draw up the offer. She'll have it in her hands by nine tomorrow morning, but I've already given it to her verbally, and she said it's good. She's going to take it. And today Suzanne gave me a hard time about not charging enough billable hours. I will be so glad to get out from under that corporate stuff. I can't believe it, but I'm doing it, Drake! I'm buying Shift!"

"Whoa, babe. Slow down," he said, trying to keep up with her and tamp down the sting about how much she'd done without even communicating her decision to him first. He knew he had no business being irritated. This was her decision, her life, but he still felt left out. "That's great news, but how did you get the money?"

"Oh my gosh. I'm so excited I forgot to tell you! Gavin and I are partnering together. Fifty-fifty, right down the middle. Mallery and Wheeler! Can you believe it? It's perfect!"

Drake bit back a curse. "Babe, you won't take my money, but you'll take money from a guy you've known for a *month*?"

"I'm not *taking* his money. We're business partners, Drake, like you, Rick, and Dean."

"Whom I've known my whole life. How do you know you can trust this guy?"

"I just *know*. Why are you so upset?"

"Because I don't want you making a mistake," he said as he paced. "Partnering in business is complicated on so many levels. You have no idea if this guy is honest or not."

"Actually, I *do*," she snapped. "He's been nothing but honest with me about everything—work, life, friendships. I trust my instincts, and you should, too."

"You're talking about a ton of money, babe. You're sinking twenty-five grand into this with him. Anything can happen."

"It's twenty-*nine* grand," she said harshly. "We have to pay for the attorney and our partnership agreement and other things. But you know what?" Her voice escalated. "I'm not arguing about this with you. You're right, Drake. *Anything* can happen, and I'm confident something *wonderful* will happen. Tomorrow, after Justine officially accepts our offer, I'm giving my notice, and in two weeks I'll be back at the Cape, with *you*, and that's pretty damn wonderful if you ask me."

His hand curled into a fist. "You're right, it is. But I'd feel better if I had Gavin checked out. My buddy Reggie Steele is a PI. I'll call him tonight and get a report before you sign off on the deal. Just in case."

"Whatever. You do what you have to do."

"It's for *your* protection, Serena. Not for me."

"Is it? Or is it jealousy?"

"*Jesus.* This is business. I trust you. You have to know that.

You're with the guy every frigging day. You have drinks with him, sing karaoke with him. The guy brings you *cookies*, Serena. If I didn't trust you, I wouldn't still be with you. But you're my girlfriend, and you might not be willing to take my money, but I'll be damned if I'll sit back and watch you possibly make the biggest mistake of your life."

"Way to trust my instincts."

"That's not what I mean. *Damn it.* Listen, if he's on the up-and-up, then I'm all for it. But how can you know without doing your due diligence?"

He was answered with silence.

"Serena," he said in a softer voice. "I love you. If this is what you want, I want it for you. But can't we agree that having him checked out is *smart* business? It has nothing to do with not trusting you, or being jealous, and everything to do with wanting to protect you."

She was quiet for a second, and then she said, "Shoot. That's Justine calling on the other line. I really need to take it in case something's wrong. I'll call you back after."

The line went dead.

"*Fuck.* Fuck, fuck, *fuck.*"

Rick and Desiree came around the corner of the building. "What's going on?" Rick asked.

Drake shut off the grill. "Serena's making an offer on Shift—with Gavin as her business partner."

Rick and Desiree exchanged an *oh shit* look. "Okay, well, you said he's a good guy, right?"

Drake glared at him. "I meant for hanging out with, not handing everything she's ever worked for over to. She's so damn stubborn. I told her I wanted to get him checked out. You know, due diligence, as we would on *any* business partner. We don't know this guy from Adam."

"But she does," Desiree reminded him.

He scrubbed a hand down his face. "Yeah, I know."

Rick held his stare. "What are you going to do?"

"You mean besides having Reggie Steele check him out? Fuck if I know." He stalked toward the office.

"Drake—"

Rick started to follow, but Drake stopped him with a cold stare. Then he stormed inside, taking the steps two at a time.

Chapter Twenty-Three

"I KNOW, CHLOE!" Serena said into the phone. "I'm over-the-moon excited. Once you told me to take M-O-M out of the equation, everything fell into place."

"You know if you *were* doing this for Drake, it would be okay, right? You're not Mom. You could never be her."

Serena nodded, even though they weren't on a video chat. "I know. Thank you. Listen, I gotta go. Justine and I were on the phone forever, and I've been trying to reach Drake. He's not answering my calls or my texts."

"He's probably at the music store or out for a run."

"Maybe, but he was pretty pissed at me. He wanted to have a PI check out Gavin and I was…less than okay with it."

"Oh shit. You're so fucking bullheaded. He was only trying to look out for you."

Tears burned in Serena's eyes. "Yeah, I know. I gotta go." She ended the call and tried Drake again. It rang three times before sending her to voicemail. She didn't leave a message this time. How many times could she plead for forgiveness?

She called the music store, and when that went to voicemail, too, she realized she was an idiot. If he wasn't answering *his* phone, why would he answer the music store phone?

She called Mira next, and the second she answered, Serena said, "Have you seen Drake?"

"No. Why?"

"We had a fight. I've been calling him for almost an hour and he's not answering. If you see him, *please* ask him to call me." She pushed the gas pedal to the floor, needing to get rid of her frustrations.

Less than two minutes later, red-and-blue lights appeared in her rearview mirror. She threw her purse over the bottle of champagne on her seat. "Fucking perfect."

By the time she reached Bayside, she was a teary-eyed, angry mess, and so damn relieved to see Drake's truck, she nearly kissed it. She sprinted up the stairs to his apartment, hearing music vibrating through the closed door. She didn't even slow down to knock. She pushed open his door and stormed through his living room.

"Drake!" she shouted. "We're supposed to be celebrating, not fighting!" There was no way he could hear her with the music blaring, and he only played music that loud when he was pissed.

She plowed into the bedroom, stopping cold at the sight of her clothes neatly stacked inside a suitcase. Tears sprang from her eyes. She clutched the champagne bottle in one hand, the cookie box in the other, feeling like a fucking idiot. Why had she argued with him? Why was she so damn stubborn?

"Serena." Drake's deep voice boomed through the blaring music as he strode out of the bathroom in a towel, his toiletries bag in one hand, shampoo bottle in the other.

"I've been trying to call you," she shouted over the music. "I'm sorry. I know I'm stubborn and a pain in the ass. I shouldn't have argued with you about Gavin. You're right,

Drake. I should have checked him out. Oh God, please don't end us because I'm an idiot."

He tossed the toiletries bag and shampoo into the suitcase and closed the distance between them. "I fucking hate fighting with you," he shouted. "But that's who we are, Serena. *Two* bullheaded people."

Tears slid down her cheeks. "But we can make it work! I'll be less stubborn. I promise."

He cupped her face, shaking his head. Breaking her heart one move at a time. His thumb brushed away her tears, but it did nothing to slow the river of sadness consuming her.

"You can't be less stubborn, and I don't want you to," he said loudly.

"But you packed my stuff! I don't want you to pack my stuff. I want our stuff together. I can learn to shut up."

He shook his head again with a disbelieving smile. "No, you can't."

"Oh God..." Tears blurred her vision, and the music vibrated inside her chest, making her ache with grief.

"Your unwillingness to sell yourself short or step back for anyone is what makes you so strong!" he shouted. "And my unrelenting need to protect you is what will ensure you won't get hurt. Don't you see, Supergirl?" A genuine smile curved his lips. "We are perfect for each other. We were each other's first loves, and we'll be each other's last."

"But...?" She looked at the suitcase, trying to process his words against his moving her out.

"I was packing *our* stuff, coming to Boston to be with you until you moved here. I called Reggie, and he said he'd have a report on Gavin tomorrow. I wanted to be there with you when Justine called to accept your offer."

319

Happy sobs bubbled out, and Serena lifted the champagne bottle and the cookie box. He took them from her and set them on the bed. Then he lowered his lips to hers, healing her shattered heart one loving kiss at a time. His body was warm and damp from the shower. The deeper they kissed, the hotter he became.

"Drake! Turn it down!" Mira's voice approaching from down the hall pulled them apart. "Serena's trying to reach—" She appeared in the doorway.

Drake moved behind Serena, his hard heat pressed against her back. She couldn't suppress her giggle.

Mira shifted her eyes away. "*Oh.* Never mind."

Rick burst into the room behind her. "What's all the racket?"

Drake put his arms around Serena's waist, speaking above the music. "Just two passionate people talking. You won't have to deal with it much longer. I'm going to Boston."

"For real?" Mira shouted.

"For real," Drake said as he turned Serena in his arms, gazing down at her like she was the love of his life—and she knew she always would be. "For very, *very* real."

Epilogue

SERENA PULLED UP in front of the offices of Mallery and Wheeler Interior Designs and sat in her car for a moment, taking it all in. It had been eight weeks since Reggie Steele's report on Gavin had come back clean, seven weeks since they'd sealed the deal with Justine, five weeks since she and Gavin had left KHB, and three weeks and five days since they'd opened their new offices. Serena hated secrets, and she'd told Gavin about Drake hiring Reggie Steele to check him out before Justine accepted the offer. She'd been relieved to hear that Gavin had also checked *her* out long before suggesting they partner together. Apparently, he was as cautious and business savvy as Drake. Needless to say, the two men in her life had since become fast friends.

"Just in time for me to leave for a meeting," Gavin said as Serena stepped into their office and set her things on her desk.

"I'm sensing a pattern here. You left when I arrived yesterday, too."

"Two ships passing in the night, I guess," Gavin said as he gathered his things and pushed to his feet in his jeans and dress shirt. For the most part he'd ditched his classy suits, and he fit right in on the Cape and with her friends.

"You taking off soon?" he asked.

"About a half hour or so. I have some things to get ready for tomorrow. Good luck with the meeting. Who is it with?"

"Small retailer in Brewster. I'll fill you in at breakfast tomorrow. Rick promised to up his game. I'm hoping for those custard tarts Desiree made last week."

She smiled to herself as he left the office. They'd had some bumps and bruises at first, figuring out how to approach certain aspects of marketing and introducing Justine's clients to their new firm, but they'd worked through them and had continued to work well together. They were learning when to give each other space and when to stock up on cookies.

She sent a quick text to Drake. *Miss you. Home in forty mins or so.* She added a kissing emoji and then set to work preparing for her meeting with Seth and Jared tomorrow. She couldn't retain them as clients for the project they'd commissioned to KHB, but after she'd quit, Jared had contacted her about a restaurant they were opening in Provincetown. She was thrilled to be working with them again and couldn't wait to get started. She'd been working closely with Donovan for the redesign of Swank, but he was a tough man to please. They'd finally nailed down a concept last week and were ready to move forward.

Half an hour later she packed up her things and headed home. Her days were busy, and sometimes she had to work on the weekends, but her nights were filled with the man she adored and the friends she loved. Life was better than it had ever been, and as she drove down the dusty road toward her rented cottage, she didn't regret spending her savings on her future.

She and Drake had moved into the cottage after Violet had caught them *not* sleeping on his balcony again. He'd given up his apartment to Daphne, who was working out well at the resort. She had been staying with her sister. Serena's decision to move back to the Cape had affected Drake and the others more than she could have ever imagined. After much discussion about dreams and the importance of spending quality time with friends and family, the guys had decided to hire Everett Adler to run the resort office on weekends. Everett was a middle school music teacher who was already teaching a few music classes at Bayside Music and Arts. He was young, divorced, and working out fabulously.

Serena parked beside Drake's truck in front of the cottage. The sky-blue shutters and wildflowers used to bring the sense of relief that only being home could provide. But that had changed over the last few months. As she stepped from the car, she knew it didn't matter where she lived, as long as she was with Drake. He had become her grounding force, her comfort zone. *He* had become *home*.

An envelope was taped to the front door. She plucked it off and pulled out the card. The top half of the card read *You're my favorite thing to do*, with a red heart scribbled next to it. The bottom half of the card showed a picture of a man and woman from their bare thighs down. The woman had on red high heels, a red thong hanging around her ankles. The man wore socks, and a pair of black briefs were puddled around his feet.

She opened the card and read Drake's familiar handwriting. *Meet me at the beach.* He'd drawn another heart and had written *Superman + Supergirl* inside it.

God, she loved him.

She ran inside and stripped naked as fast as she could. Then she slipped on the slinky, backless white halter dress she'd bought a few summers ago and had never had the guts to wear. The neckline plunged loosely to her navel, and two slits ran up the sides all the way to her waist. *Perfect.*

She slipped on a pair of flip-flops and rushed out the front door. She ran all the way to the woods and hurried down the path toward the beach. As she stepped free from the woods, she kicked off her flip-flops, the warm sand slipping between her toes. Drake was gazing out over the water, his back facing her. The sun glowed against the night sky, highlighting his masculine silhouette and spreading ribbons of orange and gold over the dark water. Her heart beat faster as she stepped closer, taking in the flames of the bonfire casting shadows over the seashells he'd laid out in the shape of a heart.

As if he sensed her presence, Drake turned, taking her in with a slow slide of his gaze down her body. He closed the distance between them, his eyes narrowing, filling with lust and love as he reached for her. His hair had grown out a little, giving him that rough look she loved.

"Damn, Supergirl," he said in a low voice that made her insides clench with desire.

He placed his hands on her hips, then dragged them lower, his fingers pressing into her skin in the slits of her dress, hot and demanding. Spikes of heat and longing tore through her core.

"I loved the card," she said as she wound her arms around his neck.

He brushed his lips over hers. She loved that intimate touch. Sometimes when he was getting ready to kiss her, she'd draw back just enough to feel the graze, to sense his simmering desire.

"I missed you." He kissed the edge of her mouth. "I bought you a little something today."

"You did?" she said breathily. It was silly that she still lost her words at his touch, and she hoped it never changed.

"Yes. You know how you wanted to use your savings to buy

the cottage?" He kissed the other side of her mouth. "It's ours now."

She gasped. "You can't—"

He silenced her with a kiss, holding her tight as she murmured into the kiss, wanting to tell him he couldn't do that! She wanted to be an equal partner in their relationship, to contribute half to expensive items. But he didn't even give her the chance to breathe, taking the kiss deeper, making love to her mouth as his hands glided over her body, and he kissed her stubbornness away, leaving her reeling.

He gazed deeply into her eyes and said, "I know you want to contribute. Baby, you contribute to my life every single day. You make me happy, horny, and hotheaded, and I wouldn't change any of it."

"Drake," she said softly, feeling teary and loved. "You can't buy us a cottage."

"Let me finish, Supergirl."

He dropped down to one knee, and the air rushed from her lungs. Tears tumbled down her cheeks, and suddenly she was shaking all over, barely able to remain standing.

He must have noticed, because he put his strong hands on her hips, steadying her as he said, "You are my life, baby, my reason for being. I have loved you for as long as I can remember. I adore your strength, your intelligence, and that sassy mouth of yours makes me crazy in the best of ways. You found a partner in business, and now I think it's time you have a partner in life. When we came together, I promised to make all your dreams come true, and that cottage is one of your dreams. So, I'm thinking you'll just have to marry me, baby. Let me be the first and the last man you've ever loved, because you are, and will always be, the *only* woman I've ever loved."

She dropped to her knees, tears sliding down her cheeks. "You've always been my one and only. Yes, I'll marry you."

He swept her into his arms, pressing his lips to hers, both of them saying, "I love you," between kisses. Cheers rang out around them as their friends and family stepped out of the shadows and pulled them to their feet, crushing them in a group hug. They were passed from one set of loving arms to the next, congratulated and wished happiness by all the people they loved most. Even Gavin was there, grinning at having pulled the wool right over her eyes. There was no potential client, just the most romantic secret proposal waiting in the wings.

Serena was still shaking when she finally landed back in Drake's arms and he said, "I've always wanted to be your hero, Supergirl."

She gazed into his loving eyes and said, "I never thought I needed one. But I guess that's because you've been by my side all along."

Ready for More Bayside?

Hold on to your hat for Violet's wildly hot love story! Lizza is up to her old tricks again, and Violet is in for the surprise of a lifetime!

Fall in love again in BAYSIDE ESCAPE

Have you met the Bradens?

Fall in love all over again with Treat Braden and Max Armstrong!

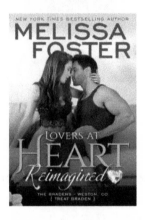

Treat and Max have a very special place in my heart. Their love story is the beginning of my beloved Braden series, and it introduces you to some of my favorite characters and to a family that has become so real to me, they're always by my side.

One of the greatest things about being a writer is the ability to reimagine worlds and create new stories. For the past several years, I have had the nagging feeling that there was more to Treat and Max's story than I had originally thought. I wanted to give two of my favorite characters a more mature story without losing the essence of who they are. This is Treat and Max's story, *reimagined*, and I hope you adore it as much as I do.

Have you met the Montgomerys?

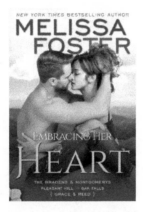

Fall in love with the newest Love in Bloom family

Welcome to Oak Falls, Virginia, home to horse farms, midnight rodeos, bookstores, coffee shops, and quaint restaurants where you're greeted like family and treated like treasured guests. Buckle up for a wild ride. Like any Southern girls worth their salt, the sweet-talking, sharp-tongued Montgomery sisters can take men to their knees with one seductive glance or a single sugarcoated sentence.

In *USA Today* bestseller EMBRACING HER HEART...
Leaving New York City and returning to her hometown to teach a screenplay writing class seems like just the break Grace Montgomery needs. Until her sisters wake her at four thirty in the morning to watch the hottest guys in town train wild horses and she realizes that escaping her sisters' drama-filled lives was a

lot easier from hundreds of miles away. To make matters worse, she spots the one man she never wanted to see again—ruggedly handsome Reed Cross.

Reed was one of Michigan's leading historical preservation experts, but on the heels of catching his girlfriend in bed with his business partner, his uncle suffers a heart attack. Reed cuts all ties and returns home to Oak Falls to run his uncle's business. A chance encounter with Grace, his first love, brings back memories he's spent years trying to escape.

Grace is bound and determined not to fall under Reed's spell again—and Reed wants more than another taste of the woman he's never forgotten. When a midnight party brings them together, passion ignites and old wounds are reopened. Grace sets down the ground rules for the next three weeks. No touching, no kissing, and if she has it her way, no breathing, because every breath he takes steals her ability to think. But Reed has other ideas...

Dear Readers,

The Bayside Summers series is just one of the subseries in the Love in Bloom big-family romance collection. You may enjoy starting with SEASIDE DREAMS, the first book in the SEASIDE SUMMERS series (free in digital format at the time of this publication). But you might enjoy starting at the very beginning, with SISTERS IN LOVE, the book that started the sensation (free in digital format at the time of this publication). Although characters from each subseries make appearances in future books so you never miss an engagement, wedding, or birth, each of my books may be enjoyed as a stand-alone novel, so jump in anytime!

Not all of my future releases will have preorders. Please be sure to sign up for my newsletter and follow me on Facebook so you don't miss them.
www.MelissaFoster.com/Newsletter
facebook.com/MelissaFosterAuthor

Keep track of your favorite characters with the essential Love in Bloom Series Guide:
www.melissafoster.com/LIBSG

Get your FREE first in series Love in Bloom ebooks here:
www.MelissaFoster.com/LIBFree

See the full Love in Bloom series here:
www.melissafoster.com/love-bloom-series

More Books by Melissa

LOVE IN BLOOM SERIES

SNOW SISTERS
Sisters in Love
Sisters in Bloom
Sisters in White

THE BRADENS at Weston
Lovers at Heart, Reimagined
Destined for Love
Friendship on Fire
Sea of Love
Bursting with Love
Hearts at Play

THE BRADENS at Trusty
Taken by Love
Fated for Love
Romancing My Love
Flirting with Love
Dreaming of Love
Crashing into Love

THE BRADENS at Peaceful Harbor
Healed by Love
Surrender My Love
River of Love
Crushing on Love
Whisper of Love
Thrill of Love

THE BRADENS & MONTGOMERYS at Pleasant Hill – Oak Falls
Embracing Her Heart
Anything For Love
Trails of Love

THE BRADEN NOVELLAS

Promise My Love
Our New Love
Daring Her Love
Story of Love
Love at Last

THE REMINGTONS

Game of Love
Stroke of Love
Flames of Love
Slope of Love
Read, Write, Love
Touched by Love

SEASIDE SUMMERS

Seaside Dreams
Seaside Hearts
Seaside Sunsets
Seaside Secrets
Seaside Nights
Seaside Embrace
Seaside Lovers
Seaside Whispers

BAYSIDE SUMMERS

Bayside Desires
Bayside Passions
Bayside Heat
Bayside Escape

<u>THE RYDERS</u>

Seized by Love
Claimed by Love
Chased by Love
Rescued by Love
Swept Into Love

SEXY STANDALONE ROMANCE
Tru Blue
Truly, Madly, Whiskey
Driving Whiskey Wild
Wicked Whiskey Love

BILLIONAIRES AFTER DARK SERIES

WILD BOYS AFTER DARK
Logan
Heath
Jackson
Cooper

BAD BOYS AFTER DARK
Mick
Dylan
Carson
Brett

HARBORSIDE NIGHTS SERIES
Includes characters from the Love in Bloom series
Catching Cassidy
Discovering Delilah
Tempting Tristan

More Books by Melissa
Chasing Amanda (mystery/suspense)
Come Back to Me (mystery/suspense)
Have No Shame (historical fiction/romance)
Love, Lies & Mystery (3-book bundle)
Megan's Way (literary fiction)
Traces of Kara (psychological thriller)
Where Petals Fall (suspense)

Acknowledgments

In case you're wondering, the Chocolate Orgasm doughnut is real, and so is Kane's Donuts. I'm thrilled to announce that I have teamed up with Kane's Donuts, located on Oliver Street in Boston, where much of this story is set, and Kane's has created the Perpetual Bliss doughnut just for Drake and Serena! When you're in the Boston area, be sure to stop by and try it out!

Nothing excites me more than hearing from my fans and knowing you love my stories as much as I enjoy writing them. If you haven't joined my fan club, what are you waiting for? We have loads of fun, chat about books, and members get special sneak peeks of upcoming publications.
facebook.com/groups/MelissaFosterFans

As always, thank you to Lisa Filipe and Lisa Bardonski for our fun chats and headbanging. Heaps of gratitude go out to my meticulous and talented editorial team. Thank you, Kristen, Penina, Juliette, Marlene, Lynn, Justinn, and Elaini for all you do for me and for our readers. And as always, I am forever grateful to my main squeeze, Les, who allows me the time to create our wonderful worlds.

Meet Melissa

Having sold more than three million books, Melissa Foster is a *New York Times* and *USA Today* bestselling and award-winning author. Her books have been recommended by *USA Today's* book blog, *Hagerstown* magazine, *The Patriot*, and several other print venues. Melissa has painted and donated several murals to the Hospital for Sick Children in Washington, DC.

Visit Melissa on her website or chat with her on social media. Melissa enjoys discussing her books with book clubs and reader groups and welcomes an invitation to your event.

Melissa's books are available through most online retailers in paperback, digital, and audio formats.

www.MelissaFoster.com
www.MelissaFoster.com/Newsletter
www.MelissaFoster.com/Reader-Goodies

CPSIA information can be obtained
at www.ICGtesting.com
Printed in the USA
LVHW02s1824240718
584774LV00003B/641/P